Until Proven Innocent

Until Proven Innocent

A Novel
By Carol Kinsey

Until Proven Innocent
Copyright © 2014 by Carol Kinsey
Published by Breautumnwood Publishing

This is a work of fiction. Names, character, places, and incidents either are the product of the author's imagination or are used fictitiously. Any resemblance to actual persons, either living or dead, events, or locales is entirely coincidental.

First Printing – September 2014

ISBN-13: 978-1495973703
ISBN-10: 1495973700

Edited by Rachael Woodall
Cover design by Bethany Anglin
Special thanks to Samuel Hart and Bethany Anglin
Cover photographed at Roscoe Village, Coshocton, Ohio

"Scripture quotations taken from the New American Standard Bible®,Copyright © 1960, 1962, 1963, 1968, 1971, 1972, 1973,1975, 1977, 1995 by The Lockman Foundation Used by permission." (www.Lockman.org)

Coming Soon
from author Carol Kinsey
Three new novels

Greater Love
Witness Protection
Special Ops and the Grace of God

See Also
Under the Shadow of a Steeple
Published in 2013

Dedication

To Von, Autumn and Breanna. Thank you for believing in me.
I love you.

To my Lord Jesus Christ. May You be glorified.

Thank you, Bethany, for loving my books. You know this one's for
you.

"Whatever you do, do your work heartily, as for the Lord rather
than for men, knowing that from the Lord you will receive the
reward of the inheritance. It is the Lord Christ Whom you serve."

Colossians 3:23-24

Chapter 1

The cold barrel of a Colt .45 pressed against her temple brought Bethany Young out of a restless sleep. This was it, the end of the line. She squeezed her eyes shut and wished away the nightmare that haunted her life for almost four weeks. *Just take me home, Jesus… please just take me home.*

"Bethany Young, you're under arrest," the voice at the other end of the .45 said without feeling. "For the murder of Patrick Webber."

There was no running this time. No getting away from the accusations. Bethany was trapped. She rolled over in the hotel bed and faced her captor in the dimly lit room.

Tanner Brenly narrowed his dark brown eyes on the tired young woman. "Sit up and put your hands together."

It was early dawn. Bethany could barely make out the man's face, but she knew what she was wearing underneath the blankets and had no intention of letting him see. "I'm only wearing my slip." Her tone was barely a whisper. "Please let me dress before you place me in cuffs."

Bethany heard the click of his .45. "My orders are to bring you in dead or alive, Miss Young," the officer said coldly. "If you so much as reach for your gun, mine will go off."

Holding the sheets against her chest, Bethany reached for her dress at the foot of the bed. "I have no gun." As quickly as possible, Bethany pulled the long dress over her head and slipped her arms through the lace-covered sleeves, allowing the sheets to drop away as the blue and brown floral gown took its place.

1

Still pointing his gun at her, Tanner motioned toward her boots. "Put 'em on."

Bethany pulled on her ankle high boots with shaky hands. She rose to her feet and held both wrists together without resistance.

Icy metal bracelets slipped over each wrist while a tear slipped from Bethany's hopeless eyes. She trembled with fear and tried to steady her breathing. She was trapped. Every part of her wanted to scream. But it was hopeless.

A strong hand turned Bethany toward the door while the man's other hand held his gun firmly pointed at her back. "It's time to go."

Bethany didn't speak. It seemed pointless. Witnesses said they saw her. Patrick Webber was dead. The only thing was—she didn't do it.

With a final glance at the dim little room, Bethany let the man walk her toward the stairs.

The hotel was small. Only the eyes of the hotel proprietor were on her as she walked through the lobby to the police wagon waiting outside the door. How humbling to have the curious old man glare at her as if she were a common criminal. He didn't know. No one knew.

The early morning sun reflected on Bethany's golden brown hair. Her curls hung, slightly mussed, down her slender back.

"Get inside," Tanner said without a hint of compassion in his voice.

Bethany obeyed. She watched the doors to the wagon close and with them any chance of proving her innocence.

The policeman returned to the hotel for quite some time, leaving Bethany to watch from behind barred windows as the businesses along the small western town opened and merchants set up their wares along the roadside. Inquisitive onlookers glanced at the wagon, likely wondering who had been arrested.

Bethany leaned her head back, hardly noticing the cold steel bars, and waited, wondering why this was happening to her. This wasn't the life Bethany knew. She should be waking up in her own, comfortable bed, eating breakfast on the terrace and enjoying the view of the Santa Rosa countryside.

Moments that felt like eternity passed before the young officer approached the window carrying her small garment bag. "Where is the money?"

"I have no money," she answered without emotion.

The lawman narrowed his eyes and blew out a frustrated sigh. Without another word he mounted the front of the wagon and set the horses into motion.

It wasn't a very long ride to the jail. Vacaville was a small town and the horses seemed in a hurry.

Bethany tried to clear her mind. She'd had very little sleep over the weeks since her life turned upside down. Posters of her face made it impossible to walk anywhere during the day and her presumed guilt made asking for help seem futile. Even with a bonnet worn low over her face, she could feel curious eyes on her everywhere she went.

The wagon stopped abruptly and Bethany trembled as she glanced at the bleak stone building she knew must be the jail.

"Let's go." A hand reached inside to help her step down.

Bethany avoided eye contact with her accuser, not wanting to read the judgment in his eyes.

His gun to her back as she walked toward the building served more for Tanner's assurance than it did to actually control her. The idea of running away never entered her mind.

As soon as Bethany and the officer stepped through the redwood doors, a shadow fell across the entrance. "So this is her?" Sheriff O'Brian studied Bethany curiously. "You can put her in that cell over there until you are ready to move her north." The man opened a cell and watched as Bethany was ushered inside. "There's not much to the little lass, is there? It's hard to believe one lady could wreak so much havoc on a town."

Bethany took a seat on the hard, dirty mattress and kept her eyes on her handcuffs. *It wasn't me. I would never have killed Uncle Patrick.* Bethany wished she could defend herself. The sorrow of his death grieved her as much as the accusations.

"Where'd you find her?"

"She was holed up in that hotel across from the mill."

The two men walked away, but Bethany could still hear their conversation.

"Did you find the money?" O'Brian asked. He poured two mugs of coffee and set one beside Tanner.

"No. Not even a penny. She must have hidden it." Tanner glanced toward her cell.

O'Brian shook his head. "Did she confess to anything?"

Tanner took a seat across from O'Brian and lifted the coffee to his lips. "I haven't really felt like talking to her." He took a sip and set the mug down. "This woman killed her own uncle in cold blood and shot down two of her household staff. I don't have the patience to hear her lies."

"You search her stuff?"

Tanner nodded toward the bag. "There's nothing—just a change of clothes, a few garments and personal items. Nothing of value and nothing that would lead us to the money."

O'Brian drained his mug and walked to the cell. "So you're Bethany Young." His lips curled as he spoke her name with disgust. He opened the cell door and stepped inside. "Where's the money?"

"I don't know." Bethany shook her head and kept her face down. "I didn't do it."

O'Brian smacked his fist against the bars. "Don't lie," he raised his voice.

Bethany felt herself cower under his reprimand. She stared at the stone floor. What could she say to make him believe her?

"Look at me when I'm talking to you," O'Brian demanded.

Nothing in Bethany's twenty-three years had ever prepared her for the situation she now found herself in. A tear ran down her face and she shuddered.

He took a few steps closer and grabbed her face with a rough hand, lifting her chin to look at him. "You've got no need for money with your neck just days away from a noose. Tell us where you've hidden it. Where are the contents of the safe?"

How could she answer? What could she say? She had no idea where her uncle's money was.

"Answer me!" The man raised his hand as if to slap her and Bethany flinched.

"I don't have any money," her voice trembled. "I don't know what you mean." She recoiled from O'Brian and buried her face in her cuffed hands. Sobs shook her slender form.

4

"Don't play dumb, Miss Young. You were seen. You forced your uncle to open his safe. Then you murdered him. There are witnesses!"

Tanner stepped into the cell and placed a hand on O'Brian's shoulder. "It's not worth it. Don't get yourself all worked up. She doesn't want to talk. Just let her sit and wallow in her own guilt and shame."

Bethany glanced at Tanner out of the corner of her eyes. He wasn't as tall as O'Brian, but his broad chest and muscular arms could be seen through his clean, blue shirt. He had dark brown, well-groomed hair and a clean-shaven face. If he wasn't treating her with such contempt, Bethany might have thought he was handsome.

"I'll remove her cuffs," Tanner said.

O'Brian clenched his fists and turned around. "The only thing worse than a mouthy woman is one that's giving you the silent treatment."

***

Tanner watched O'Brian walk from the cell and turned to look at the woman for whom he'd searched more than three weeks to find. In his four years as a deputy sheriff, Tanner never had to apprehend a female. He did his best to keep her crimes at the forefront of his mind in order to prevent any chivalry from surfacing. Bethany Young was a cold-blooded murderer. She deserved all that she was going to get.

He reached for her hands and unfastened the cuffs. Bethany turned her face to him for the first time. Blue eyes, brighter than the sky on the sunniest of days, peered up at him through dark, wet lashes.

Expecting to see at least a hint of remorse, Bethany's frightened eyes seemed to plead with him as a victim. There was something raw and vulnerable in her expression that caught Tanner by surprise.

As quickly as he'd been pierced by her glance, he turned to follow O'Brian from the cell. *I will not let this murderous charlatan fool me.*

"I need to leave with her first thing tomorrow morning."

***

Lying in his comfortable hotel bed, Tanner did his best to erase the imprint of Bethany's eyes from his mind. After their futile endeavor to uncover the hidden stash, Tanner and O'Brian met with a man named Zane Daniels.

Zane was a local whom O'Brian hired to accompany Tanner and the prisoner to Santa Rosa and return the wagon to Vacaville. Zane was older than Tanner and his rough manners and bad language made him a less desirable companion, but Tanner knew O'Brian needed to stay in Vacaville. The bustling town couldn't afford to have its sheriff gone for over a week.

Tanner reviewed the plans in his mind. Zane and Tanner would be taking Bethany close to sixty miles across rocky terrain to Santa Rosa where she would be tried and punished. The trip would take several days.

Bethany would ride in the wagon, with their crate of supplies and Tanner's saddle, while Tanner and Zane would take turns driving the two horses and keep tabs on the prisoner.

More than anything, Tanner wanted a good night's sleep before the trip, but all he could do was stare at the dark ceiling. His heart was unsettled.

Tanner never intended on becoming a deputy. The job simply fell into his lap four years ago during a chance encounter with a couple of would-be bank robbers. He'd simply been at the right place at the right time.

Having served for the north during the Civil War, Tanner learned to look death in the face to promote justice. He wasn't afraid to use a gun and he'd gained skills in combat.

The scene in the bank still made him smile when he thought about how easy those two thugs were to bring down. The sheriff arrived on the scene just as Tanner bound the second man with a pair of suspenders given to him by one of the bank tellers.

Sheriff Alan Thacker offered him the job on the spot.

Tanner never anticipated staying in Santa Rosa as long as he had. Going out west had been his way of dealing with pain.

He rolled over and faced the dark window on the other side of the room. After he delivered Bethany to Santa Rosa, maybe he'd leave. Go home. Regular letters from his parents told him this was what they wanted.

"Isn't five years long enough?" his mother had written in her last letter.

Tanner shut his eyes. It was hard to believe it had been five years. Sometimes it still felt like yesterday.

Sleep finally came, but painful memories and sky blue eyes haunted Tanner's dreams.

***

Commotion in the sheriff's office brought Bethany out of her fitful sleep. She could hear voices and knew preparations were being made to take her back to Santa Rosa.

Sitting up from the lumpy mattress, she brushed the wrinkles out of her dress and tried to smooth her curls with her fingers. She'd taken a bath at the hotel the night before and let her hair hang dry, now the long ringlets hung loosely down her back.

The dirty, cramped cell was a cold reminder that she was trapped. She kept herself quiet, dreading interaction with her accusers. She'd been alone on this terrible journey for over three weeks, but felt even lonelier being with people who hated and distrusted her.

"Well, missy," a man Bethany hadn't met yet came to her cell jangling keys. "Looks like it's time to take a little trip." His eyes scanned Bethany's pretty form and his sinister grin sent shivers down her spine. "Get up. I need to cuff you." He grabbed her arm and yanked her to her feet.

Bethany glanced with fear at the tall, wiry man. His greasy brown hair was in good need of a cut and his lined face was leathery from the sun. Bethany didn't resist the cuffs but stepped away abruptly when she felt the man's hand run along her arm.

"Come on, sweetie, I'll be your travel companion for the next few days." Zane grabbed her wrist.

"Step away from her, Zane." Tanner's sharp tone broke through the tension.

As Tanner approached Zane, Bethany noticed the contrast between the two men. She admitted to herself that Tanner was ruggedly handsome and carried himself with confidence and dignity. Zane reminded Bethany of a snake.

"Oh, come on, Brenly," Zane slung the deputy's name with a snort. "She's about to hang. May as well have a little fun with her."

Tanner's dark eyes narrowed and he took Bethany's arm. "You touch her and you'll be the next one in cuffs." He walked her out of the cell and to the same doors she'd been led through the day before.

O'Brian had the wagon waiting and locked the back after Tanner helped Bethany inside and uncuffed her. Bethany glanced out the barred window to the sky. Large gray clouds hid the sun making the day feel dark and gloomy. The sky fit her mood.

"You really trust this Zane guy?" Bethany heard Tanner ask the sheriff.

"I've had Zane help out on a few jobs," O'Brian said. "He's rough around the edges, but he's stayed out of trouble."

Tanner shrugged. "I don't like the way he was looking at Miss Young," he spoke in a soft, serious tone. "Murderer or not, she's still a woman. I told him I'd be cuffing him if he caused me any trouble."

"Do what you need to." O'Brian patted Tanner on the shoulder.

***

It was slow going over the rocky road toward Santa Rosa. Tanner wondered where Bethany had been headed that she'd made it all the way to Vacaville.

Murders as public as the one Bethany was accused of were rare in Santa Rosa. Her uncle was a prominent figure in town, owning thousands of acres as well as several businesses.

When Tanner first left Santa Rosa to hunt down Bethany, Sheriff Alan Thacker was busy trying to notify Patrick Webber's son, James. Bethany's cousin was several years older than Bethany and owned a successful business in San Francisco.

8

Tanner pitied the man. To lose one's father in such a way at the hand of a woman, raised as his sister nonetheless, would be a great sorrow and cut deep.

The details of the Bethany Young case ran through Tanner's mind as he drove the wagon.

Thursday morning, Bethany was reported having gone to the bank for her uncle where she requested a large sum from his personal funds. She had a letter, written in her uncle's handwriting, asking that she be entrusted with the money as they'd had a family emergency.

Unsettled by the unusual request and behavior of Miss Young that morning, the bank owner then notified the sheriff.

Both Sheriff Thacker and Tanner arrived at the Webber estate that afternoon to verify that everything was okay. What they found was a brutal crime scene of murder and theft.

Patrick Webber was tied to his desk chair with a bullet hole in his head. One of the maids, although not dead, had been shot and was found just outside Patrick's office door. One of the Webber's drivers had also been shot with evidence of a struggle. Patrick's safe stood opened and empty, and the house drained of jewelry and other valuables.

The cook and the other maid arrived home later and explained that Miss Young requested they go into town that morning to run a few errands.

From there, a search for Bethany Young began.

The search lasted three weeks. But Tanner admitted to himself, catching her was easier than he'd expected. An anonymous tip initially set his feet in motion. Although she'd paced herself well, Bethany was reported having used her uncle's stolen gold coins in a couple small towns southeast of Santa Rosa. Patrick Webber had a rare gold coin collection, which had been stored in the safe and robbed the day of the murder. A description of the coins was sent out to many of the banks and business establishments within a hundred mile radius.

Sheriff Thacker knew the Webbers and their niece. Although he'd only met Bethany a few times, it was difficult for him to imagine her involved in such a scandal. But he was no stranger to the fact that her uncle had cut her from his will upon

9

her insistence in pursuing her new "fanaticism," as Thacker's lawyer explained it.

Patrick Webber practically washed his hands of his niece and only cared for her out of respect for his deceased wife, who was the sister of Bethany's mother. There had been rumors that Bethany planned to find her father's family back East due to the tension between her uncle and herself.

Tanner wondered if Bethany's fanaticism was only a front. It would be a nice alibi to weep innocent tears, telling the world that she'd been at the Ladies Missionary Society meeting while her poor uncle was being murdered. But Bethany actually had no alibi. She'd been seen at the bank and she'd personally sent away one of the maids, the cook and the other stage driver. It was as if she'd dug her grave and lay herself down in the coffin.

"Clouds gettin' pretty ugly," Zane broke through Tanner's thoughts. "Let's stop for dinner and set up camp. We're lookin' to get soaked if we keep ridin'."

Tanner nodded. The sky had grown dark and the winds picked up. "I've got a tarp. We can string up a tent between the wagon and these trees."

"I'm sleepin' in the wagon." Zane winked and climbed down from his seat to help Tanner tie the horses.

"That wagon's not big enough for the three of us." Tanner patted one of the tired horses. "And anyhow, we need to give the woman privacy."

"Who said anything about three of us?" Zane put a pinch of tobacco behind his lip. "It aint' very often I get to be alone with a beautiful woman."

"Well, you're not gonna be alone with her." Tanner unrolled the tarp and gave it a flick in the air to shake it out. "And I'd better not catch you anywhere near her."

"Yeah, yeah, deputy boy." Zane spit brown liquid on the ground. "I hear ya. But I'm sure you've noticed that purty little face of hers."

Tanner chose not to continue the conversation. He unlocked the wagon and asked Bethany if she needed to take care of personal needs. "You've got exactly two minutes. If you aren't back I'm coming after you."

Bethany lifted her sad blue eyes to his and nodded quietly.

Tanner watched her walk into the woods and turned around. Bethany's quiet demeanor was unnerving. He wasn't sure what he expected when he found her, but it wasn't this quiet, dignified lady. Her submissiveness made his job easier, but he almost wished she'd give him a fight.

When Tanner returned to the wagon with Bethany, he found Zane rummaging through her belongings. Tanner snatched a lace garment from Zane's hands and stuffed it back into her bag. "What do you think you're doing?" he asked, helping Bethany into the wagon.

"Looking for clues." Zane gave an unconcerned grin and sauntered to the tent. "I got some beans. You hungry?"

Tanner was hungry, but the pot of dried up crusty brown beans Zane made was less than appetizing. After locking Bethany into the wagon, Tanner took a seat on the ground next to an old tree stump and hoped their makeshift tent would hold up under the increasing winds.

"That girl walked away with over seventy-five thousand in cash." Zane handed Tanner a bowl of beans. "Not to mention the gold and jewelry." He sat down on his sleep sack. "That's some money."

Tanner didn't answer.

"Aren't you at all curious where it's stashed?" Zane asked through a mouth full of beans.

"We're not responsible to find the money. Our job is to take Bethany to Santa Rosa."

Zane made a few annoying chewing sounds and shoved another spoonful of beans in his mouth. "You collectin' that reward?" The look of greed in his eyes was disconcerting.

"Apprehending criminals is my job." Tanner gave up trying to eat the beans and dumped his plate. "My reward is the satisfaction of justice."

As the first few raindrops began to fall, Tanner carried a bowl of beans to Bethany. Home was sounding better every day.

***

Bethany pulled the scratchy wool blanket close around her shoulders and tried to make herself comfortable on the floor of the

11

wagon. Rain pelted hard against the walls and blew into the windows. Bolts of lightning lit up the night sky and loud bursts of thunder rattled the carriage. She was mentally exhausted but sleep wouldn't come.

In less than a month her life had gone from one of comfort and security to fear and want, but none of it made sense.

She knew that her uncle was dead. She knew that she was being accused of the murder, but why? It all seemed so unreal.

Bethany rolled onto her side and rested her head on her hands. She'd spent hours praying, hours asking God for help and direction. She wanted answers. *Why do they think it was me? How can people say there are witnesses?*

As the wind howled outside, Bethany's despair grew. Did God not hear her prayers?

Where are You? She whispered softly to God. Tears welled up in her eyes and she blinked in the darkness. *I feel so alone...*

Chapter 2

The storms that blew through camp during the night left numerous trees down. Tanner's makeshift tent was blown to strips and hung dripping from the three trees where he'd tied it. He and Zane were both soaked and Tanner was tired of Zane's constant whining that the murderer stayed nice and dry while he and Tanner had a horrible night's sleep underneath the wagon.

The two men hurried to pack up camp and continue west but found that all their hurrying did little to help once they hit the road. Downed limbs every several hundred feet made the ride slow moving.

"I say we shoot her, throw her body over a horse and ride back to Santa Rosa," Zane suggested. "I can pick up the wagon on my way back."

Tanner shook his head. "We're not shooting her."

Zane let out a frustrated sigh. "Reward poster said 'dead or alive.'"

"This is my mission, Zane," Tanner said dryly. He was growing weary of Zane's endless complaining and talk of money. Tanner's motivation was to uphold the law. It was clear that O'Brian's man, Zane, was in it for himself.

It was Zane's turn to hold the reins and Tanner rolled up his sleeves and tried to get comfortable on the hard wooden seat.

The road showed signs of wear from the heavy rains the night before. With a gray sky still looming overhead, and an eerie stillness leaving the trees almost motionless, Tanner worried that they may be in for more.

This would have been a beautiful ride. With tall redwoods and scenic cliffs overlooking a wandering creek, Tanner let himself daydream about hiking the road all by himself.

***

A crack of thunder brought Bethany to the edge of her seat. From inside the wagon, she could feel every bump, but suddenly her prison walls were sliding down the hill as her wagon and the horses that controlled it met with the forces of nature. She crouched to the floor and tried to hold on to whatever wasn't moving while the sound of frightened horses mingled with rain and thunder.

The wagon rolled several times and crashed into an immovable tree. The walls, which once held her captive, now lay in fragments along the path. Bethany wasn't sure why she was still alive. Her hands shook as she rose to her feet. There was a bump on her head and her shoulders were bruised from the somersaulting. But she was in one piece.

After she caught her breath, Bethany made her way out of the debris and saw Tanner lying under part of the wagon. His gun was only a few feet from him and he moaned as he tried to free himself.

"Zane," he said through a strained breath. "Get this off me."

"Well this is just too bad." Zane brushed the dirt off his pants and walked down the hill toward the wagon. "The poor young deputy was killed trying to recover a known murderer…"

"What are you talking about?" Tanner tried to free his arm in order to gain more control. "Move the wheel, then I can get out."

Zane laughed. "This lady's worth a thousand dollars, and if I can get her to talk, she'll be worth even more." Zane had to step out of sight for a moment in order to get to where Tanner lay under the wagon. "Did you hear that Miss Young? I'm willing to be your partner!"

Bethany didn't question Zane's intentions. *Dear Lord… don't let him kill the deputy.* In the pit of her stomach, Bethany knew she was far safer in the hands of this upright lawman than she was at the mercy of Zane. Impulsively, Bethany reached for Tanner's gun and crouched behind the broken pile of debris not far from Tanner.

"You're talking crazy, Zane. Get me out of here." Tanner worked his arm free and moaned. He had a sizeable gash in his arm and very little strength to push free from the wheel.

"You don't seem to get it, deputy. I was planning on killin' you anyway. This little accident just makes it easier." Zane stood over Tanner and grinned.

"Zane… don't do this." Tanner had absolutely no defense.

Silently, Bethany readied Tanner's Colt .45 and peered out from behind the wreckage.

"Say goodbye." Zane raised his gun.

Bethany pulled the trigger and watched Zane drop his gun to grab his leg. She quickly handed Tanner his .45 and tried to pull the wheel off his body.

Zane dragged himself to his gun and reached for it, yelling expletives at both Bethany and Tanner. "You think you can stop me? You're both gonna die!" He raised his gun but never got to pull the trigger.

Another shot from the .45 silenced Zane forever.

***

It took every bit of strength Bethany had to pull the wheel and debris off Tanner. Using his good arm, Tanner slid free from the painful trap and leaned his back against a rock. His head was still reeling from everything that just happened.

Bethany knelt beside him and looked at his arm. Splinters of wood and dirt mingled with raw flesh. The urgency of the situation wasn't lost on Bethany. This man had a severe injury. "We need to do something to stop your bleeding."

He stared at her curiously.

"You can set your gun down. I'm not going anywhere." Bethany stood up. She almost smiled. "I'm the one who handed it to you, remember?" She walked toward the wagon remains and began investigating. "Do you have any kind of medical supplies in all of this?" She rummaged through the supplies O'Brian had provided for them and found alcohol and several bandages.

Tanner clenched his teeth while Bethany pulled away the fabric from his wound. Was this murderer helping him? He studied her face while she worked. His head ached and he leaned it back on the rock, watching her while she cared for his injury. Why didn't she let Zane kill him? Surely Zane would have worked out a deal with her—her freedom for a portion of the money she'd stolen. Something. Why save him?

She wrapped his wound tightly and encouraged him to lie down. "I'll try to use what's left of the wagon and its top to give you some shelter."

Too weak to even help, Tanner watched Bethany work to use boards from the wagon walls to shelter him from the rain. She'd gathered her bag and the supply box and secured it from the weather.

"I keep hearing a horse down below," she said. "Why don't I head down the hill and see if I can't find out where they are?"

Tanner nodded. He wasn't sure what to think. "Take rope."

Bethany slipped away, leaving Tanner to wonder what kind of murderer she was.

***

Bethany found one of the horses dead at the bottom of the hill. It was a gruesome sight and she turned away to see if she might find the other.

The rain stopped, but water droplets fell from the tall redwood trees onto the wet forest floor. Bethany walked quietly, listening for movement in the woods. Another whinny signaled a distressed horse.

"Where are you, buddy?" she called in reply. Surely even a strange horse, if it were tame, would appreciate the call of a human.

The horse returned the call and Bethany followed the sound until she saw him walking toward her. His nostrils flared with fear and she approached slowly, talking in a soothing tone. "You're okay... come on, boy."

The frightened gelding sniffed her hand and pressed his muzzle into her shoulder. She rubbed his face and talked calmly to him, recognizing that this was a trusting animal.

"You like people, don't you, boy?"

Bethany was convinced the horse wanted to be caught. Without a flinch, he let her place a rope around his neck and lead him up the hill. Bethany talked to him the whole way, stopping to pet his face and reassure him that she would take care of him.

It never ceased to amaze Bethany how a twelve hundred pound animal could let a hundred and twenty pound person control him. She stroked his chestnut hair and rubbed the white diamond on his muzzle.

Walking beside this strange horse brought back memories of her horse in Santa Rosa. Bethany wondered how Sophia was doing. Her Paco Fino was a beautiful mare and even though her uncle had a stable hand to care for the horses, Bethany usually gave her mare special attention.

On her way up the hill, Bethany spotted a crop of enormous rocks. Upon closer inspection, she found an overhanging rock shelf that would make a nice shelter, far better than the bits of broken wood she'd used to make a roof for Tanner. Bethany thought she could even light a fire under it. She tied the horse to a nearby tree and completed the climb to see if Tanner would be able to move.

Tanner was half asleep when Bethany reached his side. "Officer," she wasn't sure what she should actually call the man.

He glanced up and struggled to return to a sitting position.

"I found the horses. One of them is dead. The other I've tied up to a tree right outside a rock shelf. I think it will be better if we move there for the night." It seemed strange to be explaining all of this to the man whose job it was to take her to the gallows.

Tanner did his best to stand but Bethany could tell he was suffering. His face was pale and he was shaky on his feet. He reached for his gun and placed it in his holster.

"Is your leg broken?" She asked. *What will I do if it is?*

"No. It's my ankle. I think it's just sprained."

Bethany stepped closer to Tanner. "Why don't you put your weight on me?"

Tanner stared at her as if she had two heads.

"I can take the weight." She grabbed his good arm and put it over her shoulder. "It's not far."

Reluctantly, Tanner let her help him to the cave.

"I'll get the rest of our stuff."

***

Tanner sat on the ground and leaned against a rock. He watched Bethany start a fire just outside the cave.

She'd carried everything that could be salvaged to their campsite. Including Zane's gun and Tanner's handcuffs. She set them beside Tanner without a word and went to work gathering wood.

For a young woman raised with wealth, Tanner was surprised Bethany was willing to work so hard.

The clouds cleared away and a few stars could be seen through the treetops. Neither Bethany nor Tanner had spoken many words to one another since the accident. Tanner wasn't sure what to say. This murderer saved his life and was caring for him. Was she still his prisoner or was he hers?

"I made corn cakes." She carried a plate to Tanner and sat beside him with her own. "I'm not a very good cook, so I'm sorry if they're not palatable."

Tanner took the offered food and leaned back against the rock wall. "Thank you."

Bethany closed her eyes and bowed her head quietly for a moment before eating her food. Tanner watched her curiously and waited out of respect. Was this real? Was she thanking God for her food?

Bethany ate quietly. It was nothing like eating with Zane. Tanner finished eating his corn cake and blew out a sigh. "Are you always this quiet?"

A few crickets made night sounds and Bethany swallowed. "I don't really know what to say."

"Start with what happened up there?" Tanner finally let the words out.

Bethany lowered her eyes.

"You shot him in the leg and then you handed me the gun," Tanner watched the top of her head. "You were less than fifteen feet away from him. Are you really that bad of a shot or did you do that on purpose?"

Bethany blew out a shaky breath. "I just wanted to bring him down."

"Why didn't you kill him?" Tanner pressed.

"I've never killed anyone…"

Tanner set down his plate and wished he could get up and pace the cave. "How can you say that? Remember why I arrested you? You murdered your uncle!"

Bethany shook her head. "You're mistaken. I did not kill anyone."

Tanner didn't know what to believe. Bethany could have killed Zane. He was sure of it. For that matter, Tanner knew she could have killed him. She could have let Zane kill him. Why didn't she? Why did she get him out from under the wagon and then bandage his arm?

"You saved my life," he finally said softly. "I don't know why you did it. I don't know what your motives are. But thank you."

Bethany wiped a tear from her face. "You're welcome."

***

Bethany's body ached when she woke the next morning. The hard, wet ground made sleeping on her bruised shoulders almost impossible.

Tanner was still sleeping so Bethany slipped out of the cave to take care of personal needs and change into her other dress. She planned to wash clothes along with the bedrolls today and hoped everything would dry in the sun.

When Bethany returned, she knelt beside Tanner and wondered if she should wake him. After clearing her throat a few times and getting no response, she touched his good arm but only got a pained moan. His arm was hot.

"Officer," Bethany tried once more to awaken him. "Sir?" She grew suddenly frightened. She touched his face. Tanner was hot and clammy.

What should I do, Lord? The prayer rolled off her lips.

Tanner's face was beaded in sweat. She had no doubt he was fighting off infection from the cut in his arm. It would need to be washed and re-bandaged.

As carefully as she could, Bethany removed Tanner's blue shirt. She unwrapped his arm and tried not to become squeamish.

During her Aunt Olivia's last year of life, Bethany took on many of the responsibilities of nurse. While the family had plenty

19

of money to hire a nurse, her aunt was not comfortable allowing anyone else to clean her bedsores. It was unpleasant work, but it made her aunt's last months more bearable.

Tanner's swollen, deeply torn flesh was worse than her aunt's bedsores. Bethany knew an injury this serious needed proper care and she was the only one here to do it. Working as quickly as possible, she cleaned his wound with the alcohol and applied fresh bandages.

Dear Lord, please don't let this man die... She prayed softly for her captor.

Later in the morning, Bethany left Tanner to rest and washed their laundry in the creek using the soap from her bag. Their bedrolls and blankets got muddy from the wreck and Bethany wasn't sure how long they would be trapped there. Doing her best to scrub the blood from Tanner's shirt, Bethany glanced up at the blue sky and felt the sunshine on her face. What a contrast from yesterday.

Bethany didn't know what to think of the situation she now found herself in. With Zane dead and the young deputy lying lifeless in a cave, she could easily take the horse and run away. It would be days before anyone even knew she was gone.

But this man needed her. Bethany wrung water from his shirt. How strange to be needed by the man who two days before held a gun to her head.

I'm not sure why You've allowed all this to happen, Lord. She gazed at the sky while she prayed. *But please just guide me.*

Once the laundry was dry, Bethany laid out Tanner's bedroll and carefully moved him onto it. Throughout the day, Bethany did her best to keep his temperature down with a cold damp rag applied to his forehead, but it all seemed futile. Tanner was even hotter than he had been in the morning and he moaned and mumbled as if in great pain.

In the night, Bethany woke to the sound of coyotes howling and calling to one another from the hill above them. *They must have discovered Zane's body.* She shuddered at the thought. It seemed inhuman to leave his body to the dogs, but Bethany wasn't sure what else she could do. She had no shovel and struggled with the idea of seeing his dead form. She moved her bedroll closer to

Tanner and watched his silhouette. It was comforting to have another living person near by.

Tanner groaned and his rate of breathing increased.

Bethany poured more cool water from the canteen onto the rag and placed it on his forehead.

"Ruth…" Tanner spoke the name through a pained voice.

Bethany could barely make out his face in the moonlight.

"Ruth?" His breathing quickened and his tone began to take on the sound of panic. "Ruth?"

Bethany wasn't sure what to do. This man was a stranger to her but he obviously needed to be comforted. While caring for her ailing aunt, there were many nights when the touch of Bethany's hand brought comfort to the woman and allowed her to rest. Bethany wasn't used to caring for a man. Should she hold his hand as she had her aunt's?

"Ruth…" He moved his head from side to side.

She reached for his hand and he clutched hers.

"Ruth…" His breathing slowed as the panic left him. "Where's Rachel?"

"She's not here," Bethany wasn't sure how else to answer.

"I want to hold her—where is she? Where's Rachel?"

"It's okay," Bethany placed a tender hand on the man's strong, handsome face. "You're sick. You can't see anyone else right now."

"Don't leave me, Ruth… don't go." He reached up and grabbed her arm with his other hand.

"I won't leave." Great tears welled up in Bethany's eyes. Was he calling for his wife? The thought grieved her. This man could be dying and wanted Ruth… *She may never know what happened to him.*

***

By early morning, Tanner was back to a restless sleep. Bethany only left his side long enough to gather more water from the creek. When she returned, her heart stopped cold. Two Indian men stood in the cave watching Tanner.

The men heard Bethany and stared at her curiously. Trying to remain calm, Bethany lowered her eyes and carried the water to Tanner.

One of the men knelt beside her and motioned toward Tanner's wrapped arm.

Bethany turned to the man and his eyes grew suddenly wide. He motioned for the other man and reached for Bethany's face. She wasn't sure what the man wanted but knew it was best not to show fear.

The two men spoke and stared at her eyes.

My blue eyes... It dawned on Bethany that they may not have seen eyes as blue as hers.

They returned their attention to Tanner's arm and motioned for her to remove the wrap. She had still not changed the bandages from the day before, so she unwrapped it, exposing Tanner's red, swollen arm. One of the Indians covered his nose.

Bethany watched as the men spoke to one another. One nodded and got up to leave the cave. The other man touched Tanner's face and shook his head.

He got up and walked around the cave, seeming to investigate the items lying around. He then walked outside to the horse.

Please don't steal the horse. Her hopes dropped when the man untied the horse and began walking the animal away from the cave. She glanced at Tanner's gun, which she'd kept near her bedroll. If the horse was stolen, she'd have very little hope of ever getting out of this place.

She covered the gun with the edge of her bedroll. A horse was not worth a human life. Let him take the horse. God would take care of them.

The man returned after several minutes and retied the horse to the tree. Bethany couldn't believe her eyes. Had the man simply taken the horse to the creek for water?

"Thank you," she said. She was sure the man did not understand English, but at least he could tell from her tone that she was appreciative. She walked to their food supply and offered him a piece of jerky.

He put up his hand and motioned for her to put it back. Perhaps he understood that this was all the food she had to care for herself and Tanner.

Bethany wasn't sure what to do. She returned to Tanner's side and was about to begin working on his arm but the Indian stopped her and motioned toward the outside.

It seemed like hours passed before the other Indian returned carrying a leather bag. The two men began to work quietly on Tanner's arm. What they put on him, Bethany had no idea, but they covered his wound with some kind of leaves.

They motioned for a cup and Bethany brought them one. One of the men rekindled Bethany's fire and she realized they must want to make something warm. She brought them a pan and watched curiously as one of the men heated water with several leaves.

Filling the cup with the liquid, one of the men took a sip and nodded to Bethany. She figured he was showing her that what he'd just made was not poison. He motioned for Tanner.

Bethany used a spoon to slowly seep some of the liquid into Tanner's mouth. The Indian nodded.

One of the men pointed to the cup and motioned to Tanner. *They must want me to give him the whole thing.* She nodded and attempted to smile.

Without another word both Indians left.

***

Through the day, Bethany did what she could for their survival. She made sure the horse was watered, refilled the canteen, and ate only enough to keep up her strength.

In the evening, Tanner called for Ruth again and Bethany sat beside him.

His head turned back and forth and he mumbled things Bethany couldn't understand.

"Where's Rachel?" He stopped moving and clutched her hand. He opened his eyes for a moment and Bethany wondered if he was coming out of it.

"I'm so sorry Ruth… I'm so sorry…"

Bethany saw tears flow down Tanner's face and she touched his cheek tenderly. "It's okay," she tried to keep him calm.

"Don't leave me, please don't leave me," Tanner held her hand as if his life depended on it.

"I won't leave." Bethany swallowed hard. It was difficult to watch this man suffer. She let him hold her hand while he drifted back into a fitful sleep.

Through the night she held his hand and talked to him. She quoted verses of scripture she'd memorized and sang hymns. Her voice seemed to bring comfort to his restless body.

***

The next day the Indians returned. This time, they brought her two large pelts of animal fur and lay them on the ground beside her bedroll. They almost seemed to be laughing at her thin quilt.

Without another word, they moved Tanner onto the thick fur, removed his bloodstained pants and covered him with his quilt.

Bethany kindled her fire for the men and watched as they repeated the same steps as the day before. She studied the leaves, curious where they could be found and whether they would actually do anything to help Tanner.

Before leaving, one of the Indians handed Bethany a basket filled with fruit and vegetables. Her eyes beamed with appreciation and they seemed satisfied with her joy.

After spoon-feeding Tanner with the Indian's medicine, Bethany ate several handfuls of blackberries and lay down on her own fur bed, letting its softness comfort her sore muscles and weariness.

In the evening Tanner broke out in chills, pulling Bethany from her sleep.

"I'm so cold... so cold..." he mumbled.

When Bethany touched his forehead, Tanner was roasting. She worked for over an hour trying to bring his temperature down using cool water from the stream.

His teeth chattered and he thrashed about in pain. Bethany lay beside him on her own fur bed with her hand on his. Her eyes were heavy and she wanted to sleep, but the young deputy needed her.

24

It was strange holding this man's hand. She'd never held a man's hand this way. Bethany ran her thumb over his knuckle to calm him. His hands weren't rough, but they felt strong.

Bethany wondered how Ruth would feel about another woman comforting him in this way. Was it wrong to hold his hand?

When she tried to pull it away, Tanner stirred. Her hand was his comfort.

***

On their third visit, Bethany's Indian friends brought another Indian and motioned to Bethany's eyes. The new visitor took Bethany's hand and led her outside into the sunlight. He seemed mesmerized by the blue in her eyes.

After the other two men were done helping Tanner, they joined their friend and talked about her in words she could not understand.

They motioned to the hill. Bethany figured they wanted to know if the wreckage belonged to them. She nodded. One of the men motioned for her to follow them. She hesitated. Zane's body was still there.

The men began to climb the hill and Bethany did her best to keep up. She slipped a few times on the moist undergrowth but reached the sight of the wreckage close behind them.

The men motioned to the wagon wheels and pulled them out of the wreckage. One of the Indians touched a wheel and patted his chest.

How could she explain to these Indians that the wagon actually belonged to the Vacaville police department and was not hers to give away? There was not much hope of rebuilding the wagon, most of the boards were broken and scattered along the hillside. Would Sheriff O'Brian even bother with it? She wanted to remain in good standing with these men who helped her the past several days. "You can have them," Bethany said, realizing they probably couldn't understand her. She pointed to them and nodded.

The Indians seemed pleased and began rummaging through the wreckage.

She turned around and noticed what was left of Zane's carcass. Her stomach heaved. Impulsively she covered her face. One of the Indians noticed her response. He gently took her arm and led her back to the cave entrance. He motioned toward Tanner as if encouraging her to continue caring for the injured man.

Throughout the day, Bethany could hear them working on the wagon. By early evening one of them motioned for her to follow and led her back to the wreckage.

Bethany first noticed the pile of rocks where the remains of Zane's body had been. She nodded her appreciation. She saw that the men had disassembled the broken wagon and stacked the shattered wood to the side. She motioned to the wheels and other scraps and pointed to them. "You may have it all."

The men seemed to understand and nodded. One of them helped her down the hill while the other two began carrying their spoils away.

***

For two more days the Indians came and helped Bethany care for Tanner. Her fear of them was completely gone now and she looked forward to their visits. It comforted Bethany to know these men were looking out for her.

One afternoon, they brought Bethany a pair of moccasins. The Indian holding the moccasins motioned to her stylish side-lacing boots and shook his head in disapproval. He said something that made Bethany think he was insulting her choice in footwear and insisted she take them off.

Bethany removed her boots and tried on the moccasins, allowing her new friend to show her how to tie them up. He nodded and spoke approving words.

"Thank you." She graced him with a sparkle in her blue eyes.

After they left, Bethany sat beside Tanner and ran her hand over his forehead. He was definitely cooler. She also noticed as the men doctored his arm that it was beginning to heal.

He moaned a few times and moved his head from side to side. Bethany wiped his brow with the cool rag and took his hand. Holding his hand always seemed to comfort Tanner.

"Our Indian friends brought me a pair of moccasins today," Bethany said, as if Tanner could hear her. She blew out a heavy sigh. It was strange talking to someone who was unconscious. "I think it was their way of thanking me for the wagon." She gently brushed his sweaty curls away from his forehead. "I gave them what was left of the police wagon the other day. I figured it was better to keep them happy than refuse them the right to the few undamaged wheels and metal scraps."

She leaned back against the cave wall and watched his restless sleep with concern. Would he ever come out of this?

Some time in the early morning, Tanner began to stir. Bethany sat up immediately, acutely attune to even his slightest movement. She reached for him in the dimly lit cave. "I'm right here," she said softly.

"Where are we?" This was not the delusional voice that had called for Ruth the past several nights.

"We're in a cave—we're safe." She touched his forehead and found it was much cooler. "You've been very sick."

Bethany realized this man probably still saw her as a murderer, a stranger, and a woman not to be trusted. But she'd spent six days with him, praying for him, caring for him, nursing him, and holding his hand.

Tanner reached for his arm and felt the leaves. "What is this?"

"They're leaves. I don't know what they're called," Bethany reached for the canteen. "The Indians brought them." She held the canteen to his lips and encouraged him to drink.

"Indians?"

"They helped us." She made sure Tanner's head was properly supported by the pillow she'd made for him out of a clean shirt and leaves.

"Is that where this pelt came from?" Tanner ran his fingers over the soft thick fur bed.

"Yes."

Tanner tried to sit but quickly gave up. "Where are my clothes?"

Bethany cleared her throat. "The Indians undressed you," she felt herself blushing. "I've washed them and have them ready for you."

Tanner glanced at her in the early morning sunlight. Bethany figured he had a lot of questions, but she encouraged him to rest.

***

Midmorning the Indians returned and Bethany met them at the cave entrance with a smile. "He is awake." There was relief in her voice. She led them to his bed and knelt beside him. "Sir." she gently touched his arm.

He turned his head and opened his eyes.

Without a word, the Indians began their morning routine. Tanner watched them curiously as they nursed his arm. Bethany urged him to sip the warm medicine they just made for him and he stared at her curiously.

"It's okay. I've been giving this to you for the past few days. I think it saved your life."

Tanner allowed Bethany to prop him up so that he could sip the warm liquid by himself.

One of the Indians motioned to Tanner's arm and held up one finger, made a motion toward the sun and held up another finger.

"Two more days," Bethany nodded. "Thank you." She reached for the Indian's hand and gave it a gentle squeeze.

He seemed to understand and gave her a nod.

Tanner watched the interchange and waited until the men left to speak. "How long have I been down?"

"This is day seven." Bethany knelt beside him and took his cup. "They've been coming for six days."

"How did you find them?"

"They found me." She leaned against the cave wall. "I think they heard the coyotes that went after Zane's body and undoubtedly they saw my fire."

Tanner lay his head down on the pillow and sighed. "I'm going to have to take care of Zane's remains."

"The Indians already did. They covered him in rocks." She got up to throw a few more twigs on the fire. "I gave them what was left of the wagon. I hope that was fine."

"These men… they treated you well?"

28

"Perfectly," Bethany smiled. "I think God sent them. I only wish I had a way to talk to them about God… to tell them about Jesus. They have been more than kind."

Tanner licked his dry lips and pulled the quilt up closer to himself. Bethany could tell he was still tired.

"Why don't you sleep? I need to water the horse and give him a new place to graze." She rose to her feet. "I won't be far. Your gun is right under my pillow."

***

The next two days were slow for Tanner. He wanted to be up, walking around, doing something, but he was too weak and tired. The Indians came back both days, medicated his arm and replaced the leaves. He was also urged to drink the bitter tasting liquid that Bethany said saved his life.

The Indians brought leather bags to Bethany on the second day as well as some extra friends. Tanner watched them cautiously as they took Bethany into the sunlight and took turns studying her eyes.

"Thank you for all you have done," Bethany spoke to them slowly in English. "I would like to pray for you." She reached for the two men's hands on either side of her and motioned for the other men to join hands.

Tanner could tell this was not something these Indian men were used to doing but they complied with the blue-eyed lady whom they all seemed to adore.

"Dear God. Thank You for these men," she prayed.

The Indians seemed to understand that she was talking to her God. There was a quiet reverence in the circle.

"Thank You that You created these men and have shown them ways to help others. Please help them to know and love Jesus. Show them Your Son."

She ended the prayer in Jesus' name and thanked each man individually for his help.

When they left, Tanner watched Bethany return to the cave. "I've never seen anything like that in my life."

"What?" she asked.

"You had a whole group of Indian men circled up in prayer… They adore you." He grinned.

She smiled shyly. "They brought us these leather bags. I think they meant for us to pack our belongings in them to make everything easier to carry." Bethany held the heavy leather containers curiously.

"It looks like they also made you some shoes." Tanner noticed her moccasins.

Bethany nodded. "They thought of everything."

Tanner glanced around the cave. "Miss Young, I'd really like to get dressed."

"Of course." Bethany brought him his clean clothes and stepped outside of the cave to give him privacy.

Tanner dressed as quickly as he could, but his sore arm made it difficult to do anything fast.

***

Bethany made stew for dinner using a rabbit the Indians brought her that day and what was left of the vegetables.

"When do you think you'll be well enough to travel?" Bethany asked.

Tanner took a bite of the warm food and savored the flavor. He looked up into Bethany's eyes curiously. "I'm hoping I'll be ready in a couple days."

Bethany nodded. Tanner noticed she did this a lot.

They ate quietly.

"Would you like more, sir?" Bethany asked after a few minutes.

Tanner declined. "My name is Tanner," he said. "You don't need to call me 'sir.'"

"Thank you. I wasn't sure." She smiled shyly.

Tanner studied her face. He'd only seen her smile a couple of times and it was when she talked about the Indians. The way her eyes lit up when she smiled was stunning. No wonder the Indians practically worshipped her. "I want to know what happened," Tanner finally said, setting his empty bowl aside. "I at least owe you the chance to tell me your side of the story." Tanner took a drink from the canteen. "You said you didn't kill your uncle. You said you don't have the money… I want you to explain."

Bethany lowered her eyes and her face took on a very serious expression. She licked her lips and blew out a steadying breath. "I went to church on that Wednesday evening as I always did," she began. "I had to walk because my uncle refused to allow me the use of a carriage for 'religious activities' as he called it." Bethany set her soup bowl aside. "On my way home, a man I'd never seen before approached me. At gunpoint he forced me into the back of a wagon where he gagged me, covered me with a tarp and held me down while the driver took us out of town."

Tanner could see the intensity in her face. This was not an easy story for her to share.

"We rode for what felt like half the night to a deserted cabin. It was dark and I could barely see anything. They brought me in the cabin and locked me in a room. The window was boarded up and there was nothing in the room but an old mattress and a couple of dirty smelling quilts." Bethany wiped away a tear and rubbed her forehead. She tried to still her breathing and held her lips together.

"Go on." Tanner was eager for her to continue.

"I was all alone in that room for about three days. I lost track of time because the room was so dark that I couldn't tell when it was day. They left me water and dried meat, but that was all." She brushed away another tear. "I thought I was going to go insane waiting. I pounded on the door until my knuckles were bruised. Whoever these men were, they planned on me being locked up and secured every escape."

Tanner narrowed his eyes. None of this made sense.

"When they finally returned, they left me locked in the room. They brought me food and water each day, but hardly spoke to me. I could hear their voices in the cabin. There was laughing and talking. But I could never make out what they were saying. I didn't know why I was there or what they planned to do with me." Bethany brushed a stray hair from her face.

"I was alone in that little room for about a week. Then one day they opened the door and told me I was wanted for murder." She shook her head. "They warned me if I returned to Santa Rosa I would be hung." Bethany lifted the canteen to her lips. "I didn't believe them at first. I didn't know what to believe, really. They gave me a bag of my belongings, several gold coins, and wished me good luck."

"They let you go?" Tanner asked.

"Yes. They just mounted their horses and rode away.

Tanner furrowed his eyebrows. "Could you identify these men?"

Bethany shook her head. "The night I was first taken, it was dark and I didn't get a good look at them. After that, they always covered their faces with bandanas and wore hats."

This story sounded hopeless.

"I was eager to leave the cabin, but I had no idea where I was. It took me two days to find a town. I ended up in Saint Helena, where my face was plastered on a wanted poster in the town's post office. It said I was wanted for murder, just like my captors told me. But I didn't know what it meant."

Tanner tried to read Bethany's eyes.

"I purchased a bonnet in one of the shops in Saint Helena and took a room at the hotel. For two days I wandered around the town inquiring as discretely as I could as to who this 'Bethany Young' was and why she was wanted for murder." A sob escaped her lips. "That's how I found out about my uncle." Her shoulders shook and her eyes welled up with tears. "A lady in Saint Helena told me that 'Bethany Young' murdered her uncle in cold blood." Bethany wiped her eyes. "I was shocked. Not only was I being accused of murder, but my uncle was dead. I couldn't even mourn for him." She lowered her face in her hands and cried.

Tanner watched her curiously. Was this show of emotion real?

After she calmed down, Bethany wiped her face on her skirt and continued her story. "I pried more, trying to understand why I was being accused. Eventually people started watching me. I paid for my room and slipped out of town the following night."

There had been a report that Bethany was seen in Saint Helena and used some of the gold coins stolen from her uncle's safe. But Tanner couldn't figure out how this story fit with the murder. "Where were you going?" he asked.

"I didn't know for sure. At first I planned to go to San Francisco to find my cousin, James. I sent him a letter, telling him what happened, but I had no way of knowing if he got it or if he would even believe me. I decided to go to Sacramento and search for information about my family."

"You were only another two days from Sacramento."

Bethany nodded. "I planned to leave Vacaville the morning you caught me." She took a deep breath. "How did you find me there?"

"I followed the gold."

Bethany waited for Tanner to explain.

"I wasn't far off your trail. The gold coins you used were some of the coins stolen from your uncle's safe. I tried to hit every small town between Santa Rosa and Vacaville seeing where you'd spent them."

"I don't understand." Bethany shook her head.

"Bethany," Tanner tried to explain. "Those coins were part of a collection of small, rare coins your uncle collected. Patrick's lawyer said your uncle kept them in his safe."

Bethany shook her head. "I didn't know."

"How could you not know?" Tanner was growing frustrated. "You used the coins you found in the safe… that points the crime right to you."

"I didn't take the coins. They were given to me… those men…" Bethany pleaded with her eyes.

"Miss Young," Tanner sighed impatiently. "Even assuming you didn't steal the coins, did you not recognize them?"

"My uncle never showed me those coins. He and I didn't talk much. Especially after my aunt's death." Bethany lowered her eyes. It was obviously painful to speak of her family. "He never talked to me about what was in his safe."

Tanner stared out the opening of the cave at the changing colors of the sky and tried to process what Bethany just shared in light of what he knew from his own investigation. It almost sounded like she'd been set up… framed. But how? The banker saw Bethany. Three of the servants saw Bethany. He glanced at her soft fine features and golden brown hair. Anyone who knew Bethany would recognize an imposter.

She turned her soft blue eyes on his.

There's no way anyone could imitate those eyes. He shook his head. *It had to be her…*

Chapter 3

The next two days Tanner worked to get his strength back. With his arm secured in a sling, he did his best to help Bethany pack their belongings in the new packs and explored the area around the accident. Bethany's Indian friends did a thorough job cleaning it up and took every bit of metal they could find.

Their food supplies were dwindling and Tanner knew they were still a couple days from the nearest town.

He hiked down the hill and found Bethany by the creek with the horse. They hadn't talked much since she shared her story. Tanner turned her story over and over in his mind, trying to look at it from every angle. She seemed so earnest… could someone fake that emotion? *Anyone cruel enough to kill her own uncle could fake her emotions.* Tanner was convinced there was no way her story could be true. *But why would she save my life? Why would she willingly let me take her back to Santa Rosa?* Was there something he was missing?

"I found some wild raspberries," Bethany called to Tanner as he approached.

Tanner glanced in the basket and grinned. "That's a whole meal."

Bethany nodded. "The Indians dry their berries. But I don't know how they do it."

"It would take days and we need to leave." He took the horse's lead rope and walked with Bethany up the hill toward the cave. He watched Bethany carry the berries into the cave while he tied the horse to a tree. "Bethany," he followed her to one of the animal furs and sat beside her. "You do know that I plan to take you to Santa Rosa."

The light quickly left her blue eyes. "I know." She picked through the ripe red berries and divided them between the two mugs. "I figured you didn't believe me."

Tanner sighed. "How could I? You were seen." He studied her face for some response.

"I have no explanation. I told you everything I know. I wasn't in Santa Rosa when my uncle was murdered. But I have no witnesses... only a small little shack in the middle of the woods somewhere east of Santa Rosa.

"A two day's hike from Saint Helena," Tanner added.

Bethany handed Tanner the mug of berries and drew in a shaky breath. "I'm really not afraid of dying..." she was quiet for a moment. "Only of people believing something not true of me. I guess I shouldn't care. God knows the truth. That's all that matters." Tears welled up in her eyes and Bethany set the bowl down. "I need to take a walk."

Tanner watched Bethany leave. Was she going to try to escape? It seemed unlikely. If Bethany was going to leave, she would have done it by now.

***

What felt like an hour passed and Tanner grew worried. What if she had run away? What if she'd gotten hurt? Both guns were still in the cave. Bethany had no real self-defense.

He made sure his gun was loaded and left the cave in search of her.

Tanner walked along the creek calling her name. The gentle sound of water rushing over the rocks drowned out his voice. Tanner almost gave up his search when he spotted her on a large rock in the middle of the creek.

"Bethany!" he called to her.

She wiped her face and put on a fake smile. "I'm sorry," she stood up in her bare feet and reached for her moccasins. "I lost track of time."

Tanner removed his boots and waded through the water toward Bethany. "This is a beautiful spot."

"I came here a couple times while you were sick." She moved over to make room for Tanner.

Tanner sat beside her and let his feet dangle into the water. "I thought maybe you'd run away."

Bethany shook her head. "What good would that do me? I have no alibi. I'm guilty until proven innocent."

Her words touched Tanner's heart. "That's not the way the law is written," he studied Bethany seriously.

"But that's the way it really is." Her eyes darted up to his. "And the worst part of it is, I'm going to die for no reason—it's like being murdered."

Tanner clenched his teeth and stared at Bethany. She had no way of knowing the sensitive nerve she'd hit in Tanner's heart.

"Someone set me up and I'm never going to find out who." She slid down from the rock and lifted her skirt from the water. "We should leave early tomorrow so I'm going try to get some sleep."

Tanner left her go and let his mind wander to the reason he first came to California. *Justice...*

***

Tanner and Bethany loaded the horse with all their belongings and began their long walk along the small road where they'd first traveled over a week ago. The weather was good and Bethany appreciated the comfortable moccasins for such a journey. The small town of Fairfield wasn't very far and Tanner hoped they'd be able to purchase a horse so they could both ride.

Bethany tried to see their week in the cave as an extra week of freedom. Had the accident not happened, they'd have made it to Santa Rosa by now and she would have met her end.

However, she was also thankful for Tanner's recovery and often wondered about Ruth and Rachel. They would surely be happy to see Tanner returning. He seemed like a good man, even if he did believe her to be guilty.

She glanced at Tanner out of the corner of her eye. Tanner had no way of remembering the hours she held his hand. It seemed strange to think about now. Bethany turned her face back toward the trail ahead of them. Ruth would never know the words he spoke for her while he was in a delirium. Whoever she was, Tanner loved her. What would it be like to be loved by a man like Tanner?

Bethany could almost feel the warmth of his hand holding hers. There was something comforting in it for her, too. For those hours, she was Ruth... he talked to her. He trusted her. He cried to her.

These thoughts were not helping her at all. Bethany took a deep breath and resolved not to let herself think them again.

"I figure when we stop for dinner, we can set up camp for the night," Tanner interrupted her thoughts. "We should be able to reach Fairfield by tomorrow."

Bethany nodded. "You should probably cuff me when we get to Fairfield." Her tone was somber.

"I was thinking I'd bring you into town with a disguise."

His response surprised her. "Why?"

"After what happened with Zane, I'm not sure it's safe to bring you through town. Even in cuffs, every bounty hunter this side of the Rockies will be looking for you."

"But if you've captured me, surely no bounty hunter will make a move." Bethany placed a hand on the horse to steady her steps.

"I'm not willing to take the risk."

Bethany was quiet for a moment. "Why does it really matter who brings me in? Unless you want the reward too..."

Tanner stopped and turned to Bethany. "I want justice, Miss Young. I'm not sure a bounty hunter cares. I don't plan on letting them just hang you—I aim to search out the truth."

"You mean there's a little bit of you that believes me?" Bethany felt a glimmer of hope.

Tanner didn't answer. He gave the horse a tug and they continued walking. "I'm thinking about taking a different way home," he said. "When we get to Fairfield, the better road dips south toward Vallejo. But if we head west toward Napa we can go through Saint Helena. When we had the wagon it might not have worked. But on horseback, the smaller road shouldn't be a problem."

"Why Saint Helena?" Bethany asked.

"I want to ask around about any abandoned cabins."

***

Fairfield was a sizeable town. Considered the midway point between San Francisco and Sacramento, it was a stopping point for many travelers. Tanner knew Bethany needed a good night's sleep in a clean hotel, but worried that bringing her into town would put her in danger unless he could somehow disguise her.

Tanner left Bethany well hidden in the woods several miles outside of Fairfield and promised to return before dark.

Finding a small shop in the center of town, Tanner purchased several yards of dark material and a cane.

Bethany's blue eyes were a blessing and a curse. It would not be so difficult to hide her lovely hair and her delicate facial features if they weren't the frames for two windows to the sky. Tanner decided to disguise her as a blind woman.

"Wear this black material over your head and keep your eyes closed," Tanner explained. "The cane is only for appearances. I will guide your steps."

Bethany did as she was told and kept her head bent low.

"I'll walk you in on the horse," Tanner explained as they neared the town. "There's a hotel just inside the town. We'll get two rooms and I'll make sure you are left to rest. Don't look at anyone."

Once in town, Tanner helped Bethany down from the horse and gave her the cane. With her eyes closed and her head bent low under the black head covering, one might have taken her for a very old woman.

"My sister and I need two rooms," he said to the hotel concierge.

Bethany let him lead her to a room and open the door. Once inside, he carried her bag to the bed and let out a heavy sigh.

"You lied to him," Bethany said in a disapproving tone as soon as he closed the door.

Tanner shook his head. "What choice did I have?"

"You could have said, 'this woman', 'this person,' 'my friend'…" Bethany gave him suggestions.

"Friend?" Tanner raised an eyebrow. "I'm about to turn you in for murder. Don't you think 'friend' would be a lie too?"

Bethany turned and walked to the mirror, which hung over a small oak washstand. She stared in the mirror and watched Tanner's reflection behind her. She studied his serious, dark brown eyes and thought about how expressive they were. "You're right," she said softly. "That would be a lie."

Tanner knew he'd just hurt her. With a sigh, he turned around and left.

***

Tanner left her alone. Bethany hadn't felt this alone since she'd been locked in the dark cabin in the woods. A bath had been brought to her room shortly after they arrived, and Bethany did her best to wash in the cold water.

Donning a clean slip, she pulled back the floral quilt from the double canopy bed and climbed into the clean white sheets.

Like salt in an opened wound, the realization that Tanner really wasn't her friend hurt Bethany. He'd arranged for Bethany to have a good night's sleep in a nice, clean hotel… wasn't that something you'd do for a friend? She'd sat up with him for a week, nursing him, helping him through the roughest nights. Didn't that make her his friend?

She pulled the sheets close to her face. The faint smell of lavender met her senses while a deep sense of loneliness engulfed her.

God, why? She buried her face in her hands and let herself cry. *Why is this happening? What do I do? I feel so alone…*

"I have called you friends…" Bethany remembered Jesus' words to her from John chapter 15 and it comforted her. *I think You're my only Friend right now…*

***

Sunlight streamed through the lace curtains in Bethany's hotel room and a cool breeze blew through the opened window. Bethany sat quietly, waiting for Tanner to arrive with instructions for the day.

Bethany appreciated the comfort of the soft featherbed and fine sheets, but she'd found it difficult to sleep. While she and

Tanner were in the cave, she was free. Now that they were in the real world, she was a prisoner again.

She stood by the window and watched as wagons rode past and townspeople hurried from one place to another. It would have been nice to explore the little town. *But I can't leave this room...* Bethany knew the risk. Her face was on posters all over these towns. Men like Zane would be scouring California, looking for a chance to earn a living.

But even if she got back to Santa Rosa alive, she would only be prolonging her death. Bethany sighed and stepped away from the window. *Someone committed the perfect crime and I'm the one who will take the fall.* It all seemed hopeless.

Tanner knocked on Bethany's door and she let him in. He carried a plate of warm biscuits and gravy from the hotel kitchen and a glass of fresh, cold milk.

Bethany thanked him.

"I plan to buy supplies." He set down her plate and averted her eyes. "I'll also be sending Sheriff Thacker a telegraph."

Bethany nodded. She could feel the tension in the room.

"Do you need anything from the store?" Tanner asked.

Bethany sat at the desk and took a sip of milk. "Whoever packed my bag for me neglected to pack my Bible." She glanced toward the opened window. "I really need a Bible."

"I'll see what I can do," Tanner walked to the door and slipped out quietly.

***

Downtown Fairfield was full of activity. Tanner knew he needed to hurry if they hoped to leave the next morning. His first goal was to send a telegraph to his boss. Vacaville was not yet wired with a telegraph so Tanner had not been able to send word to Sheriff Thacker that he'd apprehended Bethany. With a limited number of words, he told Sheriff Thacker that Bethany was in his custody, but that the search for Patrick Webber's murderer should still continue.

Tanner and Sheriff Thacker had a mutual respect for each other. Tanner hoped his senior would understand the telegraph's intended message.

After sending the telegraph, Tanner made his way to the general store. A bell over the door announced his arrival.

"Good morning," a friendly young woman greeted him.

Tanner returned the greeting and began collecting the things he and Bethany would need for the next week.

The bell over the door chimed again and Tanner heard the store clerk greet someone else.

"Morning, Sheriff," her friendly voice rang through the store.

"Morning, Elizabeth. Is your father around?"

"No, sir. He had to help Mr. Lawrence find one of their goats this morning."

The sheriff handed Elizabeth a poster. "Well, I need you to switch out that wanted poster with this one. The reward's been raised to five thousand dollars."

Elizabeth lifted the poster and studied the face. "Why this lady don't look no older than me."

"She's a heartless murderer, Elizabeth."

Tanner's arms were getting full. His healing arm ached under the weight. He roamed around the store wishing the sheriff would leave.

"Do you want to set your things down, sir?" Elizabeth called out to him.

The sheriff turned and noticed Tanner.

Tanner was sure the lawman would stick around now to see who this strange face was in their general store. Tanner carried what he'd gathered to the counter and hoped he could get done with his shopping without engaging in a conversation with the sheriff.

Elizabeth turned to Tanner. "What else do you need, sir?" She returned to the role of saleslady.

"I need a half pound of corn flour, a pound of oats and a Bible, if you have one." He glanced over his list in an effort to appear busy.

The sheriff leaned sideways on the counter, studying Tanner. "Where you visiting from?" he asked. "You look familiar," the sheriff pressed. "Do I know you?"

Tanner knew he needed to be honest with this fellow lawman. He'd have a hard time explaining himself later if this man ever learned Tanner was a deputy. "Santa Rosa." Tanner opened his vest and exposed his badge. "Deputy Brenly," he introduced himself.

"I thought I knew you," the sheriff said. "I'm Sheriff Baker. I was up in Santa Rosa a year ago. Brought back a couple of cattle rustlers."

Tanner remembered the case, although it looked like Sheriff Baker had put on a few pounds since then.

"So I guess you're familiar with Miss Young," Sheriff Baker turned the poster toward Tanner and watched his reaction carefully.

"Been investigating that crime for the past month." He glanced at the poster and played it casual. "When did they up the reward?"

Baker motioned toward the poster. "Just got word this morning. I guess the victim's son upped the ante with his own money." The sheriff turned the poster back to himself and smoothed it out. "Got any leads?"

Tanner kept a straight face. "A few. But I'm not totally convinced Miss Young is guilty." Tanner figured he'd shed some doubt on the rumors going around about Bethany.

His comment piqued the sheriff's curiosity. "Really? I was told this was a cut and dry case. Witnesses and all."

"There are some holes in the accusations that need cleared up." Tanner kept it vague.

"Well they'd better get cleared up before someone finds her. This poster here says 'dead or alive'. For that kind of money, she won't have no time to be explaining."

Tanner questioned the justice in that.

"I've got two Bibles left," Elizabeth interrupted the conversation for a sale. "Is this for you?" She gave him a flirty smile and turned her wide, brown eyes on his.

Tanner reached for one of the Bibles and flipped through a few of the pages. "No, ma'am. For a friend." As soon as he said it, Tanner's mind went back to the evening before. He knew he'd hurt Bethany when he told her she wasn't his friend.

It made sense. He couldn't be her friend. She was wanted for murder. She'd probably hang. Tanner didn't want to see any more people he cared about die.

"Is that all you need today?" Elizabeth pulled him from his thoughts.

"It is." Tanner could still feel the sheriff's eyes on him. He pulled out his money and counted what he owed.

"How long are you in town?" the sheriff asked.

"Leaving tomorrow." Tanner gathered up his packages. He knew the sheriff was hoping for more information, but Tanner was reticent to give any. The small lead Tanner had was thin. A cabin within a two-day walk of St. Helena was about as vague as he could get. He might be a fool for even following this lead.

Tanner headed back to the hotel and wondered how he was going to purchase a horse and get Bethany out of town without looking suspicious to the sheriff.

After taking his packages to the hotel, Tanner visited the stable where he was boarding his horse and asked where he might buy one more along with a saddle.

"I got this little mare here I'd sell," the stable owner walked toward a stall. "She's a pretty good horse. Had a guy boarding her for about six months and then he stopped paying. I told him she was mine to sell now."

Tanner looked her over carefully. "I'll take her. Got any tack?"

"I'll throw in everything the man left," the stable man said. "Got a saddle, a blanket, reins, bit, and even a couple saddlebags. Not in bad shape either."

Tanner gave the man his price. "I'll pick her up when I leave with this fella," he patted his own horse and rubbed his muzzle.

"What time you want them ready?"

"Before dawn," Tanner handed the man a wad of bills. "I'd like to leave quietly."

The man glanced at the money and grinned knowingly. "I won't even see you leave."

Tanner nodded. He hoped the man would keep his word.

***

Sheriff Alan Thacker held the telegraph in his hands, leaned back at his desk and read Tanner's short message for the

43

third time that day. *He's got Bethany Young but he wants me to keep investigating the murder?* Alan set the paper down and scratched his head. Tanner knew the details of this case. Several witnesses not only saw Miss Young take the money from the bank but she'd been home that morning to dismiss her servants.

Tanner's message troubled him. It wasn't like Tanner to question a case with this much evidence. The older man was unsettled. Just a few days ago the reward for Miss Young had been raised to five thousand dollars, an unheard of amount for a murderer. But her cousin, James, was determined that the woman who murdered his father be brought to justice.

It took almost a week for Alan to track down James Webber, whose business took him away from San Francisco regularly. As soon as James learned of his father's murder, he put his business aside and came to Santa Rosa to deal with his grief.

The man was greatly distressed to learn that his own cousin, raised as his younger sister, was the murderer. Showing no compassion, James increased the reward in his determination that she be punished.

In the weeks that followed the murder, Patrick Webber was buried and his lawyer was set into motion on the will. The stable hand that had been shot was Manny King. He was doing well and healing from a minor concussion and gunshot wound at the care of his brother and sister-in-law at their farm.

The head maid had no family in town. In her late sixties, Marie Chavez had served the Webbers since she was in her early twenties. She told everyone the Webbers were all the family she needed.

Marie had suffered a serious gunshot wound that only missed her heart by inches. Her recovery had been slow, but the doctor visited with her regularly at the Webber estate where she was being cared for and said that she appeared to be pulling through.

Alan questioned Manny King as soon as the man was well enough to talk. The stable hand's story was vague. Miss Young had asked him to have a carriage ready to take into town. She'd mentioned needing to go to the bank.

He'd gotten the horses ready quickly but wondered if the lady would prefer the open carriage since it was such a lovely day.

He had just opened the front door and called for Miss Young when he'd heard shots fired. Instinctively he ran back to the stable. Manny couldn't be certain who followed him because he never looked back, but the person shot him while he was climbing the ladder to the loft where he kept his own gun. He thought he saw Miss Young just as he fell from the ladder and landed unconscious on the ground.

Alan had no trouble connecting the dots. Manny witnessed her just after she shot Patrick and Marie. She then followed him to the stable in a vain attempt to silence him.

The only thing he hadn't figured out was, with Manny unconscious on the floor of the stable, who drove Miss Young to town?

***

It was late when Tanner knocked on Bethany's hotel door carrying a tray of food. He handed her a full plate of fried chicken, carrots, fresh cornbread and a baked potato. It was the nicest meal Bethany had seen since her last night in Santa Rosa.

She carried the plate to her desk and began to eat as soon as she prayed. It had been a long day. Tanner had dropped by in the mid-afternoon to bring her some fruit and lemonade, along with the new Bible he'd bought. But he didn't stay to talk.

He seemed distracted but Bethany was afraid to ask questions.

"We need to leave before dawn," he studied her face and then paced the room.

"Okay."

"The sheriff in this town knows I'm looking for you." Tanner took a seat at the edge of Bethany's bed.

"He knows that you're looking for me or that you've found me?" Bethany wanted to clarify.

Tanner shrugged. "He knows I'm on the case." Tanner took a sip of his lemonade and set the glass down on the nightstand. "He recognized me, so I had to tell him who I was." Tanner shook his head. "I was a fool for bringing you into this town."

"Would I have been much safer on the outskirts?"

"I don't know." Tanner shook his head. "We should have just headed northwest."

"We needed to get supplies," Bethany wondered why Tanner seemed so upset. "Sheriff O'Brian knew about me. What is the danger of this sheriff knowing?"

Tanner sighed. "You're wanted for murder, Bethany." Tanner ran his fingers through his dark curly hair. "When you travel with a murder suspect, it's customary to have a traveling companion and make sure the suspect is properly secured."

"So cuff me." Bethany knew what the metal bracelets felt like. How much worse could it get?

"I don't want this sheriff getting involved. Not if we're going to try to find that cabin. There's not enough evidence to warrant such a search. All I've got is a story from you and the fact that you saved my life." Tanner's eyes softened and he searched Bethany's face intently. "For whatever reason, I need to see if that cabin exists." He lowered his face. "I need to know the truth."

Bethany's heartbeat quickened. Tanner may not be her friend, but she knew he cared.

Tanner rose to go but stopped when he reached the door. He turned and looked at Bethany. "When I was sick you prayed for me, didn't you?"

Bethany nodded. His dark eyes were expressive.

"You kept repeating a Bible passage to me. It was familiar."

"The Lord is my shepherd, I shall not want." Bethany recited from memory. "He makes me lie down in green pastures; He leads me beside quiet waters. He restores my soul; He guides me in the paths of righteousness for His name's sake. Even though I walk through the valley of the shadow of death, I fear no evil, for You are with me; Your rod and Your staff, they comfort me. You prepare a table before me in the presence of my enemies; You have anointed my head with oil; my cup overflows. Surely goodness and lovingkindness will follow me all the days of my life, and I will dwell in the house of the Lord forever."

Tanner nodded. "My..." he paused. "A friend from my past used to recite those verses." His voice was thick with emotion.

"It's Psalm 23. It's a very popular passage of scripture."

46

Tanner took a deep steadying breath. "But it's not always true."

Bethany stared at him curiously. "What do you mean?"

"Sometimes goodness and lovingkindness don't follow us. Where is the Shepherd then?" There was passion in his eyes.

"The passage tells us He is always with us," Bethany said. "Sometimes bad things do happen, but we have to trust that He is still in control. He promises us that one day we will sit at His table and that we will dwell in His house forever. It's not always about this life."

"But what about those who are still in this life? What about us?" Tanner's eyes flashed.

"To us He provides comfort."

Tanner shook his head. "I haven't found that to be true." He opened the door. "I hope it works for you."

***

Tanner had the horses to the hotel before dawn the next morning. After paying the bill, he led Bethany to the horses and helped her mount. She was quiet. Tanner wasn't sure if she was upset about their conversation the night before or if she was just tired.

Tanner's nerves were on edge. He'd not told Bethany the reward for her head was now five thousand dollars. With numbers like that, Tanner knew the search for her could get ugly. Even though Sheriff Thacker would have received his telegraph by now, she was still free game until she got to Santa Rosa.

A thick fog lay low over the town. Bethany mounted the horse and pulled the dark covering over her head. She glanced quickly at Tanner for direction.

"Just ride beside me and keep your head down." Tanner knew his 'blind sister' act wouldn't fly if he came upon the sheriff. The man already knew Tanner was investigating the Bethany Young case.

The sound of their horses' hooves echoed in the fog and Tanner held one hand on his gun while they rode.

Tanner heard the other horseman before he was upon them.

"Leaving kind of early aren't you?" Tanner heard the click of Sheriff Baker's gun.

"Is there a problem?" Tanner knew it was futile to run.

Baker brought his horse closer. "Only problem is you telling the owner of the hotel livery that you'd like to leave quietly." He steadied his gun on Tanner. "Care to explain?"

"Sheriff Baker, I assure you, my intentions were to keep myself clear of bounty hunters who would rather take the law into their own hands rather than trust those whose job it is to uphold the law."

"So my hunch was right," Baker drew his horse closer to Bethany. "You've got Miss Young." He reached over and yanked the dark covering from Bethany's head, exposing her golden brown hair and frightened eyes.

Tanner clenched his jaw. For some reason he didn't feel good about Sheriff Baker knowing this information.

"I saw you two riding in together the other night," Baker said. "I'd heard Santa Rosa's only deputy was hot on her trail, but somehow I didn't expect you to bring her into town un-cuffed and unattended."

"Do you really need to point that gun at me?" Tanner's nerves were mounting. "There's a lot you don't understand about this case and Sheriff Thacker is expecting us in a few days."

"Yeah," Baker pulled out a telegraph note. "He wrote you back yesterday evening." He glanced at the paper. "Said he'd investigate your concerns, but that the reward was high and to watch your back."

"You intercepted my message?" Tanner eyed Baker coolly. "That's highly illegal."

"It's a message from one lawman to another," Baker shrugged. "I thought maybe I could help."

"What do you want?" Tanner could see there was more to this than an offer of assistance.

"Where are the cuffs on the girl?" Sheriff Baker asked accusingly. "She looks pretty comfortable for an apprehended criminal. Where were you taking her?"

Somehow Tanner knew the story of Bethany saving his life wasn't going to go far with this shady sheriff. "Miss Young knows better than to try to escape and I'm taking her to Santa Rosa."

"Not today you're not," Baker narrowed his eyes. "I need to investigate your intentions. I'm a little surprised you'd be making disguises for her and ushering her through my town as your sister if you're really planning to take her to Santa Rosa."

Tanner shook his head in frustration. "This disguise is to protect Miss Young while I get her to Santa Rosa. You know as well as I do that with a bounty as large as she's got on her head, I'll be lucky to get her there alive."

"Well then, wouldn't you be better off letting me give you aid taking your prize back to Santa Rosa, Deputy Brenly?" Baker motioned to someone in the shadows. "I've got a few good men willing to lend a neighborly hand."

Tanner watched while two more riders approached through the lifting fog.

"Let's take her back to the jail while I send a little message to your sheriff asking him why you'd be sneaking off alone with her before the sunrise."

Tanner's heartbeat raced as he watched one of Baker's men pull Bethany from her horse. "Leave her alone!" Tanner reached for his gun.

"Get your hands in the air where I can see them," Baker warned. The sheriff motioned for another man to remove Tanner's gun from his holster.

"Cuff her." Baker ordered.

Bethany gave Tanner one helpless glance as the man cuffed her and gave her a shove back toward town with the barrel of his gun.

"You'd better come too, deputy." The sheriff motioned with his gun.

Chapter 4

Once again, Bethany found herself handcuffed, sitting on a hard mattress in a small dirty jail cell. This time, however she listened while Tanner argued for her—not against her.

"You do not have authority to apprehend my prisoner!" Tanner smacked Officer Baker's desk. "You've compromised my mission and now there's a dozen bounty hunters outside that door drooling for the chance of ushering her back to Santa Rosa."

"Well, maybe if you'd have worked with me when you first got here instead of sneaking around on your own private mission, this wouldn't have happened." Baker glanced at his deputy and grinned.

"So, what are you planning? You're going to let the one who'll give you the most money take her in? Is that it?" Tanner paced the room.

Baker narrowed his eyes. "You do realize I'm the sheriff in this town and you're just a deputy miles away from your jurisdiction. Don't sass me, kid!" Baker slammed both hands on his desk and leaned forward toward Tanner. "You're just bringing me one step closer to arresting you for teaming up with that little tramp to run off with whatever money she's got in hiding."

"Sheriff Thacker knows better."

"Does he?" Baker grinned. "I've got witnesses that say you got her a hotel room across the hall from yours and that you were seen going into her room multiple times. There's also the question of minimal security. Since when are murderers given their own private rooms, a horse, and not hand cuffed?"

Tanner slapped the wall. "She's not a murderer!"

Bethany's head shot up and she caught Tanner's eyes for just a moment. He believed her.

50

Tanner rolled up his sleeve and exposed his arm. "See this. I was trapped under a wagon with a piece of wood jammed in my arm. Bethany Young saved my life. She spent a week nursing me back to health, knowing I was the one taking her to Santa Rosa to meet her fate. This woman isn't a murderer."

"And you're just a kid whose been duped by a pretty face," Baker laughed. "This makes the story even better."

Tanner shook his head.

"There's no way I'm letting you take this girl in," Baker gave Tanner an icy stare. "You can't be trusted."

It all began to sink in for Tanner. Sheriff Baker wanted the reward for himself. This wasn't about Tanner sneaking out of town with a prisoner. Sheriff Baker was determined to find reasons to discredit Tanner. This was about a woman worth five thousand dollars dead.

"Where are my horses?" Tanner's glared at the sheriff.

"I'm holding them for investigation."

Tanner tried to still his breathing. "My stuff?"

"Yes." Baker flicked a piece of dirt out of his fingernail. "I have a question about that extra gun. I believe it was in Miss Young's saddle bag."

"That's not true." Tanner took a few steps closer to the sheriff. "You have no authority to hold my belongings." Anger burned in his eyes. "You're nothing but a criminal with a badge!"

Before he could react, Sheriff Baker's deputy grabbed Tanner by the collar and threw him into a wall. Searing pain shot through his wounded arm and Tanner clenched his teeth to hide the pain.

"You don't talk to the sheriff that way," the deputy spat. He used his backhand to slap Tanner across the mouth.

Tanner wiped away the blood and moved toward the door.

"Watch yourself, kid." Baker sat down and leaned back in his chair. "And remember, you're not a deputy in this town."

***

Tanner stormed out of the sheriff's office with a burning mission in his heart. He had to get Bethany out of that jail. He paced back and forth in front of the sheriff's office trying to work off steam.

She was alone in a jail cell with a corrupt sheriff in control of her future. Where was her Shepherd now? Was He comforting her? Was He leading her beside quiet waters? Was He restoring her soul? Tanner kicked a rock into the road.

He regretted the words of hopelessness he'd unleashed on Bethany the night before. She needed that hope, especially now.

Instinctively he knew he was being watched. Did everybody in this town work for the sheriff? Even his telegraphs weren't safe.

Without a horse Tanner was trapped in this town. *This is insanity.* Tanner headed toward the hotel. He needed to find a place to cool down, away from all the eyes.

"Back so soon?" the hotel concierge glanced up from his desk when Tanner walked through the door.

"I think I'll stay another night." He feigned a smile.

"And your *sister*... will she be returning?" The man eyed Tanner knowingly.

Tanner's temper was hot. He contemplated grabbing the man by his shirtfront and saying a few nasty words, but this was the only hotel in town. "She has other accommodations tonight." Tanner challenged the man with his eyes.

"I'm so sorry. Well, our rates went up a little bit since yesterday." The man set a room key on the desk. "They're actually double."

Tanner glanced angrily at the key and back at the concierge. He clenched his fists and reflected quickly on the potential consequences of using them. He shook his head. "This place isn't worth it." He knocked the key across the desk and walked through the doors, fantasizing about slamming the man's face into the wall.

He scanned the town for some place safe from the eyes of Sheriff Baker's informants. Two drunk men stumbled out of the small saloon only a few doors down from the telegraph office. *Drunk before noon... Are these more of Sheriff Baker's friends?* Tanner walked toward the saloon and slipped in quietly. At least he could sit and think for a while.

"What can I get you?" the bartender asked as soon as Tanner took a seat at the far end of the bar.

"Whisky, straight." Tanner leaned back in his seat and scanned the room.

Tanner rarely drank. At one time in his life, he would never have touched alcohol. But today he hoped it might serve to make him credible with someone the sheriff didn't have as an informer. *Surely the man has at least one enemy… and I hope to find him.*

Tanner paced his drinking, making time his friend. He watched discreetly as various customers moved in and out of the saloon. A couple of the men Tanner recognized. He'd seen them hanging out near the sheriff's office.

"Hey, Walt," a tall, skinny man took the seat next to Tanner and greeted the bartender.

"Hi, Charlie." Without a request, the bartender handed the man a beer. "What's going on at the sheriff's office?" Walt said so quietly Tanner had to block out all other sounds to hear.

Charlie glanced at Tanner and picked up his beer. "Don't know nothing."

Walt nodded and went to tend another customer.

Tanner was sure this man knew something. It was time to play drunk and mouthy.

"Oh come on…" Tanner downed his shot and rocked unsteadily on his seat. "When even the visitors in town know the dirt, don't pretend you don't know," he laughed and pounded his glass on the bar. "One more!" he called out and grinned at Charlie. "Pretty things like her don't make it far when they've got a bounty on their heads."

Charlie glanced nervously over his shoulder and narrowed his eyes. "Aint' you that deputy that tried to sneak off with her?"

Tanner scratched his face and slapped down a few bills for Walt. "I aint' saying who I am. Not in this shady little town full of secrets."

Walt leaned forward on his elbows and slid the glass toward Tanner. "What's the scoop?"

Tanner bent forward. "Some lady worth five grand is holed up in the jail…"

"Heard you were bringing her to Santa Rosa and Baker took her right out from under you," Charlie spoke softly. "That true?"

"What if it is?" Tanner slurred. What did these guys know? Did they approve of Sheriff Baker's practices?

Walt shook his head. "If it is – that no good excuse for a lawman needs to be taken down a notch that's what."

"What are you saying?" Tanner narrowed his eyes. "You're not one of his spies?"

Walt let out a dry chuckle. "You've got to be clan for that. This town is run by Bakers. The only reason my saloon survives in this town is because I provide them with cheap liquor."

Tanner studied Walt for a moment. Could this man be trusted? Very discretely Tanner exposed the badge he wore under his leather vest and eyed Walt knowingly.

Walt nodded. "That dirt bag…"

Tanner quit the drunk routine and spoke in hushed tones. "How do you feel about hanging a woman before she's proven guilty?"

Charlie leaned in close. "They said she murdered her uncle and took off with over two hundred thousand dollars worth of cash and gold."

Tanner shook his head. "Don't believe everything you hear."

Walt pretended to wipe down his counter top. "Is she innocent?"

"Until proven guilty," Tanner said.

The bartender needed to step away for a few minutes to wait on other customers but returned with another beer for Charlie. "My brother was hung in this town a couple years ago," he said softly. "He was accused of murdering his wife. After they hung him, they found the real killer. Sheriff Baker never did his work, and the real killer went free." There was bitterness in Walt's eyes. "The killer was a Baker."

Tanner just found Sheriff Baker's enemy.

"They're talking about hanging the girl," Charlie glanced around to see if anyone was listening. "Guess the poster said dead or alive."

Tanner ran his fingers through his hair and shook his head. He had to get her out of here. How much should he tell these two men? Were they really sympathetic or were they just better than he was at putting on a show?

"Listen," Walt watched a group of men who just slipped into the saloon. "We can't talk now. But I want to hear your story. I take a break at three. Meet me at the water tower."

Tanner nodded. Walt's eyes told him the men who'd just entered the saloon were Baker's friends. It was time to leave.

***

Tanner stepped from the saloon doing his best 'drunk' routine again. He stumbled into the street and headed toward the telegraph office.

He wished there was some other way to communicate with his boss, but once he left Fairfield there wouldn't be another telegraph office for days.

The telegraph attendant glanced with mistrust at this deputy who, rumor had it, tried to sneak out of town with a known killer.

"I need to send a telegraph," Tanner knew he smelled like whisky and hoped he could convince the proprietor that he planned to send a drunken plea to his boss in order to save his job. He also hoped Sheriff Thacker would read between the lines.

"What's the message?"

Tanner leaned on the edge of the counter, pretending it was the only thing holding him up. "What do you think I should write? I'm about to lose my job… that's what I get for getting tangled up with a pretty face."

The telegrapher gave a knowing grin. Tanner was sure this man had been given some kind of story that would fit Tanner's lie.

"Tell him you're sorry…" the man suggested.

"I've done that before," Tanner slurred. "He's tired of me giving him words. How about, 'Trust me. No more words.'"

"It might work." The telegrapher sounded unconvinced.

"Then that's what I want!" Tanner smiled and slapped a few bills on the counter. He watched as his message was sent and hoped Sheriff Thacker would understand.

***

Tanner found Walt smoking a cigarette on the far side of the water tower at three. The afternoon sun was high in the sky and there wasn't a cloud in sight. The water tower was far enough out of town that anyone watching would be easily spotted.

"So this woman…" Walt studied Tanner curiously. "You're sure she's innocent?"

"How honest can I be with you?" Tanner was desperate for someone who would hear him out and tell him if he was a fool.

"Let's take a walk. My house is just around the corner. Have you eaten?"

Tanner shook his head. He'd been too stressed for food.

Watching their backs carefully, Walt and Tanner headed to a nicely kept cabin a quarter of a mile from the water tower but off the beaten track.

"I'm not the best cook." Walt pulled a loaf of bread out of a breadbox. "It's just me living here."

Tanner looked around at the nicely furnished cabin and figured Walt must be doing pretty well as a saloon proprietor. He took a seat at an ornately carved oak table and realized how hungry he really was.

Walt made them both sandwiches and placed a mug of hot coffee in front of Tanner. Then he walked to a back room and returned carrying a well-worn photograph. "This was my brother, Roy," he set the photo down in front of Tanner. "That's his wedding picture. He and Gina got married in Indiana. That's where I'm from. They moved out here to chase gold." Walt sighed heavily. "He wanted me to go into business with him opening the saloon. It paid better than farming and took a lot less work, so I sunk a few hundred dollars in with him and became his partner."

Tanner took a few bites of his sandwich and listened quietly.

"Gina was a bit of a flirt. Being exposed to all those men at the saloon wasn't good for her. One night, she and Matthew Baker slipped off and compromised her marriage covenant."

It was easy to see where this story was going.

"My brother was heartbroken. But he said he'd forgive her if she'd break things off and never see the man again. Gina promised. But she wasn't a woman of her word. A few months later, Gina was found shot dead in her lover's bedroom. Matthew claimed that my brother caught them and that Roy shot her." Walt shook his head. "I knew better. Roy was with me. We were at the bank taking out a loan when Gina got shot. But the banker wouldn't own up to it. Roy was hung and two months later the truth came out. It was Matthew's wife who caught them. She confessed to killing Gina but instead of punishing her, she and Matthew took off and were never found."

"Convenient." Tanner understood what it was like to have a killer slip away before justice could be served.

"So, you going to tell me your story?" Walt took a drink of his coffee and gave Tanner the floor.

Tanner started from the beginning and held nothing back. He needed some perspective and this sympathetic ear seemed sharp enough to give an honest assessment.

Walt asked several questions along the way and finally got up to refill his coffee. "So she had opportunities to kill you multiple times."

"Yeah. And she could have killed Zane. But she let me do that."

Walt glanced toward the window. "If she wanted to escape, it would have been so easy."

"She nursed me for over a week." Tanner let his eyes travel to Walt's kitchen window. "I don't remember much. I had a terrible fever." He steadied his eyes on Walt. "I have faint memories of someone holding my hand and speaking words of comfort to me though the hours of my sickness...she could have run away and left me to die in that cave. Instead she nursed me back to health."

"Doesn't sound much like a murderer."

Tanner agreed. "There's something about her story. As crazy as it seems, I believe her."

"She deserves a fair trial." Walt said.

"But with a five thousand dollar reward on her head, who's going to give it to her?"

Walt studied Tanner for a moment. "I'll help you get her out."

Tanner breathed a heavy sigh. "You're willing to do that?"

The saloon proprietor smoothed out his salt and pepper hair and rubbed his rough chin. "You know, I've been serving these drunk idiots for about eight years. I watched them kill my brother. I've watched Sheriff Baker take bribes and I've watched him turn a blind eye. There's nothing I'd like better than to give back to him a little bit of what he's been dishin' out."

"But I don't want you end up there. If we fail, we'll be the ones with our necks in a noose." Tanner tried to count the cost.

Walt shrugged. "Someone has to stand up against his injustice. And hopefully your boss will hear you out when you get back to Santa Rosa."

Tanner hoped he would. "You know, running a saloon isn't the only way to make money in California." He steadied his eyes on Walt. "I don't really want to see any more saloons in Santa Rosa, but we're not a town run by Bakers."

"I'll think about that," Walt grinned. "What do we need to do for a jail break?"

***

Bethany leaned her head against the hard, stone wall and closed her eyes. It was quiet in the sheriff's office. Sheriff Baker and his men left hours ago, leaving her with a piece of hard bread and a tin cup of dirty water.

This was no different than being locked in the dark cabin in the middle of the woods. She felt so alone. If only they would have given her the Bible that Tanner had purchased for her the day before. She asked the sheriff for it but he'd refused to give it to her.

Father... she prayed softly in her cell. *Why is this happening? None of this makes sense. Why would someone want to frame me for murder?*

Bethany thought about the peaceful life she lived in Santa Rosa. Her circle of friends was small. It wasn't that she was unsocial, but her uncle rarely entertained. She had a private tutor during her years of education and spent most of her free time with her aunt, until the dear woman passed away. Occasionally, Bethany attended a dinner party with her uncle, but he was not fond of mingling in society.

Recently, she was beginning to get acquainted with a few ladies from her church but her closest friend was Marie, who'd worked as a servant in her uncle's house for as long as Bethany could remember.

After her aunt passed away, Bethany looked up to the woman like a mother. *Does Marie think I murdered Uncle Matthew?* The thought grieved her. *Wouldn't Marie have told the police that I was missing? Surely Marie could testify for me. Unless...* Bethany covered her mouth at the thought. Was Marie okay? She remembered hearing that two of the household staff had been shot. *What if one of them was Marie?*

Tears welled up in her eyes and she covered her face with her hands.

The Lord is my Shepherd...

***

Tanner woke up on the soft feather bed in Walt's guest room and stared at the ceiling. Walt's cabin had all the amenities. It was clean, well furnished, and comfortable. In spite of the comforts, Tanner had a restless night's sleep, thinking of all the things he could have done differently to prevent Bethany's capture.

Why didn't we just bypass Fairfield? What if I'd left Bethany outside of town? Why didn't we just leave after I sent my telegraph to Alan?

Tanner could hear Walt moving around in the kitchen. The smell of bacon and coffee reminded him once again that he'd been fortunate to make this new friend.

Walt wanted to help. He offered Tanner a place to stay and helped devise a plan for breaking Bethany out of jail. They'd stayed up half the night working out the details. Tanner hoped their plan would work.

"Do those clothes fit you alright?" Walt asked Tanner when he stepped into the kitchen.

Tanner glanced down at the almost brand new pair of blue jeans and clean brown and white checked shirt he now wore under his leather vest. "Like they were made for me."

Walt scraped two fried eggs and a couple slices of bacon on a plate and set it at the table for Tanner. "I figured you were about my size."

"I still feel like I should pay you for all this." Tanner said.

Walt had given Tanner another clean pair of pants, a shirt, two thick quilts, and an abundance of food and camping supplies.

"You don't owe me a thing." Walt slid a Colt Walker across the table toward Tanner. "I've been waiting a long time to pay Sheriff Baker back for what he did to my brother." He nodded toward the gun. "That was Roy's gun." He stared at it for a moment. "I haven't touched it in years. Take it."

Tanner lifted the smooth six shot revolver and turned it over in his hands.

"It's a single action revolver," Walt explained. "Ever shot one of those?"

Tanner nodded. "It's a powerful gun. I can't take this." He glanced up at Walt. "It was your brother's. You should keep it."

Walt shook his head. "I've got other keepsakes from Roy. The gun holds no special meaning." Walt sat across from Tanner. "You need a gun, especially if we're about to break someone out of jail."

It was doubtful Sheriff Baker would give Tanner back his own gun. "I can't thank you enough." Tanner set down the firearm and began eating his breakfast.

The two men continued talking through their plans.

Tanner was pleased to learn that in spite of Walt's minimal connections in Fairfield, he was friends with a man who owned a livery stable. They planned to strike up a deal with the man for two fresh horses off the record.

"My buddy, Ivan, can equip you with a couple nice saddles and saddlebags, too," Walt said. "We'll head on over there after breakfast."

Tanner tried not to think about the potential consequences of what they were about to do. There was no turning back once this plan was set in motion. He hoped his instincts were correct.

***

The word in town was that they were going to hang Bethany tomorrow and take her body back to Santa Rosa. Tanner's eyes scanned the gallows in the center of town and wondered how many innocent victims met their fate at the end of that rope.

Unconsciously he rubbed his neck and turned away.

Walt's friend proved to be an asset. After meeting with Ivan that morning, Tanner was now the owner of two fresh horses and everything he and Bethany would need to ride.

Tanner made his way to the saloon after arrangements were made for his horses to be readied and delivered at the specified time. Ivan gave his word and even added several rounds of ammunition to Tanner's assortment of supplies.

It seemed Sheriff Baker had more than one enemy in Fairfield.

Their plans were laid in place, now they just had to wait.

Tanner headed into the saloon and caught the eyes of the man who'd pulled Bethany from her horse the day before. The man glared at Tanner as he made his way to the bar. Tanner sat at the bar and waited for Walt.

"The place is crawling with Bakers," Walt whispered. He slid a shot of whisky across the bar and accepted Tanner's payment. "I'll tell you when."

Tanner downed the shot, glanced around at his audience and turned on the show. "Give me another one of these," he ordered.

People came and went over the next couple hours. Tanner kept to himself and waited for the signal from Walt.

"This is it," Walt spoke softly as he wiped down the counter in front of Tanner.

Doing his best drunk impersonation, Tanner wobbled to his feet, paid Walt and staggered out the door to an empty bench in front of the post office, making sure the men he'd seen with Sheriff Baker witnessed him leaving.

With one quick glance at the sun as it lowered itself in the western sky, Tanner waited for the plan to unfold.

***

61

Walt grinned when Ben Baker stepped into the saloon. Ben was one of Walt's favorite drunks. He had the temper of a hot volcano and the alcohol tolerance of a grandma. When Ben ordered a shot of whisky, Walt made it a double and claimed all his single shot glasses needed washed.

Once Ben downed his double, he was ready for more. Walt hid his grin and kept the whisky coming.

The saloon was filling up quickly. There was a lot of talk about the hanging scheduled for tomorrow. Watching a hanging usually got people outside talking. Walt pieced together the town gossip and figured out Sheriff Baker's story. He'd caught the deputy of Santa Rosa trying to help Miss Young escape but didn't have enough evidence to arrest him. Instead the poor fool was sitting in a drunken stupor outside the post office. Bethany Young was going to hang tomorrow and Sheriff Baker hired two respectable men to deliver her body and bring home the reward.

Walt tried to hide a grin. *We'll see how that works out for you...*

Ben was well on his way to severe intoxication when he called Walt over for a refill. "Are you sure you should have another?" Walt spoke his concern loud enough for witnesses to know he was doing his part to keep Ben out of trouble.

Ben slapped his fist on the table. "Shut up and bring me a drink."

Walt watched Ben talk to another drunk named Frank. It was no secret that Frank was a womanizer and turned the eyes of half of the women in Fairfield. This was just perfect.

After Frank walked away, Walt set the drink in front of Ben. "I'd watch him," Walt whispered.

Ben narrowed his eyes and tried to scrutinize Walt through blurred vision. "Why?"

"Come on, Ben... haven't you heard the rumors?" Walt shook his head knowingly and walked away.

The match was lit. Now he needed just a few more bombs.

At the bar, Walt scanned Baker's top henchmen lined up in a pack. He refilled their drinks and shook his head in disapproval.

"What's the news?" One of the men leaned forward to interrogate Walt who was known as the source of all juicy information.

"There's a lot of gossip about the plan for Miss Young, after she's been hanged."

"What kind of gossip?" the man leaned closer.

"That those of you delivering her dead body better watch your backs." Walt watched the man glance around the room. "There are quite a few men interested in that five thousand dollar reward."

Baker's man scanned the saloon and let his eyes rest on several shady bounty hunters. "Those guys are just jealous because the sheriff has us doing the job."

Walt shrugged. "I'd just be careful if I were you."

He wiped off the counter and poured a few beers to deliver to the shady bounty hunters.

"Here's your drinks, men," he set the beers in front of the men and wiped off their table. "Don't let those other men bother you. I don't need any problems in my saloon." Walt acted like he was eager to walk away.

One of the bounty hunters grabbed his arm. "What are you saying?"

"Just that those men seem to think you men are jealous and well… you know how they are." He took a few steps back. "Look, the beer's on me, okay?"

Walt was barely back to the bar before the fuse began to smoke. Ben and Frank started having words and Walt was shocked to learn that his hints had more truth in them than he knew. The heat in the saloon grew when the bounty hunters marched over to the bar to tell the henchmen to watch their backs.

It pained Walt a little to see things erupt. He knew it was going to mean quite a clean up for him tomorrow, but he stepped into the shadows while the brawl began.

"Call for the sheriff!" he finally ordered one of his employees. The noise in the saloon had reached the streets outside and already people were headed inside to see what was going on.

***

This was Tanner's cue; he sat on the sidelines and watched the sheriff and one of his deputies hurry across the street with guns waving in the air. Chaos had erupted in Fairfield and Walt helped

63

orchestrate it. *Thanks, Walt*... Tanner slipped into the sheriff's office unnoticed.

"Bethany?" he called as he walked into the vacant office.

"Tanner?" Bethany rose from her bed and hurried to the cell door. Her eyes were wet with tears and she watched him in disbelief. "What are you doing here? Its not safe for you..."

"I'm getting you out of here. Did you happen to see where they keep the keys?" He seriously hoped they weren't with Sheriff Baker.

Bethany shook her head. "I don't know." She clutched the iron bars nervously. "But, Tanner, that sheriff is just looking for a reason to arrest you..."

"So I've heard." He searched Baker's desk, hoping the fighting in the saloon would last long enough to give them time to get out. "I think these are them." He hurried to the cell and unlocked the door just as the door to the office opened.

Tanner was fast. He had his gun on Baker before the sheriff knew what was going on. "Hands in the air."

"You don't want to do this, Brenly." Baker slowly raised his hands.

Tanner motioned for Bethany to follow him while his gun was aimed at Sheriff Baker. "Move and I'll take your head off," Tanner eyed the man evenly. "Bethany, grab his gun."

Bethany glanced nervously at Tanner. She pulled the sheriff's gun from his holster.

"Once you go down this road, you can never go back." Baker watched Bethany hand his gun to Tanner.

Tanner ignored Baker's threat. He set the sheriff's gun on the desk. "Now cuff him." Tanner motioned to the cuffs on the man's hip.

With trembling hands, Bethany put the handcuffs on the sheriff and Tanner walked him toward the cell at gunpoint.

"You'll hang for this Brenly. You'll be on more wanted posters than Miss Young."

"Maybe." Tanner snapped the cell door shut. "But at least I won't be guilty of letting you hang someone before she's been proven guilty. Hand me your set of keys."

"You've got them." Sheriff Baker argued.

Tanner clicked his .45 into position.

"You'd shoot a fellow lawman?"

"Give me the keys. I'm sure you've got an extra set." Tanner said in a steely tone.

Baker used his cuffed hands to pull the keys from his pocket and handed them to Bethany on the other side of the cell.

Tanner found what was left of their belongings and shoved them into one of their Indian bags. Tanner blew out the kerosene lanterns and walked toward the door.

The sun had set outside and noise from the saloon still filled the air. "You can't do this," Baker's angry cries were drowned out by the commotion in the street. "You're a criminal! You're going to hang!"

With one hand on the leather bag and the other hand in Bethany's, Tanner led her through dark alleyways to two horses, saddled and ready to go. He tossed the sheriff's keys in a pond on their way out of town.

Chapter 5

Bethany and Tanner were quiet as they hurried their horses northwest toward Napa. They weren't following a well-worn trail, but their horses were swift and they both knew how critical it was not to get caught.

Bethany was thankful for the years she'd spent learning to ride. Even though the Quarter Horses she and Tanner rode now couldn't compare to the light gait of a Paso Fino, she had a good sense of riding and controlling a horse.

They rode for hours. Bethany wondered if Sheriff Baker had any idea of the direction they went. The cool breeze felt wonderful on Bethany's face. She closed her eyes and fought the tears that wanted to overtake her.

Only a few hours ago, Bethany sat in a cold jail cell listening to Sheriff Baker's plans to have her hung and collect the reward.

"She's a cold-blooded murderer." She could still hear his words ringing in her ears. "Cared more about money than the man who'd raised her."

In all her life, Bethany couldn't remember anyone glaring at her with so much contempt.

"Ungrateful trash!" Sheriff Baker called her.

"It's gonna be a pleasure watching her swing from that rope!" his deputy added.

"And it's gonna be a pleasure handing her corpse over in exchange for five grand," the sheriff added with a sinister grin. "I might just retire with my share."

The sheriff made all kinds of promises to his men and laughed at the stories he planned to tell about Tanner. She was sure he would tell stories now.

Tanner just broke a wanted criminal out of jail and forced a town sheriff into his own cell. What did that mean for Tanner? Would he really hang if they were caught? Why was he risking so much for her?

Bethany never dreamed Tanner would get her out of that jail cell. It seemed unreal. After they'd been caught trying to leave town, Bethany thought for sure her life was over. She'd laid on that hard, cold mattress trying to picture the moment she would step into heaven and all these trials would be gone.

As a young believer, Bethany had no doubts about heaven. She knew that one day she would be in God's presence and it would be amazing. But she'd never before felt such a longing to go there. She was young. There were things she wanted to do. She used to dream about marrying a wonderful man who shared her faith, serving the Lord together, and having children. Strange how those dreams could be stripped away in one day.

Bethany clutched the reins and listened to the steady hoof beats echo along the wooded path. She was weary and discouraged. It all seemed hopeless. With a warrant out for his arrest, how could Tanner help prove her innocence?

The sun was almost up before Tanner slowed his horse to a stop. They'd reached uneven terrain and the thick forest of redwoods made it difficult to maneuver without light.

"I think we should get some rest." Tanner dismounted and walked his horse to a tree. He tied up his tired gelding and reached for Bethany's reins. "Do you need help?" He offered her his hand.

Bethany accepted and hopped down, hoping her legs hadn't fallen asleep.

She did her best to help Tanner unsaddle the horses and spread out their quilts. She wished there'd have been a way to retrieve their animal furs, but at least she had her moccasins.

"We'll have to cook without a fire," Tanner said emotionlessly.

"I'm not hungry anyway."

"Did they feed you?"

"A few slices of bread. But it was enough."

Tanner lay down on his quilt and took a few deep breaths. He stared wordlessly at the sky. "Did they hurt you?"

"No." Bethany sat beside him on her quilt. "Only with their words."

"That man doesn't deserve to be a sheriff."

Bethany agreed. "He was making up stories—lies, that he planned to tell about you in order to make sure he got the reward and not you."

"And undoubtedly he'll tell those lies." Tanner never took his eyes from the star filled sky.

"You broke me out of jail." Bethany moved closer to Tanner. "There will be a bounty on your head now too."

Tanner sighed. "Well, we're not supposed to fear evil, right?"

Bethany studied Tanner's face in the dim morning light. "Are you follower of Jesus, Tanner?"

Tanner was quiet for a few minutes. "No."

"Why not?"

"What kind of question is that?" Tanner turned to glance at her.

"It sounds like you've had Christians in your life."

Tanner closed his eyes. "A few."

"So you know the message of Jesus Christ? That God so loved the world that He gave…"

"His only begotten Son," Tanner continued. "That whoever believes in Him shall not perish but have eternal life."

"That was pretty good," Bethany studied him curiously.

"My parents made me learn it." Tanner opened the quilt and pulled it over his legs. "They filled my head with all kinds of Bible verses. They believe that stuff."

"And you?"

Tanner cleared his throat and sighed. "I had to go off to war. Fight the south. Kill men whose fate was determined by their location on the map." Tanner's tone was cynical.

"You fought for the freedom of the slaves." Bethany defended his actions.

Tanner kept his breathing controlled. "I fought for the right thing. But it still wasn't easy." He paused. "Killing a man like Zane in self defense… I have no regrets. But some of those southern soldiers were just boys like me. They had wives. They had families." Tanner turned his face away from Bethany to hide the emotion in his eyes. "If I had to do it all over again, I'd still fight for the North. But sometimes you make enemies."

Tanner stopped talking.

Bethany wondered if he'd gone to sleep. She leaned back on her bedroll and listened to Tanner's breathing. *He restores my soul...* her eyes filled with tears for this man. This man who wasn't her friend.

***

Sheriff Alan Thacker sat across from his wife in their bright kitchen and set out the three telegraphs he'd received from Fairfield over the past several days. A cool breeze from the outside blew through their bay window and the couple sipped on iced tea and talked.

"I just don't understand," Alan confided in his wife. "Five days ago Tanner told me he had Bethany Young in his custody but urged me to continue to investigate and find the murderer. Three days ago, I got this one," he passed Tanner's cryptic message across the walnut table to his wife.

"'Trust me. No more words,'" Jane read. She shook her head and waited for Alan to continue.

"Then, yesterday, I got a message from the Sheriff Baker telling me that Tanner and Miss Young were trying to sneak out of town to find her hidden stash and were apprehended. Sheriff Baker wrote that Tanner broke Miss Young out of jail, held Baker at gunpoint and locked him up in Bethany's cell. Baker now has a thousand dollar reward out for the capture of Tanner Brenly."

Jane shook her head and placed her hand over her mouth. "That just doesn't sound like Tanner."

"Sheriff Baker sent the same message to James Webber and Webber's furious." Alan said. "I keep thinking Tanner was trying to tell me something deeper when he wrote 'Trust me.'"

"Do you think he was referring to breaking Miss Young out of jail?" Jane asked.

Alan nodded. "That's what my gut tells me. But he'd have to have a pretty good reason for breaking someone out of jail. He knows that I can't protect him from the consequences." Alan shook his head with grave concern.

Jane got up and walked to her husband. She massaged his shoulders tenderly and kissed the top of his head. "It sounds like we need to pray for Tanner."

Alan nodded. "That's a good idea."

***

Mapping their own course to Napa through rugged California terrain wasn't easy. Tanner hoped he knew his direction well enough to stay on target. Once in Napa, he planned to pick up the road to Saint Helena and from there search for the elusive cabin Bethany said was her alibi.

Tanner still hadn't figured out his next step. Things got thrown off in Fairfield. Breaking Bethany out of jail hadn't been part of his original plan. The fact that he was now an outlaw did complicate things.

Traveling though the forest meant riding slower, but Tanner didn't mind. There was something peaceful about the high redwood trees and the lush forest floor. Ferns and wildflowers made the woods feel mysterious.

They'd been riding for hours. Tanner was lost in his own thoughts. He wanted to explain the whole story to Sheriff Thacker and a telegraph would never do. It needed to be a letter.

Without a doubt, Baker already sent a telegraph making Tanner look like a common criminal. But Sheriff Thacker had discernment, which was one of the things Tanner respected about him. Alan was a sensible man who would not allow others to sway his judgment without a thorough understanding of the facts.

I hope he'll hear me out.

The sun was setting in the sky and the woods were getting dark quickly. Tanner brought his horse closer to his fellow fugitive and suggested they find a place to camp for the night. "Provided I got my direction right, we should make Napa by tomorrow afternoon," Tanner said. "We need a plan for when we get there."

"Will there be wanted posters?" she asked.

"I'm sure there will be."

"Can we bypass the town?"

Tanner shrugged. "We could. But they've got a good post office in Napa. I'm not about to use the telegraph again after seeing how it was misused in Fairfield. But I'd like to get a letter off to Sheriff Thacker, telling him a little bit more of what's going on."

"I can stay outside the town," Bethany suggested. "But do you think you'll be recognized?"

"All Baker could possibly have by now is a drawing of me. They're never perfect. I think I can slip in and out unrecognized." He rubbed his chin. "I haven't shaved in a couple days," he sounded hopeful. "That should help."

Bethany closed her eyes. Tanner thought she was lifting up a silent prayer.

"Just please be careful."

Tanner promised he would.

They found a secluded place at the base of a large boulder to set up camp. Tanner refilled their canteens from a nearby spring.

Bethany busied herself getting a meal made and laid out their bedrolls.

Tanner thought about how Bethany always put their quilts beside one another. He figured it was a habit she started while he was sick. But he'd never asked her.

There was nothing extremely intimate in their sleeping arrangements. Bethany usually turned one way while he turned another. He wondered if she felt more secure beside him.

"Walt gave us a lot of food." Bethany carried a bowl of tomato and bean soup to Tanner and sat across from him on a large rock.

He politely waited for her to pray and then began to eat. It was nice to have a hot meal again.

"Do you think Sheriff Baker has his men out looking for us?" Bethany asked.

Tanner hated to scare her but he had no doubt. "I'm sure he does."

Bethany was quiet. It was obvious that she was struggling with her thoughts. They'd hardly talked since their escape.

Tanner wrestled with his feelings. He'd just broken a suspect out of jail and held a sheriff at gunpoint.

He hardly knew this woman. He'd been tracking her for weeks, convinced that she committed a heinous murder. All the evidence pointed to Bethany. He thought for sure she was guilty.

But then she saved his life. She didn't run. Why would a woman who murdered her uncle for money bother saving the life of her arresting officer? It didn't fit the rest of the story. Was personal character enough proof to risk his career?

"Tanner," she interrupted his thoughts. "I'm sorry you got dragged into this because of me."

"You didn't drag me into this. I made a choice." Tanner took another spoonful of his soup.

Bethany held her bowl on her lap and gazed out at the dark woods beyond their campsite. "You made a choice because of me." She turned her eyes to his. "A choice that makes you a wanted man."

Tanner was thoughtful for a moment. "You saved my life, Bethany… more than once. Why?" He studied her eyes for answers. "You could have let Zane kill me. You could have killed Zane and left me to die. But you didn't." He shook his head and blew out a heavy sigh. "Whoever killed your uncle did not have the kind of compassion you've shown me. I plan to do everything in my power to prove your innocence."

"Thank you for believing me."

Tanner gave a nod. *I hope I'm not crazy.*

***

It was close to noon when they approached Napa. They found a secure hiding place far enough from town to keep Bethany safe. Tanner slipped away, leaving Bethany to hide among the shadows of the rocks.

Napa was a busy town. Several hotels, saloons and gambling emporiums graced the busy streets. Tanner scanned the storefronts for wanted posters.

The post office was located just past the general store. Tanner went to the general store first to purchase paper, pen and ink.

The town seemed too busy to notice him. Tanner stepped into the post office and looked for a place to write his letter. He noticed a collection of wanted posters just inside the door but didn't see Bethany's. Tanner realized it didn't mean the poster wasn't there, only that there were so many, hers was not on top.

He penned a short, descriptive letter to Sheriff Thacker, explaining that he had reason to believe Bethany was innocent:

I'm sure Sheriff Baker's stories have met your ears and I hope you will give heed to mine. Baker is corrupt and while I did assist Miss Young in escaping from his jail, you must trust me when I say I did so to promote justice, not to scorn the law.

Without turning this letter into a long epistle, I must tell you briefly that Bethany Young saved my life. In doing so she proved both her integrity and gave me reason to trust her. While her alibi is not entirely clear, it is not impossible. I still plan to bring her to Santa Rosa. But I ask as my friend and respected boss, that you would further your investigation. Is there any way Miss Young might have been framed?

Tanner signed his letter and addressed it to Alan Thacker's residence. Would his boss be willing to listen? Had Tanner already been labeled a felon? He mailed the letter and slipped through town without a hitch.

***

Diverting themselves away from Napa added extra miles to their journey, but eventually Tanner led them to the main road and they headed towards Saint Helena.

"Tell me any landmarks you saw while you were wandering away from the cabin." Tanner was trying to ready himself for the search.

"There was an abandoned vineyard."

Tanner grinned. "Okay, so that narrows it down - you were in northern California."

Bethany knew he was teasing her.

"When did you come upon the vineyard?"

"After about a day and a half," she said. "I was so disappointed because I'd hoped to stumble upon people."

"But the real question is… were you able to eat some grapes?" There was a twinkle in Tanner's eyes.

"No," Bethany feigned genuine disappointment. "They weren't ripe yet."

Tanner shook his head. "Terrible."

Bethany laughed. This was yet another side of Tanner she'd not seen. He was teasing her. She forced herself to think about the details of where she'd walked and what she saw. "The cabin wasn't far from a creek."

Tanner nodded. "That's a good clue. Was it a small creek or something more substantial?"

"Just a little smaller than the creek near the cave."

"Well then, let's try to find this place."

***

They rode until the sun began to set and Tanner found another place to camp. "If I ever get the chance to have that sheriff arrested, I'm going to demand those animal furs back." Tanner unrolled his bedding.

"Who gave us these quilts though?" Bethany asked. "They're very nice."

"Walt. The man who owned the saloon in Fairfield."

"The man who prompted a saloon fight to help me get out of jail?" Bethany remembered the story from Tanner, but still found it hard to believe. "Will we ever learn how he did it?"

Tanner shrugged. "I hope so. I liked Walt."

Bethany set to work preparing corn cakes on the griddle and Tanner refilled their canteens at a natural spring that he discovered just a few hundred feet from their campsite.

"We still have another full day of riding before we will hit Saint Helena." Tanner took the corn cake Bethany offered him and waited for her to pray.

"I'd like to talk to people in the town… I want to see if anyone knows about a cabin somewhere between Saint Helena and Santa Rosa."

"I spent two days in that town, Tanner. I'm afraid I'll be recognized."

"What if we went in holding hands and told people we were newlyweds looking for a cabin where we could raise a family…"

"You mean lie?" Bethany's face sobered.

"It's a necessary evil sometimes, Bethany." Tanner seemed suddenly frustrated. "We don't even have to say we're married. We can just look like it. You're not afraid to hold my hand are you?"

Bethany turned her eyes on Tanner evenly. She didn't appreciate his sudden turn of attitude. "Not at all. I spent hours holding your hand back in that cave, Tanner. But that time you called me Ruth."

Tanner looked like she'd just knocked the wind out of him. He stared at Bethany for just a moment and then got up to walk away. He was noticeably upset.

"Tanner, wait," Bethany rose to follow him. "I'm sorry…"

"What else did I say to you?" He turned abruptly and stared coldly into her eyes.

Bethany felt like she was treading on forbidden ground. She considered just answering 'nothing' but that would be a lie. She lowered her face and prayed for wisdom. "You asked about Rachel."

Tanner closed his eyes.

"I assume Ruth is your wife." Bethany wasn't sure why Tanner was becoming so emotional. "I'm sure you miss her… and I'm sure she misses you."

"Misses me?" Tanner glanced curiously at Bethany.

"You've been away from Santa Rosa for several weeks."

"Ruth never lived in Santa Rosa." Tanner turned his face away from Bethany. "And I don't have a wife."

He walked away and Bethany felt certain he did not want her to follow. *Why did I have to say that to him?* She wanted to kick herself. She didn't know who Ruth and Rachel were, but obviously Tanner had a lot of hurt when it came to them.

***

He'd heard enough. Alan held up his hand in an effort to silence James Webber. "Please, Mr. Webber, would you let me speak?"

James slapped his desk and rose to his full height of six foot three. "We've been down this road. You told me your deputy is an upright lawman. You said we could trust him." James shook his head and reached for something he could tear to pieces. "But from all vantage points, it looks like he ran off with my cousin and however much money she managed to abscond from my father before she killed him."

"Tanner wouldn't do that."

"That's what you've said." James paced his office and ran his fingers through his dark hair. "But you need to look a little closer at your deputy."

"Trust me, James," Alan said. "I'm looking closer at everything. I'm still trying to figure out who drove the wagon for Miss Young when she went to the bank."

James laughed. "You've got a deputy who broke her out of jail and you wonder who drove the carriage? I'll tell you who drove the carriage. It was your deputy. Tanner Brenly. Mark my words."

Alan attempted to shove that thought far from him. *Tanner, drive the carriage? That's impossible.*

"Were you with Deputy Brenly Thursday morning when Bethany went to the bank?" James asked.

Alan preferred not to answer the question.

"This is all going to the mayor, I hope you know," James hissed. "You were asked to bring down one simple criminal and she runs off with your deputy."

"But what if she didn't commit the murder? What if there is something else going on here?" Alan tried to get James to look at the case through a different lens. "You've known Bethany practically all her life. Does her character match the crime? My wife tells me Bethany recently began attending church. Jane is a pretty good judge of character. She said Bethany was a gentle-spirited, sweet, young Christian who prayed regularly for both you and your father."

James swore under his breath and sat down across from the sheriff. "Trust me, Sheriff Thacker. This is as difficult for me to understand as it is for you. Bethany was like a little sister to me. I taught her to ride, to hunt, even how to climb a tree. But after my aunt died things changed. Bethany changed." He shook his head. "Sure, for the past couple of years people in town saw her going off to church every Sunday and Wednesday night. But my father said the changes in Bethany at home were different."

Alan watched the emotion form in James' eyes.

"You know he took her out of his will…"

Alan nodded. *This fact gave motive to the case. But did motive override character?*

"Don't let the picture Bethany painted of herself, with all her church going, blind you from the quality of paint she was made of." James stared evenly at Alan. "Bethany's father came from a rough family. Even though he was never accused of any crime, a little digging will show you what kind of apples grow on the Young tree." James crossed his arms over his chest. "She can use religion as a front to the rest of the town, but she'll never blind me."

Alan needed to go. He had a meeting with his assistant deputy at noon and he had a lot to think about.

Chapter 6

Tanner didn't speak much as they neared Santa Helena. Instead of feigning marriage, Tanner insisted she wear her hair in braids and wear his cowboy hat. He'd get another hat in town and simply be her riding companion.

"I want you to change into these pants and white shirt," Tanner handed her one of the spare outfits Walt provided for him.

Bethany raised her eyebrows. "Pants?"

"You can use this to hold them up." He tossed her a long strip of woven material. "You're going to be a cowgirl."

Bethany understood that a disguise was necessary. Separated only by Hood Mountain, Santa Rosa was only another twenty miles away.

"Whatever you do, don't look people in the eyes." Tanner reminded her. "I can't afford two jail breaks in one week."

Bethany thought Tanner was teasing, but his demeanor was still professional and distant. She changed into Walt's clothes and stuffed her dress inside one of the saddlebags.

They rode into the busy town mid-afternoon. Tanner found the general store and tied his horse out front.

Bethany froze. "I don't know if it's wise for me to go in there," she spoke in low tones. "That's where I bought my bonnet."

Tanner nodded. "You stay here."

Bethany stayed with the horses. Two long braids hung in front of her shoulders and Tanner's hat lay low over her eyes. She scanned the town discretely, praying she wouldn't be recognized.

Even though she didn't know what lay ahead for her in Santa Rosa, Bethany felt like she and Tanner were on the road to uncovering truth. She didn't want to meet another roadblock.

"Morning," Tanner greeted a tall, skinny bald man behind the counter. He forced a smile and glanced over the counter at the small array of cowboy hats. "I'm thinking I'd like that one," Tanner pointed to a brown cowboy hat, much like the one he'd just given Bethany to wear.

"Looks nice on ya," the store clerk returned Tanner's friendliness and watched as Tanner tried it on. "You're a new face."

"Name's Morgan," he said, using his middle name and leaving it up to the storeowner to decide if that was his last name or first. With possible wanted posters out on him now, Tanner couldn't afford to use his first or last name.

"William Ross," the proprietor reached out to shake Tanner's hand. "What else can I get for you Mr. Morgan?"

Tanner gave William a firm, friendly handshake. "I'm here to check out Santa Helena. Looking for a nice little cabin. Know of any that might be for sale around here?"

William scratched his scalp for a moment. "There's a couple just outside of town."

Tanner nodded. "Got any acres with them?"

"No. 'Fraid not. But if you head down to the barbershop you can ask Ed. He sells real estate."

"Sells property and shaves beards. Sounds like a pretty versatile guy," Tanner said good-naturedly. He rubbed his rough chin. "I could use a good shave. Maybe I'll check him out." He paid for the hat and gave William a parting wave, hoping he'd find out more from Ed.

***

Tanner donned his new hat and found Bethany waiting nervously on her horse. "There are two hotels in town. Tell me which one you stayed at so we don't stay there."

"I stayed at the Hood Mountain View." Bethany remembered the name clearly.

Tanner sighed. "Great. That leaves the hotel across from the sheriff's office." He mounted his horse and readied himself to ride.

"We could set up camp," Bethany suggested.

"I need to talk to people. Make them trust me. I can't do that if I'm hiding out in the woods." They rode slowly toward the hotel. Tanner glanced at Bethany. With two long braids hanging down in front of her and his cowboy hat over her eyes, she looked entirely different. He grinned. *I'm sure it's easier to ride a horse in pants than wearing that long dress of hers.*

They tied their horses to the hitching posts and Tanner whispered to her before they walked into the hotel. "Just look disinterested and anti social - don't smile, don't greet anyone. You're a woman in pants, everyone will assume you have a bad attitude."

"Great." Bethany muttered and followed Tanner into the lobby.

"I need two rooms for tonight," Tanner greeted the concierge in the friendliest tone he could muster. "Been riding a far piece and need a couple nice soft beds."

"I have a small room on this floor and one upstairs. Would that work for you?" A sweet middle-aged lady replied with an equally friendly tone.

Tanner wished the two rooms could be closer to one another, but he shrugged. "As long as they have beds." His eyes twinkled.

"Are you just traveling through, Mr...?" The woman handed Tanner two keys.

"Morgan," Tanner took the keys. "And it's interesting that you ask." He leaned one arm on the desk and spoke slowly. "Betty here is headed back to her family now that we're done working. But I'm thinking of finding a nice place to settle down.

The woman glanced at Bethany who was standing near the fireplace studying the stones along the wall.

"She's a worker?" the woman whispered.

Tanner raised his eyebrows and gave a knowing smirk. "A cranky old bat if you ask me," he spoke softly. "Got the temper of a mother bear. But, she ain't afraid to work, that's for sure."

The concierge studied what she could see of Bethany and shook her head. "I don't know what gets into these women. Next thing you know they'll be wanting to vote."

Tanner walked Bethany to her room. He let her carry one of the saddlebags to keep up the show. Once inside, he turned and gave Bethany the first smile he'd given her all day.

Bethany's eyebrows held more expression than the rest of her face. "And so this was you being as honest as possible?"

Tanner shrugged. "My middle name is Morgan and Betty could be short for Bethany."

"And I'm meaner than a mother bear?" She put her hands on her hips.

"We've created a new identity for you, Bethany. The last time you were in Saint Helena I'm betting you were sweet, ladylike and timid."

Bethany shrugged. "I was scared."

"Exactly. Now you're a she-bear with an attitude. No one will want to mess with you to find out any different."

Tossing the hat on the bed, Bethany walked to the window and looked out at the sheriff's office directly across the street. "And what about you? What if the sheriff of Saint Helena is on the lookout for you?"

Tanner rubbed his scruffy face. "I was thinking about leaving a mustache."

Bethany turned to face him. They'd never talked about the night before. Bethany knew she'd hurt him when she mentioned Ruth and Rachel. But why? Who were these women?

"I'm off to meet Ed the barber," Tanner picked up his own bag and walked toward the door. "We can get something to eat when I get back."

"Be careful." Her eyes softened and she watched him leave.

***

"Are you Ed?" Tanner stepped into the barbershop and did a quick scan of the room.

"Sure am. You look like you need a shave." The man greeted Tanner with a handshake and motioned for him to take a seat.

81

"Name's Morgan." Tanner removed his hat and made himself comfortable. "I think I want to keep my mustache this time." He leaned back in the chair and closed his eyes. "The ladies seem to like it."

Ed got his blade ready and stirred up his shaving cream. "So who told you about me?" The man lathered the foamy white cream across Tanner's chin.

"Man named William Ross at the general store." Tanner heard the bell ring over the door and tried to ignore it. "Said you might be able to tell me about some real estate."

"Oh, yeah," a voice Tanner didn't recognize chimed in. "Old Ed here can set you up with some beach property in the Grand Canyon." The man chuckled.

"You'd better watch it, Sheriff, or I'll be shaving off your mustache when I get you in this here chair," Ed bantered back.

The sheriff... Tanner tried to act normal. *Am I just a magnet for sheriffs?*

"Mr. Morgan," Ed patted Tanner's shoulder. "Don't you pay my friend no mind. Everybody knows the best beach property is in Arizona."

Tanner laughed. He opened his eyes and glanced quickly at the sheriff. *Not anyone I recognize. I hope he doesn't know me.*

"Did you hear Maryanne had her baby last night?" The sheriff made small talk with Ed.

"No. Did Eldon get the son he was praying for?"

The sheriff chuckled. "Nope. He's got his sixth daughter."

Both men laughed. "Okay now, stop talking to me... Mr. Morgan wants to talk real estate." He tilted Tanner's head up so he could properly shave under Tanner's chin. "What are you looking for?"

"Just a small cabin. I'd like some land."

"How much you wanting to spend?" Ed asked.

Tanner grinned. "Wanting to spend? I'd like it to be free. But I reckon that ain't gonna happen."

Ed nodded.

"I don't want to spend too much. Just a roof over my head is good enough for me." Tanner let the man wipe away the excess shaving cream.

"How far from town?" Ed handed Tanner a mirror.

"I'm flexible." Tanner assessed his new shave and chuckled inwardly at the mustache. He hated mustaches. "Can you take a little bit off my hair?" Tanner liked having Ed's undivided attention. It kept him from having to talk to the sheriff.

"Do you mind, Clarence?" Ed asked the sheriff. "I know you were wanting to get done quickly, but you know I make more money off new customers than I do you." There was fun in his tone.

Clarence set down the newspaper he'd been reading and rose to his feet. "I don't mind. I'll head back by on my way home from the livery. I need to check on that lame horse of mine. Maybe you can sell this fella my lame horse too," he said with a laugh.

Tanner liked this sheriff and watched the man walk away, regretting that it was necessary to be under cover. Clarence seemed like a man Tanner would enjoy getting to know.

Ed was back to talking about real estate. "I know a couple properties just outside of town."

Tanner listened to the various options. "Santa Rosa is only about twenty miles west of here isn't it?"

Ed nodded. "But to get there takes some pretty rough riding."

"The roads aren't real good?" Tanner already knew this but played it off well.

"No." Ed snipped Tanner's hair carefully.

"But I heard the soil's good." Tanner needed to find out what was there. Searching out a cabin in the middle of the woods was like looking for a needle in a haystack. He needed some direction.

"The soil is good. Best around for growing grapes." He chuckled.

"Do you know of anything between here and Santa Rosa?" Tanner held his breath.

A few more snips while Ed thought about it. "I reckon you might find a few cabins if you head west toward Spring Mountain." Ed combed through Tanner's curls.

"Not too much off the back," Tanner spoke up.

"There's a few folks living out that way." Ed offered him the mirror again.

"I don't know of anyone selling. But Spring Mountain Road will take you straight out and maybe you can talk to someone."

Tanner nodded and paid the man.

"But I'll keep thinking. Where are you staying?" Ed asked.

Tanner hated to give away any information but he didn't want to act suspicious. "Tonight I'm at the Porter White Hotel."

Ed nodded and smiled at the nice tip he'd been given. "Good thing I sent Clarence away. The locals never tip."

***

Bethany was asleep when Tanner knocked at her door. A quick glance toward the window told her it was probably close to dinnertime.

When she opened the door she tried to hide a smile. Tanner cleaned up nicely, but she didn't like the mustache.

"Don't say a word," Tanner walked past her into the room. "I plan to shave it off as soon as we're out of Saint Helena. But here's the deal," Tanner sat across from her on the bed. "Tomorrow we're heading out toward Spring Mountain." He studied Bethany closely. "Do you remember any springs?"

Bethany furrowed her eyebrows and tilted her head. "I really wasn't looking for springs."

Tanner understood. "Are you hungry?"

"Starving."

"Grab your hat. We'll eat downstairs in the hotel. I asked for a table at the back, since you're so unsocial." His eyes held a glint of humor.

Together they walked to the hotel restaurant and were seated at the most secluded table in the room. Bethany removed her hat and faced the wall. Tanner kept his eyes on the rest of the customers.

"So what's the news about me in town?" she asked softly.

"I didn't hear a thing.

That was a relief.

"You need to keep up your act," Tanner whispered. He silenced her while their plates were being carried toward the table.

Bethany winked at him and gave a mischievous grin.

"Thank you." He gave the waitress a friendly smile.

"Why, you're welcome, sweetie." The waitress set his plate down and gazed at him with interest. "Here's your drink." Her tone was buttery smooth.

"They call this food?" Bethany mumbled looking down at the mashed potatoes and hamburger gravy. "I've seen pig slop that looked better."

Tanner almost dropped the water he'd just taken from the waitress. *Did Bethany just say that?* He glanced at the waitress apologetically. "Don't mind her," he mouthed and gave the woman a knowing nod.

Bethany looked up after the waitress walked away and raised her eyebrows. "Did I do okay?"

"That was pretty good." Tanner took a sip of his water and chuckled. "I didn't know you could be mean."

"I've been taking lessons." Amusement twinkled in her blue eyes and played with the corners of her mouth.

Tanner ignored her joke and watched their waitress talking to another woman while glancing at him. "I think she liked my mustache."

"Then she's the only one." Bethany cleared her throat.

"Should I be offended?" Tanner knew she was only having fun with him but it felt good to lighten up. He glanced down at his plate. "In spite of what you said, this food looks pretty good."

Bethany nodded. "It does." She folded her hands in her lap and bowed her head to pray.

Tanner scanned the room hoping no one noticed the mother bear praying. "Did you have to do that here?" he whispered.

Bethany leaned closer. "If I ever needed to do that, it's here."

"Fair enough." Tanner dug into his food with one eye on the door.

Things seemed safe until Tanner noticed the sheriff walk through the door. *Oh no...* Tanner watched as the man greeted the hotel proprietor and nodded at the flirty waitress. He was obviously well liked in this town.

"Just take your favorite table, Clarence," the waitress said pleasantly. "I'll bring you some sweet tea."

"Be careful." Tanner tried to speak without moving his lips. "That's the sheriff."

Bethany kept her head bent low and did her best to eat fast.

While taking his seat, the sheriff recognized the newcomer in town and started walking toward Tanner with a welcoming smile.

"Bethany, your eyes. You can't look at him…"

Tanner didn't know what hit him when Bethany stood up and threw a handful of food in his face.

"Would you stop spitting at me? If you can't eat with your mouth closed then eat in the barn." She covered her eyes. "You got something in my eye."

The sheriff was upon them in a matter of seconds. "Are you okay, miss?"

"Just need to wash his spit out of my eyes," she said rudely. Bethany rubbed her eyes and shook her head and snatched her hat. "I'm done. I'll be in my room."

Tanner watched her leave and let out a relieved sigh.

"She's some work." The sheriff took a seat across from Tanner. "Do you mind if I sit down?"

"Go right ahead." Tanner minded quite a bit but wasn't about to tell the sheriff that.

"Do you need to help your friend?"

Tanner laughed. "She'll be fine. I'm sure she won't be in the mood to talk to anyone the rest of the night."

Clarence didn't question it. "I'm glad I caught you," he began.

Tanner's heart dropped to his stomach.

"I wanted to apologize." The sheriff brushed a few of Bethany's crumbs into a pile.

"Apologize?" Tanner was not expecting this from the sheriff. "What in the world for?"

"I shouldn't have made all those jokes at the barber shop," Clarence confessed. "You're a stranger in this town and I don't want to be a bad witness."

Tanner couldn't believe what he was hearing. This conscientious sheriff was apologizing for his jokes. "No need to apologize," Tanner said sincerely. "I actually appreciate your sense of humor."

The waitress walked up carrying Clarence's plate. "Are you moving to this table, Sheriff?"

"If my new friend here doesn't mind." Clarence waited for Tanner's response.

This is not happening... "Of course not, please stay."

Clarence made room for the plate. "Do you mind if I pray?" He glanced at Tanner.

Is he really asking me this? I just scolded Bethany for praying... "No. Go right ahead." *Is this punishment for something?*

Clarence bowed his head. "Heavenly Father," he prayed out loud. "I thank You for this bounty which You have so graciously provided. I also thank You for the opportunity to share a meal with a new friend. Help this friend, Lord, to know You and Your salvation."

Tanner stared at the food he still had left on his plate. This was not the way he intended on spending his evening.

"So tell me about yourself," the sheriff began.

This is not happening. Tanner did his best to give a blank look. "Not much to tell."

Clarence smiled. "I guess you heard my name's Clarence. Clarence Moore. I'm the sheriff." He took a few bites of his food. "Did I hear Ed call you Morgan?"

Tanner nodded.

"Where are you from, Mr. Morgan?" Clarence seemed to be making small talk.

"I was born in Maine." Tanner took a sip of his drink and wondered if Bethany was worrying.

"You're far from home."

Tanner shrugged. "Yeah. A little." He tried to keep himself aloof.

"I'm from the east coast too," Clarence offered. "I was born in Virginia but grew up in Connecticut. Moved west after the war." He took a sip of his iced tea. "Needed a change of scenery."

Tanner's ears piqued. "Did you fight for the north?"

Clarence's face sobered. "I did, although half my family fought for the south. Brother against brother, right?"

"I fought for the north." Tanner wasn't sure why he just offered that information.

"What brought you out west?"

This man's questions were just a little too personal. Tanner studied his fingernail for a few minutes and sighed. "Justice."

The sheriff studied Tanner for a moment. "Did you get it?"

Tanner looked past Clarence to the little bit of light coming through the window across the room. "Not yet."

Seeming to sense Tanner's need to gather his thoughts, Clarence was quiet for a moment. "Were you hoping to bring about that justice at your hand?"

Tanner lowered his fork and rubbed the strange new hair above his lip. "Yes." He finally said, looking straight into the sheriff's eyes.

"This person must have hurt you pretty bad." Clarence's expression softened.

Tanner clenched his jaw. This was not the conversation he expected to be having tonight. He was not in Saint Helena to talk about his personal life. He was on a mission.

Clarence was still watching him. Waiting for an answer.

"He took from me everything that mattered in this life." Tanner said with emotion. "And I hate him. I hate him with everything that's in me." Tanner turned his eyes away.

Clarence reached for Tanner's arm. "I understand your pain, son." His voice was kind. "But all hatred does is kill the one who's feeling it."

"I don't care." Tanner wished this nosy sheriff would just leave. He was worse than Sheriff Baker.

"I don't believe you." Clarence didn't take his eyes off Tanner. "You don't want to live your life with all this bitterness."

"And you're going to tell me that I need to take it to the Lord. Let Jesus wipe away my pain… Everything will be all better." Tanner's tone dripped with sarcasm. "Am I right?"

Clarence sat back in his chair and studied Tanner for a moment. "Actually, son… While I do believe that Jesus will wipe away your pain, my first question for you is what about your sin?"

This was not the answer Tanner expected. "My sin?" He shook his head. "I'm not a ruthless murderer."

"But you hate him. You want him dead. Am I right?"

Tanner tried not to let his temper flare. "He deserves to die. He destroyed the lives of many noble Union Soldiers. Killing their wives… killing their children…" Tanner could feel his hands shaking. He was about to lose it.

"But what about your sin?" Clarence repeated.

Tanner tried to steady his breath. "I fight for justice. I've never stolen anything. I've never murdered. Right now I've put my own life in danger to uphold what is right. You have no idea!" He threw his napkin down, tossed a handful of bills on the table and walked toward the door.

Clarence followed him outside. "Morgan," he called when they reached the street. "Morgan!"

Tanner turned around. His eyes were red with unshed tears. His heart ached. Everything ached. "You don't understand!" Tanner felt like his knees were going to buckle underneath him. He wanted to run. "Don't judge me!"

Clarence was by Tanner's side in a moment. He placed a tender hand on the younger man's back and Tanner began to unleash a torrent of tears.

"I'm sorry, friend," Clarence spoke softly. "I didn't mean to rip out your heart."

Tanner staggered a few steps, immobilized by emotions he hadn't let himself feel in years.

"Please come talk to me." Clarence urged. "There's no one in the sheriff's office. We can talk privately."

Tanner glanced at the building across the street. The building he never planned on seeing up close. What was he thinking? Was he walking into a trap? Tanner stared into Clarence's eyes. His emotions were spinning out of control right now. He lowered his head and nodded. "Okay."

***

Bethany stood by her window and fidgeted nervously with the edge of the long lace curtain. Tanner was outside with the sheriff. It almost looked like they were arguing. This couldn't be good.

She cracked the window but couldn't hear what was being said.

When Tanner began to walk to the sheriff's office with the man, Bethany's stomach dropped and she closed her eyes.

Dear Lord… Oh no… no… She grabbed the top of her head and walked aimlessly around the room. Was Tanner being arrested? Was he going to hang because of her? How long before they found her? Should she hide? *I could break him out of jail. I could use the same trick he used. Surely a saloon fight isn't too hard to start...*

Bethany's head reeled. No matter how he felt about her, Tanner was her friend. *He risked his life for me.* Tears welled up in her eyes and she knelt beside her bed. "Father... please help Tanner..."

***

Clarence locked the door and lit a tall glass oil lamp near his desk. There was still a little bit of light outside, but inside it was dim. He motioned for Tanner to take a seat and offered him a glass of water.

"No. I'm fine." Tanner was already regretting his decision to further this conversation with the sheriff. *What made me think I liked this guy?*

"Mr. Morgan," Clarence sat across from Tanner and leaned forward at his desk. "First of all, I hate calling a person 'Mister.' Can I ask your first name?"

Tanner's mind raced with dozens of names he'd used when under cover. But somehow the truth seemed like the best answer. "Tanner." He hoped the truth wouldn't get him into trouble.

Clarence stared at Tanner for a moment. "Okay, Tanner... I know I asked you some painful questions, but my job as the sheriff here, it just pays the bills. My real job in this town is telling people about forgiveness."

"I've heard all the stories, Sheriff," Tanner steadied his voice. It was time to push his emotions back under the wall he'd built to hide them. "I grew up in a Christian home. My parents were the real deal."

"So..."

"So why am I not?" Tanner knew the question before Clarence got it off his lips. "When I was younger I never really took it serious. My older brother did. He's a pastor in Vermont. But I..." Tanner tried to chose his words. "I was caught up in winning the heart of the woman I loved." There was a far away look in Tanner's eyes.

"We weren't married long when I went off to war. We'd moved to Boston before I left and Ruth... she was carrying our daughter." How many years had Tanner buried this story?

Clarence was a good listener. His eyes said he cared.

"At the time I really just didn't need God. Then, after the war..." Tanner couldn't speak the words. "Things happened and God wasn't there to help me. So I determined that I didn't need a God like that."

Clarence narrowed his eyes and licked his lips. Tanner knew the man was about to throw out a rebuttal.

"So, God didn't give you what you wanted and you rejected Him. Is that it?"

Tanner smacked the desk. "I really don't like the way you sum things up."

"Math is math, Mr. Morgan." Clarence pulled a Bible from his desk drawer. "He made Him Who knew no sin to be sin on our behalf, so that we might become the righteousness of God in Him," he read from 2 Corinthians 5:21. "God did that for you. There is nothing else that you could ever have asked for on this earth that carries more value. He took your sin and died for it. And don't tell me your sin is any less than the man who you say destroyed your life because by your very admission, you hate him and want him to die. That's pretty ugly."

"But he deserves to die." Tanner clenched his jaw and tried to keep himself from letting these words reach his heart.

"We all do." Clarence steadied his gaze on Tanner. "During that war, I killed men who were only standing there with a gun because their government told them to. Sure, I was defending something I believed in. But so were they." Clarence's face showed emotion.

"I faced my own cousin on that battle field. He knew me and I knew him. I was no better of a man than he was... but I was a better shot. It didn't take me long after that to see what kind of heart I had. I'm a sinner."

Tanner swallowed back the lump in his throat. "But sometimes we don't have a choice. There's a difference."

"I understand. And God knows the difference. He knows our hearts." The sheriff reached his hand out and touched Tanner's trembling one. "What color is your heart, Tanner?"

91

Tanner closed his eyes and leaned back on the hard wooden chair. He knew the truth. Tears filled his eyes and he narrowed them on Clarence. "He killed my wife. He killed my baby girl." Tanner's body shook with sobs. "How can I not hate him?" He held his hands to his face and wept.

"Jesus knew no sin, but He took yours..." Clarence said through his own tears. "And He doesn't hate you."

"But my sins... they aren't as bad as his." Tanner wiped his face on his shirt.

"But Jesus had none and he took yours. And he took that man's too."

Tanner slapped the table. "Why?"

"Because He created you and He loves you. There's no other explanation."

The room was growing dimmer and Clarence rose to light another lantern. When he sat back down Tanner ran his hand over his forehead. "How do I forgive the man?" Tanner sounded tired.

"By accepting God's gift of forgiveness for you," Clarence handed Tanner a handkerchief. "You need to experience forgiveness before you can give it." He leaned back and studied Tanner. "And you need to be willing to repent."

Tanner nodded.

"From the moment I saw you sitting in that barber chair I could see you were carrying around an extremely heavy weight."

"I am."

"He can take it from you, Tanner."

Tanner's mind raced with all the things weighing him down right now. Proving Bethany's innocence, explaining why he'd broken her out of jail, the threat of bounty hunters, and of course forgiving the man who murdered his family. "Not everything that's weighing me down right now is my own sin."

"That's okay. Jesus can take it all." Clarence clutched his Bible and his eyes seemed to plead with Tanner. "Are you ready for redemption?"

A new kind of emotion welled up in Tanner. A feeling he couldn't explain. "I am... I want forgiveness." He lowered his head on the desk and cried.

Together, Tanner and Clarence prayed. Tanner laid his sins at the foot of the cross and asked Jesus to make his heart clean. The two men talked and prayed well into the night.

"I can never thank you enough," Tanner said when he finally rose to go. "My parents are going to want to, that's for sure."

"I'm just doing what the Lord told me to do." Clarence patted Tanner on the back as he walked the younger man toward the door. "When are you heading out?"

"Tomorrow," Tanner answered honestly.

"Well, you know how to reach me. Stay in touch. Okay?"

Tanner promised he would. He put his hat on his head and stepped out into the night with a lighter heart and a newfound joy.

***

Bethany had gotten very little sleep when Tanner knocked on her door the next morning. She was still wearing the pants and shirt she'd fallen asleep in and her hair was a mess. With red, swollen eyes, she opened the door and stared questioningly at Tanner. "You're here?" she asked softly.

Tanner stepped inside and immediately set down her breakfast and placed his hands compassionately on Bethany's shoulders. "What's wrong? You look devastated."

"I saw you go into the sheriff's office last night." Tears welled up in her eyes. "I thought the worst." She sat down on the edge of the bed.

"Oh, Bethany," Tanner pulled up a chair and sat across from her. "I'm so sorry. I never meant to cause you fear." He gave her arm a gentle squeeze. "Everything is fine. Sheriff Moore's a good man. He wanted to talk." Tanner wiped a tear away from her cheek. "About God."

Bethany couldn't hide her surprise. "You talked about God?" It was the last thing Bethany expected to hear from Tanner. "You mean he doesn't know who you are? We're not caught?"

"He knows my first name is Tanner, but he was more worried about my name being written in the Lamb's Book of Life than he was about a wanted poster." A smile tugged at Tanner's lips. "I poured out my heart to the man."

93

Bethany's blue eyes fixed on Tanner, eagerly waiting to hear the rest of the story.

"I've never done that before," Tanner confessed.

"So what happened?" Bethany reached for the glass of juice Tanner brought her and took a sip.

"I'm forgiven." Tanner's eyes held a new kind of radiance that Bethany had never seen in them.

Joy lit up her face. "You've surrendered your life to Jesus?"

Tanner nodded.

Without thinking, Bethany moved from the bed and hugged Tanner.

***

A stream of morning sunlight burst through Sheriff Thacker's east facing office window. Alan loved mornings in Santa Rosa. A low laying fog came to life with color from the sun and Alan watched as several birds found his wife's bird feeder on a nearby tree.

Alan had a lot on his mind and he'd come to his office to sort out his thoughts. He was surprised when his wife knocked on the office door and announced a visitor.

Who would visit this early?

Jane ushered Dr. Clay Nash into the office and Alan rose to greet his friend.

"Can we talk?" Clay's eyes were wide with concern.

"Sure," Alan motioned for Clay to take a seat on a comfortable chair on the other side of the desk.

It wasn't like the doctor to make social call. He asked Jane to put on some coffee and then he closed the door. Jane would understand their need for privacy.

"What's troubling you, friend?"

Clay sat at the edge of his seat. "Marie is dead," he fidgeted nervously with the edge of his suit jacket.

Alan felt his heart sink. "Oh no. That's terrible." He shook his head.

Clay shook his head. "But something's wrong, Alan. Something's terribly wrong."

Alan studied his friend. While Clay was often more expressive with his emotions than Alan, it wasn't like him to be quite this dramatic. "What are you talking about?"

"She shouldn't have died." The doctor stood up and began pacing the floor.

Jane knocked at the door and carried in two cups of coffee. She nodded to her husband and Clay before she walked out the door.

Clay continued after the door closed. "I'm telling you, Alan, Marie was doing better. She was talking clear. She was able to walk around with assistance. She should not have died." Clay's tone was passionate.

"You can't blame yourself, Clay."

"I don't." Clay sat back down. "I know it was nothing I did."

"How did she die?" Alan was trying to understand his friend.

"She stopped breathing last night."

Considering the seriousness of Marie's injury, Alan tried to figure out why this was such a surprise.

"There was no reason for her to stop breathing. When I checked in on her yesterday afternoon, Marie's breathing was normal. She had good color in her face and she was feeling well."

"I'm sorry, Clay. I still don't understand. Are you saying someone killed her?"

Clay leaned forward and looked around the room. "A few days ago, Marie told me that Bethany didn't shoot her."

Startled by Clay's words, Alan held up his hand to clarify. "What?"

"She said the woman looked like Bethany but Marie insisted that she'd know her Bethany anywhere." Clay fixed his eyes on Alan.

"Why didn't you tell me this a few days ago?"

"I didn't really take it serious. I figured Marie just didn't want to believe that the woman she'd practically raised would try to kill her."

It sounded logical to Alan. "And besides, other people saw Bethany too. There's no way any human being could fake eyes that blue."

"I told her that yesterday when we talked. She brought it up again."

"What did she say?"

Clay scratched his head. "She said it wasn't the color of Bethany's eyes that made them unique. It was the light inside them."

Alan tried to process what his friend just said. "For someone to commit such an unspeakable crime there couldn't be any light shining through."

"I agree," the doctor nodded. "But don't you think Marie would know? I mean really know." He picked up his coffee cup and blew before he sipped. "She was like a mother to Bethany."

"Did Marie tell anyone else her theory?" Alan asked.

"Marie had more friends than any five people I know added together," Clay admitted. "She had visitors in and out every day. I'm sure she was sharing her story."

"Alright Clay, let's assume it wasn't Bethany. Then where is Miss Young?"

"She's got a five thousand dollar bounty on her head. If she's smart, she's in hiding."

Or she's with my deputy... Alan shook his head. "Okay, the better question to ask is, why did she leave?"

"I don't know," Clay raised his hands up in the air. "But I'm telling you. Marie should not have died and the only thing that keeps spinning around in my head is that Marie could have identified the killer."

"You've given me something to think about."

Clay let out a trembling breath. "But promise me something."

Alan nodded.

"Don't tell anyone where you got the idea."

This was ludicrous. "You're not afraid, are you?" Alan asked.

Clay stood up and glanced nervously out the window. "I'm terrified." He turned to his friend. "We're missing something in this story and I'm scared to find out what it is."

***

Tanner gave the hotel keys to the woman behind the counter and thanked her for the wonderful hospitality. "I'll be sure to stay here next time I'm through Saint Helena."

The woman glanced in the direction of Bethany, who was standing by the door with Tanner's hat low over her eyes, holding one of the saddlebags.

"Maybe you'd better come without her next time." She winked.

Tanner chuckled and picked up his bags. "Come on, Betty, I got the horses out front."

It was later than Tanner hoped to get on the road, but both he and Bethany were tired. Tanner felt bad that he'd been the cause of the dark circles under Bethany's eyes. Even after her night in jail the last time, Bethany's eyes didn't show so much sadness. *Was she that worried about me?*

He helped Bethany onto her horse and began working to attach his saddlebags. "I also bought a little bit of fruit from the hotel this morning," he said while he worked.

A friendly voice from across the street caught Tanner off guard.

"Tanner!" The sheriff waited for a wagon to cross and hurried to catch his new friend. "I'm so glad I caught you this morning, Brother." He reached to shake Tanner's hand but pulled him into a hug. "I brought you this." He handed Tanner a brown wrapped package.

"Clarence, you didn't need to…"

"Just open it." Clarence patted Tanner's shoulder.

Tanner opened the package and ran his hand smoothly over a black leather bound Bible and his heart tightened in his chest. "I don't know how to thank you…"

"You've thanked me plenty," Clarence said. "There is nothing that brings me more joy than seeing a life surrendered to the Lord."

Tanner flipped through the Book and touched the delicate pages.

Clarence stepped away from Tanner for a moment to express kindness to the woman he'd only briefly met the evening before. "I'm sorry, I didn't mean to be rude." He turned to Bethany with a friendly smile. "I'm Sheriff Moore."

In her tiredness, Bethany forgot about her eyes and glanced at the man who'd led Tanner to Christ and smiled.

Tanner caught the interchange and sobered. Clarence's face took on a confused expression and he studied Bethany just a moment longer than was natural.

Bethany quickly lowered her eyes.

He knows who she is. Tanner's heart sank. This would have been the moment to think fast. To come up with some story about getting Betty back to her grandmother's house or how that was the first smile he'd seen from Betty since she took down that redwood tree they logged a few days ago. But Tanner's mind went blank. In his hands he held the Word of God while Sheriff Moore just realized who they were.

Clarence turned to Tanner and glanced toward the mountains in the distance. "You do know, Tanner, that a child of God is responsible to keep his heart right with His Savior. We're not to continue in sin."

"I realize that, Sheriff." Tanner looked directly into Clarence's face. "But sometimes things aren't always as they seem. You can't believe everything you hear."

Clarence narrowed his eyes on Tanner. "Are you saying there's more to some stories than people know."

"That's exactly what I'm saying." Tanner hoped this new friend would give him the chance to prove it.

"You're taking a pretty big risk." Clarence glanced quickly at Bethany.

"But I've surrendered this mission to God and I've got no doubt that the Truth is going to set us free." Tanner slipped his new Bible into a saddlebag. "Trust me," he said softly, more as a plea than a demand.

Clarence took a deep breath and stepped back for Tanner to mount his horse. "Don't let me down, *deputy*," he said softly.

"You have my word." There was deep sincerity in Tanner's eyes. He respected Sheriff Moore and prayed the man would indeed trust him.

Chapter 7

When Alan Thacker arrived at the Webber estate his heart was heavy. Talk in town said that James was beside himself with grief. How could Alan approach James now, in the midst of this crisis?

Alan left his horse with the stable hand and took a long look at the large, three story Victorian estate where so much tragedy had occurred. Lavish gardens graced the walkway to the house and Alan let the smell of sage calm his nerves. He hoped James would be willing to talk.

The well-dressed businessman was sitting at a small table with his head in his hands when Alan was escorted onto the verandah. With his high collared white shirt, wide striped tie, and crisp suit jacket, James looked more like he was about to have a business meeting than a man grieving in his own home. But James was known for his professionalism and fine attire.

"Don't get up." Alan motioned to James sympathetically when he approached. Alan took the chair across from James and let out a heavy sigh. "I'm so sorry."

James sucked in a deep breath and glanced off toward the hills behind his childhood home. Tears filled his hurting eyes. He wiped his face and put on his wire-rimmed glasses. "You know… I loved my father. I really did… But it was different." James smoothed his thick dark hair and reached for his glass of red wine. "My father was a cold man; my love for him was more like respect." James glanced at Alan. "Do you know what I mean?"

Alan thought he did. He remembered Patrick Webber as being unsocial and all business.

"But Marie… she was different." James brushed away a tear. "She was almost like another mother to me." James drained his glass and shook his head. "I can't believe she's dead."

Alan reached out a comforting hand and patted James on the arm. "I understand."

"I thought she was doing better."

"So did Dr. Nash." Alan figured it was okay to admit this to James.

"Then why?" James smacked his hand on the table.

Alan shook his head. "Sometimes we don't have all the answers."

"Why would Bethany do this?" James shook his head. "Marie loved her!"

This was a painful conversation. Alan hated to see James suffering. "People are saying that Marie didn't think it was Bethany who shot her."

James turned his gaze to the hillside. "Marie didn't want to believe it was Bethany."

"But wouldn't Marie have known?" Alan questioned.

"Marie was grasping for hope," James said. "Bethany was like her own child." He closed his eyes for a moment. "For that matter… she was like my sister."

"And yet we believe Bethany is guilty - without even hearing her side of the story?" Alan considered whether or not this was the right time to broach the subject. He leaned forward and steadied his gaze on James. "I need to ask you something…" he hoped this wasn't going to push James over the top.

James studied Alan's face and waited.

"Did Bethany have a sister?" The words rolled off his lips and Alan watched James to gauge his reaction.

James attempted to drain the last few drops of wine from his glass. "I don't know." He fixed his eyes on the hillside. "I was only seven when my parents brought Bethany home. She was a squirmy little two-year-old who took away my mother's attention."

One of the servants stepped onto the verandah and refilled James' glass. "Would you care for wine, Sheriff Thacker?" she asked.

Alan declined.

James waited for his servant to walk away. "But she grew on me," he continued. "Eventually Bethany won my heart." He finally looked at Alan. "You have to know this is eating me up inside."

Was there any question? Alan couldn't imagine the stress James was under. To lose his father, a dear family friend, and believe that his cousin was to blame, was devastating.

"That's why I think we should take a deeper look, James," Alan urged.

"A deeper look?" James shook his head. "Why?"

"Because I know Tanner," Alan said. "He's a good man. He's saved my life more times than I can count." James glanced at the sky and paused while a gentle breeze blew through the verandah. "I can't believe that Tanner would risk everything to break her out of jail unless he was convinced it was the right thing to do in pursuit of truth."

"Have you seen Bethany?" James looked skeptically at Alan.

The sheriff nodded. Bethany was a beautiful woman. He was sure she turned many heads in their town. But he also knew Tanner. A pretty face was not enough to make Tanner compromise what was right. "I know my deputy." His tone was determined. "The law says she's innocent until proven guilty."

James reached for his drink and swirled the red liquid around the glass reflectively. "Well then, I guess we should continue the investigation." James raised the glass to his lips.

***

Bethany sat beside a clear, quiet river and leaned back on a moss-covered log. She watched the water glisten in the sun and breathed in the fresh, clean smells of spring. Tanner was down stream, doing his best to catch a fish with his makeshift pole and line.

They hadn't talked much during the day. Neither of them mentioned the cryptic conversation Tanner had with Sheriff Moore that morning. Bethany wondered if Tanner questioned his decision to break her out of jail – if they couldn't prove her innocence, Tanner would surely pay serious consequences.

What if they couldn't find the cabin? They'd spoken to a few homesteaders along Spring Mountain Road, but so far they had no leads.

Bethany noticed Tanner wading through the water proudly holding up a large striped bass. "Never let it be said that I'm not a fisherman!" Tanner wore a grin as he splashed through the river. He was as carefree as Bethany had ever seen him.

"I never said you weren't a fisherman." Bethany got up to greet him. Her lips curved into a warm smile and she tucked a stray curl behind her ear.

"No. Only that you'd personally gut and clean it if I actually caught something with my homemade fishing line." Tanner reminded her, playfully. "So, here's your fish."

Bethany sized up the large silver fish and swallowed. "I need a knife." She glanced at Tanner.

Tanner set down his pole and held up his catch with both hands. "I'm not going to make you gut him." His eyes twinkled.

"I said I would." Bethany readied herself for the undesirable task. "I'm not going to go back on my word." She found Tanner's knife in one of the saddlebags and walked to where he stood at the edge of the water. "Just show me what to do."

"You've never gutted a fish before?" Tanner knelt down and laid the fish on a large rock.

"No."

He reached for the knife. "Just watch me this time." He smiled. "I'll let you do the next one."

Bethany watched while Tanner inserted his knife into the side of the fish's gills. He made a clean slice all the way through to the other side.

"Striped bass have some spiny fins," he cautioned. "So you need to watch that you don't get cut."

Bethany carefully touched the fins that Tanner pointed out.

He glanced at her out of the corner of his eyes while he worked on the fish. "You actually seem interested."

"My Uncle Patrick and James weren't fishermen. They preferred hunting," she explained. "I've often thought I'd enjoy fishing."

"Why is that?"

Bethany shrugged. "Because it involves sitting beside the

water, usually in a quiet place. I like that kind of thing."

Tanner nodded.

After he gutted the fish, he and Bethany made preparations to cook it. They washed their hands and took a seat by the fire.

Tanner leaned against the rock with his knees bent and readied himself to speak. "I… I wanted to talk to you about something," he stammered.

Bethany's curiosity was piqued. She wasn't sure she'd ever heard Tanner stammer.

He glanced at the fire, watching the flames dance over the logs. "It's about Ruth and Rachel."

Bethany waited for him to continue.

"Ruth was my wife." He took a deep breath. "And Rachel was my little girl."

It was obvious Tanner was forcing back his emotions.

"They were murdered." His eyes filled with tears as he said the words.

"Ruth and I got married about six months before I went off to war. We moved to Boston where my aunt and uncle lived so I'd be able to get up to see her once in a while. Ruth was three months pregnant when I left. I didn't get to meet Rachel until she was almost five months old. After that, I didn't see her again until she was a year."

Bethany watched Tanner's expression intensely. She could see this was a painful story to share.

He crossed his arms and blew out a shaky sigh. "She was a beautiful little girl." He shook his head somberly. "She had short golden curls and two little dimples that came to life whenever she smiled," Tanner said reflectively. "I was so happy when the war was over. I was finally going to spend time with my wife and child. Rachel was a year and a half old and full of energy. Ruth was a wonderful mom."

Tears filled Bethany's eyes as the story unfolded.

"I'd gone into town… I was only gone a few hours, but when I came home there was a man sitting on my front porch waiting for me. He stared at me for just a moment and told me that I was about to learn what it meant to suffer." Tanner choked back a sob. "The man got up calmly and walked away. I ran inside to find Ruth and Rachel, but it was too late. They were both dead."

"Oh, Tanner…" Bethany didn't know what to say.

"The man who killed them was a confederate soldier named Thaddeus del Mar. He was a southerner with a vendetta against the Union soldiers who'd fought in my unit. He went on a killing spree and murdered the families of five other men." Tanner reached for his canteen and took a sip of water. "That was five and a half years ago." Tanner brushed away his tears. "All this time I've carried around a burning hatred for that man."

"Did they ever catch him?" she asked.

Tanner shook his head. "No. Rumors were that he moved out west. So that's where I went." He glanced at Bethany. "I came to California to kill him."

Tanner's words caught Bethany by surprise.

"I used to fanaticize about it." He confessed. "I pictured myself catching him off guard somewhere and making him beg for his life right before I shot him."

Bethany could understand Tanner's hurt and anger, but his raw honesty surprised her.

"Have you ever lived with that kind of hatred controlling your life?" he asked.

Bethany carefully considered his question. "No. But I can understand where yours came from."

"My heart grew ugly with it, Bethany." He shook his head. "And I was miserable."

Tanner took the fish from the fire and set the hot pan on the ground. Bethany handed him the plates and waited while Tanner dished out their food.

"Do you want to pray?" he asked.

Bethany nodded. She thanked God for their food and made a quick petition for Tanner in a soft, audible voice. She wasn't sure how Tanner would take her praying for him, but her heart was heavy with all he'd just shared.

The fish was delicious. Bethany took several bites, waiting for Tanner to continue his story. He seemed to be trying to gain control of his emotions again.

"So…" Tanner finally returned to the conversation. "I searched for Thaddeus for a year. I'd heard accounts that he was in California, but I never found him." Tanner took a few more bites of his fish. "I think God was protecting me. I can see that now.

Four years ago I took the job as deputy in Santa Rosa and pretty much gave up on finding del Mar. But I still carried around the hatred."

Bethany gazed at the changing colors in the sky. Streaks of pink broke through the various colors of blue. It was a beautiful evening but Tanner's story was heartbreaking.

"Last night when I talked to Clarence, he told me I needed to forgive." Tanner let his eyes rest on the same sunset. "I've asked the Lord to help me do that. It feels good." He released a deep breath. "I already told you that Clarence led me to Christ. But I thought I should tell you about Ruth and Rachel."

"Thank you for trusting me with your story," Bethany turned toward Tanner.

There was more Tanner wanted to say, Bethany could read it in his eyes. She waited quietly and pulled her legs up close to herself.

"When I was sick, you said I called you Ruth." He tried to hide his obvious embarrassment. "Can I ask you what I said?"

Bethany lowered her eyes and studied the palms of her hands. She remembered Tanner's words well. It was like she'd been the recipient of a private conversation not meant for her. "You told her how much you love her." Bethany turned her face to Tanner's. "Sometimes you just held my hand and kept saying 'Ruth.' Other times you asked to hold Rachel. But mostly you held my hand as if I was that one person whose touch gave you a reason to live." Bethany blushed. "For those hours that you needed me to be... I was Ruth."

"I remember thinking that Ruth was there," Tanner confessed. "And yet I knew she couldn't be. Even in my subconscious I knew." He watched Bethany curiously. "I remember one time I looked at you and saw your sky blue eyes. I thought you were an angel."

Bethany smiled.

"Should I be embarrassed?" Tanner asked. "For the crazy things I said?"

"No. Not at all." Bethany brushed a long golden brown strand of hair away from her face. "They were beautiful words – even if they weren't meant for me. I can only hope that one day some man will love me the way you loved Ruth."

Tanner took the complement. "Thank you for being there for me." He reached for her hand and gave it a gentle squeeze.

Feeling his hand in hers, for even that short moment, refreshed her mind to the strange intimacy they'd shared those days that he was sick. Bethany tried not to let herself think about those nights: hours of comforting him, praying for him, and even wiping away tears from his rugged cheeks. She could never tell Tanner how many hours she spent just staring at him, studying his handsome face, wiping the sweat from his brow. Those were beautiful moments, but they were hers alone to cherish.

"You're somewhere else right now," Tanner interrupted her thoughts.

Bethany turned her face away. He could never know those thoughts.

***

It was no secret that the further you got from civilization, the more suspicious the people often were who lived there. Tanner had a bad feeling the minute he and Bethany rode up to the small run-down shack nestled between the creek and a rock ledge. A fire in the woodstove sent a stream of gray smoke through the trees. Movement behind a worn set of curtains inside the house told Tanner they'd been seen. It was too late to change their minds about talking to these people.

"Stay back," Tanner urged Bethany. Unsure what kind of folks might be taking up residence here, he couldn't risk her being identified. He dismounted and handed Bethany his reins.

It took a full minute for someone to answer Tanner's knock. *Enough time to load a gun.* The minute the door opened, Tanner knew his feeling was accurate. The face that met him at the door was hard and his eyes burned with something so evil it sent shivers down Tanner's spine.

"What do you want?" The man asked behind a .44 Magnum.

"Easy now," Tanner's tone took on his best impersonation of an outlaw and he raised his hands. "I ain't here for no trouble." Tanner narrowed his eyes and glanced around shiftily.

"Tell your friend to show his gun," the man hissed.

106

"Well now – I reckon if you're going to stand there with a gun pointed at my head, it's only fair that my friend's gun remain a mystery."

The man raised an eyebrow and studied the figure across the yard. "Alright." He still held his gun at Tanner. It was not a position Tanner liked to be in. *If this man shoots me, will Bethany know how to defend herself?*

"You've got about ten seconds to tell me why you're here."

"I need to find a place to hunker down for a few days." Tanner tried to sound guilty. "Somewhere private."

The man steadied his dark gaze on Tanner. "What's in it for me?"

Tanner considered this ruffian's question. "Maybe you tell me about a few places and I'll give you a token of my gratitude."

"Or maybe I'll just kill you both and find out what kind of tokens you got." The man cocked his gun.

"Or maybe…" Bethany used her best mother bear voice, got off her horse and walked closer to both men. "I can give you a good faith offering and we can all be friends." She tied both horses to the hitching post and reached inside the bag.

What is she doing? Tanner tried not to show his sudden fear.

"This gold coin is worth enough for both a few good leads and your silence." She held the coin in one hand and Zane's gun with the other. "On the other hand, this Colt .45 will silence you if you decide we're not all friends."

The man studied Bethany curiously. "I know you… your face… You're that killer from Santa Rosa."

Bethany's lips curved into a sinister grin. "And I'll be the killer from Spring Mountain, too, if you don't get your gun out of my friend's face."

Tanner couldn't believe it. Bethany was putting on an act like he'd never seen.

"Lower your gun," she pointed hers at the man.

Something in the man's eyes changed from mistrust to uneasy respect and he lowered his gun. "You serious about that gold coin?"

"Only if you toss your gun into the yard and talk to us." Bethany said in an even tone.

The man tossed his gun and took a few steps closer to Bethany. She lowered her gun and Tanner let himself breathe.

"So you're looking for a cabin to hole up in for a few days?" the man asked.

"A cabin would be good. Know any?" Bethany was now the one calling the shots.

"I know a few. One's down river about five miles, up a little canyon... been boarded up at least eight years. There's another one west of here. No real good road to get to it, but it's about as private as they come." The man gave a brief description of how to get there and explained the location of another cabin. "Sometimes they're in use, if you know what I mean."

"We can take care of that." Bethany kept up her menacing act. "If you see the rest of my buddies, can you give them the information you gave me?" she handed the man the coin.

"I can do that."

"Just make sure they're my friends." She gave him a wink and sauntered to her horse.

"Appreciate it." Tanner tipped his hat as he walked past the man.

Bethany took the lead and headed in the direction of the most remote cabin the man told them about. Neither of them spoke until they were close to a mile away.

***

"Bethany..." Tanner rode up beside her and stared at her curiously.

"Don't talk to me right now," her voice trembled. "I think I'm going to throw up."

Tanner slowed his horse and Bethany did the same. "Are you okay? You were amazing back there."

Bethany closed her eyes and blew out a trembling breath. "I was terrified."

"How did you get your hands on Zane's gun so fast?"

"Very carefully." She took off Tanner's hat and waved it in front of her face like a fan. "Good thing I'm still wearing pants – he might not have been as afraid of me if I'd have been wearing my blue and brown floral."

"You were incredibly convincing and you used your reputation to your advantage." Tanner reached into his saddlebag and handed Bethany the canteen. "Where did you get that gold coin? I thought you used them all up."

Bethany shook her head. "That was my last one. I had it hidden in case I needed it."

Tanner studied Bethany curiously. If he hadn't seen her give up her freedom to save his life, Tanner might have wondered... her act was pretty convincing.

Bethany tossed him back the canteen and leaned forward in the saddle. She was noticeably shaken up. "I felt so deceptive." There was sadness in her blue eyes. "I let that man think he was buddying up with a murderer instead of pointing him to my Savior."

"You probably saved our lives, Bethany."

"I know, but..."

"I don't think the man was ready to hear any preaching right then." Tanner stepped down from his horse and walked over to Bethany. "He was just about to put a bullet in my head."

Bethany glanced up at the trees. Tanner thought she was praying. *This sweet woman who loves the Lord... this is the real Bethany Young.* He knew Bethany was no killer.

"Listen." He placed a hand on Bethany's arm. "When we get to Santa Rosa, I'll send a telegram to Sheriff Moore telling him exactly where this fella' is holding out. I'm sure Clarence will be more than happy to go tell the man about the Lord."

Bethany gave him an appreciative smile. "You promise?"

"You have my word."

***

Bethany's reaction to the man who'd pointed them in the direction of Bethany's potential mystery cabin put a new thought in Tanner's mind. She was more worried about the man's salvation than her own safety.

Tanner rubbed the leather reins between his fingers and stared above his horse's head to the trail in front of them. He was a new believer. Was he ready to start telling people? The first person to pop into his mind was Walt.

109

Tanner recalled Walt's story about his brother, Roy. *Walt has about as much anger and unforgiveness in his heart as I did.* Tanner knew what carrying all that hatred around did for him. A real friend would want to share the way of healing. *Guess I need to write Walt a letter, too.*

They rode quietly and Tanner tried to think through what his letter would say. His eyes scanned the rocky trail ahead of him. Low shrubs and wildflowers dotted the rolling hillside. The steady rhythm of the horses' hooves beat against the dry ground and Tanner let the peacefulness of the countryside sink into his heart.

They followed the man's directions up a steep bank and past a low-lying cliff. Tanner saw the cabin before Bethany did. There wasn't much left to it, but Tanner waited to see what Bethany's reaction to it would be.

"This isn't it." She shook her head and turned discouraged eyes to Tanner. "It seems hopeless."

What was left of the front door hung from one rusty hinge and the cabin's only two windows were void of any glass.

"If we don't find this place, I'm sure you're going to think I made it all up."

Tanner shook his head. "I don't need to see the cabin to believe you, Bethany. But I want to find it to help your case."

"Thank you." She sighed. "Should we camp here tonight?"

"No." Tanner looked at the location of the sun. "I don't want to stay at any of the places that man sent us. Just in case."

Chapter 8

Alan Thacker sat on the edge of Patrick Webber's desk and scratched his head. He and James spent half the morning looking for anything about Bethany's birth family that might tell them if she had a sister.

"Surely your mother has something about Bethany's mother. They were sisters." Alan scratched his head. "Old letters? Notes in the family Bible? Did she keep a special chest that might have that kind of information?"

"You're welcome to look, Alan." James closed his father's desk and stood up to work the kink out of his neck. "I actually have to meet with my father's lawyer this afternoon. But I'll be back by evening."

Alan nodded. He couldn't think of another stone that they could overturn. But he wasn't ready to throw in the towel.

It had been an emotional few days. Marie's funeral was the talk of the town. He and Jane attended more out of respect than of any real relationship with Marie. The Webber's servant was a recent attender of Jane's church, but the two were only acquaintances.

The funeral also served another purpose for Sheriff Thacker. He was able to hear what kinds of things people were saying about the murder case.

Comments ranged from hoping they'd catch the murderer soon and hang her from a short rope, to a genuine disbelief that such a sweet, goodhearted lady like Bethany could really have murdered anyone. The town was obviously split.

But the town was also buzzing with eyes.

Raising her reward to five thousand dollars made Bethany's capture an actual income. Alan had more visitors in the sheriff's office over the past month asking for details of Miss Young than he usually saw in a year.

James left for town and Alan accepted a cup of tea from the cook. He took a seat in the servant's kitchen and wiped his forehead with his handkerchief. The tea was hot and Alan blew on it before taking a sip. A glass of water would have been more refreshing, but he appreciated the servant's thoughtfulness. "This is good tea." He nodded appreciatively to the cook.

"Thank you," Rosa said in a thick Spanish accent. She was a quiet woman who barely looked at a person when they spoke to her.

Alan listened to the ticking of a clock over the kitchen door and watched Rosa roll out her dough in preparation for the evening meal. She worked methodically, adding flour, rolling the dough, and adding more flour.

"Are you making bread?" Alan asked.

"Yes," she answered without looking up.

"How long have you worked for the Webbers?"

"It's been three years, sir."

There was no need to question the Webber's cook. She'd already given her testimony the day of the murder. Everything she reported panned out. She'd been driven to town by one of the drivers and made purchases at several shops in town. Rosa said Miss Young gave her specific directions before dismissing her for the day. She admitted that Bethany's behavior was strange, but thought nothing of it.

Alan finished his tea and tapped his finger on the table thinking through the facts. He'd explored Patrick Webber's office, investigated the few belongings left from Olivia Webber, who died two years ago, and rummaged through a few trunks that James thought might be helpful. So far he had nothing. Either Olivia Webber and Bethany's mother had no real relationship prior to the woman's death, or any communication they did have was destroyed.

Alan was just about ready to tell Rosa that he was finished for the day when he thought about Marie. Would Marie have had anything that would point to Bethany having a sister?

"Rosa," Alan interrupted the cook's kneading.

She stopped working but never raised her eyes to him.

"Has anyone gone through Marie's things since she died?"

"I do not think so."

"Can you tell me which room was hers?"

Without a word, Rosa wiped her hands on a towel and began walking toward the servant's hallway. Alan took this as a yes and began to follow her.

"This was the room of Marie." Rosa gave a curtsy and hurried away to complete her bread.

Alan stepped into Marie's old bedroom and opened the curtains. There was a cold, empty sort of feeling in the room that made Alan shudder. It was never enjoyable investigating a room shortly after someone died. Maybe it was superstition, but Alan always felt as if he was being watched.

Her bed was empty, void of sheet or pillow.

Alan opened Marie's wardrobe and was met by the smell of cedar. Carefully he touched each article of clothing and felt along the floor. A pair of black winter boots sat on the shelf above the clothes and Alan ran his hand along the top. Nothing.

The other side of the wardrobe contained some of Marie's personal items. There was a small stack of letters written in Spanish which Alan assumed were from her family in Spain.

At the bottom of the wardrobe was one long drawer. Alan opened it and found a Bible nestled atop a pile of white, lace handkerchiefs. He sighed. *This seems futile.*

He lifted the Bible out and dug underneath the handkerchiefs. In the drawer he found Marie's rosary, her pen and ink, and a piece of fine jewelry reminiscent of Spanish craftsmanship.

Trying to return everything to the drawer, Marie's Bible slipped from his lap and fell open. Several papers slipped from the thin pages and scattered.

Alan sighed. He reached to pick up the papers and noticed a photograph. Something in the pit of his stomach leapt when he saw the image of two small girls. He turned the photo over and read the names. *Charlotte and Bethany, age 15 months.*

He sat down on the floor and leaned back against the wardrobe staring at the photograph. *Bethany was a twin...*

***

113

Alan couldn't wait. This one piece of evidence could give James hope. It pained Alan to see the way James had aged since his father's death. The man's face was gaunt and he carried himself as one without peace.

The Webber's lawyer was less than a mile a way. Alan hurried to try to catch James before they'd gotten very far into their meeting.

Asa Langley's sign hung with gold lettering over the door. Alan hurried inside and informed the lawyer's secretary that this was urgent.

Asa wasn't used to being interrupted during a meeting with a client, but his secretary insisted that Sheriff Thacker was persistent. Asa was a well-educated man, noted for his sophistication. The handsome middle-aged lawyer had thick salt and pepper hair and a dimple in his strong chin. He turned to the door and waited to hear what was so important.

"I'm sorry to interrupt your meeting." Alan's eyes had a glimmer of anticipation and he held the photograph against his heart. "But James, I found something today that might give you hope."

James stared at Alan for a moment with uncertainty. "Sheriff, I'm sure that within the past forty-five minutes you could not have found something so significant that you would need to interrupt my meeting with Mr. Langley."

"But I did." Alan held up the photograph. "This is Bethany… and her twin."

Asa stood up as fast as James did but Alan held the photo.

"This could be it." Alan was almost afraid to hope. "We need to find Charlotte Young."

"This is significant." Asa sat down with wide eyes.

Alan glanced at James to gauge his response.

James ran his hand over his face and asked to hold the photograph. He sat down slowly and stared at the two black and white figures in the print. The man seemed stunned. "I had no idea," he finally said softly. "A twin." He shook his head in disbelief. "Why would they keep that from us?"

"Well," Alan took a seat and asked for the photo back. "Separating twins is a pretty big deal." He glanced at the picture again and clutched it tight. "It seems to me if God brought them into the world together, it isn't right to tear them apart when they're young."

"People have their reasons," Asa defended. "Olivia wasn't a very strong woman. To take on two energetic toddlers at once might have been more than she could handle."

"But she had Marie," Alan argued.

"Perhaps Charlotte didn't survive. Whatever took my aunt and uncle might have taken her as well," James suggested.

"Which would invalidate the argument I think you are hoping to make," Asa said.

"Do you have any documentation about Miss Young's family back east?" Alan asked the lawyer. There had to be more.

Asa shook his head. "I've only been Patrick Webber's lawyer for eighteen years."

Alan sighed. "Who did he have before you?"

"I'd have to do some research to find that out. I know the gentleman doesn't live in Santa Rosa any longer," Asa said. "Could Marie have had more information? Did you search everything?"

"After I found the photograph I hurried here," Alan explained. "The photo was in her Bible. Nothing else I found appeared to be related to Bethany."

Asa glanced at James and gave him a wane smile. "This should give you some hope, James," he said. "It will put things on hold a little longer, but I'm sure you'd rather find Bethany innocent than anything else."

James nodded. "I'm almost afraid to let myself believe it. Do you know what I mean?"

"I do," Asa comforted his client. "For close to two months you've believed your cousin to be a murderer. I'm sure you don't want to get your hopes up until you know for sure."

Alan rose to go. "I don't want to keep you men any longer." He patted James comfortingly on the shoulder. "I just couldn't wait to tell you."

"It's better that we know now," Asa explained. "Thank you for coming by, Sheriff."

"Yes, thank you," James shook Alan's hand.

Alan walked outside into the warm California sunshine and glanced one more time at the photograph before putting it into the safety of his vest pocket. *I just hope that this gives us some answers.*

***

Sometime in the night Tanner was pulled from sleep by the sound of an animal rummaging through their camp. A full moon was all Tanner needed to make out the silhouette of a black bear. Tanner lay perfectly still and prayed the bear would leave them alone.

Tanner's .45 was just under his pillow, but Tanner knew a .45 was no match for most adult bears. Chances are it would take every bullet in his gun to take this animal down and it might only make the bear angry.

Bethany began to stir. Very slowly Tanner reached his arm out to her and held her down. He didn't say a word. Bears have excellent hearing and Tanner couldn't afford for this one to know they were there.

Bethany seemed to know what was going on. She clutched his arm as if her very life depended on it. With one hand he held the gun and with the other he comforted Bethany.

The horses sensed trouble, but Tanner was confident that they were safe from the bear.

Time seemed to stand still. Tanner was convinced that if he could have heard the seconds ticking on a clock they would have moved in slow motion. Should he stand up and start yelling? In some situations that would scare off a bear.

He sent up a silent petition for their safety and kept his arm on Bethany. He tenderly massaged her wrist, trying to still her nerves. Tanner could feel her fear. *Lord please... Bethany has already been through so much. Please send that bear away. Please protect her.*

As the bear stood up attempting to reach the bag Tanner had hung from a tree, Tanner could see the size of the animal and his heartbeat quickened. He was glad he'd thought to hang the bag with most of their food supplies. He only hoped it didn't make the bear more angry.

116

Minutes passed and the bear finished his exploring. With only a few disappointed growls, the bear sauntered off. Tanner let himself breathe and glanced over at Bethany. "Are you okay?" She still had his arm.

"I was really scared." She finally let go.

"So was I." Tanner shook his head. "He must have smelled our leftover corn cakes." Tanner stood up and rekindled their fire.

Bethany sat up from her quilt and wrapped her arms around her knees.

Tanner took a seat next to her on his quilt and reached for her hand. "You handled it perfectly."

Bethany let out a quavering breath. "How much food do you think the bear took?"

Tanner wasn't sure. The fact that he and Bethany were still alive at that moment seemed more important. "Most of our things were out of reach." He tightened his hand in hers and breathed out a deep sigh. "What a way to wake up."

"Thank you for helping me feel safe." Bethany glanced down at her hand that he still held.

"If God meant to get me to start praying, it worked," he laughed.

Bethany let go of his hand to pull her hair away from her face. "I doubt I can go back to sleep now."

Tanner nodded. He felt the same way. "Dawn will be in another half hour. Maybe we should just get an early start. We've got two more cabins to investigate."

***

Both Bethany and Tanner were tired by the afternoon. Waking up before the sun and riding all morning, trying to follow instructions without a real map, was exhausting. They stopped for lunch and Bethany fell asleep on the soft underbrush of the forest floor.

Tanner watched her while she slept. Bits of sunlight streaming through the trees brought out the golden highlights in her curls. Impulsively Tanner touched her hair. He wanted to feel its softness in his fingers. How long had it been since he'd touched a woman's hair?

117

Bethany was lovely. That word described her well. The sweetness in her smile, the way her eyes lit up when she felt emotion, and the way she cared for people, made Bethany unlike any woman he'd ever met.

It bothered him to have this thought. *What about Ruth? Wasn't she lovely? Wasn't she caring?*

Ruth had been his first love. They were both young when they started courting and both eager to get out and be on their own. Ruth was lighthearted and amusing. Tanner remembered several jokes she played on him when they first got married. One time she replaced his shaving cream with buttercream. He'd worked it and worked it trying to figure out why it wouldn't lather. She also sewed the bottom of his pant legs together one night so when he went to put on his pants the next morning he couldn't get his feet through.

Tanner smiled at the memories.

But Ruth didn't have the same sensitive spirit as Bethany. Even though he thought he was holding Ruth's hand through the many dark hours of his illness, Tanner wondered if Ruth would really have laid down her life like that. It bothered him that he'd question it. He never doubted that she loved him. But Ruth was really not that selfless. She was actually quite spoiled and made a fuss when she didn't get her way. He chuckled at the memory of some of their spirited arguments.

Tanner wondered if much of that was simply their age. Ruth was young when he'd married her. His mother teased him that he'd robbed the cradle.

Why was he comparing Ruth to Bethany? This was wrong. He took his hand away from Bethany's hair and got up to walk around.

He would be insane to allow himself to have feelings for this woman. First of all she was wanted for murder and still stood a good chance of being hanged. Never again would he live through the sorrow of losing a loved one unjustly. Tanner had no intention of letting himself get hurt again like he did over five years ago.

Secondly, Ruth was his first and only love. She represented to him all the joys of youthful romance and first time motherhood. No matter how sweet and gentle-spirited and caring she was, Bethany could never compete with that.

***

By late afternoon Bethany was awake, refreshed, and ready to ride more. She was still doubtful as to finding the cabin, but she was eager to continue the quest.

Tanner had been quiet since she woke up. Bethany had no idea of the mental battle he'd had with himself while she slept. She simply assumed he was tired.

They'd ridden for what felt like miles off the beaten track, and Bethany hoped Tanner was still able to follow the vague directions given by the man to whom she'd passed her last gold coin.

This part of the forest was different. Many of the tall redwood trees had been logged leaving a large amount of shrub brush and weeds. Something about it was actually familiar.

"Tanner," she almost whispered. "I know this place."

Tanner stared at her with a look of restored hope. "Really? That's a good sign."

The longer they rode, the more encouraged Bethany became. "There was a unique rock formation behind the cabin," she said. "I climbed down it to get to the creek. I remember it because the natural grooves were almost like steps."

"That's a pretty good landmark." Tanner scanned the creek.

Bethany slowed her horse as they neared a place where they would need to cross the shallow water. "Tanner, I think this is it." Her eyes were wide. "See the steps? They lead up that incline to the back of the property."

Tanner could see it. A giant rock face lay flush into the hillside with distinct grooves that looked like steps. "We won't be able to take the horses up that rock," Tanner said. "Let's ride a bit further down and take the horses up."

Bethany took the lead. "The cabin should be right up there." Her tone was enthusiastic and she hurried her horse up the hill.

Tanner's horse was only a few steps behind her and stopped beside Bethany, whose enthusiasm had been replaced by a look of total discouragement. Instead of a log cabin sitting in the clearing at the top of the precipice, there was a pile of ashes and burnt lumber. The cabin had been burned to the ground.

Climbing down from his horse, Tanner tied the reins to a tree and walked toward the rubble.

"It's gone." Bethany dismounted and took a few staggering steps. "We're too late. The cabin is gone."

Tanner felt through the ashes to see if there was any heat left. "It could have been done weeks ago." He studied the debris. There was nothing here to support her story except ashes.

Bethany just stared. "Why?"

"They wanted to destroy the evidence. Whoever this person is, they know you're still out here and they want to take away every little crumb that might prove your innocence." He turned to Bethany.

Her face was white and her blue eyes without hope. "I'll just turn myself in," Bethany said with resignation. "It's the only thing left to do. You head east. Go home to Maine."

"No." Tanner walked to Bethany and placed a hand on each of her arms. "I'm in this with you to the end. If you're guilty then so am I."

She shook her head. "We can't win this Tanner. They've thought of everything." She glanced at the sky and closed her eyes. "They gave me coins stolen from my uncle's safe and like a fool I used them. They burned up the cabin. And somehow… witnesses say they saw me." She ran her hand across her forehead and tears filled her eyes. "How can I prove it wasn't me when people say they saw me?"

Tanner pulled her to him and held her in his arms while her body shook in sobs. He didn't have the answers. At this moment it really did feel hopeless. But the woman in his arms was no killer. Tanner would bet his own life on it.

Chapter 9

Alan Thacker's stomach let him know it was time to head on home. He stacked the papers he'd been working on into a neat little pile. "I say we call it a day," Alan said to his assistant deputy.

Rodney Porter finished sweeping the empty jail cell and set the broom against the wall. "Would you like me to file those papers for you, Sheriff?" The young assistant was eager to help in any way he could.

"No, we'll do it tomorrow. Your mother's probably got dinner ready for you."

Rodney nodded. "Beef stew tonight," he said. "She made sure I knew so I wouldn't be late."

Alan let out a chuckle. "Are you seeing your girlfriend this evening?"

"Not tonight." There was disappointment in Rodney's tone. "She's supposed to help work on her sister's wedding dress."

"Well that's good practice for her own some day," Alan teased.

Rodney didn't deny it. "Maybe."

"Go on home. I'll close up the office."

Rodney left while Alan finished up his last minute to do list for tomorrow. In light of the new information they'd found, the mayor agreed to let Alan remove "Dead or alive" from Bethany's wanted poster. There was still a five thousand dollar reward for her capture, but Alan convinced both Mayor Watkins and James that this investigation was not over. Eager to make the changes, Alan spent the day sending out notifications.

Alan glanced up when he heard the bell over his door ring. Did Rodney forget something?

"Sheriff Thacker," Asa Langley said walking toward Alan's desk. "I got that name for you."

Alan took the slip of paper from Asa and read the name. "Drew Keene." Alan grew reflective. "That name rings a bell."

Asa took a seat across from Alan. "I think he was only here for a few years and then he moved to San Francisco."

"Is he still practicing law?" Alan asked.

Asa nodded. "He is, and from what I understand, he's doing very well."

"San Francisco can probably keep its lawyers busy," Alan chuckled. "I really appreciate you finding this for me."

"Finding Bethany's twin is a good lead—definitely worth investigating."

"We can't bring Marie or Patrick Webber back," Alan said. "But if we can prove it wasn't Bethany, at least James won't have to lose his cousin too. The poor man looks like he's about to come unglued. I don't know how he's hanging in there."

Asa agreed. "And the longer this case goes unsolved, the longer it drags out the legal proceedings."

"Why is that?" Alan asked. "I thought Bethany was taken out of the will."

"She was taken out of her uncle's will. But her aunt left close to twenty-five hundred acres in a trust for Bethany that would have become available to her upon Patrick's death."

Alan paused for a moment. "Where is this land?"

"About forty miles outside of Sacramento." Asa scratched his face. "It's not developed. From what I understand, they purchased this land many years ago with the intention of giving it to Bethany some day. Because Bethany cared for Olivia for almost a year while the woman was bed-ridden, Patrick didn't have the heart to remove Bethany from that part of the will.

"Who all knows about this?" Alan asked.

"I believe it's common knowledge. There is supposed to be some story that goes along with it."

Alan sighed. "So until all this is cleared up, you can't fulfill the desires of the will."

"I can move forward with the properties which have been clearly left to James, but I'm going to have to sit on the twenty-five hundred acres a while longer. I just hate dragging it all out."

"Understood." Alan glanced again at the name on the paper. "I think I'll be catching a train to San Francisco tomorrow."

***

San Francisco was alive with activity. Alan walked down the busy streets, taking in the fascinating contrast of foreigners and classes. Businessmen ambled along, entrenched in intellectual conversation. On the same sidewalk sat a young boy, dressed in dirty rags. Two Chinese men passed Alan speaking to one another in words Alan could not comprehend.

This was not Alan's first trip to San Francisco, but every time he went, he was struck by the disparity. Glancing down at the slip of paper in his hand, Alan refreshed his memory of the building he was looking for.

For Bethany's sake as well as Tanner's, Alan hoped he could learn something from Mr. Keene.

He found Keene's law office nestled loftily on the high end of town. Alan noted the clean marble floors and ornate wooden paneling along the walls. He found Drew Keene's office and stepped inside.

"May I help you?" A fine dressed gentleman seated behind a large walnut desk glanced up from his pen and ink to appraise his new visitor.

"Are you Drew Keene?" Alan asked.

"No. Mr. Keene is with a client this afternoon. Do you have an appointment with him?"

"I'm Sheriff Alan Thacker from Santa Rosa. It's imperative that I see Mr. Keene as soon as possible."

The secretary set down his pen and scanned Mr. Keene's appointment calendar. "He has a very busy day tomorrow, but I can squeeze you in around eleven-thirty."

"Tomorrow?" This was not what Alan was expecting. He was a Sheriff; didn't he have the right to meet with a lawyer about pressing criminal charges when it was best for *him*? "I was hoping to meet with Mr. Keene today."

"That's impossible," the secretary gave Alan a disinterested sigh. "Shall I mark you down for eleven-thirty?"

Alan stood to his full height and nodded. "That will be fine."

It took every bit of dignity Alan had to hide his annoyance from this haughty secretary. Alan hoped Drew Keene wasn't as arrogant.

***

Santa Rosa was just over the last hill. Even in the night, Tanner knew the landscape and recognized the surrounding area. He and Bethany prayed about and discussed their new plan and now it was time to move.

Sheriff Thacker's house was on the north side of town. He owned several acres with a couple fruit trees and an ample garden. Tanner knew the property well. He'd been invited to the Thacker's home for Sunday dinners on many occasions.

Alan had a sizeable barn and a wide stretch of pastureland where he grazed his horses and dairy cow. Tanner was counting on slipping into that barn for the night undetected and establishing contact with Alan in the morning.

Bethany drew her horse closer as they approached the sleeping community. Doing their best to keep to the edge of town, they crept quietly past dark farms and small vineyards.

Alan's house was set away from the road and Tanner led them quietly up the well-worn path to the barn.

Without warning, barking broke the silence and Tanner saw Alan's dog approaching with his hackles up.

"It's okay Max," Tanner tried to silence the protective animal. Max was only doing his job. Max's barks echoed through the farm and Tanner hoped it wouldn't wake Alan and Jane.

Tanner climbed down from his horse and allowed Max to smell his hand. "It's okay, buddy." He patted Max behind the ear. "It's just me... you're okay."

Max was content that these were not villainous thieves out to overrun his much-guarded domain and wagged his long black tail while they snuck to the barn.

Inside the barn, Tanner and Bethany unsaddled both horses and Tanner led them to a couple empty stalls. He handed Bethany one of the saddlebags and was about to lead her to the hayloft when he heard the clear sound of a rifle clicking into ready position.

Bethany lowered herself behind a wooden crate and quieted her breathing.

"Alan," he spoke into the darkness with his hands in the air. "It's me, Tanner."

"Tanner?" Jane's curious voice surprised Tanner. "What in the world are you doing here?"

***

Bethany sat beside Tanner on a small sofa in the Thacker's parlor while Tanner explained their story to Jane. It was close to three in the morning, but no one was tired. Jane made them both a cup of tea and listened as the details unfolded.

"Alan read me the telegrams you sent," Jane said. "We've both been worried and I've prayed for you every day."

"Thank you, Jane." Tanner's appreciation was genuine. "God did more than bring us safely to Santa Rosa," he continued. "He delivered me from my sin and saved my soul."

Jane listened with interest while Tanner shared how he'd given his life to Christ.

"Dear Tanner," she beamed. "This is an unexpected joy."

"For me as well," Tanner said.

Bethany had spoken very little since their arrival. Actually, Bethany hadn't said much since she and Tanner left the site of the burned cabin.

Sitting in a comfortable home, talking so openly about the past two months with a woman she was only vaguely familiar with was a little unsettling to Bethany. She trusted Tanner and knew he believed Alan would give them an opportunity to present Bethany's case, but what about Jane? Was she a busybody in town who would now carry the news of Bethany's arrival in Santa Rosa to her sewing circle?

Bethany was a fairly new attender of the church where Jane was a member. Growing up, Bethany was never taken to church. It was only after her aunt's passing, two years ago, that Bethany began attending.

She recognized Jane as one of the members, but they were minimally acquainted. Bethany came from a wealthy home. In spite of her desire to make friends, her perceived status was an unfortunate social barrier.

How could Bethany explain to Tanner that Jane was not someone she considered a confidant?

"What is the climate of the town?" Tanner asked Jane.

"The past two months have been insane. Alan has been inundated with curious bounty hunters and the gossip has been non-stop," Jane said.

"What is being said about Bethany?"

Jane glanced quickly at Bethany and back to Tanner. It was clear this question made her uncomfortable. "Because of all the evidence, most simply hope she is found and brought to justice."

"But what of my friends and family?" Bethany finally spoke up. "What of James?"

Jane drew in a steadying breath. "Your cousin is deeply grieved. Alan recently uncovered news that he hopes will shed new light on the case, but it has been difficult to sway opinion away from the apparent evidence."

"So my cousin thinks I killed his father?"

"Until these recent developments, I don't think he doubted it." Jane lowered her eyes. "But there is hope. Only a few days ago, James and the mayor agreed to allow Alan to remove 'dead or alive' from your wanted posters."

"But there is still a five thousand dollar reward for her capture?" Tanner clarified.

Jane nodded. "And Alan fears the changes will go unnoticed in the battle for her capture."

"What are these recent developments?" Tanner pressed to understand the situation.

"I believe it would be best for Alan to explain." Jane stood up to refill Tanner's tea. "I'd rather not disclose anything until Alan has had the opportunity to investigate this new information."

"When do you expect Alan to return?"

"He sent a telegraph yesterday that he hoped to be home within two days." Jane explained. "Alan is working to prove your innocence, Miss Young, but it is not safe for you here."

"Are there none in Santa Rosa who believe in my innocence? What about Marie?"

Jane studied Bethany curiously.

Bethany watched Jane's confused expression. Why was the woman looking at her so piteously? Was something wrong? Jane's eyes filled up with tears and Bethany knew instinctively that something was terribly wrong.

"Marie is dead," the words rolled off Jane's lips and struck Bethany's heart with a painful blow.

Bethany's eyes grew wide and she shook her head. *Marie? Dead?* "No… not Marie…" Great pools welled up in her seas of blue and she fidgeted nervously with the edge of her shirt. "How? When?" Bethany wasn't sure she wanted to know. She'd reached the end of her rope.

Jane seemed uncertain how to answer. "She was shot the day your uncle was killed. Dr. Nash believed she was doing better but there must have been internal injuries no one anticipated. It's been almost two weeks now."

Bethany grew pale and buried her face in her hands.

Tanner placed a comforting hand on her back and drew her closer to him. "I'm so sorry."

***

Tanner stepped from the guest room where Bethany had finally fallen asleep. For hours he sat with her consoling her through her grief. Bethany shared with him the friendship she had with this woman who was more like a mother to her than a servant. The death of her uncle paled in comparison to the pain of losing Marie.

"How is she?" Jane asked Tanner when he stepped into the kitchen.

Tanner shook his head. "I don't know how much more Bethany can take." He sat at the table and accepted the plate of cheese and bread. "The men who'd held her captive only told her about Patrick and while she was deeply saddened by his passing, Bethany admitted she was far closer to her Aunt Olivia and Marie."

"I confess, Bethany's reaction to Marie's death did more to convince me of her innocence than anything else," Jane said. "She was in total shock. That was not the reaction of someone who'd been the assailant."

Tanner took a bite of cheese and wondered what information Alan had and whether it would provide them with any hope. Bethany was desperate for hope.

"So tell me," Jane sat across from him with a cup of tea. "What about you." She leaned closer. "You're wanted for breaking her out of jail and threatening a fellow officer of the law. Alan knew you would never have made such a move unless you were upholding justice. But you can't be seen in this town either."

Tanner sighed. "It does make things a little more difficult. But whoever framed Bethany and killed her uncle is still out there and knows she is too. They were counting on someone else killing Bethany and burying their secret. Removing the 'dead or alive' status presents a new risk for this person. What if she lives and what if people believe her? Then they might start looking for the real killer."

Jane nodded.

"Has Alan considered that the further he investigates, the more his life could be in danger?"

The expression on Jane's face told Tanner that she had not considered that idea. "You believe this investigation could be dangerous for Alan?" She reached forward and grabbed Tanner's wrist. "Dr. Nash was scared when he was here. Alan told me Nash feared for his life."

"What does Dr. Nash know that would put his life at risk?"

"He is convinced that Marie was getting better. He said the injury had healed and it was just a matter of getting her strength back. Her death came as a total shock to him."

Tanner shook his head. "I don't understand. Why would Dr. Nash fear for his life?"

"Because Marie told Dr. Nash that the person who shot her was not Bethany."

Jane released her hold on Tanner and glanced at the window. "Dr. Nash believes someone killed Marie to silence her. He's afraid they will need to silence him too."

This was a new thought for Tanner.

Jane's eyes grew suddenly wide. "Tanner, my sister just drove her buggy up the drive. You need to hide. Rose is as nosy as a cat." Jane grabbed Tanner's dishes and hurried them to the sink. "Hide in Bethany's room but don't walk around. Rose listens for every creaking floorboard thinking she's sniffing out rodents. Go now!"

Tanner hurried upstairs to the guest room and locked the door behind him.

***

"Rose." Jane did her best to recover and sound happy to see her sister. "So glad you dropped in today. What brings you out? Can I get you a cup of tea?"

The heavier woman dropped herself exhaustedly down into Tanner's still warm chair. "Rodney was over visiting Eliza last night and mentioned that Alan is in San Francisco investigating Mr. Webber's murder." Rose hurried out her words and waited for her sister to respond.

Jane steadied her nerves. She knew that the assistant deputy was courting Rose's granddaughter, but Rodney had no right to disclose that information. "Alan is still working on the case," she answered cryptically.

"After all this time?" Rose took the offered tea and sweetened it with several spoons of honey. "I would think your husband would just open his eyes and admit to himself that he'd been fooled. That no good deputy he so entrusted got side-tracked by a pretty face and has run off with her and the money."

Jane cleared her throat and hoped the walls were thick enough to silence their voices. Tanner did not need to hear this conversation. "I trust my husband's discernment," she said.

"That's always been your problem, Jane. Too quick to believe the best in people and what does that do for you? Rodney said there was too much evidence that Miss Young is the killer and that Deputy Brenly is looking at twenty years if he's not sentenced to the rope."

"Rose," Jane took a seat across from her older sister and wished the woman would leave. "Rodney is still young. He doesn't know the whole picture and he really needs to stop giving his opinion."

"What Rodney needs is for your husband to fire that no good traitor of a deputy and give the position to Rodney so he can marry my Eliza. I honestly can't believe you won't encourage Alan to do so. Eliza is your great niece remember?" She took a quick sip of her tea and added more honey. "And for that matter, why in the world is he running off to San Francisco? Do you know what kind of den of iniquity that town is? I'm sure any investigating he needed could have been done through the good old U.S. postal service."

Jane was growing tired of her sister's endless prattle.

"Poor Eliza is just waiting for Rodney to get that promotion. I'm sure you remember how difficult it was to see your older sister plan a wedding while you're told to be patient. It doesn't seem right. I'm her grandmother and it nearly breaks my heart." Rose got up to explore Jane's kitchen. "Have you got anything to eat? I haven't had a bite since breakfast."

"Take a seat, Rose," Jane motioned to a chair. "I have some tea cakes I think you'll like."

"Thank you." Rose smiled at her sister. "I know it's difficult for you to relate to the maternal things of life, since you and Alan never had children. But honestly, nothing grieves a mother's heart more than seeing her grandchild cry because the man she loves can't afford to take on a wife."

Jane tried not to be bitter at her sister's careless comment about childlessness.

Rose helped herself to another teacake and motioned toward the barn. "So did Alan get a couple new horses?" she asked. "While I was parking my buggy, I happened to glance in the barn and noticed two new quarter horses."

Of course you 'happened' to glance in the barn. "We're keeping them for a friend. Quite pleasant horses actually. I wouldn't mind Alan owning them."

"Well you know if Alan needs another horse, my Vincent is quite the breeder."

Jane nodded. It was no secret that Rose's son was one of the best breeders in town. "I'm sure Alan won't forget that."

"Did your friend buy those from Vincent?"

130

"I don't know, but I'll be sure to ask." Jane got up to wash a few dishes.

"Whose horses are they? I can ask Vincent."

"Why do you need to know? They're already owned – what does it matter who they were purchased from?" Jane wished there was some way to get her sister to talk sensibly.

"Well I don't suppose it really does matter, only that Vincent likes to know what competition is out there. I try to help him as best I can. He is your nephew. I would think you'd want to help too." Rose sniffed. "And why would your friends want to board their horses here? Vincent has two very nice livery stables on either side of town."

Jane slapped her hands onto the counter. "Okay, Rose. I'll just spill the beans. They're our horses." Her eyes flashed with frustration. "We got a great deal and couldn't resist. It was a breeder over in Napa. Best prices around. They say he's taking over central California. Are you happy now?"

"Oh my," Ruth dabbed her eyes with the corner of her apron.

Jane felt suddenly guilty. "I was only having fun. They really do belong to a friend. But Rose can't you see the ridiculousness of your questioning?"

"I can see when my own sister doesn't want to talk to me. Why in the world you and Alan have to always be so secretive I don't understand."

"My husband is the sheriff," Jane tried to soften her tone. "We can't tell everything."

"Being a lawman doesn't stop Rodney."

"Well it should."

* * *

It was 11:45 a.m. and Alan sat in Drew Keene's immaculately furnished office waiting for the man to arrive.

"Sorry to have kept you waiting," Drew stepped in and closed the door.

Drew was in his early sixties. With thick unruly gray hair, dark eyes, and a slightly Roman nose, Alan guessed him to have been of Greek decent.

131

"I've been so busy, I meet my self coming and going." Drew walked to the desk and shook hands with Alan, standing at least three inches above the sheriff. "My secretary tells me you are the sheriff of Santa Rosa."

"Yes," Alan sat across from Drew and readied himself for the conversation. "I've been investigating a crime that was committed against one of your former clients."

"That would have been Patrick Webber," Drew straightened a few objects on his desk and glanced quickly at Alan.

"Yes."

"I've read about it. Sad story." Drew rubbed his nose a few times and sniffed. "How is my assistance needed?"

"You were Patrick's lawyer twenty-one years ago when he obtained custody of his wife's niece, Bethany Young."

Drew nodded somberly. "Sad story that. To raise a niece as your own child only to have her murder you."

"That's why I'm here," Alan drew the photo out of his pocket. "I'm not convinced it was Bethany." He handed the photo to Drew. "Were you aware that Bethany is a twin?"

Drew took the photo and studied it for a moment, reading the inscription on the back. "Are you sure this is truly Bethany Young?" He handed the photo back to Alan. "Where did you get the picture?"

"I found it in Marie Chavez's Bible." He tapped the photo a few times. "This photo could split the case wide open."

"You believe this Charlotte Young might have been the murderer?" Drew leaned back and studied Alan curiously. "Isn't that a stretch?"

"It's a lead." He placed the photo back into his pocket. "And what I need from you is anything that might help me find Bethany's family back east."

Drew sighed deeply. "I no longer have any files from my clients in Santa Rosa," he shook his head somberly. "A fire my first year in San Francisco took everything."

Another wall. "Well, what can you remember?" Alan asked. "Surely Patrick would have spoken to his lawyer about bringing his wife's niece into their home. Did he ever mention her being a twin?"

"I'm sorry, Sheriff Thacker. You're asking me to remember something that happened twenty-one years ago. I'll be honest. I'd almost forgotten all about Patrick Webber until I heard about his death."

"Can you remember anything? Where was Olivia's sister from?"

Drew rubbed his face and looked reflective. "Ah, yes… Olivia. It seems like she was from Missouri maybe?" He shook his head. "I'm sorry I'm not more of a help. I didn't stay close to the family."

Alan thought he understood.

"But I truly wish you the best of luck." Drew glanced at his timepiece. "I hate to end this conversation so abruptly, but I'm meeting a client for lunch."

Alan shook the man's hand and stepped toward the door. *Well this trip proved to be worthless.*

***

Bethany brushed her wet hair and sat in front of the small, oval mirror hanging above her washstand. It felt good to take a warm bath and finally have a clean dress to wear. Bethany appreciated the blue and white cotton dress Jane let her borrow.

Jane made a fuss about how it was probably not the quality Bethany was used to, but Bethany insisted that it was lovely. *Does Jane see me as spoiled?*

It was time for breakfast. The smell of cinnamon and coffee wafted up the stairs and Bethany felt a twinge of hunger. As much as she wanted to curl back up in the warm cozy bed and sleep away all her pain, Bethany knew she needed to go downstairs.

"The dress fits you nicely," Jane said as Bethany walked into the kitchen.

"Thank you." Bethany glanced at the neatly set table in the middle of Jane's kitchen. A lace tablecloth covered the quarter sawn oak top while delicate Rose Bud Chinz plates sat at each place.

Both women were quiet for a moment.

"Are you feeling rested?" Jane asked.

The uneasy silence between them was awkward. Bethany had slept away most of the day before, only waking up to a feeling of hopelessness and sorrow. "Yes. Thank you." She offered to put out the silver. "Where is Tanner?"

"He is caring for the horses."

Bethany nodded and carefully set each piece of silverware beside a plate. "Is it safe for him to be outside?"

"We are both keeping a close eye on the lane. I don't expect anyone until Rodney brings Alan home from the train station."

Bethany watched as Jane set a fruit cup at each plate. "You've set a lovely table."

Jane glanced up and smiled self-consciously. "I'm sure you are used to a much nicer one."

Bethany shook her head. "Actually, no. This is the same china pattern my Aunt Olivia had."

Jane couldn't hide her surprise. "But I thought…" she lowered her eyes and pulled the bread from the oven. "Never mind."

"Please, Mrs. Thacker. My family may have had wealth, but I have never believed myself to be better than anyone else."

Jane was embarrassed. "I'm sorry, Miss Young. I made assumptions. Your uncle's position in the community made me think you wouldn't want to associate with those of us below your class."

"Is that why you never spoke to me at church?"

"I'm so sorry." Jane set down the bread and lowered her eyes. "I would never have thought you noticed."

"I noticed." Bethany looked out the window and watched Tanner lead their horses into the pasture.

Jane turned toward Bethany. "You often sat with the mayor's wife… and Felicia Conway. They are not prone to socializing with the rest of the ladies in the church."

"They were my aunt's friends and they were the only ones who spoke to me."

Jane shook her head somberly. "I should not have been so presumptuous. I confess I questioned your presence at church and although you seemed sweet and nice, I thought your status placed you a notch above me."

"I never meant to make anyone feel that way."

"It wasn't you." Jane confessed. "I judged you. I was wrong." She sat at the table with downcast eyes. "Will you forgive me?"

Bethany appreciated Jane's apology. "Yes. Of course I forgive you."

Jane motioned for Bethany to sit across from her. "I know you weren't raised in the church, Bethany. May I ask what brought about your decision to start attending?"

Bethany nodded. "My Aunt Olivia was ill for a long time. The last year of her life she was bedridden most of the time. During that year, I cared for my aunt. Sometimes I would read to her, sometimes I would sing. When it became very clear to me that my aunt was not long for this world it got me to wondering about the next. I knew very little about God. Even in the midst of all of my uncle's books, we did not have a Bible in the house."

Jane listened quietly.

"I decided that the hours I spent with my aunt were only helping her in this present life. I knew there had to be more. So, I bought a Bible from Mr. Goodwin's store." Bethany smiled at the memory. "He seemed surprised by my purchase and asked me if I had read much of the Bible. When I confessed that I had never read any of it, he wrote down a list of books, chapters and verses to read that might bring my aunt comfort."

"Mr. Goodwin is a very wise man." Jane said.

"He is. He had me read the book of John, Psalm 23, parts of Romans, and so much more. So I read the Bible to my aunt every day for hours and hours. Over the next six months I'd read almost the whole Bible and some of it several times. Aunt Olivia and I could recite Psalm 23 together." There was a fond memory in Bethany's eyes. "As my aunt grew worse, however, I realized that she didn't find the comfort from God's Word that I would have thought she would. I went to Mr. Goodwin and asked him why."

Jane's eyes moistened with tears.

"He walked me through the Gospel pointing out verses to me that I'd read many times. It became clear to me. I needed to believe in my heart and confess with my lips that Jesus Christ is Lord and find forgiveness for my sins. I left his store that day a

Child of God."

Jane reached for Bethany's hands and clasped them tightly.

"Pastor Bennington and Mr. Goodwin came to our house several times and helped me walk my aunt through those same verses. It took a little longer for her to open her heart to Jesus. There were things she said God could never forgive her for. Pastor Bennington was a big help. He and his wife met with Aunt Olivia a few times to help her deal with the things she felt were beyond God's forgiveness. It was a beautiful day when she committed her life to Jesus. She died shortly after, but I know I will see her again some day."

"I remember you getting baptized at the creek," Jane admitted. "It was unexpected and sadly, I even questioned it. I'm sorry."

"I forgive you," Bethany brushed away a tear. "I know my church attendance was sporadic at first. My uncle and I had many battles about it. Honestly, when he gave me the choice between his inheritance or God's, I was finally free. I told him there was no comparison and that my God would supply all my needs according to His riches in Christ Jesus." Bethany smiled. "Uncle Patrick wrote me out of his will but I was free to go to church whenever I wanted."

"I had no idea that's why you didn't attend very often at first." Jane sighed. "God is really humbling me right now. I needed to learn this."

Tanner opened the back door and glanced at the two women curiously.

Jane held Bethany's hand in hers and smiled. "My dear sister in Christ and I were having a heart to heart conversation," she said.

***

Bethany and Tanner hid out in the upstairs guestroom later in the afternoon when they expected Rodney to bring Alan home.

Jane watched the door nervously, hoping her sister hadn't told Rodney about the two visiting horses.

When Rodney's wagon pulled up, Jane readied herself to greet her husband and the assistant deputy who helped Alan carry his bag to the door.

"There was really no need for you to carry my bag, Rodney," Alan held the door for the younger man to let him walk inside.

"I don't mind at all, Sheriff," Rodney set the bag down and greeted Jane. "How are you, Mrs. Thacker?"

"I'm doing well, Rodney. Thank you." She hugged her husband and offered both men a cup of coffee.

"I would love one, thank you." Rodney said enthusiastically.

"Whose horses are those in our pasture?" Alan asked before Jane could stop him.

Jane's eyes grew wide and she attempted to give her husband a look without Rodney noticing. "Don't you remember, dear?" She walked to the kitchen to get the men their coffee. "We told that friend of yours who was traveling through from Saint Helena that he could leave them here for a few nights." She handed Rodney his mug. "You like cream and sugar don't you, Rodney?"

"Yes, thank you, Mrs. Thacker."

Alan was obviously trying to figure out what his wife was talking about while he accepted the mug she offered him. "Ah, yes. I forgot. That's right." He watched his wife curiously.

"Why wouldn't you just have had the horses stabled at your nephew's livery?" Rodney asked.

"Oh, this friend is very protective of his horses. Isn't that right, Alan?"

"Very." Alan played along. "That's why our own horses are in stalls right now and he's got his out in the pasture, eating our grass." He glanced at his wife behind Rodney's back and furrowed his eyebrows.

"But we owe him." Jane sat on the arm of Alan's chair and placed her hand on his back.

"Who is this friend?" Rodney asked. "Do I know him?"

By this point Alan was having fun playing his wife's little game. "I think you do. Name's Orville Blythe. He owns about three hundred acres outside of Napa," Alan said in total seriousness.

Jane almost fell off the chair.

Rodney chewed on his thumbnail and nodded. "Yeah. I... I think I recognize the name."

He lies as bad as my husband. "Can I get you a teacake, Rodney?" Jane was feeling guilty that her husband just backed his assistant deputy into a lie.

"No. I'd better not. I'm supposed to eat dinner with Eliza tonight.

"Well that's nice. Tell her we both said hello," Jane stood up and carried her husband's empty coffee cup into the kitchen.

Rodney thanked her for the coffee and waved them both good evening. Jane watched him leave and sighed with relief.

***

Alan watched his wife, waiting for her to turn around. "So... are you going to tell me whose horses they really are?" he asked.

"Why don't you come back to the parlor and I'll let them tell you." Jane closed the front curtains, walked upstairs and knocked on the guestroom door. "Alan is home and Rodney is gone."

It was obvious that Alan was not expecting to see Tanner and Bethany walking down his stairs. His face showed immediate concern and he glanced around nervously as if he was expecting to get caught. "What are you doing here?"

"Good to see you too, Sheriff," Tanner's eyes twinkled.

"I'm sorry," Alan shook his head. "But did anyone see you?"

"No." Tanner motioned for Bethany to step forward. "This is Bethany Young." He glanced at Bethany. "Sheriff Thacker."

Bethany nodded. "I do believe we've met before, in town."

Alan was sure they had. "You do realize how insane this is. Two wanted criminals hiding in my house."

"Calm down, Alan. We've been very careful." Jane sat down on her favorite rocking chair and patted the chair next to her for her husband.

"Are you ready for the story?" Tanner asked. He and Bethany took a seat beside one another on the couch.

"I'm all ears."

Tanner began his story with the hotel room in Vacaville and Alan listened intently.

"So this Zane fella was about to kill you when Bethany shot him in the leg?" Alan glanced at Bethany curiously.

"She could have killed him. She could have killed me. Instead she saved my life." Tanner rolled up his sleeve and exposed the red swollen scar, still healing, on his arm.

Jane hadn't seen the scar and moved from her chair to look. "Oh Tanner…"

"Believe it or not, it looks much better." Tanner continued the story and then gave Bethany the floor.

Bethany shared her story with the sheriff. Her sad blue eyes fought tears and Tanner took her hand for encouragement.

"But the cabin has been burned to the ground," Tanner explained. "Whoever framed Bethany is trying real hard to destroy evidence."

Alan pieced the details together and glanced at Tanner's hand curiously. He'd never seen his deputy take on the role of comforter like this.

"I'd stake my life on it, Sheriff, and I've already staked my career," Tanner said. "Bethany did not kill anyone."

"How much did you tell them about my trip to San Francisco?" Alan asked his wife.

"I didn't tell them anything about it."

Alan nodded. "Bethany," he leaned forward in his seat. "How much do you know about your birth family?"

Bethany considered his question. "My mother's name was Eleanor and my father was Joel. I was born in Missouri." She sighed. "My Aunt Olivia told me that shortly after the gold rush, she and Uncle Patrick moved out west. My parents followed but settled in Sacramento. That's where they died."

"Do you know of any siblings, Bethany?" Alan's face grew sober.

Bethany shook her head. "No. When Tanner caught me, I was headed to Sacramento in hope that I could find out information about my family back in St. Louis. That's where my mother and father were from."

Alan lowered his eyes for a moment and glanced at his wife. Jane nodded.

"I found out something about your life that might actually give us some answers. The implications are actually pretty terrible. But in light of your story, it's the only thing that makes sense."

Bethany stared at Alan and waited for what he was about to say.

Alan pulled the photo from his vest pocket and handed it to Bethany. "You're a twin."

***

Bethany stared at the photo for several minutes while Sheriff Thacker's words sank in. "You're saying I have a twin and you believe she set me up for murder? A twin I never knew I even had?" She shook her head. "No. This can't be true. This can't be a photograph of me."

"I found it in Marie's Bible."

"No." Bethany turned to Tanner for support. "Marie would never have kept something like this from me. My Aunt Olivia would never. There must be a mistake."

"Bethany," Alan interrupted. "This is not a mistake. This is a real photograph and these are real names. This is you." He pointed to the photo. "Don't you see? If this is true and it was your twin, then it all makes sense. She came into your home, killed your uncle and stole enough money and gold to keep her happy for the rest of her life. All the while, everyone in town saw 'you.'"

Bethany leaned her head back on the sofa and ran her hand across her forehead. "If I have a twin, I want to know my sister. Not have her arrested."

"What if she did this to you?" Alan shook his head. "She deserves to hang."

"If she did this to me—then I am certain that she is not a follower of Jesus Christ. To hang her would be to send her to hell."

Tanner reached once again for Bethany's hand. "Bethany, if she did this then she is a murderer."

"For all have sinned and fallen short of the glory of God."

"Yes, Bethany," Tanner agreed. "But there are consequences to sin."

Bethany stared at the photograph again and read the name. "Charlotte…"

"Do you have any memory at all of a twin?" Jane asked.

"No. But I was so young." Bethany sighed. "If I came to live with Aunt Olivia and Uncle Patrick, who raised Charlotte?"

"Perhaps Charlotte went to live with someone on your father's side of the family. Kind of a fifty-fifty split." Alan suggested.

"But why would you separate twins? Why would you never tell?" Bethany tried to still the trembling of her heart. "A twin…" It still seemed unreal to her.

"This has to be our starting point," Alan said to Tanner. "It's the best lead we've got." He glanced at his wife. "I'll need to head to Sacramento tomorrow."

"No," Bethany interrupted. "I want to go."

"Bethany, you can't go," Alan argued. "If you're spotted…"

"I could just as easily be spotted here. If I have a sister in Sacramento, I want to meet her."

"I'll go with her," Tanner said with resolution. "We'll wear disguises and take the train."

"This is a tremendous risk," Jane leaned forward. "There are people all over the west looking for both of you."

"We made it to your house didn't we?" Tanner grinned.

"Alright," Alan sighed. "But I don't want to lose my number one deputy."

"I'm your only deputy… right?" Tanner questioned Alan with a grin. "You haven't gone and replaced me have you?"

Alan shook his head. "But trust me, Rodney's trying."

Chapter 10

The next morning, Jane's eyes sparkled with pleasure as she studied her handiwork on Bethany. "You look quite attractive as a brunette."

Bethany accepted Jane's hand held mirror and studied her hair amusedly. The coffee dye treatment, while not permanent, took away Bethany's golden highlights and toned them down to a soft brown.

"I personally like the smell, too," Jane smoothed Bethany's hair in the back. "Once it dries I'll set it into a bun and we'll finish it off with one of my bonnets."

From their many long days in the saddle, Bethany's face was full of color and freckles that she usually didn't have. Anyone who didn't know Bethany well might not recognize her.

Bethany appreciated Jane's help, but she was feeling the gravity of the situation. She and Tanner were wanted criminals headed straight to the state capitol. *What if Tanner hadn't stopped me before I got there myself?* Bethany was sure she would have been recognized.

"Meet Orville Blythe." Alan led Tanner into the kitchen.

Bethany's eyes grew wide. Wearing a dark suit, shirt and tie, and a top hat over his talcum powdered hair, Tanner's disguise wasn't bad. "Too bad you shaved off that mustache," she said.

"He's going to have his nose in the books most of the time. Orville here is the scholarly type. Very unsocial."

"Unsocial, like Betty." Tanner smiled at Bethany.

"I'm a different Betty this time," Bethany patted her hair and grinned.

"You're pretty as a brunette," Tanner took a few steps closer to her. "But you're beautiful no matter what your hair looks like." His tone was soft and he stared into Bethany's eyes for just a moment.

Alan placed his hand on Tanner's shoulder. "Why don't you help me get the wagon ready? We'll let the ladies finish up in here."

***

Tanner followed Alan out to the stable and assisted the sheriff getting the wagon in position to hitch up the horse.

"She is a very beautiful woman, Tanner," Alan made reference to Tanner's comment in the kitchen.

Tanner grinned. "You heard me, huh?"

"I make it a habit to hear people. It goes along with the job, you know?"

"Yeah." Tanner watched Alan walk to the stall. "But don't get the wrong idea. I just wanted to encourage her."

Alan cleared his throat and turned to glance at Tanner. "You've just spent almost four weeks with her. That's a lot of time with just one person."

It was a lot of time. Tanner nodded.

"I've known you for four years, Tanner. But I've never seen you act like that around a woman."

"Act like what?"

"The way you comforted her when she was emotional. Holding her hand. The complement." Alan shrugged and opened the stall. "Hey there, Missy." He greeted his mare and ran his hand over her black mane. The buckskin quarter horse returned the greeting with a nicker. "Ready to go for a ride?"

"Bethany's been through a lot. She needs a friend." Tanner considered what he'd just said. *A friend. I told her I wasn't her friend...*

"I'm not telling you that you're doing anything wrong," Alan added. "I don't know Miss Young very well. I know she grew up comfortable, but you've seen her camping out all over northern California, sleeping on a thin little quilt and cooking over a fire. Does she complain?"

Tanner shook his head. "Bethany never complains." He grinned. "She has a wonderful attitude and a servant's heart."

143

Alan began to hitch his mare to the wagon. "Sounds like some good qualities in a woman."

"Get those ideas out of your head, Sheriff." Tanner helped keep Missy still while Alan finished getting her ready. "I've already been down that road and I've no mind to get hurt again."

"Hurt? Who said anything about getting hurt?"

Tanner rubbed Missy's muzzle and decided to change the subject. "There is something I wanted to say before we head out."

Alan leaned against a stall door and listened.

Tanner took a deep breath. "I became a Christian while out there on the run."

"Well that's good news." Alan smiled.

Tanner shifted uneasily. "Sheriff, where are you with the Lord?"

Alan pulled a few blades of straw off his brown shirt. "What is this? You're about to embark on a dangerous mission and you want to make sure I'm a Christian before you leave in case you never see me again?"

"Pretty much, yeah." Tanner studied Alan curiously.

"I believe in God," Alan shrugged. "I don't go to church much, but I can't find Bible verses that say I have to."

"The Bible tells us not to forsake the gathering together." Tanner tried to recall the exact wording. He was thankful now for the verses his parents made him learn.

"I gather with other Christians."

"For the glory of God?"

"Tanner," Alan shook his head knowingly. "I admire what you're trying to do. I'm actually flattered. But I'm a good person. I pray sometimes. I believe in God. What else is there?"

"The Bible tells us, 'Even the demons believe, and shudder.' Believing that God exists is not the same as putting your faith in the redemptive work of God's Son, Jesus Christ, and wholeheartedly surrendering your life to Him."

"I'm a Christian, Tanner. I believe in Jesus. My parents raised me in a Christian home. We read the Bible."

"If I told you I believed in marriage, does that make me married?" Tanner asked.

"No."

"What if I told you my parents are married, does that make me married?"

"No."

"What if I did what married people do, you know, acted married? Would I be married?" Tanner watched Alan's expression as a little light went on.

Alan rubbed his chin. "I see your point."

"Believing in marriage, acting married, having married parents, even going to weddings, none of that makes me married. I'm not married until I enter into a true commitment, a covenant with that woman." Tanner cleared his throat. "It's the same with God."

"You really believe there's something different between you and God now?" Alan asked. "That you've found the real thing?"

"The Real Thing found me. I can't explain it any better than that I once was lost but now I'm found, was blind but now I see. He did it." There was a light in Tanner's eyes. "I prayed and just poured out my heart to Him, asked forgiveness for my sins, my greatest one, of course, was rejecting Him in the first place." There was moisture in Tanner's eyes. "But you know how long I was holding on to the bitterness of losing my wife. I hated that man."

"Don't you still?" Alan asked.

Tanner sucked in a deep breath. "I still have my issues, I won't deny it. But I'm getting there. I feel a heap better. I can tell you that."

Alan nodded reflectively. "You look better. I noticed that yesterday evening."

Tanner was glad.

"Well, we'd better get you two into town if we want to make the nine o'clock train." Alan cleared his throat and took a step toward the horse.

Tanner placed a gentle, restraining hand on Alan's shoulder. "Think about what we've talked about, okay?"

"I will."

***

145

The train station in Santa Rosa was a buzz of activity. Men, women and children hurried and scurried from one place to another in different forms of chaos. A train conductor called out final instructions and motioned to the people that boarding was about to start.

Alan and Jane busied themselves talking to Tanner and Bethany, trying to appear too distracted to talk to anyone else. This had to look real.

Jane hugged Bethany and whispered a quick prayer in her ear.

"You've got that money I gave you, right?" Alan gave Tanner a quick pat on the arm.

"Yes, sir. Thank you. I will pay you back."

"No need," Alan's eyes twinkled. "The city is paying for it. I'd call this police related, wouldn't you?"

Tanner liked Alan's way of thinking.

Tanner asked Alan to send a telegraph to Clarence Moore giving details of the man in the cabin. He hoped the missionary sheriff would witness to the shady resident.

"Have a good trip, Orville!" Alan called to Tanner as they boarded the train.

Once inside the train, Tanner led Bethany by the hand to a private room. The train ride to Sacramento was only a two-hour trip, but he did not wish to engage in any unnecessary conversations.

Bethany sank down on the plush, red velvet cushion and sat on her trembling hands. "I hope Alan and Jane don't get into any trouble for helping us."

Tanner slid the pocket door closed and drew the blind over the small door window. "I think they did a royal job. I had my nose in a book the whole way through town, but Alan said he never saw Rodney or anyone else that may have questioned him."

Bethany leaned back and looked out the window as the train pulled out of the station. Her mind raced with everything that she'd learned the last twenty-four hours. *I'm a twin.* It seemed unreal. Questions flooded Bethany's mind. Why had she never been told? Where was her sister and who raised her?

What would it have been like to grow up with a twin sister? Bethany thought about the fun things she might have done with a sister. *Someone to talk to… a friend… someone who really knew her.*

It seemed impossible that her own sister would have framed her for murder, that she would have murdered their uncle. *It can't be.*

"You seem lost in your thoughts," Tanner studied Bethany's quiet composure.

"I'm just trying to process all of this."

Tanner nodded. "I understand."

"If we do find my sister, what then? It's doubtful she would actually confess to anything if she did murder Uncle Patrick. How do we prove anything?"

"That's what I hope to learn by going to Sacramento. If there is something, I'm hoping we'll find it there."

Bethany sighed. "I almost hope there isn't. I don't know what would be worse. The sting of being framed for murder or being framed for murder by your own sister."

***

James Webber stared at the piles of paperwork scattered across his large, oak desk screaming for his attention. His time away from San Francisco had taken its toll on his responsibilities and James felt the weight of it. How many of his clients may have moved on to another accountant because he'd been away so long?

James removed his glasses, placed both elbows on the desk and rested his head in his hands. How could he concentrate on accounting when there was still a mess back in Santa Rosa? They still hadn't found Bethany. Marie was dead. The will was unsettled, and now there was the question of Bethany's twin prompting Sheriff Thacker toward further investigations. How long would this thing drag on?

With a five thousand dollar bounty on her head, why hadn't anyone brought Bethany to justice? Where could she be? He'd have raised it to ten had they not found the photo of her sister. Now what?

Why did everything have to be so complicated? James remembered a time when his life was simple. He'd gone off to college, planned his course, and embarked on his journey. Moving to San Francisco was a big step for him. It took him out from under his father's control and placed him in his own environment. It was his first major step away from Patrick.

James wondered how life might have been different had he not moved to San Francisco, if he'd have gone back east to start his career. If he'd never stepped foot into that law office...

**

Bethany felt Tanner reach for her hand as they walked down the long train corridor toward the exit. They were in Sacramento. The "River City," as it was affectionately called, felt more like a city than anywhere Bethany had ever been. A major distribution and transportation point for the western end of the First Transcontinental Railroad, Sacramento was a booming metropolis full of industry and people. She was thankful to feel her fingers securely intertwined with Tanner's.

"Are you hungry?" Tanner asked after they'd fought their way through the crowds to the wooden sidewalk outside the enormous stone railway station.

"I should be," Bethany gave a wane smile. "I think I would be if my stomach wasn't all in knots."

Tanner scanned the streets for a place to eat.

Bethany was even more grateful that she'd not come to Sacramento alone.

"Why don't we stay at the Western Hotel," Tanner suggested.

It sounded good to Bethany. The large, wooden structure sat on K Street and overlooked the bustling city, situated comfortably between the American River and the Sacramento River.

"Two rooms please. Preferably side by side," Tanner used his best British accent, smiled, and glanced down at a book into which he pretended to be completely absorbed.

The concierge handed Tanner two keys and quoted an exorbitant price. "How many nights, sir?"

Tanner glanced aloofly at Bethany. "We'll have to let you know. Can you please tell us what amusements we might find within walking distance?"

The concierge handed Tanner a list of local events and pointed to the newspaper stand outside. "If you purchase a paper, you're sure to learn even more."

"Thank you." Tanner nodded indifferently and assisted Bethany with her small overnight bag.

***

"How is your room?" Tanner asked Bethany when they met in the hallway.

"Beautiful," Bethany's eyes sparkled in spite of the stress she was under. "Lavender wall paper, an all white bedspread embroidered with elegant white lace, and a canopy top."

"Sounds lovely," Tanner returned to his British accent. "I'd hoped that by staying on the high end of town we would avoid looking guilty."

"Either that or we're spending stolen money," she whispered.

Tanner took her arm and walked her toward the large, winding staircase, which led to the restaurant below. "After we eat, we can start investigating the town. The courthouse is a few blocks away, but I think that should be our first stop."

"The courthouse?" Bethany's eyes widened with concern. "Do you really think that's a wise place for us to go? There's probably wanted posters with our faces plastered on them all over the place."

"And what more unlikely place for us to just walk into? You just keep your eyes low and I'll be a Brit and we'll be fine."

Bethany clutched his arm all the tighter and walked with him to the dining room.

For Bethany, the Western Hotel and all of its comforts felt more like home than anything she'd experienced over the past two months, but she kept that to herself. She didn't need these comforts. They just felt familiar.

It was no problem to eat like a lady when you were one and she found humor in Tanner's continual accent. She did her best to imitate it and made him laugh.

They dined on bison stew and fruit and drank tea the way Bethany thought tea should taste.

Tanner watched Bethany as she glanced curiously around the room. Her expressive eyes took in the atmosphere and Tanner finally reached for her hand and caught her attention. "You look comfortable here."

Bethany glanced shyly at her plate and pushed around a carrot. "I'm simply intrigued. This is a fine establishment, however much larger than anywhere my aunt and uncle ever took me."

"You didn't travel?" Tanner asked.

"They never took me to Sacramento." Bethany watched a waiter carry a platter of food over his head. "My uncle didn't care for big cities."

"Have you been to San Francisco?"

Bethany shook her head. "Never. My uncle… he didn't like San Francisco."

Tanner tilted his head curiously. "Why? His own son runs a successful business there."

"I don't know." Bethany shook her head. "When my cousin moved to San Francisco, Uncle Patrick forbid my aunt to ever visit him there."

"Didn't Patrick want to visit James?" Tanner asked.

Bethany wasn't sure how many family secrets she should share. Did other families argue the way James and Patrick argued? "Uncle Patrick and James were not close."

"I didn't realize that."

Bethany shrugged. "My family was pretty good at keeping up appearances."

Tanner waited for her to continue.

"Uncle Patrick was difficult to figure out. He was moody. When I was little, he and my aunt fought a lot. Sometimes their fights frightened me." Bethany had a far away look in her eyes. "I was just a child. I don't know what their fights were even about. But eventually the fights stopped and my uncle just kind of withdrew from the family."

"That's terrible." Tanner's eyes softened with empathy.

"My aunt always told me it was her fault." Bethany took a sip of her lemonade. "I never really understood them. Sometimes I thought my uncle really loved my aunt. He did little things for her, but he was distant."

Tanner was quiet for a moment. "Thank you for sharing all that with me, Bethany." His tone held genuine tenderness.

"You're welcome."

Tanner let out a heavy breath. "I owe you an apology."

Bethany tilted her head. "Why?"

"When we were in Fairfield, I told you that you weren't my friend." He lowered his eyes shamefully. "I was wrong."

"Tanner, you had the right to be honest."

"It wasn't honesty. It was fear." Tanner glanced at the chandelier filled with candles hanging in the middle of the dining room. "I've been afraid to care about people ever since Ruth and Rachel died. The fact is, I was afraid to be your friend because you're wanted for murder, and even though I know you didn't do it, if we can't prove your innocence..."

"I'll die."

Tanner let his gaze rest on the chandelier. "I don't want to lose another person I care about." He held his eyes opened wide to ward off tears.

Bethany was quiet.

"You are my friend, Bethany." Tanner turned his dark eyes to her blue ones and reached for her hand. "And I'm not going to let you die."

***

After lunch, Tanner and Bethany made their way to the Sacramento courthouse. Bethany wasn't sure what they would find on the other side of the huge oak doors, but she prayed God would protect them. Tanner was her friend. She'd felt that way for a while—but it was good to know he felt that way too.

He gave her a quick glance before opening the door. This was it.

Tanner walked inside with confidence. He wore his head high and greeted those he passed with his best British accent. In a matter of minutes they found their way to the clerk's office.

"Good afternoon," a gentleman behind the counter greeted Tanner and Bethany.

"Hello," Tanner's accent was chipper. "I'm looking for some information on a dear family who I believe moved to Sacramento around 1850."

"Hmmm," the clerk rubbed his chin and shook his head. "In 1854 the original courthouse burned to the ground during a fire that leveled much of our city. Records from the early 1850s are scarce."

Bethany tried not to look disappointed.

"However, if they purchased any land or had any involvement with the courts after 1854, we might be able to find something." The man glanced from Tanner to Bethany. "If you're willing to do some research, we might be able to find these friends."

Tanner glanced at Bethany.

"They died in 1851. I doubt there would be any information."

The clerk nodded. "The first courthouse wasn't even built until 1851. Completed just in time for Christmas." The man shook his head. "Pity it burned down. Although, you have to admit, this building is very nice."

"Yes," Tanner nodded. "I have great appreciation for neoclassical architecture. The ten pillars in the portico give the building a remarkable feeling of dignity and charm."

Bethany lowered her eyes and stifled a giggle. When Tanner put on an act, he put it on well.

"Well, I do appreciate your time." Tanner tipped his hat and took Bethany's arm. "Cheers."

Once on the street, Tanner glanced back up at the building and sighed. "Another dead end."

Bethany shook her head. "This is impossible. We'll never find her."

Tanner turned to Bethany and placed his hands on her shoulders as he did whenever he wanted her to look right at him. "We're not giving up," he said with resolution. "You said you were born in Missouri. Do you know what city?"

"Saint Louis."

"Then that's where we're going."

Bethany shook her head. "We can't go to Saint Louis."

"Why not?" Tanner argued. "Where else can we go? We can't go back to Santa Rosa and we've hit a wall here. Your family is from Saint Louis, Bethany. There has to be someone there…"

Bethany raised her eyes to the buildings across the street. Blue sky peaked out from behind the clouds. "How far is it to Saint Louis?"

"It will take us a little less than a week by train."

"My aunt told me that it took over five months to get from Missouri to California when I was a child."

"It would have. The rail line wasn't complete when I moved west just five years ago," Tanner said. "What miles I couldn't do by train I took by horse." He shook his head. "Thank God for trains."

Bethany fixed her bonnet and waited for Tanner to give them direction.

"I'll send Sheriff Thacker a cryptic message telling him where we're going and then we'll purchase train tickets."

"Do we have enough money?"

"As long as we don't stay at hotels like the Western any longer." Tanner winked. He reached to take Bethany's arm and they hurried to the telegraph office.

Chapter 11

"You got a message from your friend, Orville." Rodney hurried into the sheriff's office carrying a telegraph for Alan. "He arrived safely in Sacramento and will be heading toward Missouri with his wife tomorrow morning." Rodney read the message.

Alan stifled a desire to smack Rodney across the head with the gun he'd been cleaning and snatched the note from Rodney's hand. *What about a private message does Rodney not understand?*

Alan read the message for himself and tried to read between the lines. *Either they met a dead end and want to investigate Bethany's place of birth or they found her twin and she's in Missouri.* "Well this is good news," Alan said to Rodney.

"I guess this means you'll be watching his horses even longer." Rodney drew his own conclusion.

"Yes. Well, I owed Orville a lot. We just might be even after this." Alan was sure Rodney wanted to know more about this mysterious couple whose horses Alan was suddenly watching so he gave Rodney something to do. "Rodney, can you run over to the post office for me and mail this letter?"

Rodney never turned down an opportunity to do something for the sheriff and was off in a moment.

Alan reread the message. *Good ole Tanner knew his message would probably get intercepted. I just hope they find something out.*

***

When they boarded the train in Sacramento, Tanner noticed a dark-haired, brawny man with a thick beard and mustache watching Bethany closely. Tanner tried to place the man in his memory. Had he seen this fellow before? Tanner drew close to

Bethany and kept up his British act for the other passengers to hear. "Come darling, we need to find a comfortable berth in the sleeper car. You didn't forget to send that letter to your dear sister, Veronica, did you?"

"Of course I didn't forget, dear." Bethany replied.

Tanner ushered her along quickly, found an empty room and slipped in quietly.

"What was that about?" Bethany sat across from Tanner and glanced nervously at the door.

"There was a man staring at you," Tanner explained. "I was afraid he might have recognized you. We don't need any more bounty hunters circling us."

"What would we do? We're trapped on a train."

Tanner reached for her hand. "We'll be okay. Keep praying."

The train just started on its way when the conductor arrived to take their tickets. Tanner greeted him kindly and received a cordial nod in return.

Tanner sat back down after the conductor closed the door. "Well, you brought your Bible, right?"

Bethany nodded.

"The way I see it, we've got several days of nothing to do but just study the Bible." Tanner leaned his head back on the cushioned chair. "We can take turns reading."

Bethany's eyes twinkled. "Where should we start?"

"Let's read through the Psalms. David had some pretty difficult encounters with enemies and God continued to give him strength and protection. I think we could use that right now."

"How blessed is the man who does not walk in the counsel of the wicked, nor stand in the path of sinners, nor sit in the seat of scoffers." Bethany began reading from Psalm 1. "But his delight is in the law of the Lord, and in His law he meditates day and night. He will be like a tree firmly planted by streams of water, which yields its fruit in its season and its leaf does not wither; and in whatever he does, he prospers…"

***

In order to keep themselves scarce, Tanner and Bethany forwent taking their meal in the dinner car. It seemed like the best way to avoid the man to whom Tanner attached the nickname Mr. Brawny. However, it was impossible not to get up periodically and take short walks around the train.

Through the night, Tanner slept on the lower berth while Bethany took the upper. He tried not to allow the impropriety of sharing a sleeper car with a woman who was not his wife bother him. There was no way he was going to risk Bethany's safety for the sake of propriety. He knew that his intentions were pure and trusted that God would protect them from any potential wrong assumptions.

By breakfast, Tanner began to wonder if Mr. Brawny was simply admiring what a lovely young lady Bethany was. They'd not seen the man during any of their walks around the train and no one appeared to be searching for them.

Tanner suggested they take breakfast in the dining car and enjoy a hot meal.

It was pleasant to sit beside a quaint, curtained, train window in a cozy booth, while eating scrambled eggs and ham. Bethany appreciated Tanner's suggestion.

"I've never taken meals on a train," Bethany confessed.

"Never?"

"No. We never traveled far enough to warrant a meal." Bethany took a sip of her tea and glanced contentedly out the window at the moving landscape. "Everything looks so different."

"We're in Arizona." Tanner looked out the same window.

"Miss Young?" A voice asked inquisitively.

Before she could think, Bethany replied, "Yes?"

Tanner's whole body stiffened when he saw Mr. Brawny smile knowingly down on Bethany. "I thought that was you." He began to reach for his gun.

Tanner acted quickly. Before Mr. Brawny knew what hit him, Tanner leaned back in his chair and kicked the man in the stomach with every bit of strength he had. Mr. Brawny fell backwards into another table.

Securing his gun in one hand, Tanner grabbed Bethany's hand with the other. "Run!"

The rest of the customers didn't have time to understand what was going on and simply stared as Tanner and Bethany ran past, tipping chairs into the isle to slow their predator.

Mr. Brawny was not far behind. Tanner closed the door of the dinner car and hurried Bethany onto the nearest sleeper car. With no time to think, he slid opened one of the pocket doors, pulled Bethany inside, and closed themselves into one of the private rooms.

The sound of loud footsteps running past assured Tanner that Mr. Brawny was on his way to the next car. He tried to steady his breathing, certain that this wasn't over.

It took a moment to realize he and Bethany were not alone. Tanner gathered his thoughts and turned to make eye contact with the man whose room they'd just barged in on and come up with some convincing story about the brute who was following them.

"I'm so sor…" Tanner stopped his word mid syllable and his heart dropped to his stomach. After five years of searching, Tanner was staring into the eyes of Thaddeus del Mar.

Thaddeus recognized Tanner immediately. His eyes were fixated on the gun Tanner still held firmly in his hand. There was fear in Thaddeus' eyes. He was like a deer standing face to face with a hunter.

This was it. The moment Tanner dreamed of. The moment Tanner fantasized about for over five long years. Revenge.

Bethany didn't understand the mounting tension in the room. Her eyes shifted from Tanner to the stranger.

Tanner glanced at the gun in his hand and back at Thaddeus who was slowly raising his hands in the air.

"Go ahead…" Thaddeus finally broke the silence. "Just kill me."

Tanner clenched his teeth and stared. "You know who I am?"

Thaddeus swallowed hard. "I would know you anywhere… Sargent Brenly."

Tanner lowered his gun and stared at the man. Time seemed to stand still. All the hatred, the bitterness, and the murderous thoughts toward this man were gone. "As I would you."

In spite of Tanner lowering his gun, Thaddeus kept his hands in the air. "Just do what you came to do. I will put up no fight."

Tanner shook his head. "I can't." He returned the gun to its holster. A penetrating peace crept into his heart and his eyes grew moist with unshed tears. "I forgive you."

Thaddeus seemed unsure what this meant for the position of his hands and began to lower them awkwardly. "I don't understand..."

"My Jesus has forgiven me for the wretched sins I have committed," Tanner's emotions were raw. "Both sins of the flesh and sins of the heart. I can cast no stone at you."

"But I murdered your wife! I killed your innocent baby girl!" Thaddeus cried out with haunted agony. "I deserve to die!"

Tanner's legs were weak with stress and he sat across from Thaddeus. With wide eyes, Bethany sat beside him while tears streamed down her face.

"For all have sinned and fall short of the glory of God," Tanner quoted.

Thaddeus shook his head. "My sins are not like yours. I'm a ruthless murderer."

"While we were yet sinners, Christ died for us."

Tears filled the man's wild red eyes.

"He made Him Who knew no sin to be sin on our behalf, so that we might become the righteousness of God in Him," Tanner continued. "Jesus did that for us. For me and for you."

Bethany reached for Tanner's hand and held it as if it was something precious.

Thaddeus was beside himself with sorrow. He slid to the floor and buried his face in his hands. His body shook with sobs. "My life has been haunted by my heinous acts. I would find more peace in the grave than to suffer as I have these past five and a half years. Every face, every frightened pair of eyes, they haunt my dreams; they burn their way into my daytime. I'm so sorry... I'm so sorry..."

Tanner watched the man with pity. *I have sympathy for the man who killed my family... God, this could only come from You.*

"Mr. del Mar," Tanner spoke through his tears. "I forgive you."

Thaddeus wiped his face and glanced up at Tanner. "Why?"

"Because of Jesus." Tanner slipped from his seat and placed a comforting hand on the man's trembling shoulder. "And Jesus wants to give you that same forgiveness and healing from your past."

The man was quiet for a few moments, letting Tanner's words sink in.

Loud footsteps in the hallway and knocking on a neighboring door alerted Tanner that Mr. Brawny was still searching for them. Tanner rose quickly to his feet.

Bethany glanced at the door with fear in her moist eyes.

"Do you need to hide, Sargent Brenly?" Thaddeus read their expressions correctly.

"Yes."

Without another word, Thaddeus motioned for them to climb into the lower berth together and face the wall. Tight against Bethany, in a position of intimacy he'd only shared with his wife, Tanner lay still while Thaddeus covered them from head to toe with blankets.

Thaddeus closed the curtain to dim the room and sat down with whatever piece of newsprint he could find while the footsteps approached his door.

"Excuse me, sir," the conductor stood at the door with Mr. Brawny beside him, looking in curiously. "We are searching for a tall, slender, brown-haired woman wearing a blue and yellow dress and gray haired gentleman wearing a fashionable suit. They were last seen together." The conductor cleared his throat. "I hate to bother you, however I have been assured that my participation in this quest is essential to the well-being of everyone on the train. Have you seen them?"

Thaddeus pressed his finger to his lips and motioned, with annoyance, for the conductor to talk softer. "My wife has finally fallen asleep. She was up half the night and now here you come to make noise. Does it look like I have your friends here?" He shook his head and narrowed his eyes angrily. "I requested peace and quiet on this trip. Is this my peace and quiet?"

"I am so sorry, sir," the conductor lowered his voice. "Please, allow me to bring your meals to your cabin this evening.

We are having chicken and dumplings, potato soup and fresh cooked carrots."

Thaddeus nodded. "Bring my wife two portions." He glanced at the large lump under the blankets. "She is a big eater."

The conductor apologized again. "Yes, sir. Once again, I'm sorry for the inconvenience." He motioned for the man who'd caused this embarrassment to follow him. "I don't know what kind of joke you are trying to play but I won't have any more of it." The conductor's scolding voice could be heard down the hallway.

* * *

Wrapped in the intimacy of Tanner's arms, Bethany lay completely still on the berth. She listened while the man who'd killed Tanner's family diverted their would-be captor to save their lives.

She could feel the beating of Tanner's heart mingled with what she thought were quiet sobs. *Tanner forgave that man... How did he do it?* Bethany's heart warmed to Tanner more in that one moment than it had over the course of the past month they'd been running together.

After the conductor and Mr. Brawny left, they remained in place until Thaddeus told them it was safe.

The diversion had given both men an opportunity to get ahold of their emotions. Tanner sat beside Bethany and stared at Thaddeus. "You may have just saved our lives."

Thaddeus glanced toward the window. "Only after destroying your life five years ago."

The time for questions was now and Tanner wanted answers. "Why did you do it?"

This was not going to be an easy answer. Thaddeus took a few steadying breaths. "During the war, Union soldiers invaded my town," Thaddeus began. "I was the blacksmith and owned a nice home in the center of town. When we were told that Union soldiers were approaching, most of our neighbors fled. My brother-in-law sent his wife and children west. But I was determined not to give the north victory. I refused to run from everything I owned, surrender my home, my land, my business. I armed my boys and told them we would fight."

Thaddeus gazed into his empty hands. "But the Union soldiers were too strong for us. My sons were shot down and our home was burned. With it, my wife and our only daughter." He wiped away a tear. "I realized that the pain of losing a house or a business were nothing compared to losing those who meant the most to me. After that, I was determined to have revenge. I joined the Confederate army and fought with a vengeance unmatched by most of my fellow soldiers. I had nothing to live for but killing Yankees."

Bethany could see the lines of pain and sorrow etched in this man's face.

"After the war, I wasn't done. My heart beat with the passion of causing more bloodshed to those who took from me what meant the most."

"But why my regiment?" Tanner asked. "Were we the men who moved in on your town?"

"I found the information on several battalions that came up against my town that summer, your battalion was among several on the list. I sought to find each man and take from him what had been taken from me." Thaddeus shook his head in bitter shame.

"We never wanted to kill women and children..." Tanner began.

"I know. It was me," Thaddeus confessed. "It was my own selfish pride that made my family stay and fight. If I'd have listened to my brother-in-law... if I'd have listened to my wife..." Thaddeus turned his eyes to Tanner. "She begged me to let her leave with her sister." He shook his head. "But I was stubborn."

They were all quiet for a moment while the train shuffled down the track. The quiet hum of movement echoed through the small room and light flickered from the closed curtains.

"After I'd begun my killing spree, I began to see what I'd become. I couldn't live with myself, but dying seemed too merciful. I went west and tried to forget, but their faces are always with me."

Tanner moved to the seat next to Thaddeus and placed a hand on his back. "We can't undo the past but we don't have to live in it."

"I must confess, your words of forgiveness were the last thing I ever expected to hear from one of the men whom I hurt."

"Believe me, Mr. del Mar, had I stumbled upon you only a month ago, my bullet would have met your head with hostile vengeance. This kind of forgiveness only comes from God. I recently put my faith in Jesus and found forgiveness for my sins. Before that, my heart was dark with hatred toward you."

The men talked for hours. In that time, their meals were brought to the room and the conversation shifted to why Tanner and Bethany were being hunted.

"May I ask why you were running from that man?" Thaddeus asked.

Bethany wondered how much Tanner would tell Mr. del Mar.

"I am a deputy," Tanner began. "Miss Young has been falsely accused of murder and I have made it my job to help prove her innocence. Unfortunately, she has a high reward on her head, which has every bounty hunter west of the Rocky Mountains searching for her. I have no doubt that Mr. Brawny, as I've been calling him, sees Miss Young as a valuable source of income."

"I know what it means to run from punishment when you are guilty, Miss Young," Thaddeus admitted. "But I can hardly imagine running from a crime when you are innocent."

"It has not been easy," Bethany confessed. "But I have seen God's hand of protection every step of the way.

"I hope you are able to prove yourself innocent," Thaddeus said earnestly.

"Thank you." Bethany appreciated what seemed to be his genuine concern.

A voice walking along the corridor of the sleeper car could be heard calling for those departing in Evanston.

"This is my stop," Thaddeus said. He lowered his eyes. "I cannot thank you enough Sargent Brenly, for what you have given me. I never dreamed of finding forgiveness from any of the men whom I hurt."

"I only pray you will seek out forgiveness from the One Who can give you ultimate, eternal healing." Tanner said seriously.

"You have given me much to think about." Thaddeus admitted. "You have my word. I plan to do some talking with God about all of this."

"We will be praying for you."

Thaddeus rose to his feet and shook Tanner's hand. "Thank you."

Tanner nodded and watched Thaddeus step out of the sliding door. *I'm finally free...*

***

Bethany had no doubt that his encounter with Thaddeus had taken a lot out of Tanner. Tanner said very little after Thaddeus left, but Bethany could tell his mind was active with thoughts concerning his meeting with the man. After making their way back to their own sleeper car and finding their belongings untouched, Bethany asked Tanner how he was doing.

Tanner ran his fingers through his powdered hair and glanced contemplatively at Bethany. "I feel peace."

Bethany nodded. "What do you think Mr. del Mar will do after this? Do you believe he will turn himself in?"

"I don't know. I'm not the only one he hurt and he is a wanted man."

"I never expected him to protect us as he did." Bethany said.

Tanner agreed. "The whole thing was quite amazing. God knew I needed that encounter. It was healing for me."

Both Tanner and Bethany took some time to pray specifically for Mr. del Mar, that he would come to the saving knowledge of Jesus Christ and find the ultimate forgiveness he so genuinely needed.

There is no greater sermon than one we live... It was easy to see from Mr. del Mar's expression that Tanner's forgiveness preached louder than anything the man had ever heard.

Tanner was tired and fell asleep early. The sleeper car was quiet except for the hum of the train and Tanner's soft breathing on the berth below.

Bethany smiled at Tanner's reason for taking the lower berth. He wanted to make sure he could hop out of bed and defend them if someone were to find out who they were. He felt Bethany was safer on the top.

Tanner is so protective of me. It felt good to be protected. It felt good to have a real friend who believed in her.

It was difficult not to worry about what they might find out when they arrived in Saint Louis. Would they learn anything or would this trip half way across the United States be for nothing?

Del Mar's face quickly flashed across Bethany's mind. *It wasn't for nothing...*

***

After two more days on the train, Bethany was ready to be on solid ground. Tanner and Bethany had kept to themselves most of the remaining days on the train, only slipping out quickly and never taking the time to sit comfortably in the dining car. They had meals brought to their cabin and spoke to no one but each other. The thought that Mr. Brawny might still be on the train kept them both on guard.

As the train slowed into the Saint Louis station, Bethany fixed her hair and set Jane's large, light brown bonnet on her head. Tanner carried their bags and they readied themselves for departure, keeping their eyes open for Mr. Brawny.

Once off the train, it was easy to slip away into the crowds unnoticed. Saint Louis was alive with activity. With her arm wrapped in his, they stepped from the station onto the crowded street met by pollution and noise. Never had she seen so many people in one city before.

Was she really born here? In a city so large, Bethany wondered if finding information about her childhood was a hopeless aspiration.

It was too late to go to the courthouse, so they found a less expensive hotel and met in the hotel restaurant for dinner.

When they offered thanksgiving for their meal, Tanner asked God to lead them to the answers they'd come to Saint Louis for. Bethany was almost afraid to hope.

***

Tanner said he was not as worried about Bethany being recognized in the Saint Louis Court House. It seemed less likely that news of her accusations would have reached this far east.

There was a line in the county clerks office. Tanner and Bethany sat on one of the wooden benches lined up against the back wall and waited their turn.

Bethany smoothed the long, brown skirt that Jane gave her to wear and looked over the ruffled white blouse she was wearing. It was a simple but classy ensemble and Tanner gave her an approving smile.

"You look lovely," he said.

"Thank you." Bethany appreciated his complement.

Their turn to speak with the county clerk finally came and Tanner took the lead. "I was wondering if you have any birth records from January of 1849.

The clerk nodded. "If they registered the infant. Was the child born in Missouri?

"Yes. In Saint Louis."

"Parents' names?"

"Joel and Eleanor Young," Bethany spoke up.

The clerk wrote the names down and carried the slip of paper to his file room. Tanner and Bethany could see him bent over a series of long, wooden cabinets just through the door.

Bethany glanced at Tanner and blinked. It felt like they were waiting forever.

The man returned with several papers in his hand. Bethany chewed nervously on one of her fingernails.

"Well, I didn't find any birth records." the man set the papers on the counter in front of him and spread them out. "But I found quite a bit on Joel Young."

Bethany glanced at the paperwork in front of her.

"He sold a house in December 1849. Then in 1853 he purchased a small plat of land just outside the city limits. By now it's probably part of the city – Saint Louis has grown so much..."

"That's impossible," Bethany interrupted the man. "He died in 1851."

"I've got his death certificate right here." The clerk flipped through the pages. "It says he died in 1856."

Bethany shook her head. "No, there must be some mistake. There must be another Joel Young."

The clerk glanced through his paperwork. "Well, this first certificate shows his wife's name, Eleanor, and says his name is Joel Bradley Young... same name here, and here... and here..."

Bethany glanced at the paperwork.

"In 1855, he got arrested. Also in 1855, I show him putting his mother's name on the property deed."

"His mother?" Bethany asked.

"Ida Young."

"Is she still alive?" Tanner glanced curiously at the address on the paper.

The clerk returned to the back room and searched his files.

"I don't show a death certificate for Ida. She's listed as the owner of that property."

Bethany turned wide blue eyes on Tanner. "My grandmother is still alive..."

The man glanced from Bethany to Tanner and smiled. "And it looks like you can go visit her."

Tanner wrote down the address and thanked the clerk. Bethany reached for Tanner's arm and tried to still the trembling in her heart. *I have a grandmother living in Saint Louis?*

Chapter 12

"Why was I never told about my grandmother?" Bethany asked Tanner. He took her hand to help her climb into the carriage they'd hired to take them to Bethany's grandmother's house.

It seemed unreal to Bethany that they were about to meet her own flesh and blood, her father's mother. What would she be like? Would the woman believe Bethany? Would she know anything about Bethany's twin? Questions swirled through Bethany's mind.

Tanner sensed Bethany's nervousness and moved to her side of the carriage where he could hold her hand.

"I'm so scared Tanner." Bethany gazed into his eyes. "Scared of what I might find out."

"The truth will set you free, remember that."

Bethany nodded. "Thank you for being here, Tanner. I know I couldn't do this without you."

The ride to Ida Young's house took a little over twenty minutes. During that time, Tanner and Bethany prayed. When the carriage arrived in front of the old, wood-sided house, Tanner paid the driver and asked him to return in two hours.

The house was small and showed signs of disrepair. An old stone chimney graced one side of the house, with two windows on either side of the front door. An addition on the back added more space. Bethany thought it might have been a pretty house had it been better cared for.

Tanner knocked on the door and they waited quietly while movement inside told them someone was on their way.

When the door opened, a woman in her early seventies peered out and stepped back with a start when she saw Bethany. "Oh my…"

"Are you Ida Young?" Tanner asked.

"I am. And you must be… Bethany?" The woman spoke Bethany's name slowly with a question in her voice.

"Yes."

"Oh my." Ida repeated. She covered her mouth with her hand. "Please don't just stand there on the porch. Come inside. Come inside."

Bethany allowed Tanner to lead. She felt like she needed him close for moral support. *This is really my grandmother… she knows me.*

The house was decorated with low-end furniture, also showing signs of wear. Hand-made rugs covered portions of the rough sawn wood floor and faded pictures hung on the walls. Ida led them to the sitting room and motioned for them to take a seat on a small, dark green sofa. She pulled up a chair not far from Bethany.

"I always wondered if I'd ever get to see you again." Ida's eyes sparkled with pleasure at this surprise guest. "Just look at you. You're just as pretty as they come. Look at those eyes - so much bluer than Charlotte's. Oh my… if Charlotte could see you."

Bethany forced back the tears that wanted to surface. "Ma'am, I don't know anything about my family. I didn't even know I had a grandma until an hour ago." She took a very deep breath and tried to form her question. "Is it true that I have a twin?"

"Well I assumed you knew." Ida was confused. "Did you never see the photograph I sent your Aunt Olivia?"

Bethany lowered her eyes and shook her head. "The photograph was just found. I wasn't certain it was truly me."

"It figures that woman wouldn't tell you nothin' 'bout us." Ida sighed. "I knew she wanted me and Charlotte kept a secret. But I kinda always hoped she'd change her mind. I wrote her a nice long letter when I'd sent that picture, telling her I thought it was only right that she be honest with ya." Ida shook her head disappointedly. "She never did write back, but I always kinda hoped."

"So you raised Charlotte and I went to live with Aunt Olivia and Uncle Patrick after my parents died?"

Ida narrowed her eyes for a moment and studied Bethany curiously. "Your father didn't die when your momma did, Bethany," the old lady said seriously. "Your Pa died of cholera just a few years after we moved back to Saint Louis. It's a miracle Charlotte and I didn't get it. Seems like so many people did."

"I don't understand." Bethany shook her head.

"Your pa needed money," Ida said.

Bethany's eyes grew wide. "What do you mean?"

Ida blew out a deep heavy sigh that ended in a cough. "After your ma died, your pa went a little crazy. He got to running around with a wild bunch and got himself into some debt. He knew your Aunt Olivia always wanted a baby girl. She couldn't have no more children after James. So he wrote to your Uncle Patrick and offered to let Olivia raise you in exchange for a little bit of money. Not long after that he, Charlotte, and I come back to Missouri and bought this here little house."

Tanner shook his head in frustration. "A baby in exchange for a little bit of money…"

"Well, quite a bit really. But I don't reckon he was very wise with the money because it didn't last very long." Ida looked at Bethany sympathetically. "I didn't like the idea. I told my boy that your momma would be broken hearted if she could look down from heaven and see her little girl sold like a slave to cover his debt."

Bethany's head reeled trying to process all this information.

"But there was a difference. You weren't going to be raised like a slave. You were going to be raised in a nice wealthy home with a woman who would love you like her own daughter." Ida reached a wrinkled hand to touch Bethany's face. "I didn't have no voice in my son's decision. I figured I'd probably never see you again." The old lady's eyes were moist with tears. "But you grew up nice. I can see that. You ain't nothing like Charlotte."

Bethany pulled her lace handkerchief from her bag and wiped her eyes.

"You're a lady." Ida smiled, exposing a mouth full of missing teeth. "Your momma was a lady, too. I always liked Eleanor."

"If my birth father sold me to Aunt Olivia and Uncle Patrick, then why didn't he just let them adopt me? Why am I still a Young?"

"Your pa had pride," Ida chuckled. "He sold you like property but he wouldn't let them change your name."

"They told me both my parents died." Bethany wanted answers. Her head ached and she could hardly sit still. Why did they come here? Why did she have to find all this out? It hurt less not knowing.

Ida sensed Bethany's grief. She pulled herself slowly from her chair and walked into a room at the back of the crowded little house. She was gone for several minutes and Tanner reached a comforting hand to Bethany.

When Ida returned, she carried a small pile of letters. "This is everything," she handed them to Bethany. "The agreement stated that you would continue to be a Young until your name changed through marriage, but that you would be told that both your parents were dead."

Bethany accepted the letters as if they were something that would burn her fingers.

Ida stared at Bethany for a moment. "Your pa made Patrick promise that no one would know he was still alive. I think he was ashamed of what he done."

"And my Aunt Olivia went along with this plan?"

"As far as I can tell," Ida shrugged. "But Olivia wanted a baby girl somethin' awful. She probably wasn't thinking too sensibly. If you read the letters, it sounds like this was something the two brother-in-laws cooked up to give your aunt a baby girl and your pa a whole lot of money."

Bethany flipped through the paperwork and scanned the agreement. Her eyes grew wide and her hands started to tremble when she saw how much she'd sold for. She glanced at Tanner. "I was sold for five thousand dollars."

Tanner placed a comforting arm around her shoulder and Bethany leaned her face into his chest to cry. "Dead or alive, Tanner. I'm still worth five thousand dollars."

***

170

"How could anyone sell their child?" Tanner was doing his best to restrain his temper. Bethany's heart was breaking and he felt powerless to help. "How could you let him?" He hated to blame Bethany's grandmother, but the whole thing was insane.

"I didn't have no control over my boy and his doin's," Ida explained. "He had a temper that one did. You'd have not had a real comfortable life if you'd been raised here, I can tell you that."

"But what about Charlotte?" Bethany wiped her face and looked helplessly at her grandmother. "Does she know about me?"

Ida nodded. "Unfortunately she does."

"Why unfortunately?" Bethany wished to know.

"It made her hate her pa all the more."

"She hated that her pa separated them?" Tanner asked.

"No. She always resented that you got to live the good life while she had to grow up here." Ida scratched her white hair and shook her head. "I did my best by the girl. But she was about as unruly as her pa. She had more beaus than I had cats. Has those blue eyes too... though hers don't quite shine like yours do."

"I mailed your aunt a photograph of you and your sister. It was the only one I had. Your momma had it taken just a few months before she died. I told Olivia that some day maybe you'd like to know about your twin."

"Where is she? Where is Charlotte?" Bethany was almost afraid to ask.

"She's in California."

Bethany felt like a knife just pierced her heart.

"Moved out there about nine months ago. Said she was tired of being poor and planned to move west to make a fortune."

"Any idea where that fortune was going to come from?" Tanner asked.

"No. But with Charlotte, if she got a notion you didn't cross her." Ida got up again and walked to the back room. She came out carrying a thick brown package and a white, knit sweater. "She wrote me regularly. Things seemed to be going fine for her. She'd gotten a place in San Francisco." Ida handed a letter to Bethany. "There's an address."

Bethany took the envelope and numbly read the address.

"She even sent me some money and these real pretty coins." Ida held the gold coins out for Bethany and Tanner to see.

171

"She also sent me a real pretty brooch. I wore it to church Sunday and it's still pinned to my sweater."

Tears filled Bethany's eyes and she stared at the familiar gold coins in the palm of Ida's hand.

"That was over two months ago and I ain't heard from her since."

Tanner's head shot up. "How often did she write before?"

"I got at least one letter a week from my granddaughter." Ida shook her head. "I'm worried that she may have gotten herself into some trouble." Ida unpinned the brooch from the sweater. "This is the prettiest little thing I think I've ever owned." She handed the brooch to Bethany to see.

Tanner figured from Bethany's expression that she recognized the brooch immediately. One large ruby set between two pearls, framed in intricately etched gold.

Ida glanced at Bethany. "Child, why are you crying?"

Tanner rested a comforting hand on Bethany's shoulder. Bethany glanced up at Tanner and shook her head. She didn't want Tanner to tell this old lady the whole story.

"Mrs. Young, we'd like to help find Charlotte. That's why Bethany came here. She wants some answers. These letters, these documents, even the gold coins, would all be helpful in piecing together Bethany's life and hopefully finding Charlotte. Would you mind letting us hold on to all of this?"

"I don't mind at all if it helps find Charlotte."

Bethany reached her hand out and handed Ida the brooch. "Except this… you keep your brooch."

Ida took the brooch and glanced at it endearingly. She dropped the coins into the brown package and handed it to Tanner. "Use this in any way you can." She leaned forward and placed a tender hand on Bethany's knee. "Let me make you some tea, darling. You look all flushed."

Bethany nodded and Ida shuffled from the room.

Tanner made a small pile of all the paperwork she'd just given them and set it beside him on the floor. "Bethany." He rubbed her back tenderly.

"It was my sister… she framed me. She killed Uncle Patrick and Marie." Bethany leaned forward and let Tanner hold her in his strong arms.

Ida returned after a few minutes with a delicate blue and white teacup filled with a warm cup of sweet smelling tea. She handed it to Bethany and sat across from her with uncertainty in her eyes.

"I'm sorry I ain't been able to be a grandma to ya," Ida said. "I always did wonder how you were."

Bethany sipped her tea and took a steadying breath. "Can you tell me more about my family?"

"Why sure," Ida said. She leaned back in her chair and let her eyes rest on the fireplace with a look of reminiscence. "Your ma and pa met when we was living in Vermont."

"Vermont?" Bethany had to stop her grandmother there. "I thought we were from Missouri."

"You and Charlotte were born in Missouri. But your ma and Aunt Olivia are both from Vermont," Ida explained. "My husband, your grandpa, and I moved to Vermont while our boys were young men. We bought a farm there and set to raising sheep. We did pretty well until your grandfather got a terrible flu. He passed it to our son, Joseph, and they both died just a few short weeks of each other. Joel and I did our best to keep up the farm."

Bethany finished her tea and set the cup down on a lace covered side table and listened intently.

"Your pa met your ma in town. I still remember the day. He come home and told me he'd met his wife that day."

Bethany's lips curved into a slight smile.

"She come from a good family. They had six children and were regular church people. Her pa owned a fair amount of land, many head of dairy cows, and ran a store in town." Ida glanced at Bethany. "Eleanor was as pretty as a picture and as sweet as apple pie."

"How old was she?"

"I think she was close to eighteen. She was the middle daughter. The family had three older boys and then three girls. Your ma was close to both her sisters."

Bethany tried to picture her mother in a family of six children.

"Not long after they got married, your Aunt Olivia and her new husband got to talking about moving out west. Your Uncle Patrick was set on getting rich and was just certain his fortune waited for him where the sun set." Ida grinned. "Patrick and Olivia talked Joel and Eleanor into goin' with them. Since I had no one else, your pa brought me out west with him."

"What about the rest of my mother's family?"

"They stayed in Vermont. Your ma's older sister, Naomi, was married to a successful lawyer. They had a fancy house in St. Johnsbury. Her three brothers worked for their father."

"So just the two youngest moved west?" Tanner asked.

"Yes." Ida cleared her throat. "Your aunt and uncle already had their little boy. I was able to help her with him as we traveled out west. Olivia didn't pay me much mind except when I was helping her. She always thought she was just a few notches higher than me and my son."

Bethany could believe that.

"When we got to Saint Louis, you and Charlotte were born. I was one proud grandma, that's for sure. Your ma was crazy about you both. She coddled and loved on you just like a good momma should." Ida's lips curved into a smile.

"When you and your sister were just six months old, we up and moved to Sacramento. Your pa was hoping to strike it rich in gold. Olivia and Patrick continued west and settled in Santa Rosa."

"Did my pa do any mining?" Bethany asked.

"He tried his hand at it, but then your ma got sick. I cared for y'all as best as I could but she went so quickly... poor Joel was just beside himself."

"You said he went into debt?" Tanner asked.

"He got to drinking and gambling... he knew better. I think your ma's death just destroyed him inside. You and Charlotte were sad reminders of the woman he'd lost. It got so he could hardly even look at ya."

Bethany found it hard to think about those words.

"It wasn't that he didn't love you." Ida could see that her words hurt Bethany. "It's just that you both had those blue eyes like your ma. Yours the bluest. Charlotte's were more gray blue. I think that's why your pa chose to let your Aunt Olivia raise you."

174

Once again, my blue eyes…

"But child, please don't feel like your pa rejected ya. He knew that Olivia was going to be a good mamma to you. And she was, wasn't she?"

Bethany nodded.

"I do believe your pa regretted sending you away. He'd never have said it, but I know he suffered emotionally and I believe selling you to the Webbers was a part of that suffering."

Bethany lowered her eyes.

"I know he'd be proud of you if he could see you now. You're so pretty."

"Are Charlotte and I identical twins?" New questions raced through Bethany's mind.

"No. But you look enough alike that a person could easily be fooled. Anyone who really knew you could tell the difference. I could tell. I can tell now. Minute I saw you I knew who you were. You're enough like Charlotte, but you're… softer."

Bethany wasn't sure what that meant. "What is Charlotte like?" It was a bit painful to think that this twin whom she could have known and loved through childhood was a stranger to her and now, it seemed, a murderer.

"She's sassy, very spirited and strong-willed. Nothin' like your ma. I'm guessing you're more like Eleanor."

"Charlotte never married?" Bethany pried.

"No. Though she's had her fair share of proposals. None of them suited her I guess." Ida glanced from Tanner to Bethany. "Is this your husband?"

Bethany blushed. "Oh… no," she almost chuckled. "Mr. Brenly is…"

"A family friend," Tanner finished for her. "We could never let Miss Young travel alone."

"Well bless ya." Ida beamed at him. "I didn't offer you anything. Can I fix you both some supper? It's got to be past six."

Tanner realized their coach would be arriving soon.

"Oh no, now don't you go staying at no hotel while you're in town. I've got two bedrooms right here at my house and I won't be seeing my granddaughter staying at no hotel."

Tanner glanced at Bethany for her decision.

"Now don't go looking at her for an answer. I'm telling ya, this is home to family."

"Our bags are at the hotel," Tanner explained.

"You can go get them. Bethany can come talk to me in the kitchen while I put together a meal."

Bethany nodded. She still had a myriad of questions and this was the first place she'd gotten answers in over two months.

***

Bethany sat beside Tanner on Ida's stone patio in the back yard early the next afternoon while Tanner penned a letter to Sheriff Thacker. Bethany watched the curve of Tanner's well-written script and read every word. It was just as difficult seeing it on paper. It felt more real.

Tanner wrote out every detail of the evidence they found. He explained that there were documents about Bethany being sold to the Webbers, letters from Charlotte to her grandmother, and that Ida had been given Olivia's ruby brooch and a few gold coins. There was enough evidence to vindicate Bethany and have Charlotte charged with the murders. Tanner provided Sheriff Thacker with Charlotte's San Francisco address and told him they planned to leave Saint Louis in two days.

"She will truly hate me now," Bethany said.

"She already hates you, Bethany. No one could do what she did to you unless they already hated you."

"But it may have just been the greed that drove her. I was just a name on a piece of paper to her."

Tanner reached for her arm and tenderly rested his hand on hers. "I'm sorry, Bethany."

Chapter 13

Sheriff Thacker closed his eyes and breathed a long sigh of relief, lowering Tanner's letter onto the desk. After two and a half months of searching, the case was solved. Bethany was innocent.

It all made sense now: Bethany's twin committed the murder, ran off with the money and was hiding in San Francisco. Alan would have to make plans to go to San Francisco immediately and arrest Charlotte Young with the assistance of the San Francisco police.

Alan hoped they would not run into any complications. Did Charlotte have any accomplices? It almost seemed like she must in order to have had Bethany abducted. Bethany talked about two men with their faces covered. Perhaps one of them was Charlotte's boyfriend.

It was going to give Alan much pleasure to send a message to Sheriff Baker of Fairfield informing him that Bethany was innocent and that Tanner was vindicated of his crime. He'd already written the governor of California asking that Sheriff Baker's legal practices be investigated. This would just be one more chance to pay the man back for the way he'd treated Tanner.

A quick glance at his pocket watch told him it was still early enough to send a telegraph to James.

What a relief this will be to Mr. Webber. Alan stood up and tidied his desk.

Rodney walked into the office right before Alan walked out. "Where ya headed, Sir?" Rodney couldn't help but ask.

Alan's eyes twinkled. Quickest way to get the truth out there was to let his assistant deputy know. He waved the letter in the air. "Bethany's innocent. Just like I thought—and proof is on its way!"

Rodney would like to have asked a whole series of questions but he watched the sheriff walk from the office. Without a moment's hesitation, Rodney hurried to tell Eliza what he'd just heard.

***

Sheriff Thacker made arrangements for two San Francisco deputies to assist him in apprehending Charlotte Young. It was afternoon by the time Alan arrived in San Francisco and met the other two officers.

Both men were well versed with the case and Alan filled them in on all the new evidence. Neither of them questioned the new information and were ready to follow Sheriff Thacker's lead.

The apartments which Charlotte provided as her mailing address was on the low end of town. Crowded amidst a row of tightly built, tall wood framed buildings, Alan readied himself to meet the apartment manager.

"Yes, Charlotte Young rented a small apartment at the back of the house," Mrs. Little said. Her eyes traveled from one officer to the other.

"We need to speak with her." Alan wondered how ugly this would get.

Mrs. Little blinked a few times and shook her head. "I'm sorry, officer, but Miss Charlotte is dead."

Alan stared for just a moment to see if this was just a joke. *A cruel, inappropriate joke…*

"How did she die, Ma'am?" one of the deputies asked.

"A drug overdose." Mrs. Little shook her head somberly. "The doctor suspected opium."

Alan blew out a heavy sigh. "How long ago?"

"It's been a good two months now," Mrs. Little said. "She didn't have much. Most of it I donated to the poor. But I do have something." She walked to the office and carried back a few letters. "I know it's against the law to tamper with the mail, so I didn't know what to do with these." She handed Alan two unopened letters postmarked from Saint Louis. "These arrived after she died."

178

Alan accepted the letters and glanced down at them somberly. "What else was in the apartment?"

"A couple of poorly made dresses, a hairbrush, mirror, and a few other personal items."

"What about money?" Alan wondered where the stolen money went.

"There wasn't any. Sadly, she owed me for her last month." Mrs. Little shook her head.

Alan glanced at the deputies and back to Mrs. Little. "Ma'am, Charlotte Young is suspected to have stolen a large sum of money and several gold coins and jewelry. Is anyone living in her old apartment?"

"No. It's hard to rent an apartment when people hear about someone dying in it." Mrs. Little shook her head. "Somehow word always gets out." She glanced nervously at the ground for a moment. "But, okay, I did find a few pieces of jewelry." It was obvious Mrs. Little was feeling guilty. "I only took them because she owed me." The woman walked across the hall into her own apartment for a few minutes and returned carrying a carved walnut jewelry box. "I found this."

Alan glanced through the handful of high quality jewel pieces. "Where did you find this?"

"Under the mattress. I had to throw out the mattress. No one wants to sleep on a bed someone's died on. When I went to take it out, I found the box."

"Did you check the mattress for anything else? Money? Coins?"

Mrs. Little shrugged. "I did check. We even cut the mattress opened when we found the jewelry. We searched the whole apartment."

"We?"

"My husband and I. We manage this apartment together." Mrs. Little looked longingly at the box of jewelry. "I guess you need to keep that?"

"Yes, Ma'am. It's most likely stolen." Alan couldn't believe he would even need to explain this.

"Mrs. Little, it is believed that Charlotte Young stole thousands of dollars. If you are found with any of that money…"

"I promise you, the jewelry was all I found. The apartment was surprisingly empty."

"No attempt was made to find her family or notify anyone?" Alan found this to be heartless. "What about letters? Did she have any opened mail in the apartment?"

"There was nothing. Her apartment was spotless." Mrs. Little said firmly. "If there was more, believe me I would tell you. I told you about the jewelry, didn't I? There was nothing that would have given me any idea of where she was from or who her family was. Until those two letters came for her, I'd never seen anything personal and I was afraid to open them because of the law." Mrs. Little was suddenly on the defensive.

"Did you have any interaction with Charlotte?" Alan asked.

Mrs. Little shrugged. "She kept to herself for the most part. She did have a few male friends visit her a couple times, but I figured that was her business."

"Did anyone come by after she was found?"

"No. These men only came out a couple times… a few weeks before she died maybe."

"What about keys? Were there any keys to any kind of lock box or…"

"No keys. Just the dresses, a few toiletries and the jewelry. She didn't have much."

"Why did you not notify the sheriff?" Alan was frustrated with this woman.

"It didn't look like a crime scene. My husband called a doctor. It appeared to be a simple case of an opium addiction.

"Did you find any opium in the apartment?"

"Yes. There was a bottle of laudanum found in the room. The doctor disposed of it."

With the two letters in hand and the box of jewelry, Alan bid the apartment manager good-bye. The two deputies seemed as disappointed as Alan was.

Dead. How am I going to explain this to Miss Young? Alan was sure that Charlotte would have been hung for her crimes, but he knew Bethany would have wanted to at least meet her sister. *Probably tell the poor lost waif about Jesus.*

***

James received a brief telegram from Sheriff Thacker the day before explaining that Bethany was innocent, but he didn't expect the Sheriff to show up at his office in San Francisco.

"I would have sent a letter to explain it all," Alan said. "But I had to come to San Francisco anyway."

James motioned to a chair and offered Alan a cigar.

"No thank you," Alan declined. "I have wonderful news." His eyes beamed.

"I received your telegram last night. You said my cousin is innocent? I don't understand. Do you have more evidence?" James poured himself a glass of wine and offered Alan a glass.

Alan declined the wine.

"A photograph is hardly enough to prove..."

"It's more than a photo, Mr. Webber." Alan handed James the letter Tanner sent him. "We've got everything."

James read the letter slowly and turned his eyes back to Alan. "How in the world did they find Bethany's grandmother? I had no idea that my cousin had a grandmother still alive."

Alan shook his head. "All I can say is it must have been God who helped them. Tanner told me that the truth would set them free. Guess since God knows the truth, He worked it all out."

James took a sip of his wine. "This is wonderful." He almost looked stunned. "I just don't know what to say. My emotions are a bit out of synch."

"I can understand that, Mr. Webber."

The past two and a half months had been hard on James. The usually strong, athletic looking man was now thin and pale. His eyes appeared sunken and his face gaunt.

"You have been through a terrible ordeal," Alan's eyes were sympathetic. "And I'm sure your cousin will have her own issues to deal with when she arrives back in Santa Rosa."

"When do you expect her back?" James licked his lips.

"They should be home by the end of the week."

"I will make arrangements to be there." James ran his index finger over the rim of his glass.

Alan sighed heavily. "I will be bearing some bad news however," Alan said as he folded Tanner's letter and returned it to his vest pocket. "This morning I went to Charlotte Young's old apartment and learned that she died."

"What happened to her?"

"It was determined to be a drug overdose. They found laudanum in her apartment." Alan hadn't considered that this news might be painful to James as Charlotte was also his cousin. "We uncovered several fine pieces of jewelry which are at the San Francisco sheriff's department right now being documented. I plan to bring them back to Santa Rosa with me and will give you and Bethany the opportunity to tell me if they belonged to your mother."

James almost choked on his wine. "You've uncovered the jewels?"

"Yes. Unfortunately the apartment manager said they'd found no money and no gold coins."

"Where were the jewels found?"

"Under her mattress." Alan shook his head somberly. "This whole thing is very disconcerting. With Charlotte's death it will be far more difficult to find out who she had working for her."

"There is still more to investigate then?" James asked.

"Well, we still don't know who abducted Bethany and locked her in a cabin. Someone is still out there."

***

"They should be home in two days." Alan sat across from his wife at the dinner table and scooped more mashed potatoes onto his plate. "James needs to tie up a few loose ends in San Francisco but plans to be here by tomorrow evening."

Jane's face showed contented peace. "This is so good." She passed her husband a bowl of green beans. "Tell me James' reaction."

"I know James was pleased." Alan's face sobered. "But I fear the man's health has declined so greatly, that even this unexpected joy has not replaced his suffering."

"He is much worse then?" Jane asked.

Alan nodded. "He has lost weight and looks as though he has not slept since Marie's death."

Jane sighed. "Perhaps once he is reunited with Bethany some of his joy will return. The man has suffered the loss of both his father and one who was like a mother to him." She took a sip of her tea. "I am sure both James and Bethany will need time to heal."

Alan agreed. "And unfortunately, this case is not entirely solved. There is still the problem of who helped Charlotte."

"You found no clues in the apartment?"

Alan closed his eyes for a moment and shook his head somberly. "She died over two months ago. The apartment manager already disposed of most of Charlotte's belongings but assured me that there was nothing that would have pointed us to another human being. Charlotte had no opened letters, no papers, nothing... if I can believe Mrs. Little."

"Could Mrs. Little be involved?"

"It's nearly impossible to know at this point. It is very likely that whomever Charlotte was working with got their share of the money and have made themselves scarce."

Jane was quiet for a moment and took a few bites of her dinner. It was obvious that she was in thought. "Is it possible that Charlotte was murdered?"

Alan finished his bite of beef roast and set his fork down. "I talked to a few of the lawmen in San Francisco about that possibility. It is not impossible, however we have no leads. Mrs. Little remembered a couple of times Charlotte had visitors, but she paid little attention and said she would not even be able to recognize the men if she saw them." James lifted his water glass to his lips. "At this point, the San Francisco police have no plans to investigate Charlotte's death as a murder."

"So for now, we just need to rejoice that Bethany and Tanner are free."

"Yes."

***

"I gave you one simple task. One task!" An angry fist hit the ornately carved walnut desk with such intensity that James almost dropped his wine glass. "Could you not fulfill that one responsibility without error?" The man spat angrily.

James watched his lawyer walk to a large picture window and stare out at the San Francisco bay. James was noticeably rattled. "I thought I had." He turned his troubled eyes to his lap.

"You thought… you thought! That's the problem with you!" The lawyer paced the room. "You only think but you don't *know*!"

James finished his drink and set the empty glass down with a trembling hand. "I searched the entire house. I burned every letter my mother ever received from Bethany's grandmother. I destroyed all of Patrick's files about bringing Bethany into our home. I even destroyed everything that tied my mother to her family back east. There was nothing left in the house that should have given anyone any clues to Bethany's sister."

"Except the *one* photo!" The man pressed his fists into his temples. "I could kill you! How could you miss that picture?"

"It was in Marie's Bible. I never thought to check her Bible. I had no idea that Marie even knew about Charlotte. It was supposed to be a secret."

Drew Keene sat across from James and shook his head.

"I have more bad news." James ran a nervous hand through his hair. "My mother's jewelry was found in Charlotte's apartment."

The lawyer's eyes grew wide. This news did not please the man. "Where?"

"In the apartment. Under her mattress."

Drew punched his desk again. "Those worthless thugs! I told them to find everything."

"The sheriff told me nothing else of significance was found in the apartment," James said.

"How in the world did they miss the jewelry?"

James carried his empty wine glass to a counter across the room and gave himself a generous refill. "There is nothing we can do. Bethany's name is as good as cleared."

"And now she is about to become one of the richest women in California. Once that land passes to her, she will be sitting on a gold mine."

James sat back down and took several large sips of his wine. "Perhaps she will sell it to me. She doesn't know there's gold on the land. No one does, except us."

"It's too risky. If she agreed to sell it, you'd have to have it appraised. That's just asking for a gold discovery."

"We could do it off the books."

Drew shook his head. "There are surveyors sniffing out gold up and down the American River." He leveled his eyes evenly at James. "It's just a matter of time before they start sniffing up that twenty-five hundred acres."

"What else can I do?

"You and Bethany will need to write one another into your own wills and then Bethany will need to die."

Draining the contents of his glass, James wiped his mouth and blinked. "More killing…"

"If we don't kill Bethany, then everything we did was for nothing." Drew's eyes flashed angrily. "Do you know how much money we're talking about here?" He clenched his teeth. "I've waited almost twenty years for the opportunity to control that land. It's ripe for the mining and will make us more rich and powerful than any two men in California."

Chapter 14

The house wasn't home without Marie. Bethany sat on the
verandah and did her best to eat breakfast alone. Streaks of red
mingled with splashes of yellow morning sunlight reminded
Bethany of the mornings she'd woken up beside Tanner to see the
sun rise on the countryside. *Why am I thinking about Tanner
again?*

She'd seen very little of him over the past week. Tanner
had been busy with the sheriff connecting the details of Charlotte's
crime. Bethany missed him.

She'd been home for over a week. It seemed strange after
being away for over two and a half months. Nothing was the same.
Her uncle was dead. Marie was dead. And every room carried with
it reminders of a life Bethany no longer lived.

It was also strange having James home. For almost five
years he'd been living in San Francisco and before that he'd spent
four years at the University. Bethany hardly remembered what it
was like to have him living in Santa Rosa.

Bethany knew her cousin would not be able to stay away
from his business much longer. The poor man had been pulled
back and forth between San Francisco and Santa Rosa several
times since his father's death. How much more could he take?

The emotional drain of losing his father and Marie was
telling on James. Bethany believed his suffering would not be so
great if he understood the redemptive work of Jesus Christ.

James shared his father's beliefs that Christianity was for
the weak-minded and not worth his time. He had no hope of seeing
Marie in the next world because James did not know Christ and
His forgiveness. James could not even claim the peace that

186

surpasses all understanding because he did not know the Author of that peace.

In her few, vain attempts to talk to James about Jesus, he was unreceptive. He was unwilling to listen and unwilling to let her talk. In order to keep peace between her cousin and herself, Bethany simply did her best to live her faith in gentleness and love.

"Good morning," James interrupted her thoughts. "You are up early."

Bethany greeted her cousin and watched him take a seat beside her.

"I was planning to go into town later to meet with Jane Thacker."

"The sheriff's wife?" James asked.

"Yes. She is having a small group of ladies from our church to her home for lunch and invited me."

Rosa stepped onto the verandah carrying a plate of food for James. "Would you like tea or coffee this morning, sir?" she asked without emotion.

"Tea." James began eating his breakfast. "Don't you think it is a bit soon for you to be going into public?" James asked Bethany. "You are in mourning."

"I could use the fellowship, James. I think getting away from the house for the day will be good for me."

James cleared his throat and spread jam on his biscuit. "I am glad to hear that you feel that way," he said. "Because I wanted to invite you to come spend a month or so with me in San Francisco."

This invitation came as a surprise to Bethany. She'd never seen her cousin's home in San Francisco. But what would it be like to spend a month with him? Tanner was here… "When were you planning on leaving?"

"Probably not for another two weeks. We still need to meet with Mr. Langley to settle the will. As soon as all of the legal issues from the murder are settled, we can receive our inheritance."

Bethany lowered her eyes. She'd never expected an inheritance upon her uncle's death. It was kind of her aunt to think of her.

"Why do you think Aunt Olivia left me that land, James?"

"Undoubtedly because you were so good to her in her last year of life." James accepted the cup of tea from Rosa with no gratitude. "My mother loved you dearly."

"Some day I should like you to take me to that land," Bethany said. "It's that one little piece of her I still have."

James cleared his throat. "I told you that you are to keep the jewelry. I have no interest in any of it."

There was a bitter pill now associated with her aunt's jewelry. Hearing it was recovered in her sister's apartment after Charlotte's death robbed Bethany of any pleasure she might have gained from it.

"You have not given me an answer about San Francisco. I believe you will enjoy the change of scenery," James persisted.

"Perhaps. Let me think about it." Bethany wasn't sure how she felt about leaving Santa Rosa after just returning. Would it make home feel even more distant?

"I will need to get ready to go into town." Bethany set her napkin on the table. "Thank you for the invitation. I will let you know soon."

***

Your sister is not well. Complications from pregnancy. Baby did not survive. Prayers please.

Tanner read the short telegraph from his mother and sighed. His oldest sister, Brenda, was dear to him. It grieved him to hear that she'd lost her baby and was not doing well.

Upon their arrival home, Tanner sent his parents a long letter sharing with them how he put his faith in Jesus. He was sure his mother's request for prayers was in response to knowing he now shared their faith. His parents wrote him a long letter only a few days ago, rejoicing with him in his newfound relationship with his Savior.

"Why the somber face?" Alan asked. The two men had been working in the sheriff's office most of the morning.

"My sister, Brenda, is not doing well. She lost her baby… it's a telegram so my mother didn't give me many details. I expect she'll send a letter soon."

Alan leaned back in his chair and studied Tanner for a moment. "Do you need to go, Tanner?"

"To Maine?" Tanner was surprised Alan would ask.

"Yes. You haven't seen your family in over five years—and I know you're close to Brenda."

Tanner nodded. He and Brenda were close. Even after Tanner moved, Brenda wrote regularly to encourage Tanner, expressing her continual prayers for her brother.

He'd not considered the idea of visiting his family although he didn't doubt they would appreciate it. But was this a good time to take time off?

"I'm not sure this is the right time for me to leave. You're still settling things up with Bethany's case, I haven't been in Santa Rosa for almost two months to help you with anything, and you've just waged war with Sheriff Baker in Fairfield."

Alan was taking some heat for his recent recommendation that Sheriff Baker be investigated. The fellow lawman was not pleased with Alan and Tanner's accusations, but an investigation had begun and Tanner hoped Sheriff Baker might soon be losing his power in Fairfield. Tanner appreciated Walt's brave willingness to testify against the sheriff and hoped Baker would be charged with his abuse of power.

"Tanner," Alan leaned forward at his desk. "This might be the best time for you to go. After what you've just been through, I think you deserve a vacation."

"But I hate to leave Bethany right now." Tanner shifted his eyes across the room and stared out the window. *Bethany... could I really leave Santa Rosa for a month and not see Bethany?*

Alan gave Tanner a knowing grin. "You could always marry her and take her with you."

Tanner was surprised at his boss's suggestion. Tanner shook his head. "We're simply friends."

"I see." Alan and Tanner had been down this road before since Tanner and Bethany's return. It was clear that Alan wasn't convinced.

"There is too much going on in Bethany's life right now for her to even consider a deeper relationship with me." Tanner transferred one pile of papers to another pile of papers. "If it was even a consideration."

189

Alan shrugged. "Well then, I would say that taking some time away might be good for you."

Tanner could see the truth in that. He and Bethany had spent every day together for six weeks. It was difficult to see what was emotion and what was real. Maybe some time away from her would be good.

Since returning, Tanner hadn't seen much of Bethany, but he found himself wanting to. Knowing she was only a few miles away and that he was not with her made it difficult for Tanner to concentrate some days. He found himself wondering if she was okay, if she was safe, if she was hurting. Tanner had to get control of these feelings.

"Let me send a telegram home and ask my parents how critical things are," Tanner said. "If Brenda needs me, I will go."

***

Bethany was surprised how pleasant it was to sit and enjoy tea and cookies with Jane and several of her friends from church. These women were not what Bethany expected and she was certain they felt the same. Once the door to their hearts were opened to one another, Bethany found in these women kindred spirits, like she shared with Jane.

The truth of Bethany's story was now common in Santa Rosa, although several of the women asked Bethany questions which she did not mind explaining.

Jane refilled Bethany's pretty rose teacup and asked about her cousin.

"It's difficult to tell," Bethany confessed. "James and I have not been close for years. After he moved to San Francisco, I had very little contact with him. He came home for the holidays, but it was not the same as when were children."

She added cream and sugar to her tea and took a careful sip.

"James is very quiet and withdrawn." Bethany was also concerned with how much James drank. But she did not want to be that vulnerable for fear of betraying her family name. *He drinks alcohol afternoon to evening.*

"You have both suffered terrible losses," one of the women said compassionately. "Please let us know how we can come along side you and encourage you."

Bethany appreciated this extension of friendship. It meant a lot. *If only James could have this kind of support. It would be here for him if he were willing to receive it.*

Jane offered the ladies more cookies and teacakes and their conversation drifted to other things, which suited Bethany fine. She needed to give her mind a break from the circumstances she'd been recently living through.

As the women carried their teacups to the kitchen and made their farewells, Bethany pulled Jane aside to get her opinion about San Francisco.

"James has never invited me to visit him in San Francisco before. I believe it is because my uncle refused for us to ever go there. However, I wonder if this might be James' way of trying to become closer."

"It would give you the opportunity to get away from the house and its many memories for a while," Jane added.

But it would also take me away from Tanner. Bethany thought what she wasn't willing to say.

"Alan and I wanted to invite you and your cousin to have dinner after church on Sunday," Jane said. "We also invited Tanner."

Bethany's eyes sparkled. "I would love to come. I will ask James, although he has not been extremely social."

"We will not take it personally if he declines." Jane placed a caring hand on Bethany's arm. "Regardless we would love to see you and Tanner."

"Thank you."

***

Sunday morning, Bethany wore her long light gray gown, embroidered with small white flowers and trimmed with delicately tatted lace. She placed her hair in an attractive bun and allowed a few soft whips of golden curls to frame her face. Her blue eyes sparkled with anticipation as she thought about seeing Tanner. She'd not seen him since Wednesday night and it felt like forever.

True to Bethany's prediction, James had declined their invitation to dine at the Thacker's home.

"It's not too late to change your mind," Bethany greeted her cousin at the bottom of the long winding staircase. "Alan and Jane would still welcome you to dinner this afternoon."

"I wasn't aware that our social status had reduced itself to the station of dining with the sheriff," James replied rudely.

Bethany chose not to argue with her cousin.

After a quick breakfast of fresh fruit, Bethany rode to church in one of the Webber's coaches, and found Tanner waiting for her outside the building.

Tanner sat beside Bethany during the worship service and Bethany admired the attention he paid to the pastor's sermon. His enthusiasm to learn more about the Bible was encouraging.

Bethany and Tanner rode together to the Thacker's house. It was the first opportunity they'd had to talk privately for many days. Bethany listened rapturously as Tanner shared his thoughts about the sermon. "Pastor Bennington does not mince words when it comes to preaching the Bible, does he?"

"No." Bethany loved that Tanner was so eager to talk with her about his thoughts. In the two weeks since they'd been back from Saint Louis, they'd been able to attend church together three times because of the Wednesday night Bible study. "Pastor Bennington has a way of bringing his enthusiasm into his teaching."

Tanner agreed. "He believes what he is preaching. I've not always seen that in the pastors I've heard."

"What about your brother? You said one of your brothers is a pastor?"

"Yes. David." Tanner leaned back on the soft leather seat of the Webber coach. "He is a wonderful pastor. He was overjoyed when he heard I gave my life to Jesus."

Bethany smiled.

"Which brings me to some news…" Tanner lowered his eyes. "My sister, Brenda recently miscarried very close to term and is not well. They fear she may not pull through."

"Oh dear." Bethany wanted to reach out and hold Tanner's hand.

"I sent a telegram asking if they felt I should come and my parents said it would mean a lot to Brenda. We have always been close."

Bethany swallowed. "You plan to go to Maine?"

"I feel that I should."

"But it's so far..." Bethany regretted her words as soon as she said them.

Tanner tilted his head and studied Bethany for a moment with a grin on his lips. "Are you worried about me, Miss Young?" he asked playfully.

Bethany gazed up at Tanner with her sky blue eyes. "Will you be coming back?" That was all she really wanted to know.

"Of course." Tanner reached for her hand.

Bethany felt the warmth of his fingers and tightened hers just a bit. *What would I do if he didn't come back?* Did Tanner have any idea how much it mattered to her? Did he know how much she cared about him? What else was there in Santa Rosa to keep her here?

"If you still need me here, Bethany, I don't have to go." There was a look in Tanner's eyes that gave Bethany hope.

"No. You should go. Your sister needs you." Bethany would feel terrible if Tanner's sister passed without him saying goodbye. Bethany only wished there was a way she could go with him.

The Webber coach slowed in front of the Thacker's house and Tanner gave her his hand to step down. Bethany instructed her servant to come back in the evening and let Tanner lead her to the Thacker's front door.

***

"Well, I suppose I should tell you about the letter I received yesterday," Alan said after they'd asked the Lord's blessing over their food. "I received a message from the San Francisco sheriff's office. They caught one of the men who held you captive in the cabin outside of Saint Helena."

Tanner glanced up from his plate and waited for Alan to continue.

"His name is Buck Gainer. He tried to change out several gold coins for cash at the bank and the teller recognized the description of the coins. They apprehended him and he confessed to having abducted you and holding you at the cabin. The information he gave about his counterpart was vague."

"Did he say that Charlotte hired them?" Tanner asked.

"No. He claims he doesn't know who hired them."

"How could he not know?" Bethany asked.

"He said the man remained anonymous, gave them specific instructions and paid them. Buck claims it was just a job to him and he didn't ask questions."

That was disconcerting. "That means there is still someone else involved," Tanner said.

Alan nodded.

Bethany released a nervous sigh. "Do I need to fear for my life again?"

"I don't think so." Alan scooped a healthy portion of sweet potatoes onto his plate. "Whoever hired them got the money he wanted. Charlotte got the jewelry and these men got the coins. My guess is, the brains behind the operation purposely kept the money from the bank, which could not be traced, while allowing his hired thugs to take what could be."

"I'd not thought of that," Bethany confessed. "But that means my sister was willing to do her part in this crime for only a box of jewelry?"

"Bethany." Alan leaned forward. "Your aunt had some very rare and priceless jewels in her collection. Charlotte also sent your grandmother some of the gold coins, so she must have been given her share of those too."

"Alan, if you think I need to stay to further the investigation, I can," Tanner offered.

"No." Alan shook his head. "The San Francisco sheriff's office is investigating the hired criminals and it appears our job here is done. You should go to your family. They need you right now."

Tanner glanced quickly at Bethany. Didn't she need him too?

"You should go," Bethany reaffirmed. "I'll be okay."

"Did you decide to accept your cousin's invitation to visit San Francisco with him for a few weeks?" Jane asked Bethany.

Tanner had not been told of this option. He glanced at Bethany curiously.

"I had not yet given him an answer." Bethany lowered her eyes shyly. How could she explain that she didn't want to leave Tanner? But if Tanner was going to Maine there was no reason she shouldn't go to San Francisco with James. "I supposed I should go."

"Will you be coming back?" Tanner asked her the same question she asked him on the coach.

Bethany's blue eyes sparkled. "Of course."

Tanner was relieved. There was so much he wanted to say. They could write. He would give her his parents' address. Was Bethany going to miss him too? How long would she be gone?

"When do you leave, Tanner?" Jane asked.

"I suppose I should leave as soon as possible. It will take a week to get there and with my sister being so sick, I don't want to waste any time." He glanced at Alan. "Are you sure you're okay with me being gone?"

"In the four years you've worked for this town you've never taken even a week off. I think we owe you this."

There was still something in Tanner's heart making it difficult to leave. He knew what it was... Bethany.

***

Bethany did her best not to let her emotions show when Tanner gave her a parting hug at the train station. He would be gone for a month. She'd only known him for two and it felt like forever. How was she going to go that long without seeing Tanner?

Jane wrapped an arm through Bethany's and walked with her and Alan to the wagon. "I do believe you look like your heart is about to break," Jane said softly.

Bethany felt like it was. She lowered her eyes shyly. "I will miss him."

"And I have no doubt Tanner will miss you."

Bethany hoped so. She prayed that he would have a safe

195

trip and tried to let herself focus on going to San Francisco. She and James would be leaving in a week and a half.

"We will see you Wednesday night," Jane encouraged. "And you are invited to join us on Sunday for dinner again if you would like."

Bethany appreciated the Thackers' attempts at keeping her busy.

***

"And I just need your signature here," Asa instructed as the conditions of Bethany's will was completed.

Bethany signed the paperwork and sucked in a deep breath. "So I'm now a land owner."

"Yes you are, Miss Young." Asa pressed a seal onto the signature. "Twenty-five hundred acres outside of Sacramento."

"Why Sacramento?" Bethany asked.

"From what I understand, your aunt wanted to buy the land that your father owned when your parents moved to Sacramento, but that land was not available. This parcel is only about twenty-five miles west of there, so she asked her husband to buy it."

"Did she always intend that I should have this land?" Bethany asked.

"Olivia and Patrick made this decision long before she grew ill. I believe it was their way of giving you something to tie you to your parents."

Bethany appreciated hearing this story. It touched her to think that her aunt and uncle wanted to bless her in this way.

"How did you find this out?" James asked.

"I recently spoke to Jedadiah Cloverfield," Asa explained. "He used to sell real estate back when Patrick and Olivia made the purchase. I ran into him at the mill the other week and he told me the story." Asa smiled and shook his head. "That old timer's got more stories than he's got sense. But he's got a memory on him like nothing I've ever seen."

James was expressionless. "Was that all he told you about the land?"

"Pretty much. He went into another story about selling a vineyard to your father that Patrick never used."

Bethany knew of the place. Her uncle seemed more set on collecting property than cultivating it.

She glanced at the deed and ran her fingers along the fine script. "What should I do with this land?"

"I can't tell you that." Asa closed his inkwell. "You may want to hold on to it. Property near Sacramento will only become more valuable with time."

"Well, thank you, Mr. Langley," Bethany rose to her feet and handed Asa the deed for safekeeping. "I appreciate you finding out that story for me. It means a lot."

Chapter 15

Tanner breathed in the fresh smells of autumn in the air as he stepped from the train in Maine. It had been a long trip, but it was good to be home. He'd spent hours reading the Bible and writing letters.

He finally took the time to write a long letter to both Walt and Clarence. He'd shared with Walt about the forgiveness and healing he'd found in Jesus Christ. To Clarence, Tanner expressed his appreciation for leading him to Jesus. He also shared the details of Bethany's story and how much he appreciated that Clarence believed in him. He was sure the sheriff already heard that Bethany had been vindicated, but it felt good to personally give his new friend the details.

Tanner also wrote Bethany three letters during his traveling. *Will Bethany think I overdid it?*

"Tanner!" His mother's voice over the sounds of the crowd turned Tanner's head and he sought out her face.

The warm embrace of his mother met him before he knew what hit him.

"You've been gone too long, Son." Jacob Brenly shook Tanner's hand.

"I know. I'm sorry." Tanner could see that five years had taken its toll on his father.

"Are you staying?" his mother asked hopefully.

Tanner hated to disappoint his mother but he shook his head. "Not this time."

"Perhaps we can sway your decision after a couple weeks of your mother's cooking and after you've seen the improvements I've made on the ship factory."

"Oh, Father," Tanner walked beside Jacob toward the coach. "You know the ship factory is one of my favorite places." Tanner carried his trunk and told his parents about the trip.

He mailed out the letters while in town and got comfortable in the coach for the hour ride to Rockland. The thriving city sat nestled on the Penobscot Bay and boasted a beautiful view of the harbor with its many ships launching almost daily.

The town had more than one thriving shipbuilding business and was also a steady producer of lime. With twelve lime quarries and 125 limekilns, the town provided lime to various ports all along the eastern seaboard.

Tanner's eyes soaked in the sight of his hometown. Several three-story brick buildings lined the downtown street, while quaint farms and farmhouses dotted the countryside. Tanner watched enthusiastically as they drew near his parents' well-established home.

"So, you're telling me that my sister began improving after she heard I was coming?" Tanner asked.

"She did," Tanner's mother explained. "Between her excitement about seeing you and her determination to get better for Emily, Brenda has been improving greatly." Melissa Brenly took her son's hand and held it tightly.

"We will take you to see Brenda tomorrow," Jacob said. "We figured you would be anxious for a hot bath and a good night's sleep."

"Will I have my old bedroom?" Tanner grinned.

"You can choose. The house is so empty since Christopher moved out."

"How is he doing?" Tanner regretted that he was not able to come home for his brother's wedding.

"Wonderfully. He and Anne make a lovely couple."

It was hard for Tanner to picture his brother married to Anne Underwood. When Tanner moved to California, Anne was just a giddy girl of thirteen.

"Christopher was not hurt that I was unable to attend the wedding, was he?" Tanner asked.

"He said that since you went to such great extremes to make up a grand story of rescuing a damsel in distress, he would forgive you. But since he also knew you had made no plans to come home for the wedding even before the grand story, you would owe him." Melissa's eyes twinkled.

Tanner laughed. He knew his parents shared the whole story about Bethany with the family. All of his siblings had taken the time to write and congratulate him on his new faith.

"And now that your younger brother has taken a church in Camden, you do realize I have no son to run my business with... unless you come home," Jacob said in all seriousness.

"Hey, don't blame me. It was your willingness to allow David and Christopher to go off to Seminary that ruined your chances of having them be your business partners." Tanner teased his father. Tanner knew that Jacob was more than pleased to have two sons go into full-time paid ministry. But he also knew Jacob would love to have Tanner become his partner in shipbuilding. Especially now that Tanner shared his father's faith.

Before the war, Tanner loved working for his father. Of Jacob's three sons, Tanner was the one who enjoyed working with wood the most. Even in his free time, Tanner could be found out in the workshop planing a board or drawing up new designs. Tanner wondered if he still had that creativity.

Tanner spotted the house as they drove the carriage down the lane. Five windows graced the second story and a high stone fireplace stood on either side of the house. It was good to be home.

***

The next morning, Tanner went with his parents to visit his sister. Brenda's husband Andrew met them at the door. "Tanner," Andrew greeted his brother-in-law with a hearty handshake. "Words cannot express what it means to Brenda that you came all the way to Maine to see her." There was genuine appreciation in Andrew's eyes and he pulled Tanner to himself to add a hug to the greeting.

"Uncle Tanner?" A shy seven year old glanced curiously at Tanner.

Tanner grinned at the sweet, red-haired beauty and knelt down to give her a proper greeting. "Emily? Can that really be you?" Tanner felt a rush of strange emotions. His own daughter, Rachel, would have been about the same age by now had she lived.

Emily nodded.

Tanner knew his niece had been too young when he moved west to remember her uncle, but she always wrote a few lines in the letters her mother sent to him. "You're just as beautiful as Grandma and Grandpa wrote in their letters!"

Emily's eyes sparkled and she reached out to give this long lost uncle a hug. "Thank you for coming, Uncle Tanner." She glanced appreciatively at her grandparents. "And thank you for telling Uncle Tanner I'm pretty," she said to them from her uncle's arms.

Andrew placed a gentle hand on his daughter's back. "Why don't you lead Uncle Tanner upstairs to see your momma? I'm sure she can hear him down here and is probably itching to give him her own greeting."

Emily grabbed Tanner's hand and practically dragged him up the narrow wooden staircase with all the seven-year-old strength she could muster. "Momma's been talking about you ever since Grandma brought your telegraph. Did you really send the telegraph the same day we got it? I can't hardly believe we could get a message that fast all the way from California!" Emily chatted non-stop. "Momma said it was going to take you a week to get here but it only took a day for your words to get here. Isn't that funny?"

Tanner enjoyed listening to his adorable little niece talk as incessantly as her mother had when she was a girl.

"Tanner!" Brenda's eyes showed her pleasure when Tanner reached for her extended hands. "You wonderful, silly, little brother. You traveled three thousand miles to see your sister."

"And I'd travel three thousand more." Tanner sat at the edge of her sleigh bed and rubbed her fingers tenderly. Her long auburn hair hung in soft waves across her nightgown and she beamed at him with appreciation in her brown eyes.

The bedroom was well lit, with two long windows and the sun shining through. Tanner glanced around the room at the lavender wallpaper and remembered Bethany's response to the lavender walls at the Western Hotel in Sacramento. *She would probably love my sister's bedroom.* "Are you okay?" he asked.

Brenda nodded but her eyes misted. "I'm doing better." She glanced lovingly at Emily. "Emily needs me."

"And Andrew needs you," her husband reminded her lovingly from the doorway.

"As do your parents," Melissa added.

"And I need you, big sis." Tanner kissed her head. "You're the only sister I've got!" As soon as Tanner said it, he thought of Bethany and Charlotte and his expression changed.

"What is that little pouty look for?" Brenda squeezed her brother's fingers.

"What pouty look?"

Brenda chuckled. "You're being so sentimental." She stared at him contentedly. "I want to hear everything. Every detail that you wrote about in your letters—I want to watch your expression as you tell it again."

Tanner grinned. "I don't know that I can do that," Tanner confessed. "My handkerchief isn't large enough."

"I cried when Mother read it to me... each time." Brenda sniffed.

Melissa placed a hand on her son's shoulder. "We're so happy, Tanner."

Tanner had stayed up late the evening before sharing the details of his salvation with his parents, and they had not ceased expressing their joy.

"And then there's this Bethany..." Brenda tilted her head and studied her brother curiously. "You mentioned her a lot in your letters."

"Well it all started with Miss Young." Tanner purposely used her proper name to not raise questions. It had been many weeks since Tanner called Bethany by her proper name, but if Brenda knew that he would never hear the end of it.

Tanner began explaining the story again, answering questions as his sister asked. The story took a while to explain and he filled them in on the recent discovery of the man who'd been apprehended in San Francisco.

"What does she look like?" Brenda asked.

"Brenda!" Melissa shot her daughter a quick rebuking glance.

Tanner smiled at his sister. "She is very pretty."

Brenda was not satisfied. "But what does she look like?"

"She looks like springtime and her eyes are like a clear blue sky." Tanner purposely made it poetic for his sister's benefit. "She has golden brown hair, kissed by the sun, and her face is dusted with cheerful little freckles that make you want to smile." Tanner started laughing before he could say anything else. "How's that?"

"That sounds like a man in love!" Brenda raised her eyebrows.

"Brenda!" Melissa called out again.

"Did you see the way he talked about her?" Brenda glanced impishly at her mother. "That's why I wanted to hear the story from him. When he talked about her nursing him back to health, I knew."

Tanner shook his head at his sister.

"Tanner, I'd apologize for your sister," Andrew said. "But this is the most enthusiastic I've seen her in weeks."

"Thank you, Uncle Tanner." Emily nestled herself beside him at the foot of her mother's bed.

"So your mother is back to herself then?" Tanner wrapped an arm around Emily. It felt so good to be loved by this little girl. He imagined what it would have been like to hold his own daughter this way.

"Uncle Tanner, why are your eyes all wet?" She stared at him.

"Uncle Tanner was always the most emotional of my brothers, Emily." Brenda unknowingly rescued him. "I could make him cry just by refusing to hug him."

"That's mean, Momma." Emily hugged her uncle.

"I'm only teasing." Brenda kicked her brother from under the blankets.

"She's not teasing," Tanner whispered to Emily.

"Well I'll always hug you! Are you going to live with Grandma and Grandpa now?"

Tanner shook his head. "I'll be needed back in Santa Rosa in just a few weeks."

Emily narrowed her eyes. "But we need you here. Daddy said…"

Andrew touched his daughter's arm to silence her. "That we would all love it if Tanner came back to stay but that he has a job in California," Andrew finished his daughter's comment.

"But you also said that Grandpa needed him to help run the ship factory." Emily spilled the beans.

Andrew gave Tanner an apologetic shrug.

"It's okay, Andrew," Jacob said from the chair he'd been sitting in at the back of the bedroom. "I've already extended the invitation." He glanced at his pocket watch. "We're going to have to leave soon. Christopher and Anne are coming over for dinner tonight," Jacob added.

"But you just got here!" Brenda protested.

"I'll be back over tomorrow," Tanner promised. He stood up and gave his sister a tender hug.

"What day are David and Leah coming?" Brenda glanced at her parents.

"Monday," Melissa said.

Tanner knew his mother was enjoying all these family reunions. "So if you can get yourself better, you can come have dinner with David and Leah too."

"And I'll get to see my cousins!" Emily said enthusiastically.

"And you'll get to see your cousins!" Melissa echoed cheerfully.

***

Bethany spun around in front of the long beveled mirror and watched her new, long, lavender and yellow gown encircle her form gracefully. It was a lovely dress. Her cousin encouraged her to purchase a few new dresses before they went to San Francisco. He was generous with his inheritance and insisted on paying for the dresses.

In spite of the land she'd inherited and her aunt's jewelry, Bethany had very little available money. It was one of the consequences of choosing God's inheritance over her uncle's. But Bethany had no regrets. *My God shall supply all my needs according to His riches in glory in Christ Jesus,* she paraphrased one of her favorite verses.

James walked into the room and watched Bethany for a moment.

"I'm glad you talked me into getting a couple new dresses,"

204

she smiled at her somber faced cousin. "Thank you for buying them for me."

James cleared his throat. "It seemed appropriate."

Her cousin never complemented her in the dress nor did he express any opinion. She glanced in the mirror and wondered what Tanner would think.

The delicate sleeves were puffed and trimmed in fine tatted lace. The bodice was embroidered with delicate lavender roses, just slightly lighter than the dress itself, and accentuated her slim waistline.

"I am going to bed for the night," James said. "You will need to have your trunks packed by tomorrow. We leave Monday morning."

Bethany nodded. She'd arranged for their maid, Mae, to assist her packing.

James left the room and Bethany called for Mae to help her change out of the dress.

For over a week Bethany endured the heavy silence that permeated the walls. It was difficult not to think about Marie during these quiet times. It would have been Marie who would have helped her change out of the dress. It would have been Marie who would have helped her shop and prepare for the trip. Bethany watched Mae quietly hang the new dress in the wardrobe.

Other than Marie, none of the other maids treated Bethany like a friend. They did their jobs properly and with little emotion. In spite of Bethany's attempts to get Mae and Rosa to open up to her, they both treated her as their superior.

"Thank you, Mae." Bethany expressed her appreciation before the quiet maid left the room.

Bethany sat down at the edge of her canopy bed and watched the redwood door close softly. The Webber Estate lacked joy and Bethany wasn't sure how to bring it back.

***

Tanner spent the day with his father at the ship-making factory.

205

"I've always dreamed of calling it Brenly and Son, you know." Jacob motioned to the sign hanging above the new factory building.

Tanner grinned. He admired the new brick structure nestled along the bay. His father had done a nice job with the architect, creating a structure that was both functional as a factory and attractive to the eye. Jacob was conscious of the beauty of the harbor and didn't want to distract from it.

Large arched windows graced the fourth story of the factory and brought much light into the wide opened internal structure where his father was able to house several small ships during their production.

"Business must be booming," Tanner said. He gazed up at one of the ships in the yard and noted the attention to detail. Decorative but functional head rails and a fine gilded figurehead were signs that this ship was going to an affluent buyer.

"The Lord has blessed us, that's all I can say." Jacob motioned to one of the workers. "How is that stern post coming?" he yelled up.

"Finished," the worker called back.

"Wonderful, Charles!" Jacob waved and led Tanner into the building. "I can't even begin to tell you how much I enjoy finally having enough space to do what we need to do," he said. "And wait until you see my office."

Tanner enjoyed seeing his father so animated. He followed his father into a nicely furnished office where Jacob could work on plans and meet with potential clients.

"But I want you to pay special attention to this," Jacob stood by one door and opened it mysteriously. The door opened to an empty office, equally large with a desk that matched Jacob's.

Tanner eyed the room knowingly. "Nice room. Kind of underused I'd say. Perhaps you should move your accountant here."

"Andrew has his own office in town," Jacob led Tanner to a leather-covered chair. "Try this out for size."

"You truly aren't going to give up, are you?" Tanner sat in the chair and relaxed.

Jacob leaned on the edge of the empty desk and motioned for Tanner to take note of the marquetry on the top. Created out of different colored woods there was a design of a ship on the desk.

"This is nice." Tanner ran his hand over it.

"It's just waiting for you, Son." Jacob crossed his arms. "You always said you planned to come home."

Tanner nodded. "I do, father."

Jacob studied him curiously. "When? I'm trying not to be impatient, but…"

"I think I'm getting very close." Tanner confessed. "But there is a serious life decision I need to figure out before I'm ready to say goodbye to Santa Rosa."

Jacob chewed on his lip. "Does this involve Miss Young?"

Tanner steadied his eyes on his father and nodded.

"Do you love her, Son?"

Tanner let his eyes travel to the large window on the other wall and watched the sunlight stream into the unlit room. "When Ruth died, I always said I'd never love again."

Jacob nodded.

Tanner let his finger travel over the outline of the ship's mast on his desk made from holly wood. Tanner always admired holly because of its light color. "I was with Bethany every day for over a month. After we returned from Saint Louis and she was returned to her home, I missed her. Every opportunity I had I tried to see her, but it wasn't enough."

"I understand that," Jacob confessed. "That's how I feel about your mother."

"But I feel guilty," Tanner traced the ship with his finger. "Ruth was the mother of my child. She was my wife for four years. We shared so many memories." Tanner turned his eyes to his father. "How can I let that go?"

"Loving Miss Young doesn't mean letting that go. It means adding to it. It means moving forward with your life." Jacob took a step closer to his son. "Loving Bethany doesn't mean you didn't love Ruth. It means your heart has healed enough to love again."

Tanner blinked back tears and thought about his sister's teasing him for being her emotional brother.

"Do you love Miss Young?" Jacob asked again.

"I do. I love her dearly." It felt good to say the words. "She's so different from Ruth... in good ways. Ruth was her own person and so is Bethany."

"That's the way it should be."

Tanner smiled at his father. "I never knew I could feel this way again. All I wanted to do was protect her, keep her safe, you know?" He thought about her gentle touches and the softness of her hands. "At first I was afraid to love her because I didn't want to get hurt again. Losing Ruth and Rachel was the most painful thing I've ever gone through. But now I know... if I lost Bethany it would be the same." He brushed away a tear and laughed at himself. "Brenda is right. I am your emotional child."

Jacob placed a loving hand on his son's shoulder. "You feel things deeply, Tanner. But that is nothing to be ashamed of. I am proud of the man you are."

"What should I do?" Tanner appealed to his father for advice.

"Does Bethany love you?" Jacob asked.

Tanner remembered her worried expression when she asked him if he'd be returning from Maine. He smiled when he recalled Bethany tightening her long delicate fingers around his. "She's never said it, but I think so."

"Then, I think you should go back to Santa Rosa, marry her, and bring her back to Rockland." His lips formed into a wide grin. "And enjoy your new office." He spread his arms out into the air.

"What if she says no? What if she doesn't want to leave Santa Rosa?" Tanner's worried expression spread across his face.

"If this Bethany Young is as wonderful as you've made her sound, then I'm certain she will follow her man across the country."

Tanner hoped this was true.

Chapter 16

James lived in a three-story Victorian house situated along a steep road, lined with unique houses all designed to complement one another. Bethany had never seen such steep streets, but she had to admit, San Francisco had charm.

After taking Bethany to a fine restaurant where they dined on lobster and crab, James brought her to his house and offered her a choice of two guest rooms.

Bethany made herself comfortable in a room that overlooked the bay. Thick oriental carpets adorned the hardwood floors and Bethany's ornately carved bed was covered in a clean white spread.

The maid greeted Bethany with curious interest and helped her unpack her trunk.

The middle-aged woman barely reached five feet tall and hardly filled out the dress she wore. The servant introduced herself as Gloria and filled the washbasin with warm water.

"I was not aware that Mr. Webber would be bringing his cousin home," Gloria apologized for not being ready for her. "I would have made sure your room was aired out and had tea made for you."

"Everything is lovely," Bethany appreciated that this servant at least spoke to her.

"We no longer have our cook," the servant explained. "And poor Mr. Webber has been too troubled to find us another one. Perhaps you will be able to restore some hope to the man."

Bethany wasn't so sure. For the past few weeks she didn't feel like she'd had much influence. When James wasn't buried in a newspaper he was so filled up on alcohol that he fell asleep.

"Who does the cooking for my cousin?" Bethany asked.

Gloria shrugged. "I do my best, although the man usually dines out."

"Perhaps I can help," Bethany suggested.

Gloria glanced at Bethany skeptically. "I doubt that Mr. Webber will approve of that. Although he is not home enough to notice most likely." She fluffed the pillows on Bethany's bed. "If you need me to draw you a bath, please ask."

"Thank you, Gloria."

After getting herself situated, Bethany found her cousin in his sitting room smoking a cigar and drinking a glass of apple brandy. She cleared her throat from the smoke and sat across from him on a comfortable lounge chair. "What will we do tomorrow?"

"I need to go to the office," James said. "I'm dreadfully behind on my work. But you are welcome to read any of my books, Gloria would be happy to take a stroll with you, and I believe you will find the shopping downtown to be agreeable."

Bethany nodded. What had she hoped for?

"Rest, Bethany," James encouraged. "At my home you are free from the past and unencumbered by responsibilities."

***

The Brenly house was alive with activity. Six young cousins scurried through the house playing a combination of continental explorer and house. Emily explained to her Uncle Tanner that she was an Indian princess and that she and her husband, cousin Ned, were traveling out west to start a new shipbuilding factory near the Grand Canyon.

Tanner wished her and Ned the best and told her he hoped they were able to run a thriving business. "Perhaps you can call it Grand Canyon Ships."

"We've already named it Ned's Big Boats," Emily explained.

Tanner smiled. He found it humorous that David's oldest son was so willing to play whatever Emily demanded. "Emily is just like you." Tanner turned to his sister and smiled.

It was Brenda's first day away from her house. She'd been out of bed for a couple days now, but coming to see David and

Leah meant leaving the house if she could and Brenda was determined.

Tanner just finished retelling the entire story to David and Leah, making this the fourth retelling since arriving home in Maine.

"I love that he gets choked up when he tells the part about Miss Young taking care of him in the cave," Brenda interjected.

Leah's refined lips curved into a genuine smile. "I can see that your brother appreciated her care."

Brenda chuckled. "Appreciated is putting it mildly."

Leah glanced at her husband and David smiled. "Apparently our sister is still pushing your buttons, Tanner."

"It never ends," Tanner said. But he was glad.

Melissa offered carrot cake to the family and got an overwhelming response.

"Cut mine twice as big, Mother," David winked.

Melissa handed all three of her sons an equally large slice and slipped out of the room with Leah to get more for the ladies.

"Tanner," David said after savoring the first bite of his mother's carrot cake. "I need to clarify, in your story you mentioned that Miss Young's mother's name was Eleanor and her aunt was Olivia?"

Tanner nodded.

"They both lived in California but are from Vermont." David's expression was thoughtful.

It occurred to Tanner that his brother, David, pastored a church in Vermont. "Yes. There was another sister and brothers too, but I don't know who they are. Ida told us there were six children in the family."

"There's a woman from my church… a dear elderly lady, as sweet as can be. She has three sons who live relatively close by. Two of them attend my church." David ran his hand over his chin. "She had three daughters. Naomi, Eleanor and Olivia. I know this because she has talked about them on several occasions."

Tanner's interest was piqued.

"The two youngest daughters moved to Missouri and then California. Her youngest just died a couple years ago. Nora was deeply grieved because her son-in-law didn't even tell her that Olivia was ill."

Tanner could hardly believe the details of this woman's life. "Could this be Bethany's grandmother?" It all fit.

"That's what I'm thinking."

"I've got to meet her," Tanner said intently.

"I think you should." David took a huge bite of his mother's cake.

"You're saying that a woman from David's church might be Miss Young's grandmother?" Brenda clarified.

"I'm saying we should investigate it," David said. "Nora is a good friend of our family. She's a dear follower of Jesus. Our own children fondly call her Aunt Nora. She's got several grandchildren living in Vermont but I know she mentioned having grandchildren out west."

David called his wife back into the room. She was helping Melissa serve cake to the children.

"Leah," David spoke to his wife. "Do you remember anything about Nora's grandchildren out west?"

Leah sighed and leaned back on her husband's chair. "I don't recall their names. But I know she has always mourned that she never met the twins."

"Twins?" Tanner knew it had to be.

Leah's eyes widened as she connected Tanner's story to Nora. "I hadn't thought of it. But, yes, Nora said her daughter, Eleanor, had twins."

"Tanner," Brenda's playful voice rang out. "You get to tell the story again."

***

He'd not expected to travel to Vermont with his brother during his visit east, but Tanner was eager to meet Bethany's potential grandmother. Tanner's parents understood Tanner's urgency and gave their blessing on his unanticipated travel arrangements.

David and Leah lived in a quaint, saltbox style home a field away from the church where David was pastor. Their three well-behaved children, Ned, Annabelle and William listened rapturously to Tanner's stories of the west as they sat and drank apple cider near the large stone fireplace.

"The Humwichawa is probably one of the most unusual trees I've ever seen," Tanner explained. "Its recently been called the Joshua Tree. I've also heard them called Yucca Palms. They grow in the northern part of the Mojave Desert."

"Why is it unusual?" Ned asked.

"They stand big and tall amidst a desert of shrubs and dry grasses and each limb seems to just reach up to heaven. But they don't have regular leaves like the trees we have here."

"Are they more like an evergreen?" Annabelle asked.

"Not really. The leaves are more like big palm leaves. The trunk is made of thousands of tiny fibers so they have no growth rings." Tanner took a sip of his apple cider. "The Indians use the leaves to weave sandals and baskets. They also eat the seeds and flower buds of the Joshua Tree."

"Did you ever eat the seeds or flowers?" William joined in the questioning.

"No," Tanner admitted. "The smell just never really appealed to me."

"Did you see a lot of Indians?" Ned asked eagerly.

"I've met several Indians." Tanner went on to tell the children stories about the Indians he had met.

"But don't get any ideas of moving out west," Leah urged her children. "You'll not find maple syrup like this in California, that's for certain." She handed her son a maple cookie.

"We make our own maple syrup," Ned told Tanner.

"And we get to eat the maple sugar," Annabelle added. "That's my favorite part." She reached for a cookie and smiled at her mother.

"We will try to meet with Nora Farnsworth tomorrow," David interrupted the conversation.

"Will she be open to talking to a stranger?" Tanner asked.

"If her pastor is along, Nora will talk about anything." David winked.

Leah sat across from the children, smoothed her skirt and leaned forward to join in the conversation. "I have no doubt your friend, Miss Young, is indeed Nora's granddaughter. I can only imagine the joy Nora will have at learning that her Miss Young is a Christian."

"Although Charlotte's story is very sad," Tanner added.

Leah agreed. "There is also a grandson, correct?" Leah asked.

"James would be Olivia's son."

Leah was contemplative for a moment. "I believe James was born in Vermont."

Tanner nodded. "That makes sense."

"What is James like?" David asked. "Is he a follower of Christ?"

Tanner shook his head. "Sadly, no. However Bethany hasn't given up hope."

***

"Can you mail this letter for me?" Bethany handed James a letter addressed to Tanner in Maine.

James glanced at the letter and cleared his throat. "This is the second letter you've written to Mr. Brenly in a week. Are you not being a bit forward with the man?"

Bethany stood up straight and brushed a stray hair from her face. "Mr. Brenly is my friend. He asked that I correspond with him while he is in Maine."

"And yet the man has yet to write to you since we've arrived in San Francisco." James placed Bethany's letter on his brief case. "I will bring it to the office this morning and send it out with the morning mail."

Bethany lowered her eyes as James' words echoed in her mind, *and yet the man has yet to write to you since we've arrived in San Francisco...* The words stung. Tanner's silence had been plaguing her for days. *Why hasn't Tanner written since I've been in San Francisco?* Bethany wrung her hands. *I'm sure he's been very busy with his family. Maybe he misplaced my brother's address.*

"I will be gone most of the day," James interrupted her worrying. "I have scheduled an appointment with my lawyer for later in the week to designate you as the recipient of my will." He placed his hat on his head and turned to Bethany. "I advise you to make a decision concerning your estate as well. Since the land belonged to my father, it is my preference that the land be left to me, but I cannot force such a decision upon you."

"Of course I would leave it to you," Bethany relaxed her shoulders. "You're my cousin…" her eyes softened.

"Well, my lawyer is prepared to make the arrangements for both of us. We can have dinner in town that evening."

Bethany nodded. It would be good to get out. She'd been stuck in James' house for the past week and was anxious to see more of San Francisco. She watched James walk out the door and studied his thin frame. Did he work like this all the time? No wonder her cousin never married.

With a heavy sign, Bethany carried a book to her room, knowing that she was far too distracted to read. *What if Tanner's forgotten me?*

***

Cleo Crisfield was as tall as he was wide and had a presence about him that demanded attention. Asa glanced up from his paperwork when his secretary announced this unexpected visitor.

"Mr. Langly?" Cleo walked past the secretary into Asa's office. "I'm Cleo Crisfield." He extended his hand more as a demand than a greeting.

Asa stood up and appraised this mammoth of a man, taking note of his fine apparel and lack of teeth. With a clean-shaven face and hands rough from work, Cleo was a paradox.

"It's been a while since I've been over to these parts," Cleo took a seat across from Asa without being offered a chair. "Last time I was here for the same reason though. I just heard the twenty-five hundred acre property outside of Sacramento changed hands and was told you were the lady's lawyer."

"I assume you mean, Bethany Young?"

"Yes, sir, that's the name. I've been keeping an eye on that property for almost twenty years now."

"What is the nature of your interest?" Asa narrowed his eyes curiously and motioned for his secretary to close the door.

215

"That land bleeds yellow and it's crying to be mined. I've been itching to set up a mine there since I first spotted gold there, but Mr. Webber refused my offer." Cleo set a written contract in front of Asa and gave it a pat. "That was written up in 1853 by my lawyer in Sacramento. It's a mighty fine contract and believe me, Mr. Webber would have been the one to benefit the most. But he'd have nothing of it. Refused to sign and refused to talk to me face to face."

Asa read through the contract and agreed that it was well written and wholly advantageous to the landowner. "I don't understand," he glanced back at Cleo. "I was never told of this document."

"Well, you weren't the lawyer I talked to and after hearing Mr. Webber's response, I decided to turn my nose to the man and find some other land to mine." He shrugged. "My last diggings is about cleaned up and now I'm looking again. I just found out about the land transfer. Do you think Miss Young might be amenable?"

"I can't say for sure, however I can see no reason whatsoever that Miss Young would have a problem with this contract. But I am still very confused. I was Mr. Webber's lawyer for many years after 1854. I can't imagine him declining such an offer. Especially since he did not set up any kind of mine there himself. Are you sure you made it clear that gold was found there?"

"As clear as glass," Cleo crossed his arms. "His lawyer told me that Mr. Webber didn't take to my kind playing prospector on his land and to keep myself off his acreage or he'd find a way to back me into a noose."

"Did you ever talk to Mr. Webber yourself?" Asa asked.

"No never. The man refused to see me." Cleo was obviously offended.

"This does not sound like Patrick Webber." Asa glanced over the contract once more. "Mr. Webber was a savvy businessman. He'd have not taken an offer like this lightly." *And he would most certainly not have left his niece to inherit land where gold was discovered.* "Do you remember who you spoke with, Mr. Crisfield?"

"I don't recall the fella's name. Very tall, dark-haired fella'—about as friendly as my mule."

Asa appreciated the metaphors. "Does the name Drew Keene ring a bell?"

"Yes! Keene. That's the name. I only met with him twice. Once to make my offer and once to have him usher me out of his office."

Asa cleared his throat. "My client is out of town at the moment, but I believe it would be of interest to her. Can we talk again in about a week or two?"

"Absolutely. You're definitely not the lemon I expected to meet when I came to make my offer." Cleo rose to shake Asa's hand. "I'll be back to Santa Rosa in two weeks."

Asa walked the man to the door and scratched his head. This was going to need some immediate attention.

***

"Naomi was my oldest daughter." Bethany's grandmother sat in her favorite maple rocking chair with a faraway look in her eyes and smoothed her long brown and white gown. Nora was a petite woman in her early seventies. With silver hair worn in a fashionable bun and eyes the color of the morning sky, she was still beautiful.

Tanner sat beside David and Leah on Nora's beige couch and listened with interest as Nora gave the details of her daughters' lives.

"She was my quiet one," Nora continued. "As her mother, I could never tell if she was happy or not." Nora turned her eyes toward the long lace curtain hanging over one of her two parlor windows. "She was always kind and helpful, and I know she loved our Savior, but she simply kept to herself most of the time."

The others listened quietly.

"Her husband did all the talking in their family. Drew was nothing like Naomi and it's a wonder they ever married. He was an argumentative lawyer; tall and handsome with dark features and a masculine face. But he was absorbed with himself." Nora shook her head somberly. "I never like talking negatively about people, but I saw the way he hurt my daughter and found it difficult to warm to him."

Nora's big, fluffy calico provided a momentary distraction and Nora rubbed the cat tenderly.

"My second oldest daughter was Eleanor." Nora's eyes twinkled thoughtfully. "She was my sensitive one. Loved the Lord and loved His creation. Constantly rescuing butterflies, kittens, bunny rabbits and just about any other beautiful little creature that needed her. She was always looking for an opportunity to make someone smile. Without a doubt that was what drew Joel to my daughter.

"Joel swooped in and won my daughter's heart before Uriah and I knew he'd ever turned her head. We didn't know Joel well, but Eleanor was sure he was the man for her."

Nora leaned forward and reached for her tea. "Olivia was my rebellious one." A sad sigh escaped her lips. "She was the youngest. As pretty as could be but stubborn as a mule. A stronger willed child I've never seen. Uriah and I could never seem to reach her."

Tanner could see it was still painful to talk about.

"As a teenager, she moved in with Naomi and Drew. She'd made threats of running away so many times we felt that living with her older sister might help straighten her out. But it seemed to only get worse. She and Drew fed off one another. His pride mingled with her mischievousness almost drew poor Naomi to depression."

Leah moved to the chair next to Nora and took her hand comfortingly.

"When Olivia up and decided to marry Patrick Webber we were all thankful. Her decision was quick and irrational, but it got her out of Naomi's house and we hoped it would help Olivia mature.

"I always wished Olivia would have opened up to me. I wanted to be her mother. I could have helped her. But she had her best friend Violet and she was her only confidant."

Nora turned unsettled eyes on Leah. "Seven months after she married Patrick, Olivia gave birth to James." The older woman shook her head somberly. "Olivia was emphatic that James was born prematurely, but I've never seen a premature baby as big as James. With a thick thatch of dark brown hair and rolls of adorable baby fat, Olivia's boy was bigger than any of my three sons when

218

they were born."

All three of Nora's guests understood what Nora was trying to say.

"It's hard for me to imagine my daughter compromising the values she'd been raised with and engaging in a relationship with Patrick before their wedding day." Nora shook her head. "Uriah was beside himself. He confronted Patrick with harsh words, I'm afraid, but Patrick was unrelenting. He swore no improprieties and resented Uriah's accusations bitterly. Not long after, Patrick made plans to move west."

"Because of the accusations?" Leah asked.

"I believe that was part of it. There was a lot of gossip. Even Patrick's parents questioned the length of Olivia's pregnancy. But I think Patrick wanted to take his new wife where the gold was and do his best to make them rich." Nora glanced at Tanner. "They talked Eleanor and Joel into going with them… so two of my daughters moved away."

Unshed tears filled Nora's eyes. "Just a few years later, I lost Naomi. Her death came as a terrible surprise to all of us. Her husband, Drew, moved west to follow his brother-in-laws to the gold."

Tanner pondered Drew's name for a moment. "You said Drew was a lawyer… what was his last name?"

"Keene."

Tanner's eyes grew wide. "Drew Keene was Patrick's lawyer in Santa Rosa."

Nora nodded. "I'm not surprised. Olivia never told me what was going on in their lives. Any news I received about Olivia came through Violet, although Eleanor wrote often while she was alive. When she had her twins, she sent me a photograph." Nora pulled herself slowly from her chair and walked to a small frame sitting on a table in the corner of the room. "These are my grandbabies."

Tanner recognized the photograph. It was the same one Alan found in Marie's Bible.

It struck him as odd that Drew Keene was Olivia's brother-in-law and yet he told Sheriff Thacker that he had no memory of Bethany and Charlotte. How could an uncle forget that he had twin nieces?

219

"Mrs. Farnsworth," Tanner glanced curiously into Nora's blue eyes. "While in San Francisco, Sheriff Thacker questioned Mr. Keene concerning Bethany and Charlotte and yet the man made no mention of them being his nieces, nor of having any long lasting acquaintance between Olivia and Patrick."

Nora took in a deep breath and sighed. "I'm afraid you would need to talk to Violet about that. It seems Drew did have a falling out with Olivia and Patrick, although I know very little about it."

"Is Violet in the area?" Tanner felt that talking to Violet might be a good idea.

"She is my neighbor. She and her family live in her parents' old house just a couple farms away. I'm sure she would be willing to talk to you."

Tanner was anxious to do so.

"But now," Nora interrupted his thoughts. "You must tell me about my granddaughter. You said that you know Bethany." Nora's eyes lit up with a fresh burst of blue. "Please tell me all you can."

Tanner attempted to keep his own eyes from telling what his heart was feeling for this woman's granddaughter. "She looks like you," he began. "Her eyes are every bit as blue and she has that same look of joy." He smiled. "She became a Christian toward the end of Olivia's life and you will be overjoyed to learn that Olivia found forgiveness in Jesus Christ in her last days."

"Oh thank You, sweet Jesus," Nora proclaimed.

"Bethany is sensitive, resourceful and warmhearted." Tanner glanced beyond Nora and let his mind reflect on the woman he now knew he loved. "She can be funny and she can be serious." He glanced back at Nora. "She can also be very brave." He rolled up his sleeve and exposed his scar. "She saved my life." Tanner began to explain the whole story to Nora. "She knew I was the man taking her to prison to meet the hangman's noose, and yet she laid down her own life to save mine."

Tanner continued to explain how he'd come to believe her innocence and finally how the true details of the crime unfolded. Nora cried when she heard of Charlotte's fate and Leah knelt beside the older woman to comfort her.

"I am so sorry about Charlotte," Tanner said tenderly. "I know that their grandmother in Missouri could tell you more about her. Bethany was truly saddened to learn of her sister's death. She had no memory of Charlotte, but it grieved her to lose this long lost twin."

"Where is my Bethany now?" Nora asked.

"She is with her cousin, James, in San Francisco."

"Is she well?" Nora's voice quivered.

Tanner lowered his eyes for a moment. "I have not heard from her since she has gone to stay with Mr. Webber. I am sure he is keeping her busy." Tanner tried not to let Bethany's recent silence concern him. Surly her cousin must have her running around this new town, exploring, visiting shops and maybe shows.

"Mr. Brenly," Nora's eyes softened. "Your eyes tell me that you care for my granddaughter."

Tanner could keep it in no longer. His eyes warmed and his lips curved into a gentle smile. "You read me well, Mrs. Farnsworth. To be honest, I love your granddaughter."

Both David and Leah showed their genuine surprise.

"It is my intention to ask Bethany to marry me when I return to California. I suppose since Bethany has no father to ask, it would be appropriate to ask if I might have your blessing."

"My granddaughter… marry my pastor's brother? How could I refuse? You are a follower of Jesus Christ, I hope?"

"Yes, Ma'am, although I am a new Christian. In spite of my brother and my parents' many attempts, I have only just recently put my faith in the Lord." He smiled at his brother.

Nora smiled and pulled herself from her chair. "Dear Child." she reached for Tanner's hand.

Tanner rose to his feet and felt himself suddenly engulfed in Nora's arms. "You have my blessing and my prayers." She stepped back and studied his eyes.

"Will you be bringing my girl back to Vermont?"

"Maine—if that would suit you?"

Nora sniffed. "Maine is better than California. Although I would expect you to come visit Grandmother as often as possible."

"Most definitely." Tanner felt the older woman entwine her fingers in his and they sat back down on the sofa.

"How soon?" She obviously longed to see this long lost grandchild. "I have ten other grandchildren who all live near. At least I got to hold my dear little James before they took him off to California. Bethany and Charlotte are the only two I have never met. It breaks my heart."

"I will do my best, Mrs. Farnsworth. Provided she says yes."

***

Tanner was anxious to meet Violet Wilson. Nora's neighbor, and Olivia's old best friend, was a middle-aged woman with a full head of red hair softened by bits of white. She wore it high on her head, which suited her ample figure appropriately. She greeted Tanner uneasily when he explained the nature of his visit.

"I really don't like speaking of the dead," Violet explained as she led the way into her well-lit kitchen.

David and Leah dropped Tanner off at Violet's house with the promise to return for him in an hour.

"Yes, Olivia was my closest confidant. We were closer than sisters." Violet poured Tanner a cup of tea, added cream, several cubes of sugar, and handed it to him without invitation. "As I look back now I wish I'd have been a better friend to her. I didn't always speak my mind and that's why she liked me so well. But that's what I also lacked in genuine friendship."

Tanner took a sip of the tea and tried not to choke on its sweetness.

"Drew Keene was bad news." Violet shook her head emphatically. "There was a darkness about him that I never liked. But when Olivia moved in with him and Naomi, I liked him even less."

"Why?" Tanner asked.

Violet fidgeted nervously with the edge of her tablecloth. "They say it isn't right to speak ill of the dead."

"Mrs. Wilson, Olivia is with her Lord in Heaven. There is no need to fear speaking truth. Jesus is the author of truth."

Violet nodded. "Well… Olivia was only sixteen when she moved in with Naomi and Drew but she was as pretty as a spring flower and had bewitching eyes that she knew how to use. It didn't take her too long to turn Drew's eyes off Naomi and onto herself."

Tanner's stomach clenched at what he thought she might be about to say.

"When Olivia got pregnant she was terrified…"

"Drew got Olivia pregnant?" Tanner asked.

"Yes." Violet shook her head remorsefully. "She was wildly in love with Drew and he was infatuated by her beauty. But he couldn't risk people knowing he got her pregnant. He was a prominent lawyer in town. So he urged her to marry Patrick."

Tanner ran his hand through his hair and shook his head.

"Patrick always loved Olivia and it didn't take her but a few weeks to secure his heart. He had no idea she was already pregnant. They hurried and married—Patrick was probably afraid Olivia would change her mind. He was just as baffled as everyone else when his wife had a baby after seven months, but Olivia was adamant that James was simply early."

"And Patrick believed her?"

"He wanted to. His mother sure didn't, I'll tell you that. Mrs. Webber called Olivia all kinds of dishonoring words that a lady ought not speak. I think part of why Patrick was in a hurry to leave Vermont was to get away from all the speculations. The poor man wanted so badly to believe his wife." Violet sniffed.

"He was just a victim." Tanner could feel the man's hurt.

"Olivia wrote often to me when she moved. She hated the West at first. Patrick worked hard to give her the comforts she had while living with Naomi and I think she actually started to care for him. But then Drew moved to Santa Rosa."

"No…" Tanner lowered his eyes.

"Their affair didn't last long, but it all came out about James and then Patrick was never the same. He ran Drew out of town with threats that went beyond black mail. Patrick pulled away from his wife and son and Olivia could never get him back."

"What about Bethany? Where was she in all of this?"

"Bethany was Olivia's one joy," Violet said. "James was a reminder of Drew to both Olivia and Patrick. Neither of them wanted anything to do with their son. Olivia wrote long, terrible letters about how much James looked like his father and how she almost hated him." Violet shook her head. "She said she could hardly look at the boy."

Tanner couldn't imagine a mother hating her own son. "Does James know that Drew is his father?"

"I don't think so," Violet confessed. "I know that neither Patrick nor Olivia ever planned to tell the boy. I can't imagine what good it would have done for him to know that."

But to what advantage might it have been for Drew to let James know? Tanner felt suddenly fearful. Drew had lied about so much. Alan told Tanner that Drew acted like he hardly remembered this family... why? What motive could there have been in denying being Patrick's brother-in-law? Why deny knowing about Bethany and Charlotte?

"Drew is a dark, dark man, Mr. Brenly." Violet narrowed her eyes and leaned forward in her chair.

"It wasn't Patrick who broke up the relationship between Olivia and Drew." She stared steadily. "It was what Olivia found out about Naomi."

"What about Naomi?" Tanner's head was spinning with the direction this whole story was going. What else was he going to hear?

"Drew murdered Naomi."

Tanner's eyes grew wide. "What?"

"He told her," Violet said. "Drew confessed that his love for Olivia drove him to kill her sister. He killed Naomi so that he could move to California and be with Olivia. He wanted Olivia to help him murder Patrick so that she could be with him."

"How terrible!" Tanner shook his head with disgust. "Why didn't she report him?

"She told me that he agreed to keep her secret if she kept her silence. It was better to her than having the whole community know about her affair and about James."

"How did Patrick find out about James?" Tanner asked.

"She confessed to him. She wanted to make things right with Patrick. But it was too late and there was too much damage done. Patrick and James both lay victims to Olivia's wild passions and she suffered the bitterness of it for the rest of her life."

Olivia's story was heartbreaking. Tanner could hardly imagine the tragedy and sorrow Patrick and James must have suffered. Patrick through the knowledge of his wife's unfaithfulness and James through the rejection of his parents.

"But you never told Olivia's mother that Drew murdered her daughter?" Tanner wasn't sure how he felt about Violet's secret keeping.

Violet turned her gray eyes toward Tanner. "And to what end? Can you imagine the woman's sorrow at losing her eldest daughter escalated by the knowledge that the poor woman was murdered? Trust me, being the recipient of such knowledge was a terrible thing. But had I breached the silence, I may have put my friend's life at risk and at the very minimum, her reputation."

"And so this murderer was left to go free? What more damage might he have done?" A sudden realization gripped Tanner's heart. *What if Drew Keene was behind Patrick's murder? He had cause... and if he'd murdered once would he not do it again? But what motive would he have had in framing Bethany? How did she play into this picture? What would Mr. Keene have to gain by pinning the murder on Bethany? Unless he simply needed a scapegoat...* Tanner forced down the rest of Violet's sweet tea and sat up. He needed to send out a telegram. Were James and Bethany in danger? He had to reach Sheriff Thacker.

The arrival of David's wagon could not have come at a better time. He hated to tell his brother that his trip was about to be cut short, but Tanner knew he needed to get back to California. Back to Bethany.

Chapter 17

"Sheriff Thacker is in Sacramento," Rodney explained to Asa. "He had to deal with some issues concerning Sheriff Baker from Fairfield. That investigation has been like a splinter under Sheriff Thacker's fingernail I tell you. But it looks like Sheriff Baker will be losing his job." Rodney went on without a breath. "If that does happen, I've asked Sheriff Thacker to put in a good word for me. Can you imagine? I'd love to be sheriff of my own town."

Asa really did not have time to listen to Rodney ramble. "Do you know when Sheriff Thacker will be returning?"

Not one to get a hint, Rodney shook his head. "Don't know for sure. But can you imagine if I got hired in Fairfield? Even if it was only the deputy position."

"That would be wonderful, Rodney." Asa sighed. "But I need to get a message to the sheriff. Do you know where he's staying in Sacramento?"

Rodney walked to his desk and found the piece of paper where that information was written. "Yes. He's at the Fifth Street Hotel. I don't think that's a real fancy hotel. I hear there are some really nice ones in Sacramento. I'll bet you've stayed at some nice ones, being a lawyer and all…"

Asa glanced at his pocket watch. It was after five-thirty. The telegraph's office usually closed at five. "I'm going to head over to the telegraph's office. Maybe Coleman will still be there."

"I don't know. He's usually pretty good about leaving on time," Rodney said. "He brought a telegram over earlier today for the sheriff from Tanner Brenly. Tanner's in Maine, you know. But it sounds like Tanner is headed back." Rodney shrugged. "Sheriff asked me to quit reading his telegrams so I stopped myself. Only caught a few words."

Asa wondered what he should do.

"You might be able to catch Coleman at church on Sunday."

"I don't want to interrupt Coleman while at church."

Rodney grew suddenly curious. "What is it you need to tell Sheriff Thacker? Is everything okay?"

"Just some personal issues. Thanks, Rodney." He hurried out the door before Rodney could start another conversation with him.

True to Rodney's prediction, Coleman was gone for the day. Asa could kick himself. *Why didn't I get over here earlier?* He wanted to send a message to Sheriff Thacker concerning the gold on Bethany's land. Something at the pit of his stomach told him that Patrick Webber never knew about the gold and that for whatever reason, Drew Keene kept it silent.

Feeling that this was not something he should put in a telegraph to Bethany, Asa wrote a letter about the gold found on her land in Sacramento and Cleo's offer. He encouraged Bethany to get in touch with him as soon as possible.

Because of the time of day it looked like both the letter and getting a hold of Sheriff Thacker would have to wait until Monday.

***

Why did it feel like the train was moving slower going west than it did going east? Tanner sat impatiently in the dinner car staring out the window without really seeing the landscape as they moved past.

His parents understood about Tanner's need to return west early, although they both had hopes that upon his return he would be bringing a certain young lady who'd won his heart.

Tanner reached into his vest pocket and pulled out a small, leather pouch. Inside laid a simple gold ring with a fine cut blue topaz and two very small diamonds on either side and etched with a delicate design. Tanner removed the ring and placed it on the tip of his pointer finger to admire it. His lips tried to suppress the smile his eyes couldn't hide as he pictured it on Bethany's hand.

Would she have him? What if she said no?

227

This was Nora's wedding ring. Tanner remembered his surprise when Bethany's sweet grandmother pulled the ring off her finger and handed it to Tanner.

"Nothing would bring Uriah more joy than to know that his youngest granddaughter is wearing this ring." She placed it into Tanner's hand and closed his fingers around it.

Tanner opened his hand and glanced at the ring. "Mrs. Farnsworth... I can't..."

"My other grandchildren were all married before Uriah went to be with the Lord so they all have wedding rings of their own," Nora interrupted. "Anyway, I've given them presents all their lives. This is my chance to finally give something to my Bethany."

Tanner's eyes misted. "But what if she says no?"

Nora sighed. "Well then I suppose you can bring the ring when you move back to Maine." Her eyes changed to a twinkle and her lips curved into a smile. "But I don't count on her saying no. You said she's a lot like me. Well if that's the case, she knows a good thing when it's sitting right in front of her." Nora patted Tanner's arm and smiled. "I look forward to seeing that ring sparkling from her finger."

Tanner hoped Nora was right. And more importantly, he hoped his hunches about Drew Keene were wrong. Regardless, if he'd been party to Patrick's murder, Drew killed his own wife. But what could be done? It was a murder that took place over twenty-five years ago and Violet claimed she burned all the letters from Olivia. She was terrified to testify for fear that Drew Keene would turn his vengeance upon her and she also did not want Nora to know the truth.

Vengeance is Mine Sayeth the Lord. The verse popped into his mind.

Tanner tried to work though everything in his mind. It seemed clear that Drew had it in for Patrick. But why wait so long? Why wait close to twenty years? Was he just awaiting the right opportunity and Charlotte happened to be that "right opportunity"?

"Would you like more tea, sir?" A gentle voice broke through Tanner's thoughts.

"No, thank you." Tanner realized he'd been taking up a seat in the dinner car for a long time. It simply felt like a change of scenery from his cabin. Tanner wished there was a way to get to California faster.

***

Bethany's eyes grew wide as she walked into the large San Francisco church with her cousin's maid, Gloria. It was nothing like the small country church she attended in Santa Rosa. Huge arched windows of beveled glass lined the walls, while candlelit chandeliers hung from the ornately carved wood paneled ceiling. Gloria directed Bethany to an empty pew lined with soft red velvet cushions. *This is what we need in Santa Rosa... cushions.*

Bethany made herself comfortable and held her Bible tightly on her lap. It was nice to finally get out of the house.

Upon her cousin's encouragement, Bethany did some shopping in town with Gloria a couple times and had taken a few strolls in a nearby park. But Bethany was lonely for fellowship. While Gloria was very pleasant, she had responsibilities at the house and was limited as to when she could leave.

Bethany rose for the singing of the first hymn and closed her eyes as the words rolled off her tongue from memory. It was good to sing songs of worship. It was good to be in this place where she could be still. But her mind was distracted.

Why hadn't Tanner written to her since she'd been to San Francisco? Was James right? Had she been too forward? Did her letters to Tanner drive him away? The thought scared her. What would she do if Tanner pulled away from her?

She thought about the weeks they'd spent together in the saddle. Traveling from town to town, camping beside peaceful streams, gathering wood, sitting beside the fires talking late into the night. What about their time in Saint Louis? Sacramento? Bethany thought about the warmth of his hand in hers. She remembered that first time she took his hand when he was sick.

The singing stopped and the pastor led the congregation in the reading of a Psalm. Bethany did her best to concentrate on the reading of God's word.

"I will bless the LORD at all times; His praise shall continually be in my mouth. My soul will make its boast in the LORD; the humble will hear of it and rejoice. Oh, magnify the

229

LORD with me and let us exalt His name together. I sought the LORD and He delivered me from all my fears." Psalm 34:1-4 reached her ears and touched her heart. It was good to be reminded that when we seek the Lord, He will deliver us from our fears.

Bethany let herself meditate on those words again as she sat down with her Bible opened on her lap. *I sought the LORD and He delivered me from all my fears.*

Thank You Lord, for that reminder.

***

Tuesday afternoon, Bethany sat quietly beside her cousin as they rode the several city blocks to James' lawyer's office. Bethany knew nothing about the man, only that James planned on having the lawyer write Bethany into his will and was encouraging her to do the same.

With her blue eyes gazing out at San Francisco's hilly city streets, Bethany watched the landscape curiously. Tall Victorian style homes tightly squeezed along steep roads made a unique picture in her mind. Many of the neighbors paid special attention to landscaping and lovely flowers and shrubs lined the yards.

The lawyer's office was located amidst a crowded street of upscale offices. Bethany and her cousin were dropped off in front of one of the buildings and James led her inside quietly. Bethany noticed the smooth marble floor and ornately carved wood paneling on the walls. This was an expensive office building.

Bethany noted the name on the lawyer's door and reflected curiously. *Drew Keene. I know that name....*

Stepping inside, they were greeted by Mr. Keene's secretary, who led them into Mr. Keene's large, well furnished office.

"Mr. Webber, Miss Young, good afternoon. I trust you had a pleasant ride, Miss Young?" Drew motioned for two chairs on the other side of a long rectangular table.

"Yes." Bethany answered while her mind swam with questions.

"Mr. Webber, I've completed the write up for your new will and we can go over that first to make sure you do not have any questions," Drew said politely. Mechanically, he began to read through the terms of the will, making special note to Bethany of what her cousin's inheritance would mean for her.

Bethany's heartbeat quickened and she found it difficult to concentrate on this man's words. Her mind was elsewhere.

"Do you agree to the terms of this will, Mr. Webber?"

"Yes." James accepted the paperwork and signed on several lines.

"Wonderful," Drew pressed a seal beside James' signature. "Now, I have your papers, Miss Young." He began rattling off the terms of the will but Bethany wasn't listening. He turned the papers toward her and motioned for the pen.

Bethany glanced curiously at her cousin. Did James not recognize the name? Perhaps Sheriff Thacker and Asa Langley never showed the paperwork to James. Bethany shook her head. But there was more... she knew his face. His dark hair, now mixed with gray. His size. His nose. *Drew Keene... Drew Keene...* Bethany tried to draw the name from her memory. *Uncle Drew...* The realization gave her a start.

James and Drew both noticed the expression on Bethany's face.

"Is something the matter, Miss Young?" Drew asked.

Bethany licked her lips. "You're Uncle Drew." It rolled off her lips without thinking.

After a quick recovery from his surprise, Drew gave her an unconvincing smile. "You remember me?" he glanced at James and back to Bethany. "Why yes. I was married to your aunt before moving out west to become a lawyer."

"You were Uncle Patrick's lawyer."

"Yes. I was. How is it you would remember that? You were just a child..."

"You drew up the papers for my uncle when my father sold me to him." There was a look in Bethany's eyes that betrayed mistrust. "I saw those papers."

Drew scrambled to regain what trust he could. "Yes, Miss Young." He lowered his eyes. "Sadly, that was me." He exhaled. "It was an unusual arrangement, however you can not deny it proved to be for your own benefit."

"I have no regrets that I was raised by Aunt Olivia and Uncle Patrick. However, when Sheriff Thacker questioned you about me, you denied any memory." Her eyes pierced his.

"The terms of the agreement were that you were under no circumstance to be told. As the lawyer representing your uncle and aunt at the time, I am still accountable to my legal responsibilities toward them."

"But you lied." Bethany shook her head.

"In order to uphold my agreement to your parents, I was forced to maintain my silence."

"They were searching for a murderer. I would think your agreement would find within itself the sensibility to lay aside a contract for truth." Bethany felt herself recoil from this man.

"Miss Young…"

"Did you know I was a twin?" Bethany interrupted.

James placed a restraining hand on her shoulder. "Bethany, enough of this."

"No. I want an answer." She narrowed her eyes on Drew.

"Yes, Miss Young. One of the terms of the agreement, which you seem to have read, stated that you were not to be made aware of your twin." Drew used an exasperated tone.

"I am sorry then." Bethany rose from the table. "I can not have you be the writer of my will because you are a liar."

"Sit back down, Bethany," James ordered.

"No, James. I wish to leave. I will have Asa Langly draw up my will." She began walking toward the door.

"Miss Young," Drew called to her. "Bethany!"

Bethany turned to him. "Do not call me Bethany."

"I was your uncle."

"You denied knowing me," Bethany shot back. "And for whatever reason, my uncle chose to discontinue your services as a lawyer and you moved away."

"I moved because I wanted to begin practicing law in San Francisco. Your father simply wanted a lawyer who resided in Santa Rosa." Drew took a step closer to Bethany. "Ask James. He knows. I've been James' lawyer for a few years now."

"Bethany," James rose to his feet. "You can trust Drew." He used the man's first name.

"No. I'm sorry… I don't feel good about this right now. I need to think." She opened the office door. "I can find another ride home."

***

After Bethany left, Drew returned to the table with a fire in his eyes. "She remembered me?" He sat down and punched the table. "We are so close! So close!" He glanced at her unsigned will. "All I need is her signature."

"We can have Mr. Langly draw up the will. It won't change anything," James said.

"Except suspicions and control. I don't want Asa Langly having any control over that will. If he learns that there is gold…"

"I will talk with my cousin. Surely she can be convinced."

Drew shook his head. "The time for niceties is over."

"What are you suggesting?"

"I'm suggesting force," Drew said. "She's going to die anyway. It's time to pull out all the stops."

"How can you force her signature?"

Darkness peered through Drew's eyes. "Tell me… what does Bethany truly care about?"

James considered this for a moment. He reached into his brief case and handed Drew the telegraph he'd intercepted on Friday. "She cares about him." James pointed at the name.

Drew snatched the telegram. "When were you going to tell me that Tanner Brenly was coming to see her?" Angry eyes flashed at James.

"Upon his arrival, I planned to tell Mr. Brenly that my sister has no interest in him and ask the man to discontinue correspondence."

"They write?" It was obvious that Drew did not appreciate just now learning this information. "This is something you should have told me."

"I've intercepted their recent correspondence. I already had a plan to turn the deputy's eyes off my sister." James got up and walked to the counter where Drew kept his alcohol. "Their letters are simply the musings of two innocents with a crush. I've destroyed them."

233

Drew watched James as he carried his glass of brandy to the table and sat back down. "If Mr. Brenly is on his way to San Francisco, we may have found the way to get her to sign." A sinister smirk crossed the man's lips and he leaned back in his chair to consider his options.

***

With what little money she had, Bethany paid the driver and hurried into her cousin's house. She feared the wrath she would receive from James upon his return, but something deep in her heart recoiled from Drew Keene. The man scared her. She didn't trust him.

Gloria met Bethany in the hallway. "I didn't expect you back already." She held a duster in her hands and showed signs of dirt on her dress. "Is everything alright?"

Bethany blew out a sigh. Gloria was a good woman. Bethany wished she could trust her the way she had Marie. *Perhaps some day.* "I'm just a bit flustered. Legal issues are a bit complicated."

"Well, perhaps this will cheer you." Gloria hurried to James' office and carried back two letters. "I'd set them on your cousin's desk for him to give you, but since you are here." She handed Bethany the letters. "These just came today."

A letter from Tanner! Bethany could almost not contain her joy. "Thank you!" She hurried up the long winding staircase to her bedroom and climbed onto the soft white spread to read her long awaited epistle.

Tanner's letter started out with how much he missed her and longed to hear from her. "I am sure you are very busy with your cousin, but I confess I miss your encouraging letters."

Bethany couldn't understand this comment.

"Tomorrow I am leaving with my brother and his family for Vermont." His letter continued. "I am investigating a possible connection with your mother's family. So you see, even three thousand miles away I can not get you from my mind." Bethany smiled at those words. "I do not want to get your hopes up, but I promise to tell you as soon as I learn anything."

His letter continued with the things he'd done the past few days and made reference to another letter he'd written, none of which was familiar. Bethany tried to understand it. How is it she received this letter but not the others that he mentioned?

"I hope to hear from you soon," his conclusion began. "Yours dearly, Tanner."

Bethany pressed the words to her heart and felt two tears squeeze out of her eyes. She was so relieved to hear from Tanner. But where were his other letters?

The letter from Asa Langly seemed insignificant in comparison, but Bethany opened it and began to read. Her eyes widened as she read about the gold discovered on her Sacramento land and she felt suddenly overwhelmed.

"The terms of Cleo Crisfield's offer are fair. It would require the least amount of commitment from you and yet guarantee you a significant portion of the profits," Bethany read. "As your lawyer, I am willing to represent you in all business dealings with Mr. Crisfield, if you choose to name me that position. Although, no hard feelings will be felt should you choose another."

Dear Mr. Langly... of course I would chose you. Bethany felt a deeper sense of trust for her lawyer than before.

"I told Mr. Crisfield I would have an answer to him within two weeks. I would like to talk with you concerning this matter. I understand that you are visiting with your cousin, but am asking that you might consider returning to Santa Rosa for a few days."

Bethany could think of nothing she'd rather do. In spite of Tanner being away, Santa Rosa appealed to her far more than San Francisco.

***

"Well, Son, it appears that dear Mr. Brenly may have saved the day." Drew turned the telegram over in his fingers and grinned.

James finished the contents of his glass and rose for a refill. "I don't understand."

"Of course you wouldn't." Drew scowled at his son. "We will hold Miss Young captive and give her the option of signing the will and encouraging Mr. Brenly to return to Santa Rosa or witnessing the death of her dear Mr. Brenly."

"More death." James stood by the window and drank his brandy.

"You knew all along that Bethany had to die." James gathered the paperwork and walked to his desk.

"But someone else was supposed to do the dirty work. She was supposed to hang." James spun around. "You knew I wanted nothing to do with the killing. Nothing!" He finished his drink and slammed the glass down on the desk. "And what happened? I was the one who had to finish off Marie!

"You did the right thing, James," Drew told his son. "Marie knew it wasn't Bethany. She was putting things together."

"Do you have any idea what that did to me?" James ran his fingers through his hair. "To see her eyes staring at me before I snuffed out her life with a pillow?"

Drew walked to his son and stared at him with shame. "She was a servant!"

James shook his head. "She trusted me. She was confiding in me... she thought that I might be in danger."

"The only danger you were in was that she was telling others that it wasn't Bethany."

James lowered himself into a chair and massaged his temples. "She loved me."

"Don't lie to yourself! None of them loved you!" Drew spat. "Bethany was the pride and joy of the Webber household. I witnessed it when I was Patrick's lawyer. You were the bastard child who reminded both Patrick and Olivia of me." Drew took another step closer to James. "I've always been the one that loved you... my son. My only child." He stared at James. "And yet I was forbidden the opportunity to know you."

"I can't kill Bethany." James turned pleading eyes to Drew. "I can't bear to murder another soul."

"I won't ask you to." Drew turned to the window. "But she will still have to die."

Chapter 18

It was late when James returned home. He spoke very little to Bethany and went to bed. She figured he was angry with her for the scene she'd made at Drew Keene's office. It grieved her to upset her cousin, but something at the pit of her stomach told her that Mr. Keene was not to be trusted.

After taking a small meal with Gloria, Bethany returned to her bedroom for the night to reread Tanner's letter and revel in the day he would return from Maine and she could see him again. She'd counted the days. Tanner would be returning to Santa Rosa in less than two weeks. There would be so much to talk about.

Bethany could hardly imagine what it meant for her that gold had been found on the land she'd inherited from her aunt. She would need to talk with her lawyer about James. Should she give him a portion of the gold? He was her cousin and it was his parents who purchased the land. It only seemed right.

She hoped this discovery would not lead to resentment from James. It would not be worth any amount of gold to lose family. Things were already tense between James and herself and Bethany didn't understand why.

In the two weeks that she'd been with James in San Francisco, there seemed to be a wall between them. It was worse now than in Santa Rosa. Perhaps this was how James was all the time. How long had it been since she and James took a ride on their horses together or went fishing? They were just children the last time they'd really talked.

Bethany's mind raced for hours and it was late when she finally drifted off to sleep. But even her sleep was not restful. She had a myriad of unsettling dreams through the night.

Bethany felt the presence in her bedroom before she saw anyone.

When she first woke to the sound of footsteps in her bedroom, Bethany wondered if it was another strange dream. The room was dark, but someone was there. "Gloria?" Bethany whispered.

The sweet smell of chloroform met her senses as a firm hand forced a rag over her mouth and nose. Bethany's world went black.

***

Tanner found it difficult to sit still the more familiar the sights out the window became. Concern mingled with excitement made the hours feel like days and the minutes feel like hours.

Assuming that Bethany was still in San Francisco, Tanner opted to go there first, hoping he was right. James' mailing address would be enough to get him to her and Tanner kept the important street address in his vest pocket, close to his heart.

This was his last day on the train, but it felt like the longest. He'd walked through every car on the train, wrote letters, attempted to read, and drank several glasses of tea, just to make the time go faster.

Tanner hoped Sheriff Thacker received his telegraph and the letter he'd written. It would be helpful if his trusted friend got a head start on investigating Mr. Keene.

Friendly passengers stopped to talk, also in need of distractions from the miles of track they'd been traveling. A young married couple sat across from him for over an hour, swooning over one another as they told Tanner about their trip across the country. California would be their halfway point. Upon learning that Tanner lived in California for over five years, they asked him what sights they should see and the best routes to travel.

"So you're a real live deputy of the wild west?" The young bride sounded impressed.

Tanner shrugged. "I really hadn't thought of it that way. But I am a deputy."

"Have you ever met Jesse James?" she continued. "My brother said Jesse James has robbed banks all over the west. I've read about Jesse James, but I can't imagine actually seeing him for real…"

"No. I've never met Jesse James." Tanner stifled a chuckle. He was aware that people back east were beginning to create a kind of folklore about the infamous Jesse James, but he never thought about meeting the man.

"Have you ever had to stop a stage coach robbery?" she pressed.

Her new husband narrowed his eyes on her in a noticeable scowl.

"No. There haven't been any stage coach robberies in Santa Rosa since I've been deputy."

"What about wild Indians?"

"I've not had any negative encounters with Indians."

"See, Amy, all your stories about the Wild West are just myths," Amy's husband jabbed at her. "You need to get all those silly notions out of your head."

There was a lot of truth to Amy's stories, but Tanner was growing embarrassed by this young lady's apparent fascination with his position so he opted not to defend her.

"I was only curious. I've read some pretty exciting books." She snuggled up closer to her husband and seemed to make him feel a little better.

"Are you married, Deputy?" the husband asked.

"Not yet. Although I'm hoping to solve that problem." He smiled more to himself than to the couple.

"Oh really?" Amy gushed. "Are you about to propose?"

The light in Tanner's eyes gave away his secret.

"That's so exciting!" She squeezed her own husband's hand tighter. "When?"

"I'm hoping I can talk to her as soon as I get to San Francisco."

The young husband wished him luck. "We'll pray she says yes."

"Thank you. Please do," Tanner said.

***

The ropes that bound Bethany's wrists cut into her soft skin as she attempted to free herself from the metal railing she was tied to. It was useless. She was secured to a strong metal banister at the top of a narrow stairway in a house she did not recognize. Her feet were bound as well, although from her position against the banister, Bethany would not have been able to run away if she tried. She pulled herself into a sitting position and tucked her legs under the edge of her nightgown.

She glanced down the hallway, trying in vain to recognize where she might be.

Bethany had no concept of the time. From the light coming through a nearby gambrel window, she figured it was at least noon. How long had she been unconscious? Her throbbing headache was a testimony to the chloroform used to knock her out.

Where am I? Why am I here? She vaguely recalled a person walking through her bedroom. She'd not seen any faces, but she could still feel his firm hand cover her mouth, holding the anesthesia to her face while she fought to hold her breath. The fight only lasted a moment before the chloroform and the strength of her captor won out.

"Good morning, Miss Young," Drew Keene said as he walked up the staircase. He was carrying a lit cigar and smiling condescendingly. "Its good to see you're finally awake."

Bethany's heartbeat quickened and she pulled futilely at her wrists.

"You know, you're only going to hurt yourself by trying to do that." Drew pulled a chair into the hallway and sat across from her. "That railing is rod iron. You're not going anywhere."

"What are you doing? Why am I here?" she asked him the questions that whirled through her aching head.

A smooth grin moved across Drew's lips. "It's that little issue of the will."

Bethany shook her head. "And you think making me your prisoner will make me sign?"

"It's not just about signing the will, Miss Young. It's about dying."

"I will never sign anything you write."

Drew took a long draught from his cigar and blew the smoke in Bethany's direction. "I was afraid you might say that." He stared at her with a sadistic grin for a moment. "That's why I have a little insurance." He reached forward and held Tanner's telegram in front of her face. "Recognize that name?"

Tanner's on his way to San Francisco?

"I thought so." Drew read Bethany's expressive eyes. "And from what I understand, you care deeply for this young man. Twice now, you've saved his life. Is that right?"

Bethany didn't answer.

"Let's see… there was the man who tried to shoot him and then you nursed him back to health in a cave. That's special." Drew smiled mockingly. "I think you must really like him. Maybe even love?"

How does he know? Did James tell this man my story? "What do you want?" Bethany was tired of the game Drew was playing.

Drew cleared his throat. "So we're willing to listen now are we?" he laughed. "I thought that might get your attention. Apparently your friend, Tanner Brenly, is on his way to San Francisco. And since this message was sent last Friday, he is probably almost here. I've heard the train is ahead of schedule."

Bethany tugged at her wrists and tried to keep her eyes from tearing up.

Drew leaned forward in his chair and grinned.

"What does Tanner have to do with all of this?" She asked.

"He's my leverage." Drew chuckled. "It makes it too easy really. Since you messed up our plan the last time by discovering your sister, we've had to scramble to come up with another plan."

"My sister? What do you mean?" Bethany felt her breathing increase.

"Awww… you didn't know her did you?" Drew chortled. "She really wasn't much like you. I'll confess you are far prettier. That should make you happy, right?"

Bethany held her lips together tight.

"She didn't have quite the stunning blue eyes and she definitely didn't have your slim figure and graceful facial features. You look more like your grandmother." Drew took another puff of his cigar. "I hated your grandmother."

None of this was making sense to Bethany.

"But back to your sister. She actually found me." Drew laughed. "Ironic, isn't it? She was short of cash and thought that since she was Patrick Webber's niece, she should have her cut in your money. Once I realized that she and I were kindred spirits, we

241

began to really dream together. She thought she could pose as you and break into the house, steal a little money and get away just a little richer. I liked her plan. Except, I had another plan. I wanted Patrick Webber dead."

Bethany could hardly believe what she was hearing. "You killed Uncle Patrick?"

"Actually no, I had a henchman for that. But he did a great job and made it look like you did it. Charlotte was simply a decoy. It was her, however who went to the bank and made that enormous withdrawal. We forced Patrick to pen that beautiful letter before he was shot in the head. Too bad for him, he thought the signature would buy him his life." Drew laughed. "He had no idea I was behind all this. But I will tell you, he did know that it was Charlotte. So you can feel good that Uncle Patrick did not die angry with you."

"Did my sister know that you planned to kill Uncle Patrick?"

Drew grinned. "Not exactly. But once the plan played itself out, we made sure she remained silent."

"You murdered my sister?" Bethany's heart ached as the story unfolded.

"Why would that bother you? This same sister was ready and willing to have you framed for robbery. I should think you would thank me."

Bethany ignored that comment. Her arms ached as they stretched over her head. She tried to position herself more comfortably while listening to this sick man's story. "Why would you want to kill Uncle Patrick?"

"Because he took from me the only woman I ever loved and he raised *my* son."

"Your son?" Bethany tried to understand this crazy man.

"Yes, Bethany. There was a skeleton in Aunt Olivia's closet." Drew seemed to be enjoying the mental torment he was putting Bethany through. "James is my child. My only child."

Bethany shook her head.

"Why would I make that up?"

"You're a sick man."

Drew leaned forward and slapped Bethany hard across the face. "Don't you dare talk to me that way!"

Bethany closed her eyes against the pain.

"I was Olivia's first love. She married Patrick to protect her reputation. For years I had to watch while my son grew up believing he was Patrick Webber's son. My poor boy never understood why the man he believed to be his father treated him with contempt. James bore his name, but not his blood. James is a Keene through and through."

In spite of her desire to deny the possibility, Bethany could see incredible similarities between James and Drew. *Poor Uncle Patrick.*

"But it isn't only revenge I want." Drew took a final draught from his cigar and carried it to another room to douse it. "I want something you inherited." His eyes narrowed on Bethany and he smiled as he returned to the chair. "Had my brother-in-law left that land to my son, I could have left it be. But they planned to give it to you - the one who robbed my boy of his mother's love."

"Aunt Olivia loved James," Bethany argued.

"Not once you arrived." Drew leaned forward. "You with all your pretty dresses, sweet little smiles and playful personality. I watched from the sidelines, helpless while my boy got slighted."

"He can have the land—I don't care about the gold."

Drew's eyes grew wide with surprise. "Gold?"

"Isn't that what you want?"

"How do you know about the gold?" His eyes ceased being cynical and were now angry.

"My lawyer wrote this week to tell me."

"You lie!" Drew made a motion to smack her again but Bethany turned her face away.

Her eyes were wet with tears. "He can have the land. I don't care about the gold. I'll sign it over with Mr. Langly... *my* lawyer."

Drew stood up and paced the floor. "No! That's not how this game will be played. I'm writing the story."

Bethany's eyes flashed with fear and anger. "God is writing my story."

The back of Drew's hand met Bethany's cheek. "Don't sass me!"

Bethany clenched her teeth and sank lower against the railing, wishing there was a way to bring her arms down and bury her face in her hands.

"Here is my plan, Miss Young." Drew sat back down. "Deputy Brenly will be invited to your cousin's home for dinner so that you can announce your engagement to William Prescott. Since apparently Deputy Brenly is interested in you, it is important that he believes you do not return his feelings. A new fiancé should make it clear to him. At some point in the evening, you will dismiss yourself and meet me in a quiet room where you will sign the will."

Bethany shook her head.

"Deputy Brenly will return to Santa Rosa unharmed and you will be involved in a fatal boating accident just a few days before your wedding and never be seen again."

Great tears filled Bethany's eyes. "I cannot lie to him."

"The choice is up to you," was Drew's heartless reply. "You can either be a liar... like your dear Uncle Drew, or you can tell the truth and watch the man you love die right before your eyes and know it was your fault. Because I promise you," Drew leaned forward. "If you do not convince the dear deputy that you have no interest in him and if you do not sign the will, Tanner Brenly will die."

No... Bethany's body wilted under her bound arms and she sobbed into her aching shoulder.

"I will give you some time to consider your options. We will need to watch for Deputy Brenly's arrival."

Bethany heard him leave and poured her heart out to God.

***

"Deputy Brenly." James rose from his desk chair to greet Tanner at the entrance to his study. "How fortunate that you caught me at home today. Usually I'm at my office this time of the day. Bethany warned me that you would be arriving soon. How was your visit home?"

"It was good." Tanner noticed the strong smell of alcohol on James' breath. "Is Bethany available?" He didn't waste time asking.

"Ah, yes. She is with some good friends for the day. She sent her regards and hopes to see you while you're in San Francisco. How long will you be here?" James took a long sip of wine and carried his empty glass to the counter where he kept more. "Would you care for a glass?" he asked before Tanner could answer the other question.

"No. Thank you." Tanner watched James refill his drink and carry it back to his chair. "I was hoping to see Bethany. When do you expect her back?"

"She might be home tomorrow. I'm not sure. You know how it is with young love."

Tanner tilted his head curiously. "Young love?"

James downed his glass. "Did she not write about Mr. Prescott?"

Tanner wasn't sure how to respond to this. Bethany hadn't written to him in weeks. "No," he finally confessed.

"Well, I'll let her tell the story. I won't rob her of the surprise."

Tanner shifted uneasily.

"I know she will be anxious to see you. Why don't you plan to dine with us on Friday?" James suggested. "I am in terrible need of amusement. My cousin has been so busy since her arrival. It would be nice to see a face from Santa Rosa for a change." He attempted to drink the last few drops from his glass. "Although, I confess, Bethany and I both feel like Santa Rosa is just a place of bad memories. I'm not sure either of us ever care to return."

Tanner clenched his jaw and tried not to let himself arrive at any conclusions. Not until he saw Bethany. Why would she not plan to be home when she knew of his upcoming arrival? He'd explained that he had important news.

"I do hate to rush you off, Deputy," James tidied a pile of papers on his desk. "But I am swamped. Between business and home responsibilities, I have gotten so little done since my father's passing. Will Friday work for you?"

"Yes. Friday will be fine. Please notify me if Bethany arrives home before that time." Tanner asked. He quickly scribbled down his hotel and room number. "This is where you can reach me."

"Wonderful," James glanced with pleasure at Tanner's address. "Have a nice stay in the city."

Tanner walked from James' study with his mind in absolute confusion. This was not the reception he'd been prepared for. *Where is Bethany? Who is Mr. Prescott? Is he the 'young love' James referred to?*

Prepared to let himself out, Tanner walked to the front door by himself.

"Excuse me," the woman who'd let Tanner into the house spoke softly from behind him.

Tanner turned, with one hand still on the door. "Yes."

"Miss Young misses you dearly." She walked toward the door. "I have never seen her blue eyes sparkle so much as they did when she received your last letter."

Tanner's expression conveyed his confusion. He wanted to ask questions. He wanted to understand. "When did she leave?"

Gloria glanced over her shoulder. "I am not sure. Mr. Webber sent me to town early this morning to pick a few things up. Miss Young must have left sometime after I did."

Tanner nodded.

"But I know she will be disappointed that she missed you."

"Thank you." Tanner walked outside and watched Gloria close the door.

***

Sheriff Thacker walked into his office and sighed when he saw the pile of papers and mail scattered carelessly all over his desk. Alan never expected to have to stay in Sacramento for a week over this Fairfield sheriff incident. Because Tanner was in Maine, Alan was required to present any and every statement he could concerning Tanner and Bethany's treatment while they were in Baker's custody. He also provided the judge with Baker's misleading telegraph.

But his time there was not fruitless. Baker was no longer sheriff of Fairfield and the family was completely exposed for their unlawful control of the town. While Alan's involvement was minimal, he was asked to stay during the proceedings to aid in protecting those testifying against Mr. Baker.

The former sheriff and several of his accomplices were now serving time for their criminal deeds.

Alan poured himself a cup of cold coffee and sat at his desk to sort through the mess. *Couldn't Rodney have taken care of any of this while I was gone?* Alan sighed.

For several hours Alan dug through the letters, filed paperwork and gave a few quick replies where needed.

Tanner's letter and his telegram were toward the bottom of the pile. Obviously they'd been here a few days.

Alan read Tanner's cryptic message that he was going to San Francisco and that this thing was not over. The letter that followed gave the specifics.

Alan rubbed his forehead as the details unfolded.

"Unfortunately, we have no proof that Mr. Keene murdered his wife," Tanner wrote. "But this is telling of the man's character. His elicit affair with Mrs. Webber and his resentment toward Mr. Webber would give him motive to murder his brother-in-law. Please begin your investigation as soon as my letter arrives. I will be home shortly."

The sound of Rodney whistling a happy little tune broke through Alan's thoughts.

"Rodney," he motioned toward the telegram. "Why did you not notify me that Deputy Brenly was coming home early?"

"Well I figured he'd get a hold of you himself." Rodney approached the desk and smiled. "I gave Asa Langly your address. Did you get a telegram from him? Look at how much you got done today."

"Yeah, well, I'm behind..." Alan stood up and carried the telegram and letter toward the door. He had received a telegram from Asa Langly while he was in Sacramento and wondered now if there could be some connection.

***

Sitting alone at a table in the hotel restaurant, Tanner stared outside the large, picture frame window, watching people as they

247

walked past. In spite of the many different faces and new sights, he was distracted. His reception hadn't been what he'd expected at Bethany's cousin's house and Tanner wasn't sure what to do with his emotions.

Tanner recognized that Bethany would not have known what time to expect him to arrive in San Francisco and he couldn't expect her to sit around waiting. But who was Mr. Prescott and why had James made that comment about 'young love'? Was James drunk? Was that just the alcohol speaking?

A friendly waitress brought Tanner a refill on his iced tea and he thanked her aloofly.

From his pocket, Tanner pulled out the little leather pouch where he kept Nora's ring. It wasn't as large and fancy as rings he'd seen on some of the wealthier women he knew. Would Bethany resent its simplicity?

Tanner took a sip of his tea. *No. Bethany would love that it belonged to her grandmother. She's not attached to showiness and wealth.* He studied the delicate stone and gold setting. *If she doesn't like it, I'll be able to afford something bigger once I start working for my father.*

Another worry crossed through Tanner's mind. What if Bethany didn't want to move to Maine? What if she wanted to stay in San Francisco as her cousin suggested? Tanner had no desire for the big city. He also lacked a career opportunity here. In Rockland he could work for his father and be certain to provide for his family.

Why am I worried about these things, Lord? He prayed silently. *I know You have this under control.*

He slipped the ring back into its leather pouch and into his vest pocket, close to his heart.

He'd be seeing Bethany tomorrow. How could one day feel so far away?

***

A cold, dirty jail cell was nothing compared to this. Bethany's arms ached from their position on the metal railing. Her head throbbed and her mouth was dry with thirst. She was too frightened to feel hunger, but she longed for just a sip of water.

The man apparently dismissed his staff for a couple of days because Bethany heard no servants and Drew assured her that no amount of screaming would bring help.

He'd given her until the morning to make her decision. Would she lie to Tanner to save his life or watch them murder him when he arrived at her cousin's house for dinner Friday evening? Drew promised her that it would be a slow and painful death.

Bethany prayed and cried and prayed some more, asking for direction… any kind of hope. She had no doubt of her own death. Drew made it clear that after the paper was signed she would meet her end and be buried at sea. Her own death didn't frighten Bethany. But hurting Tanner did.

What would be worse? Breaking his heart or watching him die? Both options tore her heart to pieces. But Bethany knew which one she had to choose.

Perhaps Tanner did not feel the same for her that she felt for him. Maybe he would be happy for her 'engagement.' Bethany tried to find hope in those painful thoughts.

When her uncle found her, still sitting on his cold, hard floor, she'd made up her mind. She would lie to save Tanner's life.

Chapter 19

"How do we put these pieces together to actually form a case?" Sheriff Thacker sat across from Asa Langly in the lawyer's office and reread Cleo's offer one more time. "We know Mr. Keene was made aware of the gold and it appears he never told Mr. Webber."

"But because Patrick Webber is deceased, we have no proof that he was never told," Asa added.

Alan leaned back in the leather-covered chair and scratched his head. "Then there is the case of Bethany and Charlotte. We know Mr. Keene knew about the twins and lied about it, but we can't prove anything with that."

"And as to these accusations that he murdered his wife," Asa held Tanner's letter in his hand. "Without any testimony from the woman in Vermont, nor any existing evidence, we can't prove this either."

"So what do we actually have on the man?" Alan blew out a heavy sigh. "We know from Tanner's letter that Mr. Keene is James Webber's actual birth father, but even that doesn't give us a case."

Asa got up from his desk and walked to the window. The two men had been talking for hours and they were both tired. "I'm unsettled, Alan," Asa turned to the sheriff. "Something at the pit of my stomach doesn't feel right about giving up on this."

"The man they arrested in San Francisco said that he didn't know who hired him," Alan remembered. "That could be something."

"It's a lead... but its not conclusive evidence." Asa sat back down. "Do you know if Tanner has arrived in San Francisco yet?" he asked.

"No." Alan shook his head. "I had hoped he'd send another telegraph."

"Why don't we just go there?" Asa suggested.

"Just go to San Francisco?" It didn't sound like a bad idea. "But where do we start?"

"Let's talk to Mr. Keene about his wife." Asa shrugged. "Let's see how he responds to a few questions about her death."

"We have to be careful not to put this woman from Vermont in danger." Alan reminded Asa.

"Well, there are plenty of things for us to ask him about. If he's innocent, he shouldn't have a problem with our questions."

Alan agreed. "When do you want to leave?"

"Tomorrow morning."

"I'll talk to Jane tonight and make sure Rodney is ready to run things in town for another day or two." Alan fully expected another desk full of unfinished paperwork when he returned.

***

Gloria had been dismissed for the day and Bethany was brought to her cousin's house as a prisoner. Drew shoved her through the door with the end of his gun and ushered her into James' study, where he sat talking with another man.

Bethany stood trembling in her long white night gown. Her hair hung in long loose curls down her aching shoulders. She was weak with hunger and thirst and her world was falling apart before her. Bethany's blue eyes implored her cousin. "James... please..."

James turned away to refill his glass of brandy.

"Well hello, Bethany." The other man walked toward her and extended his hand. "It is good to finally meet you face to face."

She recognized his voice immediately. This was one of her captors from the cabin. His green eyes peered out from a young, world-hardened face, but instead of the denim pants, dirty flannel, and bandana he'd worn the last time she saw him, he wore a new dark suit of exemplary fashion and a smug smile. *Why is he here?*

"Bethany, meet William Prescott, your fiancé." Drew motioned toward the man.

"My dear," the man who'd adopted the fictitious name reached for Bethany's hand but she recoiled.

"Put that on," Drew handed Bethany a large diamond ring. "It was your aunt Naomi's. I'm going to allow you to borrow it."

Bethany held the ring curiously. She'd never met Aunt Naomi. How strange to hold something that belonged to her mother's older sister.

Drew motioned for Bethany to be seated and took the chair across from her. "I want you to understand the seriousness of this situation." His eyes bore heavily into hers. "You've got to play this well. If Tanner so much as suspects that something is wrong, he will die. Do you understand me?"

Bethany lowered her frightened blue eyes and licked her dry lips.

"William Prescott is your new fiancé. It needs to be convincing. Tanner needs to see no reason that he should remain in San Francisco. If you do your job and he leaves, then he will live." Drew's sinister eyes bore into Bethany's. "But if you try to give him any hints, any secret message, and he lingers… then the man you love will meet William's .44 Magnum. Am I clear?"

Bethany nodded.

"I asked you a question!" Drew raised his voice.

"Yes." She glanced past him toward her cousin. *Why? Why is James doing this?*

"Deputy Brenly will be here in a couple of hours," Drew continued. "My personal cook has prepared a wonderful meal for you to enjoy."

"Where is Gloria?" Bethany realized she'd not seen the one person who would recognize this fabricated story for what it was.

"James gave Gloria the day off."

Bethany prayed it wasn't the same "day off" they'd given Marie.

"You are to go to your room and clean yourself up. Your cousin selected your gown. William will be right outside your door in case you think of trying to leave." Drew motioned for William.

"But know this fact, Bethany." Drew clutched her arm before she walked passed him. "If any of this falls through… Tanner Brenly will die."

William grabbed Bethany and led her through the house and up the stairs to her room at gunpoint.

As soon as Bethany stepped into her room, she locked the door and let her tears finally fall. How could she do this? How could she pretend she had no feelings for Tanner? How could she let the man she loved suffer the pain of believing she'd given her heart to another?

Bethany sank to the bed and buried her face in her hands. *I can't do this, Lord...* Her body shook in quiet sobs.

"You best be getting ready in there." A knock on Bethany's door drove her from her tears.

The options were clear. If she didn't play this game, Tanner would be murdered. There were three of them, armed and ready to kill, and while she was sure Tanner would be wearing his gun, he was unsuspecting and outnumbered. What else could she do?

As much as she longed to soak her pained muscles in her small tub, Bethany hurried to clean herself up. The smell of her lavender soap did little to calm her nerves.

One of her new dresses hung from the wardrobe door, ready for her to wear. Bethany was glad it was not her favorite one. She didn't want Tanner to see her in the dress she'd purchased while she'd thought of his tastes.

The long light brown satin hung gracefully over her slim form. A trim of white lace graced the sleeves and neckline and tiny tatted flowers dotted the bodice. Bethany smoothed the wrinkles from her dress and did her best to set her hair into an attractive bun. Her eyes were still red from crying and she rubbed her bruised sore wrists, wondering how she would keep Tanner from noticing them.

Another knock told her to hurry.

Bethany stepped from the room and faced William nervously.

"You clean up nicely." William gave her a shameless grin. "You need to present a nice act, Miss Young." He put his arm out for Bethany to take. "Because Deputy Brenly's life depends on it."

Bethany nodded.

It took every bit of strength Bethany had to place her hand through this murderer's arm. He placed his other hand on top of her wrist and clutched her tightly. She felt like a mouse caught in a trap being carried away by the cat.

James was well beyond his usual place of intoxication and greeted Bethany with the same kind of smile he'd greeted Tanner the day before. "You must be thirsty, cousin," he handed her a glass of what looked to be water. "I even gave you a lemon in the water, just as you like it."

Bethany was thirsty. She'd been given very little to eat or drink for two days. She accepted the glass and sat emotionlessly in the chair provided for her.

"I will be in the kitchen listening to the conversation," Drew explained to William and James. "If for any reason Mr. Brenly shows suspicion, ask my cook where the olives are and I will arrive on the scene."

After only half the glass of water, Bethany felt a strange sensation overtaking her. The nerves that only moments ago were tense and guarded were now relaxed and numb. She blinked a few times to try to undo the strange feeling in her head. Why was Uncle Drew smiling at her?

"Are you feeling better, Bethany?" he asked knowingly.

Bethany closed her eyes for a moment to clear the fog. "What did you do to me?" she turned her eyes to James.

"Its just a little bit of laudanum to calm your nerves. Your sister seemed to like it." He gave her a knowing smile. "We thought you might find it helpful this evening."

"You drugged me?" Bethany ran her hand over her face, trying to restore feeling. "Tanner will know… he'll see right through you."

"For his sake, lets hope he doesn't." Drew rose from his chair. "You will walk into the kitchen to sign the will when your dessert plate is placed in front of you. If you sign, Mr. Brenly leaves. If you refuse…" Drew grinned. "Well, just don't refuse."

Bethany watched Drew disappear and felt herself escorted to her cousin's parlor. The act was about to begin.

***

Sheriff Thacker would know the way to Drew Keene's office with his eyes closed. The two days he'd been in San

254

Francisco to meet with the man were burned into his head. He led Asa across the marble floor resentfully.

"Apparently, San Francisco pays well," Asa took in the wood paneling and decorative trim.

It took several knocks before Drew's secretary answered the door. "I'm sorry, but we are closed for the afternoon." The man made no motion of recognition toward Sheriff Thacker.

"Of course you are." Alan shook his head knowingly. "But this time, I'm going to use my badge to tell you that I need to see Mr. Keene immediately."

"Unfortunately, your badge cannot make Mr. Keene magically appear," the secretary said sarcastically.

"Where is Mr. Keene?" Alan wanted to slap the man.

"I am not at liberty to say."

Alan snatched the planning book from the secretary's desk and found today's date. The boxes were shaded in but nothing was placed in the margins. "Where is he?" Alan was tired of playing this game and pulled out his gun.

"He had errands all over town today." The secretary raised his hands slowly as if this was a bank hold up. "I don't know where all he went and I don't believe you are legally permitted to use your gun on me that way."

Alan was tempted to cock the gun just to put a healthy fear of authority into the fellow, but he resisted.

"You have no idea where he might have gone today?" Asa asked in a softer tone.

"Perhaps dinner. You are welcome to check out restaurants in town. Although I don't think you'll get a very positive reception if you wave that gun of yours in people's faces."

Alan returned his gun to the holster and turned to go.

"Thank you," Asa did his best to be polite. Though they both felt like they'd hit a brick wall.

***

Tanner arrived on time and stood in front of James Webber's fine town home and stared up at the grand Victorian building in eager anticipation of seeing Bethany for the first time in almost a month. Would she be happy to see him? Would they have time to themselves where they could talk? Tanner missed those many wonderful days they spent talking together and this time, he had something very special to talk to her about. Not only her grandmother, but a possible future together.

"Good afternoon, Deputy Brenly." James met Tanner at the door and welcomed him in. "You're just in time for the celebrations."

Tanner could smell the alcohol on James' breath and wondered if the celebration had been going on for quite a while for this man.

"Bethany, William, look who is here." James led Tanner into the parlor.

A man Tanner had never seen before rose to his feet to shake Tanner's hand. "Good to meet you."

Bethany rose slowly and Tanner searched her face for her reaction to him. Her soft blue eyes seemed sad but she smiled warmly and extended her hands to greet him.

The first thing Tanner noticed was the large diamond ring on her left ring finger. His heartbeat quickened and he turned curious eyes upon her.

"It is so good to see you, Tanner," she spoke his name reverently.

"Please sit down," James motioned to the chair across from Bethany and William. "My cousin and William were just sharing their news with me.

***

Bethany knew this was her cue. She tried to still her breathing. *This is to protect him… you have to say it. You've got to do it right to save his life.* "William and I are engaged." Bethany forced herself to smile and turned to William to allow him to finish for her.

"Yes. Just last night." William reached for Bethany's hand and clutched it tightly. "She said yes." He held her fingers to his lips and kissed them.

The feel of William's lips upon her cold fingers was like a dagger cutting them off. She glanced quickly at Tanner and saw the look of betrayal in his brown eyes and it pierced her heart.

"We hope for a quick wedding so that we can explore the Pacific Islands for our honeymoon." William added fuel to the fire.

Bethany sat back in her seat and let the numbness of the laudanum take her mind somewhere else. She couldn't handle the pain. She couldn't handle the hurt in Tanner's eyes. Would he have rather they kill him? She fought tears and let the men talk.

"Tell us about Maine." William did his best to keep a conversation going.

Bethany watched Tanner attempt to recover from the blow he'd been given. "Um… Maine is good." He was obviously at a loss for words.

"My cook tells me that dinner is ready," James motioned toward the dining room. "Why don't we convene there and continue our conversation."

Bethany could barely stand up. The spinning in her head made the floor look like waves of the sea. She let William help her to her feet and mechanically she walked down the long hallway to the dining room.

James had a lovely dining room. A long oval table with four large ball and claw feet graced the floor and a clean, white, linen tablecloth covered the top. James motioned for Tanner to take a seat across from William and Bethany.

Bethany was starving. As soon as her cousin gave the invitation, she reached for a roll. Tanner watched her curiously and Bethany lowered her eyes. *He knows I usually pray.*

Bethany closed her eyes but the room felt like it was spinning. She reached for her drink and wondered if this was drugged too. Tanner was obviously studying her, watching her motions, questioning this sudden engagement. Bethany had to put up an act. James and William watched him carefully to see if he was buying any of this.

"You mentioned in your letter that you may have found a relative of mine," Bethany forced out the words.

Tanner cleared his throat. "Yes. Your maternal grandmother." He studied her eyes.

"Really?" Bethany blinked back tears. "What is she like?"

"She is like you." Tanner took a sip of his water. "I would like to talk with you about her if we may take a walk after dinner."

Bethany desperately wanted to take a walk after dinner but the look in her cousin's eyes told her she needed to find an excuse. "Can you not share it now?"

Tanner glanced around the table. "There is much to share, Bethany."

Bethany ached to hear it. But she sensed Tanner was trying to communicate that it was personal. Did she really want these two men to hear about her precious grandmother and whatever Tanner learned about her? "Perhaps you can share it with me at another time then."

Tanner nodded.

Bethany took a small piece of roast and reached for the carrots across from her. As she reached, her long sleeve slipped back to her elbow, exposing the raw, bruised flesh on her wrist. Bethany quickly pulled her hand away and placed it on her lap. "I think I will pass on carrots today. There is so much good food on your table, Cousin." She did her best to play it off.

Tanner's eyes bore into hers and she lowered her face. She knew Tanner saw the dark circle around her wrist. *Dear Lord, please don't let him ask...*

In spite of how hungry she was, eating was torture. She was reminded of Jesus' last supper. He knew he was about to die... *Am I about to die, Lord?*

***

Tanner could tell Bethany was hiding a bruise on her wrist. Was that a rope burn? He watched her other hand to see if she wore a bruise there as well. Why would she have such a terrible bruise?

"Tell me, how did you come to meet our grandmother?" James broke the silence and turned to Tanner.

"My brother is the pastor of her church." Tanner faced James. "She spoke of you as well."

"She and my mother were never close." James feigned an indifferent attitude.

"Nora loved your mother dearly," Tanner said. He took a bite of his sweet potato and tried to focus on the conversation.

"My grandmother could never accept that my mother did not share her religious beliefs." James gave Bethany a challenging glare.

Tanner knew that Olivia gave her life to Christ in her last days, but he chose not to start what he was sure would be an argument. "Your grandmother simply loved her daughter so much that she wanted Olivia to know Jesus."

"She was a controlling old bat who tried to dictate to her daughters who to marry." James downed his wine and motioned for the cook to refill his glass. "Eleanor was the only one who married a man who grandma moderately approved of. The old woman did her best to sway my Aunt Naomi from Drew and she did not care for Patrick."

Tanner noticed that James did not refer to Patrick as "my father." It was significant. "I am sure she was only doing what she believed to be best for her children."

"What was best for her children was to allow them to follow their hearts," James snapped.

"Even if that heart belonged to another?" Tanner wasn't sure what James knew, but the man obviously had some issues with his maternal grandmother.

James narrowed his eyes curiously on Tanner.

Tanner chose to play it off and took another scoop of sweet potatoes. "These are wonderful. Is this brown sugar and pecans?"

"My grandmother spoke to you of such things?" James' eyes were wide.

"She suggested her concerns." Tanner knew they were speaking in code now. "But nothing could change her love for Olivia."

Bethany watched the conversation curiously.

James lowered his fork and set his arms on the table beside his plate. "And yet she would share such concerns with a total stranger?"

Tanner could feel the challenge. He glanced at Bethany. "A total stranger who was able to share with her about the granddaughters she'd never met. I assure you, Nora Farnsworth keeps that part of her family history in the closet."

Bethany's eyes widened and she glanced from Tanner to James.

"She is a dear older woman who loves you both," Tanner assured them. "It grieves her deeply that she does not know you but she prays for you daily."

William let out a disruptive chuckle. "Well this table conversation is quite the appetizer." He finished his drink and set down his glass. "Bethany dear, are you almost ready for your dessert?"

Bethany took another scoop of sweet potatoes. "Not quite."

Tanner watched Bethany's wrists carefully. He'd seen her right one; he desperately wanted a glance at her left.

"Tell me, William," Tanner decided to play the game. "Where did you meet Bethany?"

"I am a friend of her cousin's actually. As often as I am here visiting James, it only seemed natural that Bethany and I would be thrown into one another's acquaintance." He reached for Bethany's right hand. "Isn't that right, Love?"

Bethany's eyes seemed clearer now than when Tanner first arrived. She accepted William's hand but Tanner watched to see if she squeezed William's fingers the way she had Tanner's on so many occasions.

"What line of work are you in?" Tanner pressed.

"Banking." William stared at Tanner evenly. "And I hear you are a deputy? That must be challenging."

"Yes." Tanner glanced from Bethany to William. "We are always watching for lawlessness and counterfeits."

William chuckled. "I bet." He brought his chair just a bit closer to Bethany's and placed his hand affectionately on her back. "You must see quite a bit."

James motioned for the cook. "I believe we are about ready for our desserts."

Bethany's eyes shifted nervously.

The cook removed everyone's dinner plates and offered them each a refill on their drinks. Bethany reached for her glass with her left hand and her sleeve fell to her wrist. Tanner eyed her bruise intently.

She's been tied up... there's no way her wrists would both share that kind of bruise unless it was a rope burn.

The cook walked in with Bethany's dessert plate and set it in front of her.

"Perhaps we could all carry our desserts into the parlor," James suggested. "Bethany, can you notify the cook?"

Bethany picked up her plate mechanically and walked toward the kitchen while James and William strolled casually toward the other room. Tanner lingered long enough to watch Bethany disappear into the kitchen and watch the cook walk out carrying two more desserts.

This was his opportunity - a moment to catch Bethany alone. He hurried after her toward the kitchen.

***

"You've done well today, Bethany," Drew gave her a slimy smile when she walked into the kitchen. He was sitting at the servant's table with the paperwork she needed to sign in front of him. "You know what to do." He motioned toward the ink well.

"And how do I know you will still allow Tanner to leave alive?" Bethany took a few cautious steps across the black and white tile floor toward her uncle.

Drew laughed tauntingly. "All you really can be sure of, Bethany, is that he won't live if you don't sign."

Tanner stopped himself at the door. He'd clearly caught the tail end of Bethany's conversation with whoever was on the other side of that wall. He took a few steps back and let the door quietly close. Whatever it was that she was supposed to sign seemed to matter significantly to the person in that room. Tanner couldn't let her sign it.

"Bethany!" he called from outside the kitchen. "Are you in there?" He loudly moved to open the door, figuring neither Bethany nor the man in the room wanted Tanner to walk in on their conversation.

Bethany hurried to leave the kitchen. "Tanner!" she almost walked into him. Her eyes were wide and her hands trembled. "Did you get your dessert?" She spoke loud enough for her uncle to hear and began to lead Tanner down a long hallway. "The parlor is this way."

Tanner stopped her before they reached the parlor, grabbed her hand and pulled up her sleeve. His eyes questioned her earnestly.

"Don't, Tanner," she whispered. "Please." Her face revealed intense fear.

Tanner studied her frightened blue eyes intently. "Just answer one question," he whispered softly. "Do you love him?"

"Please Tanner," Bethany shook her head. "I can't…"

"Just that one question." Tanner pleaded with her tenderly. He needed to know.

"No." Her voice was soft but clear.

Tanner released his hold upon her and followed her into the parlor. Whatever was going on right now required a plan.

***

"That fella makes me wish I could shoot first and ask questions later," Alan confessed to Asa as the two men walked from yet another restaurant empty handed. He'd not stopped fuming about Drew's secretary since they'd left the office a couple of hours ago. They'd been to Drew's house and gotten no response and now they'd visited the last of the five restaurants Drew's secretary suggested.

Asa laughed and placed an encouraging hand on Alan's shoulder. "Maybe I need to hire him to be my secretary."

"Do that and I'll run you out of Santa Rosa." Alan joked back.

Asa stopped on the wooden sidewalk and crossed his arms. "Where do we go from here?" He asked the sheriff.

Alan shook his head. "We can always get a couple rooms at the hotel and hope to meet up with Keene first thing tomorrow." Alan watched as a wealthy couple passed him to go into the restaurant.

"We could." Asa glanced at his pocket watch. "Why don't we visit Miss Young this evening and find out if she received my letter. I've not heard back from her yet."

"Do you have her cousin's address?"

Asa did. He dug through the few papers he'd brought in his briefcase and found it.

***

"Come sit beside me, dear." William made a motion for Bethany to sit beside him on the sofa.

Bethany walked nervously past her cousin and took a seat next to William. He immediately wrapped an arm around her waist and used his free arm to reach for her hand. Tanner read the discomfort in her eyes. What was this game all about?

"Were you able to solve that little problem in the kitchen?" James asked curiously.

"Not yet." Bethany lowered her eyes nervously.

"When do you plan to return to Santa Rosa, Deputy?" James asked.

Tanner sat in a chair across from Bethany and took the dessert plate left for him on the small table beside his seat. It was time to change the game and Tanner decided to attack with truth. "I'm not sure, actually." His eyes bore evenly into James'. "You see I'm in a bit of a conundrum." He reached into his vest pocket and pulled out the leather pouch. "I'd come to San Francisco to ask Bethany to be my wife." He slipped the ring out of the bag and held it on his pointer finger. "I even have this lovely ring that was given to me by your grandmother. She knows I plan to propose." He glanced quickly at Bethany and saw the emotion in her eyes. "But now I've come and found that she has already accepted an offer of marriage from another." He turned his face back to James. "And I sincerely don't know what to do."

James glanced at his cousin. Bethany turned her face away from the men in an attempt to hide her emotion.

"The fact is, Mr. Webber, I love your cousin." Tanner turned his eyes to Bethany. "I love her deeply and I want to spend the rest of my life with her."

Bethany covered her face in her hands, unable to contain her emotions any longer.

"But more than anything I want her to be happy." He focused his conversation on the two men. "Mr. Webber, if you feel that Mr. Prescott is the best suitor for your cousin and will love, honor and care for her as she deserves, then I will choose to accept it."

James shifted nervously in his chair.

Tanner reached to return his dessert plate to the table but it fell, spilling vanilla custard all across the Oriental rug. "Oh, my!"

Tanner quickly rose to his feet. "This is a terrible mess. I am so sorry. Let me get something to clean it up."

"Don't worry yourself, Deputy." William shot a quick glance to James and stood up. "Are there rags in the kitchen?"

James nodded.

"Do you need anything else?" William asked. "Would you like me to bring any olives?"

"No." James answered a bit too abruptly. "Not at this time."

As soon as William walked from the room Tanner turned to James. "Don't do this, James," he whispered. "She's your cousin… she loves you. Your grandmother loves you. Whatever your father is trying to get you to do – it's not worth it."

James turned tortured eyes on Tanner. "Don't tell me what to do. You have no idea."

"I have an idea that whatever you need Bethany to sign in that kitchen will not give you the peace you are looking for. You're only going to find that in Jesus."

Bethany's eyes grew wide and she clutched the edge of the seat. "James, please…"

"Its too late, Bethany." James searched his cousin's face and sighed. "I killed Marie…" tears filled the drunk man's eyes. "I killed her."

"James…"

"Well this is just great!" Drew and William walked into the parlor together with their guns drawn. "You're confessing to a deputy. This was not the plan!" He waved his gun angrily. "You were this close! Only one signature away."

Tanner's hand was almost on his gun before Drew snatched Bethany by the arm and held the gun to her head. "Throw your gun to the floor, Brenly."

"Don't kill her." Tanner tossed the gun on the floor and raised his hands in the air.

"Do you really think not killing her is an option?" Drew spat sarcastically. "Enough of this. You're dead, Brenly!"

In only a moment, Drew turned his gun toward Tanner to shoot just as James shoved Tanner out of the way and took the bullet.

"James!" Drew threw his smoking gun to the ground, and ran to his son.

William was about to take down Tanner when a shot fired from the hallway brought William to the ground.

Alan and Asa stepped onto the scene with guns drawn at Drew, who knelt sobbing over his son.

James lay in a pained heap on the ground and stared with emotion at his father.

"James, no…" Drew cradled his son's head in his lap. "I didn't mean to shoot you. Son… my son…" He bent over James and cried.

Chapter 20

In only a moment, Bethany found herself engulfed in Tanner's arms. He held her slim form against him while tears coursed down her face.

"I'm sorry I lied to you, Tanner… I didn't want to. They were going to kill you."

"I know," Tanner rubbed her back tenderly. He stepped back and reached for her wrists. "What did they do to you?"

"It was Uncle Drew." She turned to see James on the ground while Sheriff Thacker worked on him. "This was all about gold." Bethany shook her head somberly. "There was gold found on the land I inherited from my Aunt Olivia. It was kept a secret for all these years and my Uncle Drew finally found a way he thought that he could obtain it."

The gold was news to Tanner. "I hurried back to tell you about Mr. Keene—and about his relationship to James."

Bethany nodded while Tanner wiped a tear from her face. "Uncle Drew told me." More tears followed. "He made me wear this ring," Bethany removed it and shook her head. "He told me he would kill you if I didn't sign that will and convince you to leave San Francisco." Bethany wrapped her arms around Tanner and cried on his shoulder. She was emotionally spent. "I was so scared. I didn't want them to kill you… I love you, Tanner."

Tanner soaked in the joy of those few words. "I love you, too."

Asa approached wearing concern for them both. "Are you all right?"

Bethany nodded. "How is James?"

"Alan is doing his best," Asa said. "I'm going to try to find a doctor."

"I need to see James." Bethany glanced toward her cousin.

"He saved my life," Tanner said.

They approached the suffering man who was still lying on the floor with a tourniquet pressed to his side.

Asa hurried away to find a doctor and the police.

The cook stood at the entrance to the parlor, her face as white as snow. Mr. Prescott lay dead at one end of the room and James was obviously in danger for his life on the other side. "Mr. Keene…" she trembled at the battle scene. This was not what she'd been paid to see.

Drew lost his desire to fight. He knelt beside his son with his hands cuffed and his head bowed in sorrow. Alan had already seized his gun, but Sheriff Thacker would let the San Francisco sheriff take the man in.

Bethany held James' hand and prayed for him.

"You saved my life, Mr. Webber," Tanner knelt beside Bethany and spoke gently to the suffering man. "Thank you."

James turned hurting eyes on Tanner. "Please take good care of my cousin," he asked in a soft, strained voice.

"I will," Tanner promised.

"I'm sorry, Bethany." A single tear streamed down James' face. "I don't know why I did it. I'm just so sorry."

"I forgive you, James." Bethany clasped his hand tighter. "But only Jesus can give you true forgiveness… only Jesus can take away the pain."

"Why would He forgive me? I killed Marie." James coughed dryly. "I don't deserve His forgiveness. I don't deserve yours." More tears followed the first and James apologized again.

"None of us deserve forgiveness," Tanner explained. "For all have sinned and fallen short of the glory of God."

While they waited for the doctor, Tanner and Bethany shared the gospel with James. The weaker he became, the more pressing their desire to see him find the forgiveness he so passionately longed for.

Alan continued to press the tourniquet into James' bleeding side and allowed himself to hear the gospel message in an all new way for the first time in his life.

When Tanner finally led James in a prayer of forgiveness, Alan repeated each word as well. Both men were crying by the end of the prayer.

"Am I really forgiven?" James asked after another dry cough.

"You are," Bethany squeezed his hand.

"We both are," Alan said.

***

Jane arrived by train the next afternoon to help Bethany through the next few long days. Drew was arrested and charged with murdering Patrick Webber and Charlotte Young. Tanner, Alan and Asa worked with the San Francisco sheriff's department to file reports on the man who'd called himself William Prescott and provided them with all the information they had concerning Drew and James.

James was left to be cared for in his own home during the last days of his life. After making his peace with God, James wanted nothing more than to hear his cousin read to him from the Word of God.

Bethany read many of the same words of hope she'd read to James' mother and held his hand through his final hours.

She and Tanner could only pray that Drew would also find the forgiveness he so desperately needed. With his own death sentence hanging over his head, the man was in desperate need of Jesus.

In spite of the sorrow and tears, joy was found in knowing both James and Alan were new creatures in Christ.

Gloria returned and helped the women with all the final arrangements.

"Thank you both for everything," Bethany told her two new friends. "I don't know what I would have done without you."

Jane wrapped her arm around Bethany's waist and spoke loving words of encouragement. "And my God shall supply all your needs according to His riches in glory in Christ Jesus."

***

Only a few weeks before Christmas, Bethany and Tanner boarded an eastbound train as husband and wife. They'd had a small wedding at the church and said their good-byes to Santa Rosa and all their dear friends there.

Arrangements had been made for Asa to manage profits from the mine in Sacramento, and to keep communication with Cleo Crisfield. Asa was also in charge of selling the Webber estate and James' house in San Francisco. Bethany felt good about both Asa and Cleo's ability to manage things in California, and was excited to find creative ways to use the money to bless others in need.

Much to Rodney's joy, he was now granted the title of deputy and took over Tanner's responsibilities heartily. Jane told Bethany that another wedding would soon follow now that her niece's suitor had a better paying job.

Bethany watched out the window for only a moment and turned to face her new husband. Tanner took her hand and kissed it tenderly. Her grandmother's wedding ring graced her ring finger beautifully and Bethany could hardly wait to meet the dear woman face to face and express her appreciation for the special gift.

"Are you ready to begin our new adventure?" Tanner asked playfully.

"With you." Bethany leaned closer to Tanner.

There would be snow in Vermont and Maine when the Brenlys arrived, and Bethany looked forward to her first sleigh ride. She remembered her aunt telling stories of sleigh rides, snowball fights, and ice-skating on the ponds. They would all be new experiences to this California girl and Bethany could hardly wait to begin.

"I love you, Mrs. Brenly," Tanner spoke her new name affectionately. "I didn't have to arrest you this time to make you come with me."

"Well, if the crime I'm being accused of is loving you, then I'm guilty as charged." Bethany turned her face toward Tanner and kissed him tenderly on his lips. "I love you, Mr. Brenly."